Girls' Night Out

Books by Roz Bailey

PARTY GIRLS

GIRLS' NIGHT OUT

Published by Kensington Publishing Corporation

Girls' Night Out

ROZ BAILEY

KENSINGTON BOOKS
http://www.kensingtonbooks.com

STRAPLESS BOOKS are published by

Kensington Publishing Corp.
850 Third Avenue
New York, NY 10022

All Kensington titles, imprints and distributed lines are available at special quantity discounts for bulk purchases for sales promotion, premiums, fund-raising, educational or institutional use.

Special book excerpts or customized printings can also be created to fit specific needs. For details, write or phone the office of the Kensington Special Sales Manager: Kensington Publishing Corp., 850 Third Avenue, New York, NY 10022. Attn. Special Sales Department. Phone: 1-800-221-2647.

ISBN 0-7582-0198-2

First Kensington Trade Paperback Printing: July 2003
10 9 8 7 6 5 4 3 2 1

Printed in the United States of America

This one's for the girls, you know who you are, or do I have to name drop? Okay, then . . . for Sue, Roz, Denise, Maureen, Ellen, Kristen, Carrie, Whitney, Amy, Eloise, Tina, Liz, Nancy, Kelly, and Susan. What would I do without my partners in crime and confidantes, always willing to do a little research at Jo Allen's.

With special thanks to John Scognamiglio, who always calls at the right time with the best ideas.

PROLOGUE

Tell the world that you were giving away a million bucks, and the weirdos came out in droves. Or maybe it was the lure of television: the chance to have your image broadcast from coast to coast, your personality analyzed in workplaces across the country, your face stretched across the big-screen TVs at sports bars, your love life the topic of Internet chat rooms.

As far as Executive Producer Max Donner could discern, the biggest problem with reality programming was that it attracted the exhibitionists of the world. Viewers didn't want to watch weirdos, but it was difficult to get normal people to apply for a chance to expose their emotions and share the details of their sex lives with the viewing audience.

Max tossed another application into the rejection stack; then he skimmed the next one until it became clear that the applicant was an advocate of sex with domestic animals. "We'll just rename the show 'Lassie Is a Big Tease,' " Max grumbled as he pushed the application aside.

In one season of producing the show, Max had encountered all sorts of sexual behavior. There were the "straight sex" types, as Max had come to label them. Those ordinary Jane and John Does who offered to let the cameras come into their bedrooms, under the sheets, up their orifices—whatever it would take to show the world that they "had it goin' on." Then there were the "dysfunctional sex" types, many of them totally whacked, some creative, who were willing to turn bisexual for the day, pop out of Russell Crowe's birthday cake, have sex standing in the skyroof of a limo cruising down Sunset Strip or strip in the window of Macy's at Herald Square.

Not that Max was surprised by any of it . . . just tired of the freaks and geeks his show attracted. So many people were willing to sell their sexual secrets for a million dollars. Unfortunately, most applicants failed to understand that *Big Tease* was not really about sex. What captured and held audiences, at least in the first season, were the emotional relationships plotted out before the viewers' eyes: the roller-coaster ride, the thrill of falling in love, the crushing blow of rejection, the negotiation required to keep it all together. People didn't want to see the physical mating; they wanted the mating dance, fully choreographed and edited with a rock 'n' roll soundtrack. Not to mention that the three women they featured last season lived in Los Angeles, Boston and San Francisco. Film it in Frisco and you've got a hit; that was one of Max's rules of television and film.

The top Nielsen-rated television show *Big Tease* had been conceived as a joke, a spoof of reality shows and soap operas, a stupid idea born of the haze of Dewars and the sting of unemployment. At the time, he'd still been reeling from the cancellation of the daytime drama he had directed for eight years. He'd even relocated from Los Angeles to take the job here, working in the Kaufman Astoria Studios. And then, faster than a thirty-second commercial break, Max and the rest of the cast and crew had learned that it was all over. Canceled. He was godfather to the AD's child. His sister had married one of the cameramen. Those people were family, and they'd been forced to say good-bye with less than twenty-four hours' notice.

Bringing the crew back together had been the most satisfying aspect of producing *Big Tease.* That day in the bar, a network executive for CBN had overheard Max's slightly inebriated "concept." In a nutshell: cat fights via satellite. Three lovely, single women were chosen, and guerrilla camera crews followed them around in their private lives and well-publicized dates. Then, while on camera, each woman watched the others' dates via satellite and ranked them. After eight weeks, the audience voted for the woman who turned out to be the most worthy date, and that woman won a million dollars. Since CBN had been looking for a show to rival *Survivor,* the executive, Paul Eberheart, had asked Max to come in and pitch it to the development team, and the rest, as they said in the trades, was "broadcasting history."

Max pushed another application into the rejection stack and took a hit from his coffee. Would there *be* a second season of the show? From the looks of these applications, if he proceeded, the concept of the show would be totally skewed. He'd have to rename it "Sex Freaks." Or he could bring on the sadomasochistic couple who favor a poker iron and call it "Some Like it Hot." Or he could document the romantic strikes and gutter balls of a big-haired, fortyish Alabama bowling league and name it "Alley of the Dolls."

"Hey, boss," Lucy Ng said, breezing in on a cloud of billowing scarves. Today it was red, orange and black, sort of a flame motif. Sixty-something Lucy always dressed in black, with lots of scarf action. She'd worked with Max since the beginning of his career, when he'd been an assistant director for ABC, and Lucy had been working in Standards and Practices. "Hold onto your hat, boss," she said. "I'm about to make your day."

"Oh, really?" Max sat back and swiped a hand over his bristly dark hair. "I'd say that's a pretty tall order, but go ahead."

She waved a folder in front of his nose. "I hold in my hand three perfect applications for the second season. Three beautiful girls, none of whom escaped from mental institutions or have outstanding warrants for their arrest. I already started the background checks."

"No way." He stood and snatched up the folder from her hand. "Are you sure they're not aspiring actresses looking for exposure?"

She shook her head. "Already checked with the Guild. They seem to be legit. A photographer, a magazine editor, and a corporate type. And even better, the three women are friends. Applied together. How do you like that angle?"

"I like." He nodded, glancing at the photographs on their applications. Sad eyes bordered by a tangle of wild red hair. A buttoned-down African-American beauty in a business suit. A smart-looking brunette with a cute Irish nose. Hell, he was looking at Charlie's Angels.

"Down, boy." Lucy wagged a finger at him. "You wouldn't want to violate the no fraternization rule. This is a contest we're running, and we've got to follow the rules."

"A contest?" Max leafed through the file. "I thought it was a network TV show."

"And I've got paperwork out my ears! Network forms and policies. *Sheesh!*" Lucy was already turning to go. "Next time, please, pitch the show to cable. And let me know when you want me to call these girls in, boss."

"You're that confident?"

"Please . . ." She waved off his question. "I've already budgeted in my bonus."

Pushing back his coffee, he dropped the folder onto his desk and spread out the three applications.

The redhead was a photographer, mostly portraits and weddings, but she aspired to have a show of her own eventually. Max didn't know anything about art photography, but the woman looked the part of an artist. A downtown girl, loaded with class and angst. When he saw that her name was Apple Sommers, he began to suspect a setup. A chick named after a fruit? Get out! But her personal statement offered some explanation.

> *A weird choice of name, I know, but my parents did it to me. We've got this family tradition of fruit names—my mother is Cherry, and my grandmother was Clementine. At least it's distinctive, which is an advantage in the art world. People remember my name, even if they do forget my work.*

Max turned to the statement from the corporate type, Chandra Hammel. Born in a poor section of Philadelphia, she lost her parents at a young age and was raised by her grandmother in Queens. She had an MBA from New York University's Stern School, was planning to marry a man who was tragically killed two years ago. Hadn't dated since, but felt ready to move on now. A workaholic who'd made a swift, steady climb up the rungs of the corporate ladder. "A rags-to-riches story," he said aloud, tasting the ratings shares.

The third friend, Maggie the magazine editor, was not as classically beautiful as the other two; however, her personality came through loud and clear.

I know definitely if I am going to sleep with a guy in the first ten minutes, Maggie McGee claimed. Max nodded. Right. And does the guy have any say in this?

He read on . . .

> *And it's not just about looks. We're talking chemistry. If it's not there, the guy could be Matt Damon and he's not going to get anywhere. Which is the reason I'm still looking. I could fill the dance floor of Au Bar with all the guys I've met who are perfect on paper: gorgeous, successful, social, funny, wealthy or rising stars. But if there's no sizzle when he smiles, I've learned that he's meant to be with some other fearless female. Big sigh. And that's just a qualifier for getting into bed with me. For a proposal of marriage . . . well, I don't know what it will take because I've never met a guy who comes close to being Mr. Maggie McGee. But I'd certainly like to explore those options on Big Tease. And hey, I don't mind at all if the cameraman comes along. One of my boyfriends once accused me of being an exhibitionist—like it's a crime to play in public! How about the drink called SEX ON THE BEACH? Anyway, don't worry; I'll behave. So when do we start? Just so I can run out to Victoria's Secret and update my lingerie.*

Max rubbed his chin. An interesting trio—photogenic, witty, smart.

He sprang from his desk and called down the hall. "Lucy! You are a genius."

"Compliments get you nowhere," she called back.

He handed her the folder. "Call the network and get the ball rolling. Tell them we've got a killer season lined up, with a new twist." He paused, scratching the bristled growth at his chin. "I never thought the same city thing would work, but since they're friends, it'll be juicy. Lots of conflict and angst . . . betrayal." He grinned. "Great stuff. And since they're all in New York, we won't need a satellite hookup. And we'll save on travel expenses for the crew. I'm liking this more and more."

Lucy tapped the file, tossing a red silk scarf over one tiny shoulder. "Do I make your job easy, or what?"

"Are you kidding? I could kiss you!"

"Sexual harassment," she said. "But I'll take that raise."

"You got it," he said. "Raises all around," he called, as if he were buying a round for the guys down at Darcy's.

One of the production assistants leaned out of a cubicle with a curious stare, but Lucy waved at him dismissively. "He's joking," she said pointedly. "Kidding." She slapped Max's shoulder. "Big mouth. Don't tease the children."

Part One

Three Ways to Wrangle Your Romeo

1

"Never in a million years," Chandra Hammel said emphatically. She emptied her Perrier bottle into a stemmed glass and took a demure sip. "My answer is no, for various reasons. One"—she held up her hand, enumerating her points with firm resolve—"I have no interest in that low-concept reality trash they're putting on TV right now. Two, my appearance on such a program would not be in keeping with the profile I need to project in the corporate sector."

"I'd say your image is secure in the corporate sector," Maggie said, folding her arms to evaluate her friend. An African-American woman in her early thirties, Chandra wore her black hair short and stylish with flame highlights, her suits crisp and sleek. The woman was stunning and didn't really have a clue, sort of like Halle Berry when she stretched for *Monster Ball.* Maggie thought Chandra acted way too straight, and never hesitated to tell her so. "You don't fish off the office pier," Maggie went on. "You don't complain to your boss. You don't even show toe-cleavage. If I ever start covering cleavage of any kind, promise you'll shoot me."

"I'm sure that could be arranged." Sipping her Diet Coke from a straw, Apple turned to Chandra. "You are the most conservative dresser I know, Chandra. You should have renamed yourself Prudence."

"This is not about me or my sense of style," Chandra said defensively. "It's about the way people perceive television and reality shows and . . ."

As Chandra rattled on, Maggie McGee smelled defeat. Damn! Ten years in the magazine business had given her the sense to recognize a failing pitch. She needed to turn this conversation around as soon as Chandra took a breath. Which might take a while, since Chandra herself was a supreme negotiator. The girl could filibuster for hours.

"Three," Chandra went on, "it would be an embarrassment to Grayrock Corporation, and—"

"No one has to know you work for Grayrock," Maggie interrupted her friend as the waiter brought three Caesar salads, two with grilled chicken, one with tiger shrimp. The three friends were doing lunch at Saloon Le Funk, a favorite spot of theirs midway between Chandra's Rockefeller Center office and Maggie's 57th Street hub at *Metropolitan* magazine. "You know, Chandra, you're getting way too devoted to that job. How long have you been at Grayrock as . . . what's your title? M&M?"

"M&A . . . Mergers and Acquisitions, and I do it because I love it. That job is the only thing that's gotten me through these last two years."

"Well," Maggie went on, "before you continue the boardroom presentation, let me remind you that we're your friends. It'll be fun if we do it together."

"Oh, right," Chandra said, "catfight with your friends."

"Like we never argue!" Maggie felt herself straining to keep her composure. "Might as well get the heat on video and make some money on it!"

"Not worth it," Chandra said. "Not worth spending time on the application."

"I'll take care of the application, the photos . . . everything."

"I can do photos," Apple volunteered. "Hell, I think I have a roll of the three of us at Christine's wedding. Granted, those celery-silk bridesmaid gowns were deadly, but I can crop."

"Right, great!" Maggie nodded vigorously, her dark hair bouncing into her face. "You can be in charge of photos."

Chandra stabbed a square of chicken, a determined gleam in her brown eyes. "Not interested."

"Come on!" Maggie couldn't believe Chandra was squashing her idea so quickly. Time to bring out the big guns. "Look, I have a friend who works for the network. He doesn't work on *Big Tease,* but he thinks my idea is fabulous. The guy is in development meetings all the time, and he says the concept of three friends is irresistible. The producers will jump on it in a minute."

"I have to admit, I sort of liked that show last season." Apple swallowed a mouthful of salad and tilted her head thoughtfully. The gesture always reminded Maggie of a slender swan basking in the sun. Apple's thick hair was piled atop her head, gleaming orange whorls held in place by half a dozen clamps, a hairstyle that would have looked messy on anyone else, but somehow, Apple wore it with elegance. "It was sort of like a bad car accident. Once I started watching, I couldn't look away. Before I knew it, I was tuning in every Wednesday night, routing for the schoolteacher to get her man."

Both Chandra and Maggie swiveled their heads around to gape at Apple.

"You watched *Big Tease?"* Chandra said.

"You wanted the schoolteacher to win?" Maggie rolled her eyes. "I thought she was a total fraud with that damsel-in-distress crap."

"Oh, please!" Apple's eyes narrowed as she scowled at Maggie. "That woman was so real, I could feel her pain. Besides, she reminded me of my eighth-grade science teacher."

Chandra dabbed at her mouth with a napkin, still staring at Apple. "You, the WASP girl, the Bennington graduate from upper-class, upper-crust Westchester?"

"What's with the Westchester crap? I grew up in Queens with you guys."

Chandra was shaking her head. "I can't believe you watch that mind candy."

"Okay, consider me duly embarrassed, but the show is addictive." Apple popped a crouton in her mouth and crunched for a moment before focusing on Maggie. "But Maggie watched it, too. Why aren't you disgraced by her?"

"Maggie works for *Metro,*" Chandra said. "It's her job to keep her finger on the pulse of the lowest common denominators in pop culture."

"Well, thank you, Margaret Meade," Maggie told Chandra. Sometimes it was hard to believe that her buttoned-down best friend had grown up in Queens. Was this the girl who'd led the charge sledding down the hill next to P.S. 203? The bikini-clad teenager who'd done cannonballs from the lifeguard stand at the Bay Terrace Pool Club? But then, Chandra was definitely a chameleon. She'd gone from being little Sharon Humphrey in the projects of South Philly to a middle-class teen in suburban Queens to a shareholder in a doorman building on the Upper West Side, and all along the way she had managed to fit in. Looking at her now in her silk suit and Prada heels, Maggie was dying to soften things up with a glittery pin or jangly bracelets . . . or a shiny nose ring. Ha!

Apple shifted in her chair, absently running her fingertips over the camera strap that dangled from the ladder-back chair. "Are they still giving a million dollars to the winner?"

"Absolutely." Maggie nodded eagerly. "A million, can you imagine? That kind of money would definitely bail me out." She flipped a lettuce leaf with her fork, imagining what she would do first. Quit her job? No, she would throw an awesome party at the magazine for all the good people who constantly got trounced by management. *Then* she would quit her job. Then, a day of beauty at Elizabeth Arden on Fifth Avenue, where women in cheery pink uniforms would trim and exfoliate and condition and soothe her body from head to toe. She could even afford a hot-stone massage to open up meridian channels and get in touch with the energy from the cosmos.

"A million dollars could definitely buy me a chunk of happiness," Apple said.

"Ladies, would you listen to what you're saying?" Chandra's eyebrows shot up as she cast a critical eye on her friends. "Money isn't everything. And contrary to popular belief, you can't buy happiness."

"I'm not too sure about that," Apple replied. "It does give you freedom, the freedom to make so many more choices. And certainly freedom from the stress of wondering how you're going to make next month's Visa payment."

"Amen, sister," Maggie said, reaching across the table for a crusty onion roll.

"Wealth has its advantages, yes," Chandra admitted, "but let's not fool ourselves into thinking the wealthy are problem-free. And material goods do not bring happiness."

"You sound like my father," Apple said. "And it's easy to disparage the worth of money when you have it. You're doing okay, but Maggie and I are perpetually broke."

"Really!" Maggie held a forked shrimp in the air. "I can't even afford this. I'm eating on borrowed money. Why do we come here, anyway?"

"You love it," Apple answered.

"It's close to the office," Chandra added.

"Oh . . . right. Anyway, there's nothing like an influx of cash to lift your spirits."

"Money is not a long-term motivator for employees," Chandra insisted. "Countless studies have proven that."

"Ah, but do they consider the tingle in your fingertips at the moment of purchase?" Maggie asked, wiggling her fingers. "The last time I was depressed I bought a leather bag—a buttery soft duffel in the warmest shade of toffee—and I'll be damned if that thing didn't cheer me up. It improved my mood by seventy percent. Countless studies have proven that shopping eases depression."

"I'm sure you were euphoric," said Chandra. "Until the bill came."

"Right! And if I had the money to cover the bill, maybe the euphoria would have lasted." Maggie tore off a piece of roll and popped it into her mouth, trying to think of a way to get her pitch back on track. Since it looked like Apple was her ally here, she turned to the willowy redhead, trying not to come on too strong.

"So you're interested?" Maggie asked. "I'm sure we can find someone else to be the third."

"If you're trying to make me jealous, it's not working," Chandra said.

Apple was already shaking her head. "I don't think so. You know how I freak in front of the camera." It was one of the many ironies of Apple; the woman who lived behind the lense always felt incredibly awkward when she was photographed.

"They're not looking for models," Maggie argued. "Oh, come on, Apple. Just think what you could do with that money! You could probably buy your own studio. And no more fights with Coop about who pays for what."

"Oh, please. With a million dollars I'd buy my own place and charge Coop rent. Not that he'd be there that often. Do you know, he hasn't made it home before midnight once this week?"

"Still entertaining clients?" Chandra asked sympathetically.

Apple frowned. "Only the drinking ones."

The stench of "guy trouble" hung in the air. Maggie knew that the honeymoon period had been over between Apple and her boyfriend, Brandon Cooper, for quite some time, but Apple usually spared the details about her relationships with men.

In fact, Apple's romantic life had always been a source of wonder for Maggie, who considered herself an expert in the area of relationships and sex. Or, at least, an expert practitioner. But then, when it came to relationships, Apple was on a different planet. A few years ago, Apple had left a group-share apartment to move in with her boyfriend—boyfriend #1, was all that Maggie could remember of him—and now here she was living with Coop, boyfriend #6. With few tears and very little counseling, Apple simply moved from one guy's apartment to the next, feeling that her life was very Zen and streamlined, not bogged down by furniture. How did she do it? How did she survive without her own bed, a favorite hutch, a room full of prized possessions? Maggie wasn't sure, but she was beginning to sense that it was time for Apple to move away from boyfriend #6.

"So Coop is drinking again." Maggie tugged a strand of dark hair behind one ear. When Apple nodded, Maggie went on,

"See? See how this show could change your life?" She raised one small but well-manicured hand toward some fictitious path in the ceiling. "Go on the show with me and take your shot at a million dollars."

Apple lowered her head shyly, poking her salad with a fork. "I could never go on TV and talk about personal stuff . . . seductions and turn-ons and orgasms." She reminded Maggie of an adolescent who'd slapped open a *Playboy* centerfold for the first time. Curious but horrified.

"Apple, on a normal day I've edited pieces about striptease studs and erotic butt massages before I've even had my second cup of coffee," Maggie answered. "Surely you can make up a story or two about playing hide the salami under the covers."

Chandra waved a breadstick at Maggie. "Young lady, we've got to do something about your manners."

"Excuse me?" Maggie grinned. "I'm not the one menacing with a breadstick."

"Well, lookee there." Apple's gray eyes were alert and focused on the street activity beyond the restaurant's plate-glass window. She reached for her camera and stepped away from the table. "Look at the size of that entourage. God, is that Michael Jackson?" She squinted. "Is he supposed to be in town this week?"

It proved to be a rhetorical question, as Apple was already far from the table, sprinting through the restaurant lobby and out the door in pursuit of a pop idol. Although most of her income came from shooting portraits and weddings, she made a nice amount from selling the occasional celebrity photo to a tabloid.

Maggie turned back to Chandra, who seemed to be waiting for a cue. "Did I mention that the show is a venue for meeting guys? And not just any guy. They help you set up at least one high-profile date."

"Like I have time to date. Yesterday, I didn't even have time to breathe until I got home from work. At nine."

"Come on!" Maggie jabbed at the shoulder of Chandra's silk suit. "Loosen up, girl. A date doesn't have to be dinner or a movie. Today's woman is on the lookout for relationships around the clock. Riding in the elevator at work. Chatting at the coffee bar. Competing for a cab. I know two people who agreed to share a taxi to the Upper East Side and ended up getting married."

"Maybe in *Metro* magazine. Not in real life."

Maggie was about to argue when she noticed a young waiter eyeing their table. He sauntered over and cocked his head to the side, as if he were afraid to interrupt. In one look, Maggie knew she wanted him.

His brown skin was dark against the white uniform, his chocolate cheeks gleaming with a soft sheen. She longed to reach up and touch his beautiful face—broad mouth, high cheekbones, shiny shaved head. A perfect head.

He was an African-American god.

"Is everything okay?" he asked, gesturing to the empty place at their table.

"Everything's just fine," Maggie answered, hoping that lettuce wasn't stuck in her teeth as she flashed an enormous smile. She pulled her shoulders back, the better to show off the boobs.

Chandra gestured to Apple's empty chair. "She'll be back. We're used to having her disappear." She lowered her voice, adding, "She's paparazzo."

The waiter nodded politely.

"I think that would be paparazza," Maggie corrected. "Singular, feminine. But you say that as if it's a religious cult or something." She turned to the waiter, trying to engage him. "The first time we ate here, DeNiro was having lunch. Right over in that booth. Apple nearly fell out of chair, but we restrained her. She doesn't take photos inside restaurants, anyway. Too tacky. But once he got outside—*ka-blam.* Not one of his best hair days, but with that jaw line, who cares?"

"That's very interesting." The waiter lowered his chin.

Maggie licked her upper lip. Did he not get it, or was he being coy? *Oh, big man, give it to me!* she wanted to shout. How she longed to run her hands over that smooth, shaved head. Shiver her fingers down his chest. Down, down, down . . .

"After that, this became our favorite restaurant," Chandra

went on, oblivious to Maggie. "You're close to the office, and good for Apple's celebrity photo stock."

The waiter smiled. "I'm glad you keep coming back."

"Oh, we'll just keep on coming," Maggie said suggestively.

His eyes met Maggie's. *Click. Kah-ching!* Contact!

She was in.

And then, the moment seemed to scatter as Chandra prattled on about something Maggie couldn't follow. She was too distracted by the feeling of ants in her pants. If only she could swipe the china off the table and clear out the hungry patrons. He could ravish her right here on the green linens.

Maggie started to send him a hot vibe, but he was listening to Chandra. No . . . no! The connection was fading!

On second thought, maybe she could slip him her business card?

He gestured to their food, backing away. "Enjoy."

Chandra dug into her salad as he retreated. Maggie watched him with her smokiest, sexiest leer. Chandra was chewing when her eyes met Maggie's.

"Don't say it," Chandra told Maggie.

"I'd love to get under his apron," Maggie said.

"Oh, please. You can't be in love with every guy you meet."

"Who said anything about love?" Maggie knew that her moral scruples were quite different from Chandra's. Her friend claimed that she hadn't had sex since her boyfriend's death two years ago, and Maggie believed her. Of course, she couldn't imagine abstaining that long, but for Chandra sex was an extracurricular activity. Sort of like the occasional dessert or a weekend hobby. For Maggie, sex was a daily essential, like breathing and drinking.

Across the table Chandra's face was a study in restraint. "What?" Maggie asked. "What? What!"

"Where is Apple when I need her? We've been wanting to talk to you about this, but—"

"About sex?" Maggie rubbed her hands together. "Oh, do tell. After all, I am the *Metro* sexpert."

"That may be so, but you seem to be missing one important

point." Chandra's eyes softened as she let down her guard. "Oh, Maggie, it's not just about sex. I thought you were going to focus on finding a meaningful relationship."

"I am, I am! But in the meantime, you can't expect a sexually actualized girl like myself to sit at home watching MTV." When Chandra shook her head with a look of disappointment, Maggie groaned. "Yeeps! Don't pull the guilt trip, because it doesn't work on me."

"So don't feel guilty. But do try to pull yourself out of this slump. Really. There's got to be someone out there with whom you can share your life."

Maggie toyed with a spoon. "Yeah, yeah . . . now you're sounding like *Metro* magazine." Maggie wanted to stop the Maggie-bashing, but suddenly she realized that she could make this work for her. "You know, Chan, maybe you're right. And the best way for me to find a guy worth dating is to go on *Big Tease.*"

"Not that again." Chandra stabbed at her salad. "Have you talked to your parents about Thanksgiving? I think it would be fun for the three of us to go up to Westchester together."

"Don't change the subject," Maggie said firmly. "I'm still determined to get you to give in and sign up for *Big Tease.*"

Chandra groaned.

"No complaints. Just say yes."

"What is with you and this TV show? I know you're bull-headed, but I've never seen you quite so stuck on something so frivolous."

"A million dollars is frivolous?" Maggie quipped. "Not to mention a chance to meet Mr. Right?"

"And you think a decent guy is going to appear just because I reveal my personal life on television?" Chandra cocked an eyebrow. "That show is an invitation to every money-grubbing loser in America. And the way those women behave on camera." Her deep-timbered voice took on a whiney tone: " 'Love me! Protect me! Validate me!' " She rolled her eyes. "No, thank you. I prefer to earn my money with hard work, and you know upper management would disapprove of a Grayrock employee on that show."

"Since when did your life become all about Grayrock Corporation?" Maggie persisted.

"It's not." Chandra folded her arms defensively. "Grayrock isn't the only reason I can't do the show. There's always . . ." She stabbed her fork into a piece of chicken with a vengeance. "You know . . . *her.* The last thing I need is for her to spot me on television. And it's exactly the sort of show people like her watch."

People like her. Maggie knew Chandra was referring to her estranged mother who had passed Chandra on to relatives when she was a baby. It was part of Chandra's distant past; a piece that Maggie could barely conceptualize, knowing her friend as she was today: confident and low-key—"a gorgeous genius," as Jeff used to call her. "But you've changed your name," Maggie said. "And she hasn't seen you for years so there's no reason to think she'd recognize you."

"Why chance it?" Chandra placed her fork neatly across her salad plate and pressed her napkin to her mouth. "Look, Mags, it was a fun idea, this show thing. Ingenious. But lots of great ideas just don't pan out. Don't take it personally."

"Easy for you to say," Maggie muttered, stabbing a few leaves of lettuce with a vehemence. "You're slated for a promotion and a whopping end-of-year bonus. Me? I'm constantly in trouble with Candy these days, at least on days when she makes it into the office. I've been working for *Metro* for seven years, and my reward is to have outgrown my usefulness in a market that considers women 'ridden hard and put away wet' once they reach thirty."

"Oooh," Chandra said gently. "I didn't know we had career issues at stake here."

Maggie took a bite of salad, then chewed vigorously. "I ate ma nyob."

Chandra winced. "In English, please."

Maggie swallowed, lifting her chin. "I hate my job," she said with a British accent.

"No, you don't," Chandra insisted. "You just hate what they've done to you."

Maggie stabbed the last piece of shrimp in her salad, realizing Chandra was right. "I am so depressed."

Chandra nodded. "Aren't we all?"

Just then Apple tramped back into the restaurant looking beautifully unkempt and a little breathless. Orange strands of hair dangled over her pink cheeks.

"I take it that's the blush of success?" Maggie asked.

Nodding, Apple reached into the pocket of her khaki safari pants and dumped two rolls of film onto the table. "It wasn't Michael Jackson, but I think I got some great shots of the Artist Formerly Known as Prince."

"Really?" Chandra seemed impressed. "How does he look these days?"

Apple slung her camera over her chair and picked up her fork. "Petite but cute."

"I've always admired the way he does his eyes," Maggie said. "That smokey, mysterious look. Maybe I should use more eyeliner."

"Now, see that?" Chandra wagged a finger at Maggie. "That's the pat *Metro* response. You belong at that place. You are the magazine."

Maggie made a show of gagging. "That's a sad statement."

"But I mean it in the best possible way. If they're failing to use your talents, they need to rethink their management system."

"You go, girl," Apple said, digging into her salad again.

Chandra checked her watch. "We need to get back to work," she told Maggie.

Apple pointed to her salad. "Should I take it to go?"

"No, I'll stay with you," Maggie said, wishing she could sit here at Saloon Le Funk for the rest of the afternoon and into evening. "I have a phone interview at two, but I can do that on the cell while I'm walking back. No one will miss me."

"I don't understand that," Chandra said, taking a twenty out of her black coach wallet and leaving it on the table. "In my line of work, you need to be there twenty-four-seven. With markets open all over the world, it just never stops and everyone has to push to stay on top of it." Maggie saw that familiar glint in Chandra's dark eyes: the look of a player anxious to get back into the game.

"You love it," Maggie said.

Chandra smiled. "I do. I really do."

2

"I am so depressed," Maggie said aloud in the ladies' room. Apple had finished and headed off to her studio to do a portrait, but Maggie lagged behind, wanting to freshen up and wishing she had somewhere to go other than the editorial offices of *Metropolitan*. Staring at herself in the ladies' room mirror, she screwed up her face to give herself a bold, harsh assessment. Boring brown hair, tired brown eyes with an ashy gray shadow, and skin shiny with a sheen of oil. Okay, maybe brown wasn't boring. She had been mistaken for Sandra Bullock more than once. She cocked her head to the side, trying sultry, but she just looked tired.

She grabbed a paper towel to blot her nose and chin, and then smoothed on a layer of powder foundation from her purse, a beaded gem shaped like a fat duck. Absolutely precious and beyond her price range, but she was coming to accept her fatal flaw, a weakness for purses and clutches and bags.

She had already called to postpone the phone interview. Other than that . . . what would her afternoon entail? She thought of the work that waited on her desk back at the office: a few rough drafts of letters to Dr. Teddy Gabolski, sex therapist. Every month Maggie worked hard on the advice column, taking a few of the boring letters that came into the office or the magazine's Web site and pumping them up with verve and spice. She thought of one letter she'd read this morning, one that she could have written herself:

Dear Dr. Teddy:

It's embarrassing to admit this, but I need sex all the time, at least once a day. If I can't find a willing partner, I'll do my thing alone with a vibrator—the desire is that extreme, like eating or breathing. Because of my strong need for a guy, I've often settled for one-night stands. One of my friends says I'm a nymphomaniac. Is there something wrong with me?

Signed,
Horny Honey

And because Maggie had been working at *Metro* for so many years, she could almost write the answer from Dr. Teddy:

Dear Honey:

The desire for sex is a normal, healthy part of life, driven mostly by hormones, which some people have more of than others. But don't be embarrassed. Instead, look for a steady partner. Focus your energy on finding a hottie who is interested in satisfying your delicious daily needs.

"And *blah, blah-blah, blah-blah,*" Maggie said, turning away from the mirror. She'd read the psychobabble and the textbooks. And now to top that off she had Chandra, the spokesperson for repression, accusing her of overindulgence in meaningless sex. Oh, hell, Chandra was right. It was time for Maggie to grow up and find a real relationship. But what was the BFD? She wasn't hurting anyone but herself.

Feeling more put together, she popped out the door and walked into someone—the young black waiter. His crisp white sleeve brushed her fingers, and she found herself clutching his arm, holding on securely as he turned toward her. Up close, she caught a whiff of his aftershave, a light scent that reminded her of summer rain.

"Sorry, ma'am," the waiter said, his dark eyes full of polite restraint.

"No . . . it was my fault," Maggie said. She wanted him, right here, right now. Still holding onto his sleeve, she lifted her hand to his smooth, chocolate brown cheek.

Her touch seemed to confuse him. His eyes were alight with a question.

"Yes," she answered. "Oh, yes."

He smiled. Yes, she thought, he'd gotten the message.

Nervously, he glanced down the hall, past the kitchen doors, to the arched opening to the restaurant revealing only the back of two male patrons.

"Don't worry about the patrons. We'll only be a minute." Maggie brought her hand down over the crisp linen of his shirt, reaching under his white apron to grasp hold of his black belt buckle with a strong tug. "Where can we go?" she whispered in a candied voice.

He nodded toward the kitchen. "The storeroom?"

She pushed him toward the kitchen, following behind him. "Yes, I'd love to take a tour of the kitchen," she said as he pushed open the swinging door.

One chef glanced up indifferently from chopping mushrooms as Maggie followed her waiter into the kitchen, then turned into a small pantry on the left. He quickly closed the door behind them and Maggie switched off the harsh fluorescent light so that they could bask in the pearly winter light from the small barred window above.

As she turned toward him, she felt his nervousness, and it gave her a jolt of adrenaline. "It's okay, baby," she said, taking his hand and tucking it under her sweater.

His fingers cupped one breast, and he moaned. "What's your name?" he whispered.

"Shh." Maggie put her fingers to his lips. "No names. Just pleasure." He squeezed her breasts hard. "That's right," she whispered, distracted for a moment as she looked for a place to put her purse. She wedged it atop a giant can, then fell against him with a sigh. Heat rose between her legs as his fingertips teased her breasts. She was wet already; the excitement of forbidden, impromptu sex always did it for her. She wanted him, but when he leaned down to kiss her, she whispered, "No kissing. Just sex."

His eyes flickered as his fingers began to play over her bra. She tossed her head back, enjoying his touch. Hell, what did Chandra know about relationships or sex? At least Maggie was connecting on some level.

Connection. That's it, she thought as she tore his shirt loose and ran her hands over his bare chest. She fingered his nipples and sighed. Connection was everything.

She pulled aside his apron and tore at his belt buckle, pulling down his pants and boxers to reveal a long, thin erection. "Oh, man, you are gorgeous," she said, turning to grab her bag. He ground himself against her as she leaned her purse on one of his shoulders, fishing around for a lubricated, ribbed condom. "Got it!" she said, stashing her purse carefully. A girl had to take care of her handbags. Then, with deft fingers, she tore the wrapper open and knelt in front of him to roll it on.

"There!" she said. Rising to her feet, she flipped up her loose, flowered skirt to reveal G-string panties.

He groaned at the sight of her.

"Thought you'd like that." She tucked her skirt into her sweater and pressed against him, loving the feel of him. He thrust his hips toward her, but since he was taller, it was clear he could never enter her this way. As they ground against each other, she rolled her head to the side, searching for something to give them leverage.

The white buckets.

Huge covered buckets, filled with flour or lard, she wasn't sure, stood together in one corner. Maggie slipped away from him, turned, leaned down to the buckets and thrust her butt in the air. "How's this?" she asked, lifting the back of her skirt.

Drawers around his ankles, he shuffled over and nuzzled between her legs. She reached back to find him, but he knew the way.

With one thrust, she felt herself coming.

"Oh, oh! Yesss," she hissed.

He pulled out and thrust in again, and again, and again. Her hair fell around her face, a curtain of shimmering brown. She sucked in a deep breath scented with the tart apple of her shampoo and the dry, salty smell of the storage room and the rising odor of sex.

The thrill! Sneaky sex was so hot. Maggie felt her body surge to another climax, barely noticing the sack of rice at her head, the cold plastic buckets under her hands. Her mind focused on the motion flowing into her.

She needed this, every day.

Had to have it. Like air and water. A sex junkie.

But hey, as Dr. Teddy would say, nothing wrong with that. *Nothing, nothing, nothing,* she thought as he pumped into her.

3

If the magazine were a true reflection of the offices of *Metropolitan,* Maggie thought, it would be a sloppy stew of working girls and princesses. On the one side you had the new groundswell of industry; on the other was the old regime of gals born to know fashion because Daddy paid the rent. Maggie had always been proud to include herself in the former group, although her worklust had dissipated so much in recent months. *Ugh,* something else to worry about. Was she falling out from the group of hard-working women who churned out an endless stream of snappy phrases, clever pitches, and well-researched pieces? Exactly where she might fall *to* was anyone's guess.

Maggie's black platform boots clunked softly on the marble floor of the lobby. She nodded at the security guard, but he was engrossed in one of the tabloids at his desk. Stepping into the elevator behind a messenger, Maggie checked her watch. Nearly three. *Yeeps!* She'd spent most of the afternoon out of the office. Hopefully, Candy wouldn't notice. Although editor in chief Candy Devereaux always had a policy of giving her editors freedom to do interviews out of the office, recently she'd taken an unusual interest in Maggie's whereabouts. *An unhealthy interest,* Maggie thought. With advertisers cutting back their budgets and circulation in a slump, didn't the woman have enough to worry about without nosing in on Maggie's work habits?

When the messenger stepped out on seven, Maggie dropped to a squat and sniffed. No, no telltale sex smell. Just a heavy whiff of Ralph Lauren. She was safe, unless Candy had a speculum handy.

Maggie popped up as the elevator doors whisked open on the twelfth floor. The *Metropolitan* sign was barely visible amid the racks of clothes drooping from hangers like ghosts of high fashion. Below a pink feathered concoction and a denim jacket, two editors were perched on the low leather sofa, their heads bowed over an array of powdered eyeshadows spread on the coffee table. A thin man with delicate fingers, obviously a cosmetic company rep, sat opposite them. He spoke quietly as he brushed a pearly, luminescent gray onto the back of beauty editor Emily DePaulo's hand. Emily's assistant, Jennifer Chin, darted Maggie a harsh look, but quickly turned back to the rep, who was "so excited" about his spring colors.

Maggie stepped around them, wondering if Jennifer was trying to warn her or just being her bitchy self. Jennifer was the girl to know at *Metro,* the girl with the key to the esteemed "Beauty Closet" where all the free samples from cosmetic companies were stowed: big candy-colorful bags of cosmetics with special brushes and weird hair ding-dings, as well as sleek, minimalist black or earth-tone parchment bags of organic shampoos and meditative candles. Of course, all the samples were the property of the magazine, but once they were used or passed on for a shoot, they were free game for the privileged few who could wangle the key from Jennifer.

Maggie stepped around them and swung to the left, taking the back way into her office. It wouldn't be prudent to breeze in late through the central office, past marketing and sales and the fleet of overworked editorial assistants slaving away in their cubicles. With the collar of her coat still turned up, she felt like a spy on a mission: return undetected. Would she feel this guilty if she was late only because she'd had lunch with her friends? Was she feeling extra guilty because she'd spent company time sneaking sex with the waiter guy? Maggie didn't want to delve into those issues now as she tramped down the hall and into her office, passing only Frip the mailroom guy on the way.

With a sigh of relief, she closed the door on her closet office and tossed her coat into a heap in the corner. No amenities like coatracks or hooks in this office, but hell, she was lucky to have four peeling walls. Like most of the staff, she'd been in a cubicle until Darlene Zimmer had gotten pregnant and moved on to *New Parent* magazine. Maggie grabbed a bottle of cologne from a bookshelf and lifted her skirt to spritz her inner thighs. Then she turned to her computer and checked her e-mail. There was . . .

1. a note from her mother about folic acid research on women in their thirties (Ever since Maggie turned thirty, her mother was onto this health kick, as if she were a fossil that needed to be preserved.)
2. a message from her source on psychopathic roommates, trying to reschedule
3. a warning from the managing editor that one of her pieces was late

"Piece of cake," Maggie said, sitting in her chair and hitting the keyboard to respond to everything. She knocked off the first two responses and was in the midst of firing off a reassuring excuse to the managing editor when the knock came at her door. "Open!" she called without losing a stroke on the keyboard, and her best office buddy, Jonathon Downey, stepped in.

"Oh my God, an inputting maniac has taken over Maggie's office," Jonathon said skeptically. "Have we met?"

"Down, boy. I suffered one hellacious confrontation this afternoon and I don't need further abuse from you."

Jonathon hitched up his plaid pants and perched on the edge of her desk. "Every day is hell for you, and yes, you need my abuse to keep your ever-swelling ego in check." He picked up the green jade Buddha from her desk and rubbed its belly. "Dear God of the cosmos, please send us a pair of beautiful boys. An oversexed one for Maggie; an iron-pumping Bette Midler fan for me."

"If that thing worked, I'd be married and giving garden parties in a Park Avenue penthouse by now."

Jonathon sniffed. "Did you spill some perfume in here?"

"It's a long story." Maggie finished her e-mail to Leo, the managing editor, then turned to Jonathon. "What's up?"

"Candy's been looking for you," he said quickly. "I heard her say something to Debbie about your hours, and Debbie said she'd look into it."

"Shit!" Maggie whacked her desk. Debbie Minsk was Maggie's immediate boss, a low-key, level-headed features editor who didn't interfere with her staff unless their work was falling short. Debbie's management approach included an occasional glass of green tea and an ample supply of Midol. But Candy Devereaux, editor in chief of *Metro,* was another story.

"That bitch," Maggie said, pressing her hands to her cheeks. "She never liked me. Never. Because I didn't go to the right prep school and college."

"College has nothing to do with it," Jonathon said. "You just weren't born into the right family, you street urchin. When you were sixteen and bumming cigarettes at one of Long Island's finest bowling alleys, Candy was spending Daddy's dollars in Europe under the guise of studying art or touring cathedrals."

Maggie shook her head. "But she used to leave me alone. Now, suddenly, she's on my case. And she'll probably stay that way until something major distracts her. Like a Laura Ashley retrospective at the Met. Or a little attention from Mel Gibson at some movie premiere."

"Mel is yesterday's hero," Jonathon announced. "But Crowe . . . I'd still sit through that godawful badiator flick for a chance to meet Russell darling."

Maggie squinted at Jonathon. Over six feet tall, with sandy brown hair, high, giddy cheekbones and arms that seemed to dangle around his knee, Jonathon would have looked the part of a star basketball player, were it not for his dishy Southern lilt and his spicy fashion sense. He'd recently given up his Carrera eyeglasses for purple contacts. Purple, like Liz Taylor. You had to love the guy.

"You know," she said, "I think you and Russell would look great together."

He smiled. "Liar. You hate the man."

"Hate is a strong word," she said. "Disinterest is better. Give me a guy with a lower profile. A Kevin Bacon or a Chris Noth."

"Well, I would argue with you about Russell darling, but I actually came in here to get some quotes." Glancing down at the pad in his hand, Jonathon flipped a page over and poised his pen, ready to write. "Can you give me an upbeat, descriptive anecdote about the worst date of your life?"

"Do I have to limit it to one?" Maggie frowned. "Hard to choose between the guy who called his mommy every ten minutes and the one who got drunk and tried to pee on me."

"I might be able to use both." Jonathon sucked in his lower lip. "Though the first one is a little flat."

"He called the damned woman between every course!" Maggie said. "And then he kept complaining to the waiter that the restaurant was drafty. And after dinner I wanted to walk along the river, by Chelsea Piers, but he said it was too cold out. Nobody wants a guy who's always colder than them."

"Okay, okay, it's not a criticism of your taste if the guy is too boring to be a notorious date." Jonathon stuck the end of his pen in his mouth. "Do you think Chandra and Apple want to go on the record about their dud dates?"

"Sorry, but I can't let you tap my friends at the moment," Maggie said, turning back to check her computer for any new e-mail. "I've got the girls lined up for something big, and I can't afford to let them get distracted from my mission."

"Really?" Jonathon wiggled his eyebrows. "What's cooking?"

"Just the best idea I've had in a long time," Maggie said smugly as she watched the screen. Two new e-mails, but nothing from the show. "Fuck-a-duck. They're not getting back to me. Why aren't they getting back to me?"

"What?" Jonathan glanced at the screen. "Who?"

"The producers of *Big Tease.*" Maggie explained her plan to Jonathon, including the fact that her friends were set against going on the show, but that her friend at CBN insisted that it was a winning idea. "So I filled out the three applications myself and sent them in."

Jonathon's eyes were wide with astonishment. "All three of them? With forged signatures and everything?"

Maggie shrugged. "I submitted the application online, so there were no signatures involved. And the photos of each of us were gorgeous attachments, thanks to *Metro*'s scanner."

"Still . . ." Jonathon sputtered. "It's got to be illegal and totally unkosher. Isn't game-show fraud a felony?" He held his notepad close to his chest, adding, "I saw *Quiz Show!*"

"Get out!" Maggie found his overreaction amusing. "They're my friends; so it's not fraud. Besides, I'm the strongest writer of the three of us, and I knew exactly how Chandra and Apple would answer those questions. I should know, after so many years with them."

"But you're forgetting one important consequence," Jonathan said. "If and when you are chosen to appear on that mind-numbing show, your friends are going to kill you!"

Maggie waved off his worries. "They'll change their minds about *Big Tease*. Believe me, when that producer calls them, they'll be thanking me."

"Feeling a bit cocky, aren't we?" Jonathon clucked his tongue at her. "You know, if you did that to me, I would have no choice but to kill you."

"Only after you signed the contract with the production company," Maggie pointed out. "You'd give your Prada shoes and matching attaché to go on that show."

"You're right." Jonathon gazed up at the ceiling, as if in a daydream. "Jonathon Downey, single boy about town. Tall and lissome and full of wit. Is there a soulmate waiting for him amid the skyscrapers and boutiques of the world's most famous island of dreams?"

"Easy now. You're gonna make me cry."

The phone bleeped, and Maggie snatched it up. It was her immediate boss, Debbie, wanting to see her.

"Sure, okay, no problem," Maggie said quickly. "Two minutes?" She hung up, jumped up and grabbed her emergency bag, filled with a change of underwear and a few freshen-up supplies.

"Debbie wants to see me," she told Jonathon, "but she sounds cool. It'll be fine, but I've got to b-line to the bathroom."

"*Mm-hmm.* And what's with the emergency bag?" Jonathon's eyebrows shot up. "You didn't really spill that perfume, did you?"

"Okay, okay, I was using it as a coverup," Maggie admitted. "I had the most amazing sex with a waiter at Saloon Le Funk. Sneaky sex, in the storeroom, right there in the restaurant." Juggling her bag, she held her hands to her ears. "Geez, you know how sneaky sex blows my mind. Total blowout. *Kaploohy.*"

"Oh, my dear." Jonathon rolled his eyes. "I thought you promised yourself to put an end to quickies. Don't I remember something about this being the time to figure out what you want in a guy and stop coupling just for the sake of sex?"

"I know, I know, but he was so cute and he was right there and very interested. And you know it's hard for me to go without sex." Pulling open the door, she tucked her bag under her arm and whispered, "I slipped, just this once."

"*Mm-hmm.*" Jonathan led the way out the door, turning back to add, "Not that I'm criticizing, but it was your own plan, your commitment. What are we going to do with you?"

"I'm going to go on television and find a man," Maggie said firmly. "A gorgeous, wealthy, honest, earnest man who loves me, Jonathon. One who wants to love me again and again and again. And I'm going to do it with millions of viewers watching."

He reached for her arm, his touch warm, supportive. "Good luck," he said, his purple eyes twinkling. "Because, honey lamb, you're going to need it."

4

That night Apple lay swaddled in terra-cotta 300-count sheets, contemplating the way moonlight streamed into Cooper's apartment. It pooled around the toes of her left foot, which, wrapped in the rust-colored sheets, appeared to be emerging from a rock.

What am I doing? Why am I here? Where the hell is Coop?

She sat up in bed, wondering why she bothered trying to sleep. Apple hated sleeping alone, and these days she rarely slept without the help of pharmaceuticals. Slipping away from the sheets, she climbed down the ladder of the loft bed and saw the glaring numbers of the digital clock on its wooden stand. Three-forty. Was Cooper dead? Maybe he'd been hit by a cab, was unconscious, and that was the reason he didn't call to tell her he was working late or out entertaining clients. That would account for his cell phone being off, too. Yep. That had to be what happened.

Although it had never been the case the many times before when Coop had stayed out into the early hours of the morning without so much as a note or a phone call. Usually, he stumbled in smelling of beer, a quiet drunk. He stripped off his suit and brushed his teeth and hopped into bed like a Boy Scout back from a camping trip.

She hated him. But if she hated him so much, why was she here? Why did she care?

Okay, maybe she loved him. That wasn't the issue at the moment. Right now, Apple needed to worry less about Coop, more about herself. She wasn't getting enough sleep lately, and that was pulling her mind apart, zapping her energy so that her days were divided between a haze of hurry at the studio and a tedious paralysis in her free time, time when she should be out getting shots for her own collection, for her art.

Art? That was a laugh. Hadn't her father always told her that artists were useless unless they could make a living off their art?

At the moment Apple was having trouble making a living off her trash work—the portraits and weddings and far too occasional shoots for book covers or ad agencies. It was exhausting work, but usually it provided enough money to pay the rent on the studio, as well as her assistant's salary and other living expenses. Though recently, Apple had found herself digging into savings to make ends meet. Somehow she was two months behind on the studio rent and the landlord just wouldn't get off her back, despite her assurances that she would catch up. And she *would* catch up, with the multitude of Christmas portraits that were coming round with the season. Work like a dog and you still can't make a living. It certainly defied Dad's work ethic, though she would never, ever let him know the state of her finances. In fact, whenever Apple was in between boyfriends and out of an apartment, she often stayed in her parents' house in suburban Westchester—"the manse," her friends called it—under the guise of having her apartment painted or redecorated. Mom understood the inconvenience of having contractors in; she gave the Bedford house a facelift every three years. And Dad? Dad didn't ask Apple the same questions he barraged his lawyer son with whenever Dennis returned home. No, Dad was just glad to have his girl home.

Spying a paisley-shape of moonlight on the wooden floor, Apple thrust her foot into it for another study. The line of her toes was exquisite, the surface of the foot painted with silver, the dark shadowed lines in between like dark, velvety grooves. A human plow. Rake of the earth.

She loaded up a camera with slow film and started taking shots in the puddle of moonlight. One foot. Zoom in on a toe. The line of her calf. Two legs, nearly parallel. The bend of her knee. And her hand. The hand always fascinated her. Fingers curled. The fist. Or most poignantly, palm flat and facing upward, suppliant and begging, waiting for a handful of hope to descend from the skies.

She put the camera aside and stretched her hand into the moonlight again, this time leaning her face close to study the lines of her palm. Once, when she was goofing with her friends at a high school fair, she had paid a woman to read her palm. "Your love line is broken," the woman told her. Apple had laughed nervously, her friends giggling and cracking jokes about her latest boyfriend. "What's that mean?" Apple had asked. "I'm not going to get a date?" The woman shook her head but kept staring at Apple's palm, as if she could see something more—tiny newsflashes of information—in the thin cracks and lines. "There will be many loves," the woman said quietly, "and many loves lost."

Although the palm-reading session had ended in giggles and secret swigs from a bottle of Coke laced with rum, Apple had not forgotten the woman's prediction. Somehow it reinforced her sense of hopelessness when a relationship hit a snag that seemed hardly worth working out. "Many loves lost," Apple would say to herself, sure that this relationship, like the one before it and the one before that, was a lost cause.

A dead end.

Apple stared at her hand, fairly sure she could identify the love line. But what about the other lines on her palm? The crisscrossed etchings, the deep grooves, the endless tic-tac-toe grids and gentle arches?

She was stretched prone on the floor, leaning into the surreal moonlight when his key clicked in the door. Her heartbeat quickened as she heard the door open behind her, yet she didn't turn to him. She didn't want to give him the satisfaction of knowing she'd been waiting and worrying, knowing that she cared.

"Something wrong?" he asked.

"No."

"Can't sleep?"

"No."

She refused to look at him, but she heard the wisp of fabric; he was taking off his clothes.

"Can I ask you something?" Anger burred his voice. "What the fuck are you doing stretched out on the living room floor at three in the morning?"

Her first instinct was to run over and belt him with her camera. Fortunately, restraint prevailed. "I'm working," she said without inflection.

"The hell you are!" He threw a shoe across the room. It slapped the wall below one of Apple's framed prints and bounced down to the floor. "I can't take this. I can't come home and find you like this."

"Like what?" She sat up and turned toward him. "Awake?"

"Waiting for me. Waiting with that repressed anger, like I did something wrong. Like you're my mother and I missed curfew. Damn it, you're not my mother, and this is my apartment. *MY* apartment."

"Really?" She leaned back on her elbows and tossed her hair casually, as if it were perfectly normal to sit on the floor and argue at three in the morning. "You'd never know that, judging by the amount of time you spend here."

"Maybe I'm not here because I don't want to be with you."

She lifted her chin to see his face, sure that he couldn't mean that. He was stripping off his pants, not even looking at her. When he straightened, his gray eyes were glassy, his face shadowed with weariness and annoyance.

"Don't say that just to hurt me," she said, realizing that Coop had never tried to hurt her before—not deliberately. Difficulties arose because of his very selfish, very separate agenda, not from deliberate acts of malice.

"Why does this have to be about *you?*" He ran his hands over his hair, silver hair cut short so that it spiked up naturally. She loved running her hands over his head, feeling his arm cradle her back. When Coop held her, she felt safe, protected.

Or at least she used to.

"Do you have any idea how I feel, coming home to . . . to you? You've gotten so cold. Cold and distant. You know, it was never about love with us. We've had great sex, but love was never an issue. Now that's over too. You're barely conscious when we have sex."

"Do you want to know why?" Hitching up her nightgown, she tramped over to him, wanting to face him with her indignation. "Because you're so emotionally vacant. I hear you talking to guys you work with and you laugh and joke and . . . connect. You connect with them. But here, it's like you're already gone, even before you walk out that door."

He shrugged. "I am gone."

"Why? Why do you do that? Why do you—"

"It's too late."

"Why do you act like you don't want to be with me anymore?"

"Maybe I'm just sick of sleeping with a corpse. I may have a few fetishes, but necrophilia isn't exactly my thing."

She hauled off and slapped him, her nail scraping the line of his chin as she swiped her hand over him.

The force of the blow sent him reeling back, eyes closed. He nearly tripped on the ladder to the bed, then hunched forward, cupping his chin with one hand.

Feeling like a spectator, an outsider observing a street fight, Apple watched him dab at the skin, then check his hand for blood. "You're lucky I'm not bleeding," he said, and she began to wonder how much he'd had to drink that night.

What the hell are you doing, fighting with Coop? she asked herself. *Getting violent with your guy?*

Violence was not usually a factor in her relationships with men. This was the second time things had exploded between Coop and her. A few weeks ago when she'd burst into hysterical tears over the fact that he'd stayed out all night, he'd grabbed her, flailing and shrieking, and carried her over to the couch where he'd silenced her with forceful kisses, voracious, angry, determined attacks of his moist mouth. That morning they'd had great sex—wild and gritty, with Apple crying halfway through, Coop licking her tears as he pumped into her.

If she could press close to him now . . . just fold herself into his arms and feel his quiet strength. Maybe now, in the heat of this conflict, she could feel something in bed. Maybe now her body would respond to his, rising and falling in the climax that had eluded her for so long.

She stepped forward, bending down to touch his arm gently. "Are you all right?"

Holding his chin, he turned away. "Leave me alone." He went to the dresser and pulled out a pair of jeans and a T-shirt. "I'll expect to see you gone in the morning."

"Coop, don't say that," she said. "Don't make threats. You'll make me crazy with threats." She put her hands over her ears as if she couldn't stand to hear another word. "Don't just . . . Let's talk about this in the morning. Come to bed."

"I don't think so." He tugged the T-shirt over his head and picked up his leather jacket. "Not this time."

Without another word, without a parting glance of anger or confusion or sorrow, he went out the door.

Abandoned, Apple hugged herself, an island in the huge hardwood ocean of the sparsely furnished apartment. Why did he leave? Why did he continually do this to her, making her suffer because he had to be out, somewhere else?

And those things he'd said. Didn't he love her? She had always assumed he did. Wasn't that the foundation of attraction? Love and attraction and sex; I'm into you and you're into me. It didn't have to be anymore complicated than that. Apple always fell in love with the guy she was with. Love was not a problem for her. Why was it so difficult for Coop to admit?

And the corpse comment. That stung. Despite her recent lack of interest in sex, she'd answered his advances to keep him satisfied. She'd had sex with him, she'd moaned and writhed, pretending to come. Damn him, she'd been a really good sport. And her reward was a biting remark.

She couldn't do this. "Help me, somebody," she cried, lifting her arms to the beams of moonlight.

But there was no answer.

Xanax was the thing. She downed a pill, then took the down quilt from the loft bed and wrapped it around her body, trying to ease the shivers. The pool of moonlight had shifted, and she suddenly wished she could dive into it and disappear, like quicksilver flattening into a pool. She took a box of paper clips from Coop's drawer and brought them to the couch. She sat, huddled in the quilt, tossing silver paper clips into the silver puddle. Tedious work, but what else could she do?

She flipped a paper clip into the air, wishing she had the money to go back into therapy. If she'd had help, maybe this whole argument would have been avoided.

She yawned and wondered if the Xanax was kicking in.

A corpse. How could he say that?

She needed intense therapy. Lots and lots of therapy.

She picked up the phone and punched in the number of Maggie's cell. Men would come and go, therapists priced themselves out of her budget, but her friends would answer her calls. Thank God for her friends.

5

"Okay, then, we'll take care of the cost analysis on this end if you realign the management teams on your end," Chandra spoke with authority to the team of three managers conferencing from Grayrock's Tokyo office on the other end of the speaker phone. As she spoke, she minimized the Tokyo file and deleted another item from the calendar on her computer and checked the remaining list. So many things to take care of before she went off for Thanksgiving with her friends.

"Sounds like a plan," said one of the Tokyo managers.

"What about HR?" asked Linda, the only female manager in the Tokyo office. "Should we involve them in the realignment from the get-go?"

"Since we need to keep this as simple as possible, let's not complicate it with HR input," said Chandra. "After all, we're not relocating anyone. You guys make the decisions and HR will process them. In the meantime, I'll bring them up to speed with our plans."

"Okay, then. We'll be in touch. I'll e-mail the numbers to you today."

"Great," Chandra said, realizing that meant the numbers would be coming in sometime just before she sat down to Thanksgiving dinner. "Though Monday would be fine in this case."

"What?" Laughter came from the speaker phone. "Whoa, Chandra," said Brad. "That's the first time I heard you cut someone a break and extend a deadline."

"Tomorrow's Thanksgiving here," Chandra explained. "Or have you people been out of the country too long to remember?"

"Give me a minute," Linda said. "I'm conjuring up an image of roasted turkey with chestnut stuffing and cranberry sauce."

"Would you like us to FedEx some rations?" Chandra asked. "I'm sure the pumpkin pie would make it."

"Somehow I think we're better off with fresh sushi," said one of the guys. "But thanks anyway."

"And listen, you can e-mail your reports to my associate, Vincent Singh. He replaces Sally. Anything else?" Chandra asked, eager to wrap up the call and move on to her other work.

The Tokyo team said their good-byes and signed off. Chandra clicked open another file and called toward the open office door, "Have the numbers from London been updated today?"

Vincent appeared in the doorway. "I'll check," he said.

"Okay." She darted a glance at him, then turned back to her computer. As she clicked on a file, she could feel that Vincent hadn't moved. "Something wrong?" she asked, half-listening as she read over a document from the San Francisco office.

"I took the liberty of ordering dinner while you were conferencing with Tokyo," he said evenly.

"Oh, thanks, but I'm going to step out," she said. "I've got errands to run."

"It's almost nine."

Chandra swung around to the clock on her computer and touched her forehead. "Oh, no! Where did the time go?"

"There was the budget meeting," he said, his obsidian eyes serious. "The conference calls. E-mail and monthly reports."

"Okay, that was a rhetorical question, but you're right." She dug into her bag, wondering where she'd put the cleaners' ticket for her clothes. "You wouldn't happen to know what time the

Godiva shop downstairs closes?" she asked without looking up. She needed to pick up a house gift for Apple's parents. "I would come in tomorrow if I didn't promise my friends I'd do Thanksgiving with them. Maybe I should cancel, though Apple would . . ."

She glanced up. Vincent was gone. ". . . kill me."

Vincent reappeared holding a gift bag and a bundle of clothes wrapped in clear plastic. "I took the liberty," he said. He draped the clothes over the sofa and handed her the bag. She looked down on a gold-foil box adorned with ribbon and fake berries. It was perfect for the Sommers family, who had a penchant for naming their women after fruits.

"Oh." Chandra was dumbfounded. This was not the work of Brianna, the assistant Chandra shared with two other people. Chandra had never had an assistant who anticipated her needs, and Vincent wasn't an assistant at all but a coworker. "I can't believe this. How did you get my clothes without the ticket? How did you know where to . . ."

He held up a slender hand. "It was no problem. Next time, let me know what your errands are earlier," Vincent said, wagging a finger at her. "Your time is better spent in the office. Truly, Ms. Hammel, it's only proper that an assistant should be sent. You must learn to delegate."

"But not to you, Vincent. You're not an assistant."

"I merely made sure the tasks were taken care of." His slight British accent gave a light lilt to his words. "But there is another matter to attend to. Perhaps I should have interrupted . . . I don't know. But I did not want to disturb you."

Chandra turned to him. "What is it?" she asked, sensing his awkwardness. A naturalized citizen from India, Vincent Singh had worked his way up from an accountant to deputy manager of Finance. Most recently he'd been transferred to work as deputy manager of the Mergers and Acquisitions Team, Chandra's unofficial sidekick and right-hand man.

"While you were on with Tokyo you got a call. Please, don't be upset." Vincent pressed his hands together, stalling. "The caller said she was your mother."

Her hands froze over the keyboard.

My mother.

Chandra tried not to freeze or freak or burst into flames over this bit of news, but there was no way she could hide her feelings.

"I don't have a mother," she said.

"You don't?" The silence was heavy. "Then I am very sorry for disturbing you. It must have been a . . . a mistake."

"Did you ask if it was a wrong number?"

"She said your name, clearly. Chandra Hammel. No hesitation."

"Probably a ruse," she said. "Some kind of scam." Liking that angle, she went on, "Gee, I hope my social security number isn't floating around out there, being used by some unsavory character."

"I cannot attest to her character." Vincent disappeared into his office, then returned with a call slip. "However, she did leave this telephone number where she can be reached."

"Okay, thanks. Maybe I'll call her and clear it up." *Fat chance of that,* she thought as she dropped the slip of paper onto her desk without looking at it. She didn't want Vincent to know that she cared; she didn't want him to detect the dread rising inside her at the mention of a woman who would only drag her down at this point in her life. "So . . ." She cleared her throat. "Can you check on the London numbers?"

"Right away." He disappeared, and Chandra spent the next few minutes clicking into files, checking numbers, reading over reports and answering e-mail. Some data on a small banking institution in the Midwest caught her eye, as well as a report on a company owned by African-American financier J. Reginald Pringle. As head of Grayrock's Mergers and Acquisitions Team, it was her job to be on the lookout for worthwhile properties.

While she worked she bit her lower lip and tried to conjure an image of her mother, of the woman who had given birth to her twenty-eight years ago and then walked away. Nothing came to mind. Her grandmother had shown her a few photos from years ago—stiff, posed pictures from her mother's high school yearbook—but Gramma didn't have any recent photos that would indicate whether Rhonda Humphrey looked anything like her daughter. With any luck, there was no resemblance, nothing to tie Chandra to the woman who'd given her life and the tedious name of Sharon Humphrey, a name that Chandra had dropped in high school, sure that it pegged her as a lower-class child of the ghetto. Chandra was no longer that sad little girl, the thick-lipped waif who'd been left behind. Like Madonna, she had re-made herself, more than once. She'd morphed into Chandra Hammel, serious scholar. Then with Maggie's help she had found her fashion sense, her feminine way in the world. That had led her to grad school and Jeff, her match for life.

Jeff . . . Their time together had been magical but too short, and with his death she had been forced to reincarnate herself once again into a focused, steely businesswoman.

Come on, girl, concentrate! she told herself as she scrolled through yet another report. If she was going to spend her time moping about an irresponsible woman who'd abandoned her child years ago, she would never get out of here tonight. And Chandra was no longer that sad little girl who had been left behind.

But although her eyes skimmed over rows of numbers and bulleted items, her mind was stuck in that painful place she tried so hard to avoid, the images that haunted her. The dark closet she'd escaped to as a child to cry her eyes out. The corner of the library at Columbia University, where she'd combed news articles about Philadelphia in hope and dread of seeing a blurb about her mother. The floor of the marble shower where she sometimes collapsed under the hot spray, sobbing out the emptiness inside.

Stop this. Don't let yourself go there.

But now it was closing in on her.

She picked up the call slip and checked the number. A Philadelphia area code. Oh, man, it probably *was* her mother.

After all these years, the woman was coming after her.

6

Across town, Maggie faced equally insane deadlines with less help. It wouldn't have been a problem with the help of her assistant—or *any* assistant—but in her infinite wisdom Candy had dismissed the assistants at noon. She snatched an old issue of *Metro,* turned to Candy's column and started blacking out the teeth of the editor in chief. Ugh, that woman was infuriating.

"Fly away, little butterflies!" Candy had announced, flitting among the cubicles like a pesky insect. "Off to begin your holidays! I do love this time of year."

"But Form *A* ships today!" cried the managing editor.

"Does it?" Candy batted her fake eyelashes. "No matter. Senior staff can certainly handle it. Go, now!" she said, waving off a young assistant who had been sifting through the file drawer.

Put a sock in it, Maggie had wanted to say. Instead, she bit her lower lip and watched Candy emancipate the underlings, sure her makeup would crack open like an egg to reveal the hideous true woman inside. God knew, if Maggie wore that much makeup the seams would crack every time she smiled.

"That bitch," Maggie muttered as she stormed into the hallway. Now here she was, trying to finish off Form *A* with no support. She could kill Candy.

Maggie strode past Tara's desk and gave the assistant's empty chair a little kick.

She was traipsing to the copy machine for the gazillionth time that night when Jonathon came out of his office ready to head home. "This has to be the worst story I've ever taken part in," Jonathon said, dropping a folder into the managing editor's basket. "Thank the Lord there's no byline. And what keeps you here at this late hour? I'd figure you'd be well into your third drink at some club, cozying up to a single boy who's got a fifty on the bar and a pistol in his pocket."

"Don't torture me." Maggie bit her hand, and two of her papers fluttered to the ground. "Promise me, if I ever, ever again agree to hire one of Candy's friends' kids as an assistant, you'll shoot me?"

"Consider the gun loaded." Jonathon bent to pick up her papers, then hoisted the strap of his plaid attaché over his shoulder. "So sweet little Tara isn't working out?"

"She's working out for Kate in accounting and Heidi in marketing, but no, not for me. Seems that sweet little Tara isn't as interested in learning the business of magazine publishing as she is in seducing the staff."

"Tara?" Jonathon blinked. "Kate and Heidi? I knew about Kate, but I never thought Heidi was a lesbian."

"Maybe she swings." Maggie scratched her nose and noticed an ink smudge on her hand. "This could be *Metro*'s first case of an assistant sleeping her way to the top. All I know is, I can't keep up with Tara's love life and she can't keep up with the workload. She walks around here in a daze, like I still need to draw her a map to get to the ladies' room or the archives." She snatched the papers from Jonathon and pressed on into the copy room.

He followed her in. "Something tells me I'm going to regret this question, but how far are you from finishing?"

"I've got one story to cut and one to flesh out. The ad department lost an advertiser and I've got to fill the spot." She turned to him with her brightest, goofiest smile. "But if you help me, it would cut the time in half. And I'd be your bestest friend forever and ever."

He rolled his eyes. "Why do I always get sucked into these things?"

"Oh, Jon, you're the best!" She handed him a wad of papers and patted him on the back. "I owe you big-time. I will never forget this. Never, ever, ever!" She pressed a hand to her cheek. "Ohmigod, listen to me. Have I had enough coffee, or what? Anyway, tell me now, what do you want for Christmas? You know I love to play Santa."

"Honeychild, I don't think you can deliver the items on my Christmas list. Unless you have a tall, dark and handsome gay man in your bag of toys." He dropped his attaché on the floor of her office and unbuttoned his jacket.

"That is, indeed, beyond the realm of FAO Schwartz, but I can tell you that I did play Yenta in the high school production of *Fiddler on the Roof,* and I have had a modicum of success in matchmaking, with two happily married couples to boast of."

He pointed to her chair. "Sit down. Shut up. Finish."

"Gotcha. No problem." She handed him a red pencil. "Do you want to add or cut?"

"Give me the one that's running short," he said. "What's this about? Oh, oral sex, one of my personal favs. Let's see how much I can pump this up without being totally redundant."

They set to work. Maggie skimmed over her story on "Seven Ways to Wrangle Your Romeo" and found two loose lines to tighten and a paragraph to cut. Actually, it should be three ways to wrangle him, but somewhere along the way Candy had decided she wanted to extend all the lists in the magazine and the whole thing had spiraled out of control. Well, where was she, the big, important editor in chief on this night before Thanksgiving? Maggie slashed across the page, cutting it down to three. Let Candy complain next week, when it was too late to make the change.

Working with Jonathon, Maggie felt the injustice of the situation begin to roil inside her. Why should two senior editors have to work late before a holiday weekend when there was an entire staff to work on these things? It wasn't fair, and it wouldn't be this way if ditzy Candy hadn't slopped her power around. The bitch.

And Tara . . . what was that girl about? Maggie didn't understand how she could put so much energy into the art of avoidance. Avoiding work. Avoiding the ringing phone. Declining to learn how to summon or route a messenger, how to work the copy machine, how to research a story. The girl worked so hard at not working, she had to be exhausted by the end of the day.

"I can't believe Tara didn't stay to help me," she blurted out. "That girl has so much to learn."

"You haven't exactly been at the top of your game lately," Jonathon said without looking up from his work. "We both know you are *Metro*'s sassiest, sexiest writer when your heart is in it. But your heart has been out of it for a while now. Out to lunch. With the waiter at Saloon Le Funk."

"Ugh!" Maggie groaned, realizing he was right. "My heart and head have been so out of this magazine, these stories. Ever since Deuce. The man zapped me. He sucked away the romance in my soul."

"You give him far too much credit," Jonathon said.

Maggie just shook her head. Being with Deuce Rawlins was the closest she'd ever come to really being in love. At least, in the beginning. Deuce was a struggling downtown artist who had submerged her into his world, complete with his rat-ridden loft apartment and his maxed-out Visa bill and his funky art-world friends who pretended to hate all things commercial, like *Metropolitan* magazine. Deuce with his sun-streaked ponytail and paint-streaked safari pants. It had taken her years to see beneath the façade and recognize the fraud inside, the spoiled brat cowering inside that gorgeous bod and toothpaste ad smile. Living with him in his Soho loft, she'd learned that his hair was streaked in a salon and the safari pants came from Banana Republic. And those suffering artist friends of his? They were so quick to criticize capitalism and enterprise, but they never turned down the cash their wealthy parents sent from the suburbs of Connecticut or California or Massachusetts. Spoiled punks, the whole bunch of them.

Maggie sighed. "I miss him. I really do."

Jonathan shot her a disapproving look.

"Okay, I don't. I'm glad to be rid of him. But I miss feeling like I'm in love with someone. Coming home at the end of the day and collapsing on the pilly sofa under a fleece blanket. I miss drinking wine in sweats and thick socks. Screaming so loud during sex you could hear the rats scamper from the stairwell."

"Charming images you conjure, my dear."

"I don't miss Deuce's bohemian bullshit, but I do miss having someone to come home to. Don't you ever feel that way?"

Jonathon pressed the tip of the pencil against his smooth chin. "I've got Smelly Cat," he said. "And the top occupancy of my apartment is one person, one cat, no more."

"No room for Crowe?"

He shrugged. "Would you have me eat Crowe?"

"Ha!" Maggie laughed. She pulled her hair back into a ponytail and then let it drop onto her back. "Deuce has ruined me. I keep trying to fill the void he created, but no matter who I sleep with or where or how high I lift my legs, I still feel so empty."

"No orgasms?" Jonathon asked quietly.

"Orgasms aren't a problem," Maggie said. "But they're the knee-jerk, sneeze variety. Automatic reflex orgasms. Not the floor-pounding, take-me-to-the-mountaintop-and-beyond kind." She picked up a pen shaped like Tweetie Bird and started scrawling spirals on a scratch pad. "I'm just turning into a sex burnout. Without the romantic mind connection, sex is a mundane body function."

Jonathon nodded wisely. "A sex burnout. Maybe you should stop having meaningless sex. Isn't that what you already decided? Haven't we had this conversation?"

"Been there, done that." Maggie had made herself that promise, but then she'd met that cute guy at the gym, whom she'd hustled into a shower stall of the women's locker room on a quiet Monday night. And the guy she met at the Gap who'd wanted to do it in the dressing room. And the guy who'd bought Apple and Maggie dinner and a slew of drinks the last time they went clubbing. He'd talked about a threesome with Apple, but he'd settled for sex with Maggie on her living room floor.

Maggie sucked in her upper lip. They'd all been irresistible opportunities at the moment.

"Don't bullshit me," Jonathon said, as if he'd been reading her mind. "If you want to have meaningless sex, go right ahead. I'm not the enforcer."

"You're right; you're right. I've got to figure out a policy that works for me, and at the moment, seems to me I'm in major need of major nooky."

"Major Nooky?" One of Jonathon's eyebrows lifted. "Oh, Magpie, I do believe you're onto something. What would happen if the army recruiters got a hold of that phrase? You could have Captain Cunnilingus. Sergeant Stroke-job . . ."

"You know, you're right," Maggie said, thinking back over the meaningless relationships she'd had since Deuce. "I *am* on the road to becoming a sex burnout."

"And a sex magazine burnout," Jonathon said, pointing to the copy in his hands. "This has to be the flattest story I've ever read on one of the most titillating topics under the sun."

"Oooh!" Maggie moaned. Jonathon spoke the truth, a very painful reality. "So my sex life is empty and my career is snowballing out of control," she said. "But let's look on the bright side. Give me a minute and I'll find it."

"There is no bright side. But if you finish up in five minutes, I'll buy you a beer at Platypus."

"Make that a Cosmopolitan and it's a deal."

Turning back to his work, Jonathon adjusted his glasses with a dramatic sigh. "How do I end up bailing you out *and* buying the drinks? I've got to be doing something wrong here."

"Come on, let's finish," Maggie said, thinking of the guys who usually hung out in the back corner booth at Platypus. She'd slept with one of them once—a Derek or Dirk or something—but the whole group was just adorable and straight and into stock talk about things like options and futures and mergers. Lingo that filled the air with power. A regular testosterone-fest.

With any luck, she'd be hooked up with someone before midnight.

7

The next morning Maggie rushed around her apartment feeling festive and carefree as she tossed sweaters and jeans into a duffel bag. Her travel kit, always loaded with essentials like toothpaste, brush, shampoo and conditioner, was plopped onto the heap, along with a journal of story ideas. Hugging a mug of coffee, she paced through the apartment and tried to figure out if she was forgetting something.

Her boots clicked on the hardwood floor, a little warped in spots, but still made of rich, dark wood. The living room was narrow, with a nonworking fireplace built along the wall of exposed brick. The windows were tall, charming and drafty, but the place had character—plus a separate bedroom in the back, far enough away from 2nd Avenue to avoid the honking horns of cars waiting to go over the 59th Street Bridge. At eleven-hundred a month, the rent put a major squeeze on her budget, but the place had been a find and a necessary refuge after the Deuce Disaster.

She bent down beside the sofa to pick up the black costume she'd dropped there last night. It was a French maid's uniform, short and sassy, which Maggie had purchased for Halloween one year but held on to for role-playing with guys. Men loved to play the naughty boss taking advantage of the unsuspecting servant.

Last night Maggie had worn only a garter belt and black stockings underneath, much to the delight of her guy from Platypus. What was his name? It didn't matter. He was balding and a little too slick for Maggie's taste, but she'd wanted a quick fix and he'd produced the goods. Fortunately, he'd been happy to leave afterward, leaving Maggie free to shower and drop into her bed alone.

Hopefully, Mr. Platypus would hold her over for a few days. It was time to start straightening out her sex life. Really, this daily quest was just taking up too much of her time and energy. She was sliding the costume onto a hanger in her closet when her cell phone rang.

"I'm double-parked downstairs," Apple said. Phone pressed to her ear, Maggie went to the window and peered down to 2nd Avenue, four floors down. "Is that you in the UPS truck?" she joked. "No, wait. You must be the white Jeep."

"Ya-huh. I rented a road warrior."

"A Jeep? Isn't that extra?" Money was tight for Maggie and Apple, and Maggie hated to press Chandra to pick up the slack just because she had a high-paying job.

"It's deductible," Apple insisted.

"Yeah, but first you need an income to deduct from," Maggie explained. "And you also need to pay for the rental. That deduction stuff is a wash-out when you're broke."

"You worry too much," Apple said, tooting the horn. "Get your rear in gear and get it down here."

"All righty then."

Maggie triple-locked the apartment, tramped down the stairs and flung her bag into the back of the Jeep. "This is awesome," she said, swinging up into the front seat. "Where's Chandra?"

"She asked me to pick her up last," Apple said. "Something about a late night at the office. I think she was about to cancel, but I wasn't going to let her go there. That girl's becoming a serious workaholic."

"Well, we'll break her of the habit this weekend," Maggie said, rolling down her window an inch to savor the city sounds and cool autumn as the Jeep headed across town to the Upper West Side.

A doorman helped Chandra to the Jeep toting her sleek Louis Vuitton suitcase. Maggie had seen the line in an accessories spread that had somehow never made it into *Metro,* probably because the bag was out of reach of most of the magazine's readership. Wow. At least if Chandra was going to be rich, she was doing it with class.

"This is so great," Maggie said as they cruised up the Westside Highway toward Westchester. She was glad her parents had decided to fly to California and spend the week with Aunt Gina. She needed a break from the McGee Thanksgiving ritual of cooking frantically, eating three helpings, then collapsing on the sofa. "How long has it been since we spent a holiday together? And a cheap one at that."

"Cherry and Nelson are happy to foot the bill at turkey time," Apple said. "They love to control people, whether it's with food or funds or law suits." Apple's father, Nelson Sommers, was an attorney who'd specialized in litigation.

"It's nice of you to put up with your parents so that we can spend the weekend in the country," Chandra said. "We owe you, Apple."

"No biggie," Apple said, pushing a disk into the Jeep's CD player. "Just remember this the next time I want you to help me get a shot of George Clooney."

"I'm game," Maggie said. "Anytime you need help stalking celebs, I'm your girl."

Chandra just sat back, her arms folded over her gold Abercrombie & Fitch field jacket. She hated making a scene over celebrities. Actually, she hated making a scene at all. Sometimes Maggie wondered how she and Chandra had become such good friends, when Maggie was always the loud, wacky one who stirred the pot, while Chandra preferred to stand by quietly. She used to think she embarrassed Chandra, but recently she'd begun to suspect her friend loved being along for the wild ride—Chandra just didn't want to be in the driver's seat of the funmobile.

The ride took longer than usual, with holiday traffic bringing cars to a standstill at times.

"Can I tell you how glad I am to not be rushing?" Maggie said as she turned up the volume on the Dave Matthews Band. When that was finished, there was Nelly Furtado and the Red Hot Chili Peppers.

"So, Maggie," Chandra said from the back. "Are you going to behave this weekend? Mr. and Mrs. Sommers have that rule about boys in the bedroom."

"Ha! That worked just fine when we were fourteen!"

"I thought you made a deal with yourself about guys," Apple told Maggie. "Aren't you going to chill on the quickies and look for something more lasting?"

"Absolutely," Maggie said, touching the tender part of her skin where the stubble of Mr. Platypus's chin had grazed her just a few hours ago. She hated it when her friends made her feel guilty. "I'm definitely looking. But hello? It's not easy to find a guy that I can stand for more than one night."

"We know that," Chandra said. "Believe me, we know. But you're giving too much away. You're like an investor who moves his money from one stock to another before the stock has a chance to grow. You may not lose, but you'll never reap substantial profits."

"Ugh! I can't think of a guy as an investment." Maggie rubbed her eyes. "Do you ever get a payoff? I mean, really? Really?"

Apple pushed a curl out of her eyes, staring ahead at the road. "Don't look at me. Chandra's the financial maven."

"Come on!" Chandra was getting frustrated. "You act like they're a different species. Men are Homo sapiens, you know."

"Maybe Jeff was," Maggie said, wondering if it was a bad idea to bring up the love of Chandra's life. "Jeff was a rare breed, Chandra, and you're proof of that. Have you even dated once since he died?" Jeff's death in a car accident had left everyone stunned. It had been two years, but still Chandra hadn't completely moved on. How do you move on when your life is totally enmeshed with someone who disappears?

"Jeff was exceptional," Chandra agreed. "But he wasn't an anomaly. I'm sure there are other exceptional males out there."

"This from the woman who said she would never date again?"

Maggie turned around in her seat and cast Chandra a hard look. "What's up with that, Toots?"

Chandra squirmed. "I'm sure there are good men out there. Just not for me."

"Okay . . ." Maggie pursed her lips. "So are you saying we should take your advice, even though you don't believe it yourself? Do as I say, not as I do?"

Chandra ran a hand over the leather seat of the Jeep, then smiled. "Yes. Exactly."

"Gotcha." Maggie laughed as she straightened in her seat. "Just wanted to be sure we're on the same page."

Tall apartment buildings gave way to modest houses, then to rocky cliffs and hills dense with the last of the autumn foliage. It was after noon by the time they exited the interstate onto the narrow highway that skirted the placid reservoirs and cut through forested hills. Maggie was glad to be away from the city for a few days. Maybe the break would help her figure out her life, help her decide what she wanted to be when she grew up.

Like that was going to happen.

Gravel crunched under the tires as Apple turned into her parents' driveway, a long, curving affair that rose up the stately grass hill and snaked around the side of the sprawling Tudor mansion. Maggie popped out of the Jeep to the smells of musty leaves and moist earth and the barks of two Golden Retrievers that seemed to gallop out of nowhere.

"Easy, guys," Apple shouted to the dogs. They ignored her. One dog sniffed Maggie's crotch, while the other raced up to Chandra and jabbed his front paws on her chest, nearly knocking her over. "Stop that, Thunder!" Apple ran around the Jeep and yanked the dog away from Maggie's legs. He swung his huge head over to Apple, then jumped up to lick her face. "That's a baby," Apple cooed. "Nice kisses."

Chandra pushed the other dog away and wiped a pawprint from her jacket. "What's wrong with these dogs today?" she asked. "They used to be so mellow."

"They're probably overwhelmed by a house full of visitors," Apple said.

"Oh, there you are!" Cherry called crisply. "We expected you earlier."

Typical Mom greeting, Maggie thought as she slammed her door of the Jeep and smiled at Apple's mother. Not "so glad to see you," but "you're late!"

"We hit traffic," Apple said as Maggie and Chandra stepped forward to give Cherry the perfunctory kiss on the cheek. "What's wrong with the dogs?"

"Frightened of the babies, I think. Melonie arrived Monday, with the triplets. Dennis called last night to say he had to cancel. Something about a tech emergency, but isn't that so like him? Last minute, and he hasn't seen his family for ages. I don't know what the story is with him. I just don't know . . ."

Apple turned to Maggie and muttered: "Mid-thirties, lives in San Francisco, never married, never comes home . . . you do the math."

"Anyway," Cherry Sommers went on, "Aunt Viv and Uncle Rick are here." She smiled proudly, her gray eyes pale as she assessed the girls. "We're quite a houseful this weekend."

"Great. The more the merrier." Apple hugged both dogs, calling them her babies, then went to the back of the Jeep for their luggage.

"No," Cherry said, "why don't you leave that for Raul and take these beasts off my hands. They need a good run, so they're not going wild around the babies. The men are in the rec room watching the game. Otherwise, I'd make your father take them."

"Okay." Apple slammed the Jeep door closed, then clapped her hands madly. "Come on, guys. Come on!"

Maggie and Chandra exchanged a look of disbelief. A run in the woods? Maggie's idea of exercise was walking instead of taking a cab. "We'll bring up the rear," Maggie said as Apple chased the dogs off toward the wooded path.

Maggie planned to spend the afternoon reading a novel. As soon as the dogs got their run in, she followed Apple to the west wing of the house where two cozy rooms had been made up for Chandra and her. "The quilt room and the floral room," Apple called them. "Love it," Maggie said, kicking off her boots. "Time to bask in vacationville."

Maggie washed the sheen from her face and buried her face in a fluffy towel. She had just plopped onto the bed when Apple popped her face in the door.

"We've been summoned to service in Cherry Sommers's kitchen."

"Now?" Maggie swallowed a groan.

"Hey, dinner for twenty-two doesn't just happen." Apple folded her arms. "You know, maybe we should have skipped this trip and ordered turkey wraps at Ceecee's."

"No, no, I'm coming." Maggie slid on a strappy pair of Manolo Blahnik shoes and clacked downstairs. In the huge oak-paneled kitchen, two uniformed servants went about their tasks calmly, accustomed to Cherry's fixation with getting the meal right. At the counter, Chandra was grinding fresh cranberries into a relish. Apple was needed to peel potatoes and Maggie was put to work polishing silver. Maggie wrinkled her nose when Cherry wasn't looking. She hated the smell of the cleaner, but she sucked up her complaints, not wanting to appear ungrateful.

"I don't know why I have to make such a fuss over family, but I can't help myself," Cherry said as she added a serving dish to the cluster of silver to be polished. "My mother always said, if it's worth doing, it's worth doing right."

"That is so true," Chandra said with so much fortitude Maggie wanted to wing a pickle fork in her direction. Already her hands were sweating under the rubber gloves.

"Now," Cherry said, pushing out the door, "what are we doing for a centerpiece."

With the wicked mother out of earshot, Maggie held up a silver urn and asked Apple, "What is this used for?"

"Just for show," Apple said. "She won't put anything in it, but you've got to keep the silver polished all the time."

"Okay," Maggie said. "Guess I've been rather lax with my silver."

"Shh!" Apple warned. "Here comes Martha Stewart."

Cherry breezed in with an armful of brown brush and orange mums. "I found these in the backyard. They'll bring marvelous color to the mantel, won't they?"

"What a great idea," Chandra said enthusiastically. "And the colors are appropriate for the season."

Apple nodded. "Very nice."

Rubbing a sugar bowl in her hands, Maggie edged over to Chandra. "I'm sorry," she said under her breath, "but if you suck up anymore, I'll have to kill you."

Chandra smiled. "Is it my fault you're lacking in aesthetic sensibility?"

"Did you bring your camera?" Cherry asked Apple.

"Always."

"Don't forget we need a family portrait—sans Dennis. I'm sorry he couldn't make it, but it's his loss. The triplets have grown so much, we have to document it. You should be around more often to capture their pictures while they're playing." She circled Apple, staring cautiously at the mass of red hair that was bundled and held in place by two black lacquered chopsticks. "And what are you doing with your hair?"

"Letting it grow?" Apple said defensively.

Cherry mulled that one over, as if trying to phrase her rebuttal.

"All done," Chandra said proudly, holding up her bowl of sparkling ruby cranberry relish. She dropped the old-fashioned grinder into a sinkful of bubbles and wiped her hands on a towel. "What's next?"

"You can start setting the table," Cherry said, putting a hand to her mouth. "What did I do with those napkin rings? They're so lovely, each one shaped like a leaf." Chandra followed her to an oak hutch in the kitchen, where they searched through drawers.

"Look at these." Chandra held up a box of ceramic statuettes. "Little turkeys."

"Oh, those are place-card holders," Cherry explained. "But we could put a few out for decoration."

"What about place cards?" Chandra suggested. "I used to do calligraphy."

"Really?" Cherry was impressed. She motioned Chandra out to the dining room. "Let's take a look at the table and map out a seating chart."

"Sounds like Cherry has met her match." Apple shoved the paring knife into a potato, circling a black spot. A piece of potato popped out and shot onto the floor. "Is it me? Or is Chandra being a little too sycophantic?"

"Just like old times." Maggie wiped her itchy nose on her sleeve. "Does the name Eddie Haskell ring a bell?"

Apple laughed. Back in high school, they had loved reruns of *Leave it to Beaver* and *The Brady Bunch* and *Father Knows Best.* Simple stories about happy families. "I think I was the only kid on the block whose house was cleaner than the Cleavers'," said Apple. "Too bad my mom wasn't quite as warm as June."

"Nobody's mother was." Maggie had never expected her parents to be like the moms and dads in those shows; even as a teenager, she knew that reality sucked. Her parents didn't argue about the budget the way Lucy and Ricky did; instead they bickered about how long to cook the chicken and whether the paperboy should get a tip when he threw the paper in the bushes. And when they weren't arguing, they yelled at their kids.

"You're eating too much!" or "Eat, eat! I cooked this dinner and now you're not hungry!" "Shut up!" or "Why are you so quiet?" "You're glued to that tube!" or "Why don't you settle down and watch TV?"

No, Maggie had always known the shows were not like her life, but how tempting to lose yourself for an afternoon in three-dimensional mind candy. "They called those shows sit-coms, but they were really fantasy. Escapist TV."

The door opened, and Melonie appeared, her face puckered in annoyance. "Brianna just threw up. It's that damned dog food. Mom just doesn't get that you can't keep a one-year-old from putting everything in her mouth."

Maggie stopped rubbing the rosebud tip of a silver lid to

check out Apple's younger sister. Melon, in keeping with the family fruit motif, shared all of Apple's features, but the packaging was so different. It was as if Melonie was the Wal-Mart knock-off of a Saks Fifth Avenue gown. Her orange hair was cropped painfully short and swirled into a helmet-head. Her jade stud earrings and green sweater-set and black stretch jeans gave new meaning to the expression: Cute as a button!

"Hi, Melon," Maggie said. As their eyes met, Maggie thought for a moment that her assessment of Melonie was too mean. After all, the woman had born triplets a year ago; was it her fault if she'd fallen into the dowdy pond?

Melonie yanked open the door to the commercial-size refrigerator. "Have you seen Mom?" she asked as she took out a baby bottle and gave it a shake.

"She should be in the dining room," Apple replied. "Say hi to Maggie."

"Hi to Maggie," Melon said flatly.

Okay, maybe it wasn't mean at all. Without a kind word Melonie headed into the dining room, reminding Maggie that she'd always been a twit.

"That girl needs a make-over," Maggie said. "Or is she happy being the poster girl for the JCPenney's catalog?"

"Don't even go there," Apple said, shaking her head. "You know, sometimes I can't believe she's really my sister. We grew up in the same house and she's a complete stranger."

"Families can suck," Maggie said. "I can't tell you how glad I am to be away from home for the holidays. Cherry and Nelson, I can deal with. Not my parents, not my issues."

"Right-oh. Unfortunately, they *are* my parents, and the issues abound." Apple dropped a skinned potato into a pot. "We've got issues seeping out of the woodwork. We just never talk about them." Apple gouged out the black eye of a potato and flung it into the sink. "See, if you never talk about them, they don't exist."

8

From the minute Mom greeted them and complaining about the dogs, Apple knew it had been a mistake to come here. What had she been thinking? That her friends would buffer her from the usual agitation that accompanied a family holiday?

Bad call. But then, she'd been making a lot of mistakes lately. She just was not on top of her game, not in control of things, not sure how to return her life to the light, precarious balance she strived to maintain. She had let down her hair so that it fell over her face. Maybe if they couldn't see her eyes, they would leave her alone. Let her hide.

"Apple, help Raul get the extra chairs from the library," her mother said.

In a daze, Apple followed the orders.

"Set up Jeffey in the high chair."

"Show Chandra where we keep the pickle forks."

"Put the dogs outside."

"Pull Brianna away from the dogs' bowls."

Reaching down, Apple picked up the pudgy little thing by the waist. The baby squirmed in her arms like a worm being lifted out of the moist earth. She held the baby out, hoping that Mom or Melon or someone would take her, but they were busy fluttering around the kitchen and talking about whether it was redundant to have mashed potatoes and sweet potatoes in the same meal.

"Here . . ." Cherry grabbed a bottle from the counter and handed it to Apple. "See if she'll take this." Cherry ran her fingers through the baby's bangs. "Are you going to eat for Auntie Apple now?"

As Mom blew kisses, Apple backed away to a chair in the windowed nook, feeling more like the prison guard of a militant alien than an aunt. The baby sat in her lap and tugged at the table, not particularly interested in Apple, either. How had it happened that she was a total stranger to her own niece? Her sister had absolutely no regard for her, her mother had no respect for her skills or time, and her father didn't even care enough to come say hello during a commercial break in the football game.

The baby grabbed at the bottle and Apple pushed the nipple into her mouth. She started drinking, which was a good thing, Apple suspected. But the calm child gave her time to focus on the two women lording over the kitchen—her mother and sister. For the first time she realized they both had that same helmet-shaped hairdo and the same hard squareness to their jawline. When had Mom's face turned so square? Weren't old people supposed to grow soft and rounder as they aged?

Her face reflects her temperament, Apple thought. Though a square shape seemed so unnatural for a human face. It was the shape of boxes and buildings, synthetic robots, not people.

The pace in the kitchen quickened as the servants moved about and the men came in. Lifting her chin, Apple searched for Dad. Where was he? Why hadn't he said hello?

"Are you okay?" Maggie asked, her voice brightly animated yet contained, distant.

Apple was watching her father uncork a bottle of wine in the midst of the activity. He hadn't said hello yet, no kisses or hugs or warm smiles.

"Apple?" Maggie leaned down over her. "Why don't you put the baby in her crib?"

Brianna had fallen asleep, her body a gelatinous loaf in Apple's arms. Not sure she could walk steadily, she handed the baby to Maggie, who disappeared in the crowd of people toting platters into the dining room.

I can't believe he didn't say hello to me. It's trivial, but it matters. He only cares about me when no one else is around.

The parade moved to the dining room, and somehow Apple found herself seated in a chair before a shiny plate. A ceramic turkey held a card with her name. Apple. How silly and pretentious. As if she didn't know her own name.

I know my name.

"Who wants to say the blessing?" Nelson asked.

Someone made a joke, and across the table Chandra and Maggie laughed. Why were they sitting so far away, so far and drifting away like a raft down the river? Apple wanted to reach out and grab hold, to float off with them, but she was hopelessly stranded across the table.

Somewhere down the table a child recited grace, and then there was more conversation and chuckles and clinking of spoons as dishes were passed. The smells were overwhelming, steam rising from white and orange and brown and green and red food items, mounds and swirls and nuggets of food.

Then he spoke.

"Push your hair out of your face, honey."

Apple stared at him, wondering if she were dreaming or simply recalling a Thanksgiving dinner from twenty years ago. He scowled at her, his face a mask of disapproval.

It was real.

"How can you eat with that hair in your face?" Dad said, his tone laced with criticism.

She tucked the hair back behind one ear and wondered if he would ever ever ever leave her alone.

His blue eyes were brutal, cutting back to another evening, another dinner. An ordinary Sunday dinner when Apple didn't want to eat. There was a science lab report and a pre-algebra test and something else for school, and she'd holed up in her room to spend the night on her schoolwork.

But then the door had burst open and Dad had roared, something about dinner hour and respect for her mother. She couldn't hear him through all that fury, all that anger. Grabbing her by the shoulders, he dragged her down the hall of the Bayside Hills house. He pushed her down the stairs. She stumbled on the top step, but managed to catch the rail. Not good enough. With a growl, he pried her hands loose and pushed her again, watching her pound down. She could still hear the rhythmic thumps as she rolled down. She had landed in a ball at the bottom.

Huddled in a whimpering mass, she'd seen his shoe coming. The kick hit her backside like an attack from a stranger, some evil she had never encountered. Then he yanked her up and into the dining room, where she sobbed at the table under pressure to eat steak and rice and green beans.

How can I eat when you want to destroy me?

Someone laughed, bringing Apple back to the moment, the long table in the Westchester house, the Thanksgiving smells and foods.

"It's a wonder you can see through the lens to take those pictures," Dad went on, and she realized he'd been joking about her photography. "Not that life would end without them, mind you. The world might be a better place with fewer celebrity photos. Gods, they are, in our society. It's appalling."

It's what I do, Apple wanted to say, but she couldn't make her mouth work. The whole dinner thing was hard enough without his attack. Already it was hard to distinguish the mashed potatoes from the creamed onions. Not that it mattered. Food wasn't going to get past the tightness in her throat. She pushed a glazed carrot around on her plate and wondered how long.

How long do I have to endure?

Sticky, warm air. So hot, my fingers swelling.

Babies crying. Moaning, whining.

Cousins laughing. Not funny. Loud.

Sister, sister, do you hate your life? Screaming babies and a man who seems like a stranger to you.

Mother controlling.

Father scorning.

Do you hate your life?

"Apple," he said, louder. "Would you snap out of it and pass the cranberry relish? What's the matter with you?"

Nelson ruling. Nelson not caring. *Daddy, Daddy, what happened?*

Tears swelled in her eyes and suddenly it was all too much to take. She hoisted the cranberry dish and pushed it into another set of hands. Then, chair scraping, napkin dropping, she fled.

9

Swallowing a mouthful of mashed potato with roasted garlic, Chandra watched as her best friend left the table in a fit of tears. What was wrong with Apple? Chandra didn't get it, and the idea of disturbing everyone—the entire family and guests gathered for such a nice meal—seemed unnecessarily dramatic and selfish. Okay, something was bothering her, but couldn't she wait until after the meal and take it up in a more personal forum? Apple's public displays had always made Chandra uncomfortable, even from the day they'd met.

Chandra had just celebrated her ninth birthday in Gramma's tiny Bayside house when her grandmother got the job keeping house for the Sommers. Gramma liked it because the Sommers lived in the same town, just a short bus ride away. And since the family wanted her there every day, Gramma no longer had to travel to different parts of Queens to clean strangers' houses and apartments. For the first week or so, Gramma was reluctant to bring Chandra around. But then Cherry Sommers was thrilled to learn that Gramma cared for a girl the same age as her daughter, and she insisted that Chandra come to the house every day after school.

That first day, Chandra had dreaded the visit. The walk down the wide, treed lane with a strip of grass and trees in the center of the road. The streets near Gramma's apartment were narrow, with barely any space between the houses and the street. No front lawn to play in, no sidewalks. But that day Chandra walked on a smooth, wide sidewalk past flowerbeds of mums and late impatiens to the three-story colonial house. She still remembered knocking at the side door because Gramma had warned her not to come to the front and "put footprints all over the carpeting." Once inside, Mrs. Sommers had greeted her with a warm smile and a pat on the shoulder. Apple had approached her with reticence, but not the snobbishness she'd anticipated. There was a frisson of something in the girl's soft gray eyes—of interest or concern? Maybe pain. That first day, they did their homework side by side at the kitchen table. Within a week, Chandra met Maggie, Apple's best friend. Within a month, the three girls were inseparable and Chandra felt sure she was on a magic carpet ride into a wonderland not designed for lower-class black girls from the projects of Philadelphia. There were soccer games and bowling clubs and dance classes that Gramma couldn't really afford, though Chandra had a feeling that the Sommers footed some of the bill. Through the years, their friendships had blossomed. Threes were said to be so difficult, but somehow it worked for the girls from elementary school through high school. Car-pooling, teaming up for group projects, and hanging out at Joe's Pizzeria every Friday after school. They became an invincible threesome, a core group of friends who reached out to other people but always landed back in each other's bedrooms to cram for tests or speculate over boys. And they'd remained friends through college and first jobs and apartment-hunting in Manhattan.

When Gramma passed away, Apple and Maggie were there for her. Nelson Sommers helped Chandra handle all the funeral arrangements, and Maggie's mom insisted Chandra stay with them the week of the funeral.

Thinking back, Chandra realized that she probably felt more comfortable with Apple's parents than Apple did. But maybe that was typical, like that tired saying about the grass being greener on the other side.

Just then Maggie kicked her under the table and Chandra paused over a forkful of turkey to glance beside her. Maggie rolled her eyes expressively, though Chandra wasn't really sure whether she meant "Oh, Apple's getting dramatic again," or "Can you believe this fucked-up family?" Chandra never was good at reading other people's thoughts.

Nelson Sommers broke the strained atmosphere at the table by clanging a helping of cranberry relish onto his plate. "Got to have cranberry relish at Thanksgiving," he insisted jovially. "None of that red jelly from a can."

"Actually, Chandra made the relish this year, and it's delicious," Cherry offered, and Chandra smiled amid the glances of approval and the scattered compliments. She liked cooking, though she hadn't done much of it since she lost Jeff. Cooking for one just didn't make it.

While Cherry Sommers entertained everyone with a story about the search for a forty-pound turkey, Maggie kicked her again. This time Chandra turned to her with annoyance. What was it now? She couldn't take this nonverbal noncommunication. Maggie nodded toward the upstairs, and Chandra shrugged. "What?" she said under her breath.

"Shouldn't we go up?" Maggie grumbled.

Swinging her fork slightly, Chandra indicated the table full of food and people. "It would be rude."

Maggie rolled her eyes again. "Okay. Then eat."

Rushed, Chandra couldn't enjoy the rest of the meal. She managed to finish her turkey and mashed potatoes before Maggie stood up and lifted her plate.

"That was delicious," Maggie said, stepping away from the table.

"Oh, dear, leave that," Cherry Sommers said. "Raul will clear. And I hope you left room for pie. We have four different kinds."

"Sounds great," Maggie said cheerfully. "If you'll excuse me for now . . ."

Chandra knew a cue when she heard it. She excused herself and followed Maggie up the stairs.

"What was that about?" she asked Maggie.

"I don't know, but Apple is one unhappy camper."

They went to the three rooms that had been set up for them, but they were empty. "I know," Maggie said, leading the way down the hall to the original wing of the house. Music drifted down the hall, and Chandra recognized the voice of James Taylor singing "Sweet Baby James." It came from Apple's old bedroom, the room she had occupied during summer and semester breaks after the family moved to this house. Maggie knocked on the door and pushed it open. Stepping in behind her, Chandra felt her mouth drop open in surprise. Apple was stretched out on the bed, stripped down to her underwear—a white lacy bra and white bikini panties that showed off her flared hips and flat tummy.

"Don't come in," Apple called, blowing a gust of smoke into the air.

"Too late." Maggie plopped onto the foot of Apple's old twin bed and picked up a stack of CDs. "And now that we're here, you'll never get rid of us. We're the guests who wouldn't leave, who come to eat all your family's food, who run up the long-distance bill and stay indefinitely."

"Be my guest," Apple said. "I'm outta here in ten minutes."

"No, you're not," Maggie insisted. "Don't let them ruin your weekend."

"Really." Chandra pulled out the desk chair and sat down. "They're not that bad. And wait a minute, you don't smoke."

"No," Apple said, taking a drag, "but it really pisses my father off. I bummed this one off Raul." She folded her legs casually, reminding Chandra of a lingerie commercial for Victoria's Secret. Apple had one of those bodies that was just genetically chic, slender legs, long torso, graceful hips, champagne-cup breasts. Not that Chandra didn't have it goin' on, but she always worried that her butt was too wide, and everything she ate went directly to her hips.

"Was he the one that set you off?" Maggie asked Apple. "That comment about your hair?"

Apple blew smoke out over her head and picked up an old Garfield knickknack from the bedstand. "I can't talk about it. What's the point?" She stubbed the cigarette out in the pouch that Garfield was carrying, sat up, and crossed her legs. "Let's get out of here."

"Sounds good to me," Maggie said, looking up from a Madonna CD. "But don't you think it's a little cold out for the lounge-wear?"

"Details." Apple went over to a dresser and extracted a baggy gray sweatshirt that said "Bennington" across the front. Dressed in sweats and sneakers, she led the way down the back staircase toward the Jeep.

"A back staircase!" Maggie lifted her velvet pants to navigate the steps. "How cool is this? Wish we had it in high school."

"What about our coats?" Chandra asked. "It's freezing out."

"We'll be inside," Apple assured her, leading the way outside. "Car to bar."

"Shit! It's cold!" Maggie gasped.

"I can't believe we're sneaking out," Chandra said as she slammed the door of the Jeep. "Three women in their thirties going out the back way so Mom and Dad won't catch them."

"That's the thing with parents," Apple said. "They may grow old, but they never stop controlling."

"I wouldn't know," Chandra said as Apple started the engine. "That I wouldn't know."

10

Oh, what is happening to my wonderful Thanksgiving? Maggie wondered as Apple pulled the Jeep into the lot of the Weeping Beech, a bar she'd taken the girls to before. The music was loud, the beers were ice-cold, and besides, it was the only bar in this part of Westchester that didn't require a long drive down a series of country roads.

As soon as the Jeep landed the girls slammed out and ran inside, slapping their arms against the cold. A fire was burning in the old fireplace, the only touch of charm in the tidy room with its linoleum floors, vinyl bar stools and single pool table.

The place was quiet, with a few old-timers watching the TV at the bar and a group of teenaged girls who had commandeered the pool table. Otherwise, the jukebox blared to an empty room. Apple ordered three Rolling Rocks and brought them over to a table by the window.

"Here's to getting away," Maggie said, hoisting the green bottle. She wanted to put the ugly scene at the table behind them and party on. The red glow of a neon Budweiser sign cast a pink tint over Chandra's brown hands as she grabbed a beer.

"To getting away from the city," Chandra said.

"Getting away from life," Apple added. She took a long drink, her hair spilling down her back as she tipped back her head. Watching her, Maggie felt a niggle of worry.

"Not that you can ever get away from life completely," Maggie said. "I mean, not without dying and we're not going to go there. But it is great to get away, put everything on hold, take a deep breath and sleep in a strange bed. Maybe we should blow outta here in the morning and find a little bed-and-breakfast upstate. Just a place to—"

"I hate my life," Apple said flatly.

"No way," Chandra said enthusiastically. "You've got a great life. There's Coop and your studio and . . ."

"Nope." Apple shook her head emphatically. "Don't try to talk me out of it because I've thought about it long and hard and I know what I'm talking about. I hate my life, and my father just sort of underlined all the bad feelings tonight. My work is useless. I spend my days capturing other people's happiness on film, without a hint of that happiness in my own life. Oh, I have Coop, and I had Ray and Gerard and Anthony, but men are not the key to happiness, and neither is sex. Do you know I haven't had an orgasm in years?"

Maggie felt her eyes open wider but fought to hide her reaction. "Really? Years?"

"Maybe longer, I don't know. It's hard to remember."

Chandra clasped her hands together, as if she needed to hear more before she could make an assessment.

"It's okay," Maggie said. "That's okay. You know, it's something you can work on. Lots of women have that problem, and you can overcome it. Really. Orgasm isn't any mystery, and with women it's not about the mechanics of the clitoris or G-spot or anything like that." She pointed a finger to her head. "With us, it's so much about what's going on up here. It's about feelings and sexy images and feeling protected and strong and . . ."

"It's not that important," Apple said, shaking her head. "Really, it's not. Orgasm is the least of my worries. It's just like a symbol of everything that's going wrong in my life. I'm falling apart, and it's like my father can smell the failure. Geez. You'd think the man would just once, one time, give me a fucking break."

Maggie bit her lip. In her world orgasm was way important, at the top of the list of "things to do today," but she didn't want to drive that point home and make Apple feel worse than she already felt.

"Nelson means well," Chandra said defending Apple's father. When Apple gave her a look that said, "Oh, please!" Chandra added, "Didn't he offer to pay for your therapy?"

"That's my mother's doing," Apple said. "Dad is a rock. A mountain. An unscalable precipice." She took another swig of beer. "I'd love to know why he hates me so much."

"You want to talk about hatred?" Chandra asked, her voice catching with emotion. She turned toward the window, trying to steady herself. "How about the man who makes the baby and walks away? Or the woman who hands her child to someone else—not even a screened parent in an adoption, but to some lame relative who just happens to live nearby."

Maggie touched Chandra's hands. "Oh, honey, she didn't mean anything." She was a little surprised, especially since Chandra rarely brought up her own past. Then again, holidays often prompted people to think back over their lives.

"Really, Chandra," Apple said, "and I can't believe you can compare this to yourself. There's no comparison."

"Maybe not, but I'm finding it a little hard to totally buy that your parents hate you, Apple. Parents who stayed together and claim to care for you. They gave you a place to live, a place to go. Not to mention the tennis lessons and braces and trips to the City to see the *Nutcracker* each year at Christmas."

Maggie cradled her beer in one hand, not wanting to see the pain in Chandra's eyes. To be honest, Maggie had enjoyed most of those advantages herself, even though her parents weren't as well off as the Sommers. But Chandra—then named Sharon—had been left out of a few things here and there, mostly because her grandmother couldn't afford it. Of course, Nelson and Cherry frequently rushed to her aid and put up the money, treating

Chandra like their third daughter, but even the Sommers Scholarship Fund had foundered resentment among the girls. Apple saw it as one more act of control from her parents, while Chandra hated being the object of pure charity.

Oh, yeeps. This day sucked the big one. Raking back her dark hair, Maggie checked the bar for hotties. Nothing so far, unless she pounced on an old putz and got his pacemaker rocking. There was a new crowd over at the pool table—a few guys with potential, but they seemed to be attached to the big-haired girls who leaned against the table in their leather jackets and worn jeans.

"Maybe hatred is a strong word," Apple said. "Do I wish that they were dead? No. Do I wish that they were gone from my life? Yes." She turned to the bar, which was filling up with local patrons. "Yes, yes, yes. They may have supported me in childhood, Chandra, but support can be crippling, too. Love can be a noose. Squeeze too hard and you're choking."

"An albatross," Chandra said, swirling her finger in a puddle of condensation. "Did I tell you she called me?"

"She?" Apple lifted a piece of hair from her face and scrunched it in one hand. "She who?"

"Oh, no. You're kidding?" Maggie winced. "Are you sure it was her?"

Chandra wiped her hand on her skirt. "Vincent took the message, but the area code was right. Philly."

"Your mother?" Apple asked.

"I thought she'd never turn up again," Maggie said, thinking of the woman who had left her six-year-old daughter behind and never appeared again. Chandra spent nearly two years with her aunt in Philadelphia before moving up to Queens to live with her grandmother, her primary caretaker. Hell, Gramma had really been like a mother to Chandra. In Maggie's view, it was one thing to realize you couldn't raise your kid, and quite another to turn up years later and pretend that a special bond existed between mother and daughter.

"Well, she's back and she worries me. I just wish I knew how much she wanted. I'd write her a check and be done with it."

"Are you sure it's about money?" Apple asked. "Maybe she's driven by guilt. Or curiosity. Or love."

"Please," Chandra said. "How can you love someone you don't even know?"

"Really," Maggie agreed. "If she feels some sort of attachment, it's this romanticized notion in her head that the bond between mother and daughter is biological and not a result of constant interaction throughout childhood."

When Chandra and Apple turned to her, Maggie shrugged. "So I researched a piece on adopteds and their biological mothers."

"I just wish she would stick with her own life and stay out of mine," Chandra said. "Grayrock is a very conservative corporation. They wouldn't appreciate some crazy lady running around searching for her long-lost daughter. That and the fact that I changed my name."

"You changed it legally," Apple said. "You went through the right channels."

"But a company like Grayrock isn't happy with just complying with the law; in their eyes, the mere appearance of impropriety is enough to tarnish someone's reputation."

"That is so unfair," Apple said.

So is life, thought Maggie as she noticed two guys eyeing the jukebox. One of them, a tall guy with dark hair, had a nice butt. She leaned in toward Apple. "Who's the lumberjack wannabe?"

Apple followed her gaze and smiled. "You've seen him here before. Ozzie Hanover. Definitely from around here, but I'm not sure what he does. And you can bet he was wearing that plaid flannel shirt long before Madonna declared plaid to be back."

Noticing that the pool table was empty, Maggie smiled.

Ozzie smiled back.

Oh, he's a quick study, she thought. She stood up, her chair scraping the linoleum floor. "I say we lighten things up with a game of pool." It was the perfect way to divert her friends from their neuroses.

"Are you kidding?" Apple's freckles stood out. "With Ozzie and Eugene?"

"Oh, please," Chandra said. "I am so awful at pool."

"I bet I can find someone around here to give us a few pointers," Maggie said, turning toward the jukebox. Ozzie and his buddy were already closing up the space between them, swaggering casually like cowboys. *Looks like we found ourselves some country guys,* Maggie thought. *Yeee-haaa!*

11

"For a shot like that, you want to bend down way low, like this." Ozzie curled his body behind Maggie and leaned down, pressing the crotch of his jeans right into her ass. She could feel his package there, something firm and meaty, and for a moment she fantasized about dropping her pants and doing it right here on the pool table.

"See what I mean?" he asked.

"Definitely." She moved slightly, rubbing against him. "I think I'm starting to get the hang of this." Actually, Maggie had learned pool in her Uncle Quinn's basement, but she was willing to play dumb if it meant a few personal lessons from Ozzie. He smelled of spicy shaving lotion, and he had a slight New England accent that made him sound smarter than he probably was.

"I just wish I had the strength to hit the ball harder with precision," Chandra said, dusting the tip of her stick as she eyed the balls on the table. "Seems to me the key is to bank the ball, but I can't seem to hit it hard enough."

Ozzie's friend Eugene laughed. "What is she, a mathematician?" He laughed again, a nervous laugh like the squeal of a loose fan belt.

"Don't laugh," Chandra said, bending down to study a shot. "I play to win. Even when I don't know what the hell I'm doing."

"Fiercely competitive," Apple said, lifting her beer. "Don't get in her way, she'll knock you into the corner pocket."

Chandra tucked a strand of dark hair behind one ear, squinted, and took a shot. The balls cracked hard, scattering close to the side pocket but bouncing off the edge.

"Nice try," said Ozzie.

"Really." Eugene laughed. "You really know how to muscle that stick." He put a hand on Chandra's arm, squeezing her biceps. "What, do you work out? You bulking up on steroids?"

Chandra glanced from his face to his hand, giving off a vibe of disapproval until he pulled away. She didn't take jokes well, especially when they were aimed at her own abilities.

"Of course I work out," Chandra said flatly.

"How about you, Eugene?" Maggie asked, trying to lighten things up. "When's the last time you ran a ten-minute mile?"

Eugene cackled. "That would have to be a few years ago, when we were camping and ended up running from a bear. You never saw a group of guys hightail it outta there so fast."

"Running from a bear?" Maggie stuck her tongue out. "Get outta town. Are we still in America?"

"Yes, but you're not in Manhattan anymore," Apple said. "And last call here is at one A.M., and Santa doesn't deliver to kids over twelve."

"Oh, gad, get me another beer." Maggie held her hand to her forehead and staggered back. "I can't take reality."

"Reality sucks," Ozzie said, pulling her back against him. She let him nuzzle her neck a little as she slipped her hand down to brush his thigh. With any luck, reality wasn't the only thing that would be sucking tonight. She was dying to get into Ozzie's pants.

"Whose turn is it?" Chandra asked, trying to keep the game going.

Eugene stepped up to the table. "I think it's me."

As Eugene stepped up to the table, Ozzie laid deep into Maggie's neck, making her knees go weak.

"Give me a hickey and I'll kill you," Maggie whispered.

Ozzie froze there, uncertain.

"Look," Maggie said, "why don't we take this outside before we get kicked out of the place?"

He stroked her hair back over her ear, making the side of her head tingle. "Sounds good to me."

Without a word to anyone they snuck out the back door by the rest rooms and plunged into the cold air. So cold it nearly took Maggie's breath away.

"Ohmigod, it's freezing out here!" She danced over the gravel, stumbling in her high-heeled Manolo Blahniks.

"Where's your coat?" he asked.

"Didn't bring one. It's a long story."

He slid off this leather jacket and hung it over her shoulders, rubbing her arms.

"That's nice," she said, "but we're never going to last in this. I'm dying to fuck you, but it's not going to happen in this cold."

His eyes grew bigger as he let out a laugh. "Jesus, Maggie, do you always talk that way?"

"Isn't that why we're out here?" She grinned. "Why waste time with talking and kissing when we both know what we really want?"

"You are too much." He held his coat steady so that he could extract a set of keys from the pocket. "Way too much for me. Shit! Come on." He led her over to the parking lot, frozen grass crisp under their feet. She looked up at the sky, a little startled by the stars, so many pindots of light so close and so bright. The smell of woodsmoke filled the air. The muffled blare of the jukebox mixed with the murmur of a solitary passing car reminded her how isolated they were. The country could be so scary.

While she waited he went into a brown van. She heard the engine kick, and a moment later he ushered her into the back. The music of Dave Matthews's "Crash" blared along with the heat, and though the back was littered with tools and boxes and scraps of wood, there was a cozy little spot where he'd spread out a sleeping bag.

"Ozzie, you clever boy." Maggie knelt on the sleeping bag and flung off her sweater. "We have a nice little love nest here, and you pick out the best fuck music."

"What is with you?" He grinned. "Do you have to keep saying that word?"

She pulled him down beside her and tugged up his shirt to touch his nipples. "Oh, it is what it is. Really. But there are a million euphemisms, so what's your favorite?"

"I don't know. I guess I don't really talk about it much." He sucked in his breath as she nibbled on one of his nipples. "Damn, that feels good."

Without lifting her head, she undid his jeans and pressed her hand over the bulge in his boxers. "Ugh! I want this." She rubbed his shaft, then cupped his hard scrotum. "Oh, this is going to be great. Quick! Take off your clothes." She sat back and tugged on one boot.

Ozzie followed her orders with a subtle smile on his face. The boy could be downright handsome when he didn't talk. She slid off her shoes and velvet pants. Her black blazer whispered to the floor, leaving her only with the cover of a diamond pendant dangling between her breasts, above scalloped lace bra and panties. He groaned at the sight of her. Maybe those spinning classes were worth the sweat. As soon as they were naked, she hobbled close on her knees and pressed her body against his. His hard erection rubbed against her stomach, making her sigh.

"I am so wet already, Ozzie," she said in his ear. "Oh, wait!" She pulled away to find her jeans. "The condom! I am so into safe sex. Where is that little bugger?" She pulled the packet out of her jacket pocket and made quick work of rolling it onto him. "There. Okay, wow! You've got to fuck me now. Or wait! What do you want me to say?"

Without answering he lowered her onto the sleeping bag and stretched over her like a marine doing a pushup.

"Do me?" she asked. "Ball me? Give me a little poke in the whiskers? What do you want me to call it?"

His eyes were smokey as he lowered himself, stabbing his cock into her well-trimmed curly hairs. He found the right spot, then thrust in, giving her that first quick, knee-jerk orgasm.

"Oh, yes!" she sighed. "That's it, honey. Whatever you want to call it, that's it." She felt herself nailed against the sleeping bag as he drove in, then out. "Fuck me, fuck me, fuck me," she whispered, getting off on the sound of her own voice as he rammed into her. Ozzie held her arms above her on the mat, and she let her head loll back and forth, playing the part of the helpless fuck doll. And she was helpless, a victim of her hunger for the almighty fuck.

He moved into her again and she squeezed her muscles around him, savoring him. Lifting her head, she could see the outline of them coming together, her wiry hair, his bulging cock. So sexy.

"Wait!" She pushed him to the side and kneeled down between his legs. "I want to come, really, really big," she said, taking him in her mouth. She sucked over the ribbed condom, massaging him with her mouth as she stroked herself with her right hand. If she got herself to the peak, his cock could take her over the edge into a pounding climax that would last for a few minutes. The earth-shattering orgasm, she liked to call it.

"Oh, man, you are so good at this," he whispered as she sucked and stroked. He touched her head, weaving his fingers into her hair, and for a moment she worried that the personal gesture might throw her off her stride. No, she had to focus. Pump his dick, rub herself, and yes, yes, she was getting there, the van rocking as she dipped down on him repeatedly. She felt herself rising, the sensation inside her peaking.

"Oooh . . ." She hopped up and climbed onto him, straddling her legs around his hips. His rod dipped into her easily this time, the mere entry giving her another mini-orgasm.

"Oh, man." He groaned, reaching up to hold her hips. "You are so good at this."

I am, she thought as she rode him with the mastery of a horse-charmer guiding an untamed beast into a pasture. *I am so good at this. So good. Why would I want to stop? Why would I ever think this is wrong?*

Besides, she told herself, *you write for* Metro. *You're supposed to venture to unexplored sexual venues.*

It's research, my dear.

Otherwise, how would I ever get copy for next month's Metro *Moments column?*

12

By the time Apple was awake enough to meander downstairs the next morning, it was nearly eleven. She had actually been up since ten, but she decided to read in bed and prolong the inevitable confrontation with Mom until she absolutely, positively HAD to have a cup of coffee. The large kitchen was quiet, though the triplets had left their mark—and their mother.

"Good morning. Almost afternoon," Melon said as she scraped wet Cheerios off the floor. "But that's what happens when you party all night and sleep all day."

"Do I detect a note of jealousy?" Apple asked her sister. "Or is that just your usual animosity for me?"

"Mom's already gone. To the Galleria in White Plains. Don't expect her anytime soon."

"Woo-hoo!" Apple went over to the counter and picked up a pumpkin pie, which she planned to lavish with whipped cream for a sinful breakfast. "Free at last, free at last!"

Melonie scowled, scrubbing away with a vengeance. "I'm not laughing. You know, one of these days you're going to have to grow up."

"Maybe," Apple said as she poured herself a cup of coffee, "but that doesn't mean I have to grow boring."

* * *

"I'll never understand this antiquing thing," Maggie said later that day as the Jeep cruised down a country road that cut through densely treed areas and rocky hills. "I mean, what's the deal with going through other peoples' rejects and seeing if it works for you? Like I need more old junk in my life."

"They're antiques," Chandra pointed out. "The value of a true antique is in the craftsmanship or in the fact that it's a one-of-a-kind or a limited edition. You might find handmade furniture signed by the artist or a portrait dating back to colonial times with an important document of the Revolutionary War tucked into the back."

"Okay," Maggie said. "Junk with writing on it. I just don't get it, and I hate that bartering thing. It always makes me wonder if I could have done better, if I should have held out longer. Or if I would have gotten a better price if I were blonde or if I spoke Lithuanian or something."

"Stick with me, I love to bargain," Apple said. "I keep walking away until the price is right. And if the vendor won't go down, I just figure it wasn't meant to be."

"Wait, wait, wait," Maggie said, smiling. "The vendors go down? If I could find a vendor who'd go down on me, I could learn to love bargaining."

"Oh, behave," Chandra said. "Didn't you get enough last night with Ozzie?"

Maggie raked her hair back over one ear. "The land of Oz was delightful, but that was yesterday. I've got new lands to conquer."

Apple shook her head in disbelief. "What part of this do you not get? Do you remember our talk about being more selective?"

"Yeah, yeah, yeah, but I hate to turn down easy sex. I mean, he was right there, ready, willing and able. What am I supposed to do?"

"You think like a man." Apple banged one hand on the steering wheel. "That's it. You have sex like a man."

Maggie giggled. "I like that, Apple. I do. And the country is gorgeous, but what am I doing here, antiquing? I don't have the money, my apartment has no room for more junk, and they don't serve cappuccino." Maggie flipped her hair off the collar of her brown leather jacket and sighed. "Somehow I think I've failed before I started."

"Don't worry," Apple said, turning off the road at a sun-bleached wooden sign. "We'll cover for you."

The gravel road led to an old coach house surrounded by a clutter of paraphernalia—countless wheels, signs, tools, tables. Maggie walked up to an old Coca-Cola sign with chipped paint. "They've got to be kidding."

"Coke paraphernalia used to be hot," Chandra said, brushing past wind chimes to open the door. There was no one in the little building, which Maggie found odd, but Apple explained that people were laid-back about antiquing, often letting customers browse on their own until they came to the main house to talk. Maggie couldn't imagine a shopkeeper in Manhattan leaving the store untended—not even for a second. More proof that country people were odd, trusting strangers to sift through their pricey junk.

In thirty minutes Maggie was bored, but Chandra had found an umbrella stand she adored. She made a deal on it and they moved on to the next place, where Chandra found a Waterford crystal finger bowl she had to have. Maggie didn't see anything she even remotely admired, but maybe that was just sour grapes since she couldn't afford to buy anyway. At the third stop, a quaint red mini-barn trimmed in white, Chandra immediately bonded with the owner over a set of nesting tables, and Maggie knew she was reaching her limit. Apple had also grown tired of antiquing, but she grabbed her camera from the Jeep and went off toward the pond to take some pictures. Seeing a sign for horseback riding, Maggie decided to visit the horses and followed the gravel road past the main house and down the hill, where it ended at a weathered gray barn.

A few horses grazed in a field near the stable, and Maggie went over and leaned on the fence. "You look as bored as I feel," she said, running her fingers over the smooth splintered wood.

A chestnut horse—a mare or a gelding, how could a city girl tell?—lifted its head and blew air out through its mouth with a sputtering sound.

"Yeah, my feelings exactly."

"Hey, there!" someone called. A man appeared out of nowhere, a cowboy-type with worn jeans and an open fleece vest and boots.

Oh, baby.

"Can I help you?" he asked, closing the space between them briskly. As he got closer, Maggie picked up on his agitation.

"I was just exploring." She decided to bullshit him. With that scowl, he deserved a little attitude adjustment. "Actually, I was curious about the riding lessons. I work for a women's magazine in the City and it might be something we could do a piece on."

"What magazine?"

She fished in her pocket for the slender folder that held her license, American Express card and business card. He took the card and grinned.

"Metropolitan?" Again, big scowl. Definitely the brooding type. "No way. You don't look like an editor for a magazine like that."

Maggie felt a sting of self-consciousness, but she lifted her shoulders higher. "I'm an editor, not a goddamned model." She hated it when people had preconceived notions of her job, and she hated it more when people hinted that her body wasn't model perfect. She'd worked hard to accept the fact that she was short-waisted, that her breasts had begun to feel the pull of gravity, that she had to eat an occasional lunch of celery, yogurt and diet Coke to compensate for every piece of Godiva chocolate she consumed.

"But *Metropolitan?*" he said with disdain. "That's not a women's magazine. It's a sex magazine."

Oh, you big beef jerky, Maggie thought. "Whatever. What's the story on the riding lessons?"

He handed the card back to her. "Not sure that I should tell you. What exactly were you planning to print? I mean, what's your angle?"

She decided to play into his paranoia. "I was thinking about maybe nude horseback riding? Or maybe people would thrill to the possibilities of just riding a saddle in bed. I mean, what else are those saddle horns good for?"

His face went pale.

"Oh, chill, you big goonhead!" She pounded his chest with gentle fists. "I write for a magazine, not a porn house."

He caught her fists and held them steady against the fleece of his vest. "Yeah, like there's a difference."

Maggie laughed, hating his attitude but liking the feel of his big hands around hers. "Are you always this obnoxious, or is it just because I'm from the city?"

"You think this is obnoxious? This is nothing." He dropped her hands. "Come on. I'll give you a tour of the place."

Maggie followed, annoyed by his attitude but intrigued by the way his jeans hugged his butt. She didn't like the guy much, but somehow, that would not stop her from getting into his pants, given the chance.

Thirty minutes later, Maggie found herself crushed in his arms and writhing on a bale of hay, not so much from passion as from the fact that sharp edges of hay were sticking into her butt through her skirt. The cowboy was still lacking in the personality department, but the mere fantasy of fucking him in the barn was making her wet; it would be enough to pull her through the interlude with Outlaw El Zero.

"I want to nail you," he said, grinding his hips against hers.

"I'll bet you say that to all the editors of sex magazines."

He reached inside her leather jacket and squeezed her breasts. "Take your clothes off."

She nibbled his earlobe, then reached down to flick up her plaid skirt. "Nah-ugh. A sex magazine editor does it with her Prada heels on." She pulled her lacy black panties aside, revealing all. That seemed to get him.

His mouth formed a slow grin as he undid his belt and unzipped his jeans. She tried to focus on the sexiness of his cowboy image—his rough skin, his cold eyes. This was not a man she would want to spend much time with, with his surly comments and critical gaze. But at the moment he had everything she needed under that zipper. Good enough for the time being.

She pulled him toward her, making sure to turn her head away and avoid kissing. She eased him inside her, then jumped up and straddled him.

"Ooohf." She locked her legs around him. "That feels nice."

He pinned her against the wall and began pumping his hips as she held on tight. She imagined herself as a *Playboy* centerfold, city girl on the prairie, having sex just a few feet from the stench of manure and the odd moans of fat cows. Cowboy wasn't much for foreplay, but Maggie didn't care. The excitement of sex in this strange place, exposed and earthy and a little dangerous was enough to get her going. And then there was the anger in his eyes, the primal urges they were both acting out with a stranger.

He drove into her, pinning her to the wall. And she loved it. God help her, she loved it.

13

"It's almost five," Chandra said, stepping up to check the clock on the dashboard of the Jeep. "Do you think Cherry will be pissed if we miss dinner?"

"You know my mother; she's perpetually pissed." Apple's eyes flicked to Chandra's feet. "Look at the line of your boots on the running board of the Jeep. The folds of the leather. Nice . . ." She lifted her camera and snapped a few shots. "Actually, dinner is probably just leftovers. I don't know why we have to make an appearance."

"Because it would be rude not to show or call or anything," Chandra said, feeling like Miss Manners. She knew her friends thought she was a suck-up, but could she help it if Gramma had raised her right? When manners are drilled into you by a large, looming matriarch, you don't let them slip away. She climbed up onto the hood of the Jeep and sat there, her boots dangling over the bumper. The stringy clouds over the hills were beginning to glow pink and purple. Where the hell was Maggie?

"Besides," Apple went on, "Mom's got Mel and her whole crew of screamers there. That should shut her up."

"You still resent Melonie. Why? You don't envy any part of her life, do you?"

"Just the fact that she got the better name."

Chandra puckered. "Melon Balls?"

"Melonie. It's almost normal. The privilege of the firstborn."

"Since when did you want to be normal? No, don't answer. We don't have time for an Apple mind probe." Chandra folded her arms. "It's getting cold. Where the hell is Maggie?"

"I saw her walking around by the barn." Apple lowered her camera to point to the dirt road. "Down there."

Chandra slammed the door of the Jeep. "I'll go find her," she said, heading down the path. "But be here when we get back."

The sun rolled out from behind the clouds, a ball of gold tossed by pastel tendrils in the autumn sky. It was Chandra's least favorite time of year, the end. End of the summer, the end of green trees, the end of life cycles. And then she'd lost Jeff in November, too, on a rain-soaked highway in Houston. They'd told her the car had split in half. It was still so unbelievable. Jeff had been on his way to the airport. He'd just called on his cell to say he'd be home for dinner.

That had been the end of her romantic life. Though people constantly told her she was young and there was so much more ahead for her, she didn't feel it. That was the problem. These days she didn't feel much of anything beyond a sense of duty to her work and her friends. No longer the walking wounded, she was simply numb.

Her boots sank into the soil as she closed in on the old barn. A few horses chewed hay in the paddock, and inside she could hear the gentle mooing of cows, along with a thumping sound. A pounding mallet? Or an animal bucking to get out?

The barn door was open, though it was dark inside. Stepping into the smell of manure and hay, Chandra paused to let her eyes adjust. What was that pounding . . . and that other noise? Horses breathing? Hissing? No . . . wait.

A motion in the corner caught her eyes, and all was explained. First, she saw a man's naked butt and legs. Then she recognized Maggie's face, her dark hair tossed, her head lolling back lazily as the man pinned her against the wall.

Sex. They're having sex. Remember that?

"Huh?" Chandra's hand flew to her mouth as she wondered why she wasn't already gone. This was more information than she wanted or needed.

The man was still grinding away, but Maggie's head lifted. She'd noticed Chandra. She held up two fingers behind his back, mouthing, "Give me two minutes."

Chandra turned away, reminding herself to breathe. *Oh, God. How embarrassing. For me.* Maggie didn't seem to care at all.

Oh, man, I need a drink.

Chandra was walking up the road stiffly when Maggie called behind her. "Hey!" Maggie started running, her hair bouncing, her cheeks pink. "Was that embarrassing or what? Don't worry! He didn't notice." She linked her arm through Chandra's. "If he did, he might have wanted a three-way!"

Chandra closed her eyes, then laughed. "No thanks, that pasty white butt did nothing for me."

Maggie laughed along. "His . . . or mine?"

The awkward moment was over, but Chandra couldn't ignore the obvious. "Don't do this to me, Mags. I'm beginning to worry about you." In a way, she always worried about Maggie, who had no qualms about navigating strange places alone or going off for sex with total strangers. What if she came up against a psycho or a killer disease? Maggie's behavior was way beyond Chandra's comfort factor, and lately it seemed to be getting worse.

"Are you? That's sweet." Maggie pulled open the door to the Jeep. Apple was already in the driver's seat, listening to the radio.

"You found her!" Apple said.

"Yup. She was sewing some wild oats with the farmer. And I just got more information than I ever needed to know about Maggie."

"Get out!" Apple reached back to smack Maggie. "Bad girl!"

"Come on, guys. You know I can take care of myself. Or else I usually find a delectable male to take care of me, which is just what happened down at the barn. I had the most amazing sex right there in the hay." She fell back against the seat with a sigh.

"I've got to write this one up for *Metro.* Sex with a real live cowboy."

"Definitely preferable to sex with a dead cowboy," Apple said, glancing in the rearview mirror. "Put your seat belt on."

"Really," Chandra said, turning around to look at Maggie. "Buckle up, babe. You take too many risks as it is."

Maggie clicked the seat belt on. "Okay, Mom."

"No, really, Maggie. I do worry about you. It's one thing to schmooze up every male in sight with a trace of testosterone. But sex with strangers. And so constantly . . ." Chandra bit her lower lip. "I hope you're careful."

"Do you mean safe sex? Always. I always make them use a condom," Maggie said. "I'm a big girl."

"I'm still shell-shocked from knowing that you slept with Ozzie Hanover last night," Apple said. "He's such a local barfly. I didn't realize you were that hard up for a guy."

"Oh, you're just jealous," Maggie said. "You're in a rut, stuck having regular sex with Coop, who must be a total dud if he's never made you come."

"Excuse me!" Apple shouted. "That was private information."

Chandra glared at Maggie, who squirmed. "I'm trying to help," Maggie insisted.

"Well, you're not," Apple said.

There was a stiff silence in the car as Chandra tried to pinpoint when Maggie had begun to change. Was it somewhere around the time when she'd split with her boyfriend, Deuce Rawlins? "You know," Chandra said, "I never thought I'd say this, but I miss Deuce."

"You hated him!" Maggie shrieked. "His scrawny ponytail and his bohemian friends. You used to call them latter-day hippies."

"I know, but when you were involved with him you were more . . . even. Reliable. Less manic."

"She's right," Apple agreed. "You were definitely a better friend when you were with Deuce. It was like he kept your feet on the ground."

Chandra nodded. "Or at least he kept you from spending all your time on booty call."

"Wait, wait, wait, there," Maggie said. "You ladies seem to have forgotten that getting a little nook-nook is an important part of living. Not that I'm criticizing the ways you choose to express or suppress your sexuality, but by the same token you have to accept my means of sexual expression."

Chandra turned to Apple and in unison they said: "Booty call."

Maggie laughed. "Need I remind you, booty call is a choice, an acceptable lifestyle."

"Nope, sorry, Mags," Apple said. "It's just not working for you. This isn't just about sex, it's about your mental health. Face it, when you take a good hard look at yourself, I think you'll admit you're one of those women who needs a romantic relationship to stay grounded."

"Oh, right," Maggie said sharply. "This from a woman who hasn't paid rent in years."

"I pay rent," Apple protested. "On my studio."

"Girls, girls, let's be kind to each other, please," Chandra said judiciously. "We've never let guys come between us."

"Of course, of course," Maggie said, "but the notion that I need a man. That I *need* a regular guy? Me, need a man?"

Chandra turned around to make eye contact with Maggie.

"Okay, maybe you're right!" Maggie shrieked, her brown eyes popping. "I have felt lonely lately. Lonely and desperate, like my life is careering out of control in a downward spiral of despair and degradation."

"I hate when that happens," Chandra said.

"Maybe I'm going after quick sex to compensate for a lack of intimacy, trying to make up for the fact that there's no special person in my life. Maybe I'm becoming a sex burnout."

"Maybe," Apple said, nodding.

"But what am I supposed to do? Stop having sex?"

"Like that would be the end of the world," Chandra said, thinking of her own nonexistent sex life. Once upon a time she'd had a wonderful partner in romance and in bed, a kind, genuine guy who got just as charged up over profit and loss statements as she did. But all that had ended two years ago when Jeff had been killed. She had gotten used to the fact that she would always miss him, at least a little every day, and she'd worked hard to move on with her life. At work she was back to being a top performer, and she stepped out nearly every weekend, hanging at Birdland or M&R Bar or the Knitting Factory. Who could blame her if sexual desire was now a nonissue, a dormant little troll that reared its ugly head occasionally during a dream or a racy movie scene? Rarely a flare, easily extinguished.

"I can't stop having sex," Maggie said, as if thinking aloud. "That just wouldn't be healthy. I mean, it's not the answer."

"Right," Apple said. "Nobody's expecting you to go celibate, but you could be a little more discerning? Maybe you should make it a policy to sleep only with men who have qualities that interest you? Guys you might want to get to know. Guys you've known for more than ten minutes?"

"Thanks, Dr. Judy," Maggie said.

"What's wrong with that advice?" Chandra asked her. For an intelligent woman, Maggie was having trouble processing this concept of sex in a secure relationship. "What can we do to help you get it?"

"I don't know. It sounds all well and good in the light of day. But when those raging hormones start invading the blood, I don't know. Sometimes a girl's just got to get her groove on."

Staring out at a clump of fiery colored trees, Chandra wondered if Maggie was one of those sex-aholics, people who were addicted to sex. What a drag that would be, always needing sex. Thank God, she could live without it.

14

By the time Sunday rolled around, Maggie had maxed out on the sights and sounds of the country and was craving a nice, noisy, nasty club. The Monkey Bar. Brownie's. How she longed for the clink of martini glasses and the sound wall of voices. The smell of moldering leaves and all that cold fresh air was way too therapeutic for her city lungs.

On the way back to Manhattan Chandra dozed in the backseat, while Maggie and Apple sang along with an *NSYNC song.

"Don't you love his voice? The way he sneers when he sings?" Maggie lifted up the plastic CD cover and planted a wet one on Justin Timberlake's face. "I'll take you home any day, Justin. Which one do you like?"

"Definitely J. C., but really, guys like that are dating eighteen-year-old models?" Apple asked. "I mean, there's Justin and Britney . . ."

"Publicity ploy!" Maggie argued. "Besides, some of the guys in *NSYNC are in their thirties like us. And Justin is just so darned cute." She took her cell phone out of her purse. "I am proud to announce that I have not checked my messages once since I left home. That's the kind of totally liberated, getaway weekend that I had."

"Major points for you," Apple said.

Maggie started dialing up her voice mail. "And what about you? Did you ever talk to Coop?"

Apple shook her head.

"Really? Don't you guys miss each other when you're apart?"

"He was up in Boston at his sister's house, and we just didn't connect."

It sounded more like a business arrangement than a relationship, thought Maggie. She wondered about the future of Apple's relationship with her aloof Wall Street guy. "Do you want to work on things with him?" she asked gently. "You should probably tell him you're not having orgasms."

"I think he knows."

"Do you think he'll work with you? There's lots of things you can do together, and a few you can do on your own, that will help you come during sex."

Apple stared straight ahead at the dimly lit road. "I don't think he's interested. But thanks. Really."

"What are friends for?" Maggie tapped in her voice-mail password then pressed the phone to her ear. "And I'm going to hit the archives first thing in the morning. I know *Metro* has tons of stories about how to reach orgasm." She grinned. "I probably wrote half of them. I'll send 'em over."

"Pointers from the master. How lucky am I?"

Maggie had three messages. One from her mother who was still visiting her aunt in California, one from Tara who'd called from the office on Friday. "I told Candy you probably wouldn't be home, but she told me to try anyway," Tara whined. "But anyway, there's something wrong with one of your stories. Something that has to ship today, I think. I don't know what they're talking about. Just call the office, okay? Bye."

"Little bitch," Maggie muttered. When Apple lifted her eyebrows, she explained, "Candy's out to get me fired, and my assistant seems to be handing her all the ammunition she needs."

"Maybe you should fire your assistant."

"I would if she weren't one of Candy's minions."

The voice mail beeped again, and the third message began:

"Hey, hi, this is a message for Maggie McGee." The voice was low and rich with the wholesome twang of a radio announcer.

Hello, yourself, Maggie thought, holding a hand over her other ear to hear better.

"Maggie, my name is Max Donner and I'm a producer for *Big Tease."* He paused.

Which gave her a change to freak. "Woof! I can't believe it."

"Believe what?" Apple asked.

"It's . . . it's . . ." Maggie blinked at her friend, then held her hand up so she could hear the rest of the message.

"Yes," Max went on, "if you're doing a happy dance, it's well warranted because you and your friends have been chosen to be the contestants on this season's show. Congratulations, Maggie. And congratulations to your friends, uh . . . Apple and Chandra, too. I will be notifying them, too, though I've gone over the application and they didn't include their phone numbers. Bad girls. We're usually fiendishly strict about these details, but being the great guy that I am, I'm going to let it go this time. But call the studio as soon as you get this. We need to start shooting ASAP."

"Ohmigod. Ohmigod!" Maggie bounced up and down in her seat.

"What?" Apple persisted. "What was that about?"

"It's just . . . this guy." Maggie felt herself stall, but she wasn't quite sure how to launch into an explanation of her back-stabbing deception. What could she say? That she had overruled her best friends' decisions, ignored their opinions and forged ahead because she knew they'd all be better off as TV celebrities?

And they would, really. This was going to be the best thing that ever happened to them, if Apple and Chandra could just get beyond their own stubbornness.

"A guy?" Apple scrunched up her face. "You're flipping over a guy? I don't believe it for a second. You throw away men like most people toss snotty tissues."

"I do not!" Maggie paused. "Okay, I do, but . . ." What could she tell her friends?

Time for some fancy footwork.

"Got an idea here," Maggie said. "A deal, actually. If you and Chandra agree to go on *Big Tease,* I promise I will chasten up my sex life. Cross my legs. A regular nun."

Apple winced. *"Big Tease?* You're back on that again?"

"It'll be good for us—for all of us."

"I doubt that. And Chandra will never go for it."

"Just leave Chandra to me. Right now I think she'd do anything to see me sanitize my life."

"She is controlling, isn't she?" Apple said without malice.

"Controlling, but you gotta love her." Maggie turned to the backseat where Chandra was snoring quietly. Shadows deepened her features—her browline, her cheekbones—enhancing the quiet elegance Chandra always possessed, even in sleep.

"Oh, what the hell," Apple said. "I'll take you up on it. It's worth seeing you get yourself together. Besides, what are the chances of us getting on a show like that. Really?"

"Really!" Maggie said, turning toward the window so that Apple couldn't see her ecstatic grin.

15

Enough talk about my orgasms, Apple thought as she pulled the Jeep into the garage under her apartment building. She was glad to be alone and relieved to be home, away from the scrutiny of her parents and the banter of her friends who didn't know the meaning of the word *off-limits.* Christ, if she was worried about the orgasm thing she would have done something years ago, right?

Actually, she'd tried to get back into therapy last year, but looking at her annual budget it was clear that she just didn't make enough to cover the hundred-dollar weekly fee (and that was with a discount!) for her therapist. But getting back into therapy wasn't just about sex. Not really. She wanted to know why every guy she chose made her feel crazy, why she was drawn to the older, protective type who then turned on her with that patronizing attitude of condescension. Little girl lost. Christ, she was so sick of playing that role.

"I need to leave it overnight," she told the parking garage guy in the brown jacket. She had tried to return the Jeep, but the rental car place had already closed for the night. Just her luck. "How much will that cost?"

"Twenty-five dollars." He handed her the stub.

She hitched her duffel bag onto her shoulder and took her camera bag out of the back, all the while wondering why she'd rented this expensive SUV for the weekend in the country, an interlude that had seemed peaceful and pastoral in her mind. How wrong she'd been. Why had she invited her friends to Westchester at all, when her parents always performed a major mind-fuck that took her a good week to undo?

As she rode the elevator up, she checked her watch and shifted from one foot to the other. Eleven-thirty on Sunday, and it occurred to her that she and Coop had never talked over the weekend. Was he home? She hoped he wasn't. If he was here, she would probably feel obliged to have sex with him, and after the weekend's numerous discussions of her lack of libido, sex was definitely at the bottom of her list.

The hallway outside their door was quiet; a good sign. As Apple inserted her key into the lock, she felt a strange resistance. She went to throw the bolt, but the key wouldn't turn.

What? Dropping her duffel bag to the ground, she tried to work the key, but it was jammed. She tried the second lock without success, then squatted down for a better look. The cylinders were shiny gold, brand-new.

"Unbelievable!" The bastard had changed the locks.

Apple dug into her bag for her cell phone and punched in his cell number. She was going to give that asshole hell, blast him right out of his smug good mood. What the hell was he thinking, locking her out? And the way he did it, right out of the blue . . .

His voice mail came on and she gripped the phone ready to blast. *Bleep* . . . it was her cue, but she didn't know where to begin. What could she say? If you love me, come home and let me in? Of course he didn't love her. She knew she didn't love him.

She hung up without leaving a message. What was the point? Coop had said something about kicking her out; he'd just chosen the least confrontational way to do it, being the big wuss that he was. The man was a total loser, Apple thought as she walked the five blocks to her studio, lugging her duffel bag the whole way. She should have left him months ago when she knew it was over, that first night when she'd watched him chew foccacia across the candlelit table at their favorite little Italian restaurant and realized just how ordinary his mind was.

You should be grateful to Coop for giving you the kick in the pants you needed, she told herself as she keyed her way into the vestibule of the converted warehouse that housed her photography studio. She hiked up to the third story. Sure, it's always better to be the "leaver" instead of the one who is left. It's so much more "active" to be the one who walks out. But you must admit, you were stalled, Apple, stuck in the mud with him. This is good. This is all for the best. You'll make a new start, get back into therapy, find your own place to live.

Not on your current budget! her conscience shrieked. Or was that the voice of the accountant her father had hooked her up with? The man had set up a monthly budget for her, stipulating the minimum of bookings she had to do each month in order to pay her assistant, rent on her studio, and other basic living expenses. Apple managed to make the minimum, but there was never enough left over for luxuries like rent on her own apartment. For that she would have to double or triple her bookings, a prospect that undermined her overall goal of getting into art photography. How could she pursue her art when she was running all over her town, working her butt off at weddings and bar mitzvahs?

Climbing the last step to the landing outside her studio, she noticed the stack of bags and boxes in the hallway. Familiar boxes like the blue plastic kitchen crates and the clear plastic boxes she kept her shoes in. On closer inspection she realized those *were* her shoes . . . her jeans, her jackets and blazers and dusters. Damn it, Coop had packed up all her stuff and dumped it here, outside the door of her photography studio. She pressed a hand to her mouth as the tears came. Seeing all her things out here in the hall, she felt exposed . . . overwhelmed.

She unlocked the door, ducked inside with her camera bag, then slammed the door behind her. It was not the end of the world. She was safe here in the studio, even if it wasn't the most hospitable place with its high, unshaded windows, bare white walls and sparse furnishings. She peeled off her leather jacket, fell onto the futon couch, and covered her head with the jacket. Inside there was only darkness and hot moist air and the crinkle of polyester as her lashes brushed against the lining. Yes, she was safe in here. At least for now.

16

"You have reached the offices of *Big Tease,*" said the voice on the phone. "The offices are currently closed, but if you know the extension of the party you are trying to reach, you may—" Maggie pushed the STOP button on her cell as she hurried down the street. She was late for work, as usual, and it wasn't easy walking in these suede heels that showed off major toe cleavage, but they made her feel special (if she could stand the pinching!). She had been calling that producer, Max Donner, all night long, without success. What time did these TV people come to work, anyway?

In the elevator she grabbed her cell again, but decided to wait until she was in the office to call. If Candy was out to lynch her, it wouldn't do for Maggie to have the phone pressed to her ear as she walked in.

As the elevator doors opened on *Metro*'s floor, Maggie realized she wouldn't have to call at all. A camera crew was staked out in the lobby, lights on, camera rolling as Maggie stepped out of the elevator to a round of applause. Standing atop the black leather sofa, the cameraman shot the crowd of staffers who waved merrily to Maggie.

"Ohmigod." Maggie clutched her bag stiffly. They were here!

"There she is," Candy announced to the camera, looking all show biz with her blond hair spiked extra high with glittering gold mousse. She must have raided the cosmetics closet when she got word of the camera crew. Her eyes were open so wide Maggie was sure the stitches from her last face-lift were going to pop. "The star of *your* show, and of ours, Ms. Maggie McGee!"

More applause as Maggie grinned and swept her hand low in a theatrical bow. "Holy headlines, Batman! I just can't believe it!"

"Neither could we," Candy said. "But then again, it shouldn't be surprising. Our *Metro* Girls are the embodiment of the cutting edge, finger-on-the-pulse type of women the public adores."

Oh, enough with the Metro *shit already,* Maggie wanted to say, but with the cameras rolling she didn't want to make a bitchy first impression. Some guy stepped out from behind the camera—tall, dark-haired, dressed in black from head to toe. He had a young face with very old eyes, thoughtful eyes that seemed to pull back and glaze over as he shook Maggie's hand. "Max Donner," he said. "I'm the producer of *Big Tease.*"

"Very cool! I'm Maggie McGee," she turned to the camera to smile, "but I guess you've already figured that out."

"Yes, your boss Candy has been very helpful, showing us around, giving us the grand tour of the offices of *Metropolitan* magazine."

"I'll bet." Maggie looked through the crowd, wondering where her real boss was. Had they interviewed Debbie, or had Candy elbowed her out of the spotlight? She could imagine Candy pulling one of her devious moves, sending Debbie out to buy bagels or cigarettes or some other demeaning task. And where was Jonathon? She shielded her eyes from the light to survey the group. "Anyone seen Jonathon this morning?"

"He's got a doctor's appointment," someone answered. "He'll be in after lunch."

"Okay," Maggie said, wishing she could share her lucky break with her best bud. He'd have to get in on the act later.

"The next thing is for us to get some footage of you in your office," Max said, checking his watch. "And we'd better do that right now." He pointed down the hall. "You lead. Wherever you go, Boone will follow."

"Okay, then." Maggie swung around and felt the girls from the staff nudge up behind her as they tried to get on camera. She turned toward them. "You know I adore you guys, right? But whoever just goosed me had better back off. Besides, these guys will be a regular fixture here for a while. You'll have plenty of opportunities to say hi to get your fresh faces on TV. Make the girls back home jealous. Right, Max?"

He took a breath and pressed his hands together in a gesture of prayer. "Absolutely."

His skin was milky pale against his black hair, like a gentle vampire. *Oh, aren't you a hottie?* Maggie thought as she smiled at him. Then, she was off toward her office. As she walked she narrated a bit for the camera, talking about the *Metro* archives, the cosmetics closet, the small eating area where a supply of bunion pads, Diet Coke, microwave popcorn and ramen noodles were always on hand.

Outside her office Maggie reached into a file cabinet for a fat stack of papers, a big, messy clump. "This is so urgent," she said, handing the papers to Tara. "I need two copies of this mess, pronto! Hope you don't mind, but you're always so helpful with these things." In truth, it was made-up work to get Tara off her butt, and Maggie didn't feel one ounce of guilt. "Oh, and hold all my calls, except for my girls. Got it?"

"Okay." Tara nodded, staring at the fat file as if it were a contagious skin disease.

Boone filmed her talking on the phone, answering e-mails, kicking off her heels and rubbing her Buddha's belly. It was fun to entertain the quiet guy behind the camera. After a half hour or so Max came in, his long, lean form nearly filling her tiny cubbyhole of an office. As he perched his solid-looking butt on Maggie's desk, she slid her hands off the keyboard and picked up her Buddha again.

"Man, oh man," Max sighed, meeting Maggie's eyes. "Your boss is a handful."

"Tell me about it. She's not really my boss. I mean, basically she's everyone's boss, but I don't even see her on a daily basis." She rubbed the Buddha's belly, secretly wondering what it would be like to get into Max's black jeans. Was he a boxers boy or briefs? A slow, languorous lover, or a rock 'n' roll racer? "But you must admit, Candy is a PR dream."

"Yeah, if I were doing an industrial video for the magazine," Max said. He took the Buddha from Maggie's hand, and she marveled that he would make such a personal gesture.

"Go ahead," she told him. "Make a wish."

He shrugged. "Naw. I've got everything I want."

"Really? That's intriguing." She swivelled her chair so that she was facing him. "You're so confident. And cute, in a Transylvanian sort of way. Maybe I'll make *you* my first date for the show."

"Apparently, you didn't read the fine print on the application," he said a little stiffly. "All employees of *Big Tease* or the CBN network are strictly prohibited from involvement with any of the show's contestants."

"Really?" She flipped a strand of hair over her shoulder. "Doesn't bode well for us, does it? And what, pray tell, are the penalties?"

"You'd be dumped from the show." He returned the Buddha to her desk.

"Ouch! That's severe. Maybe we'll just have to go off-camera." She tilted her head, gazing at him through the hair falling over one eye. "We could be undercover at *Big Tease.*"

"Off camera?" He motioned to Boone, who stopped shooting and lowered the camera to his lap. "I'll tell you how it's going to be." Max's voice was deadly quiet. "I am not going to do anything to compromise my job, thank you very much. And you are going to play by the rules and let Boone follow you and your dates through Manhattan. Is that clear?"

Maggie held up her hands. "Whoa, there, buddy. You want to back off and take those issues to a licensed therapist? I give great advice, but I'm better with girl stuff."

"Just so you know where we stand," said Max.

"Oh, don't worry, I'm definitely not going to get into your

bloomers now," Maggie said, fuming. "Anything else before I get some real work done? I've got a deadline."

"Actually, I was wondering if you usually get to work on time," Max said. "Because we waited thirty minutes this morning and I hate to wait. Camera time is money."

"I bet it is," Maggie said. "Well, I'm always here late in the evening so I usually come in half an hour late, if you need to know. And I hope you can edit out most of Candy Holmes's bullshit. And you've just got to get an interview with my immediate boss, Debbie Minsk. She's a sweetie, and so much more deserving than Candy. And my best bud Jonathon. And—"

"Take it easy there, this isn't the last day we'll be shooting." Max nodded at Boone. "We'll talk to Debbie now, and I'm sure there'll be plenty of chances to hook up with Jonathon." He stood to leave, then added, "Though you have to realize, a lot of this background stuff will get edited out. We want the first shot of you, sort of like the excited sweepstakes winner, then we cut to the dates."

Maggie clutched her chest. "You've got to get Jonathon in. If you don't, I swear, I'll make him take me on a date, and since he's gay it'll be a bit of a stretch."

"You never know." Max's eyebrows rose. "Could boost ratings."

Tara poked her head in and announced, "Apple is on the phone."

"Reaction from the friends." Max grabbed Boone by the shoulders and pulled him back into the room. "We gotta get this."

Maggie straightened her red cashmere sweater so that the v-neck v-ed at the right spot and picked up the phone. "Apple!" she said enthusiastically. "Are they there? Are you dying or what?"

"Oh, I'm contemplating death, all right," Apple answered. "Yours! What the hell were you thinking?"

Maggie laughed. "Oh, honey, don't thank me! I knew you'd be thrilled."

17

Apple held her hand up to the camera. "Can I get a private moment here? I'm not even sure if I'm going to go through with this."

The other woman lowered her camera and turned to the producer, who'd introduced herself as Lucy Ng. Lifting her long cerulean scarf like a feather boa, Lucy shrugged. "You do what you gotta do. It's mostly the dates we need to film. You know, the romance."

"Right," Apple said flatly, thinking that they were going to have to search pretty darned hard to find a scintilla of romance in her life. Turning away, she blasted Maggie. "I can't believe you would go behind our backs like this. Really, Mag, this has got to be the worst thing you've ever done to us."

"Worse than when I got drunk at the school dance and you guys had to get me home covered with puke?"

"Way worse. This even tops the time we had to rescue you from that sadomasochist who chained you down in his apartment."

"Now that wasn't really my fault. He seemed like a nice guy," Maggie defended herself. "Who knew his idea of kinky included using a real firebrand?"

"I don't know, Mags. I'm really pissed." Pacing across the studio, Apple caught her reflection in one of the large windows: her red curls tossed carelessly, her skin pale and pearly. After she pulled on a black blazer, it had been hard to tell that she slept in her white T and jeans. Hard to tell that she'd had the night from hell.

"But you said it was okay, as long as I cleaned up my sex life, Remember?"

"Yeah, but . . . that was just last night. I had no idea you had already sent our applications in!"

"A minor detail," Maggie said. "And you need the money, right?"

Apple took a deep breath. "More than ever."

"Really? What's that mean?" Maggie's voice sharpened. "What's going on with you?"

"Coop threw me out," she said. "I had to sleep in the studio last night."

"Oh, Apple, I'm sorry. I mean, you sensed it was ending, but that's just rotten. Next time I see that boy I'm going to kick his ass. But don't you see, this is the perfect distraction from Coop and all the other mediocre men out there. This is your chance to strike out for someone special. Take a shot at the guy of your dreams."

Apple could feel her anger at Maggie fading already. Had she been charmed by the production crew who'd arrived with coffee and a sense of purpose? Having them here had made her feel as if progress were being made, as if the planets were spinning and revolving and somehow she was the center of that new universe. She liked feeling important. Not to mention the fact that the prize money appeared more tantalizing than ever.

"Apple?" Maggie prodded. "Oh, Apple, Apparooni, I hear you thinking. Tell me you're going to go for this."

"I'm on the verge. Just worried about competing too viciously because I need that prize money."

"That's a girl! Gotta be in it to win it!"

"That's Lotto. But, ugh! Look who I'm talking to—the girl who throws a Slutfest each year on Valentine's Day. As if I can compete with you for guys."

"But you can!" Maggie insisted. "You've got that natural thing that guys go for! I've got to work it like a . . . oh, wait. Chandra's on the other line. Hold on."

Apple waited, sure that Chandra's reaction was exponentially worse than her own. Glancing over at the cameraperson, who was smoking a cigarette in the kitchen area, Apple fantasized what it would be like to participate in *Big Tease.* She'd already seen the footage they'd shot of her this morning, as her assistant Juanita had expressed an interest and the producer had run the tape. Watching herself, Apple had felt as if she were watching another woman, a tortured artist whose words only hinted at her inner beauty. Her voice had been hoarse from crying, but somehow she sounded sexy. Her shadowed eyes had a smokey look, distant and mysterious. She had felt rumpled, but she looked world-wise, almost downtown chic.

"Are you out of your mind?" Chandra said as Maggie put her through on three-way calling. "What were you thinking! I said no and I meant it. Do you think I'm going to—"

"I know, I know," Maggie interrupted, "but Apple is getting into it, right?"

Apple swallowed hard.

Chandra cut through the silence. "Apple? Are you kidding me?"

"I don't know." Apple twisted a strand of her hair around one finger as she looked back at the cameraperson and the producer. "It's actually kind of fun, and I could use the money. And Maggie has agreed to start behaving if we cooperate."

"See?" Maggie jumped in. "Don't be the only party pooper, Chandra."

"Go poop on your own party, and don't blame me for it!" Chandra said in a hushed voice, careful not to let anyone hear her off-color language. "Did I mention that I had to miss a meeting to deal with the building security about the fact that my 'visitors,' this camera crew, didn't have clearance? And now they're sitting here, attracting gobs of unnecessary attention because they refuse to believe me when I say that I did *not* apply to be on this show. Some production assistant is on her way from CBN to bring the signed application, which I've already told them is a damned forgery."

"Oh, you didn't tell them that, did you?" Maggie asked.

"It's the truth!" Chandra said.

"You're so literal," Apple said, hoping to calm Chandra down.

"I am paid to be literal. And I am paid to avoid the sort of publicity that would be considered inappropriate for a senior analyst at Grayrock Corporation. And I shouldn't need to tell you that a fat cameraman who calls himself Mule and a funky, fast-talking producer are not the appropriate players I want to be filling my office chairs."

"Oh, right," Maggie said. "Blame it on the fat guy."

Apple smothered a laugh.

"Maggie," Chandra went on, "I am going to kill you when I see you. And that's a promise. In the meantime, I . . ." Someone interrupted her. "Okay, now I've got to go into an emergency meeting. A crisis management conference convening to manage this f-ing TV crisis."

"Okay, honey," Maggie said. "You go, rule the world. Don't worry about us. We'll hold up our ends without you."

"Oh, please," Chandra said. "Don't even try to guilt me. Goodbye."

After she hung up, Apple turned away from the window and studied the three women across the room.

"So, App, whatcha thinking?" Maggie asked.

"Actually, I was just trying to remember the last time I let myself explore a forbidden fantasy."

"Oooh! Now we're getting somewhere. So you're in? Ready to take a walk on the wild side."

"In front of millions of Americans," Apple added, sure that she was losing her mind. She'd never enjoyed being the center of attention; what made her think she'd like it now? "You know what? What the hell. It's not like I've got anything else going on."

"You go, girl," Maggie said.

Apple took a deep breath. "Okay, here I go."

18

Exposed . . . that was how Chandra felt. It was like one of those dreams when you come to work in your underwear and all your bosses and coworkers snort quietly, having caught a glimpse of what you're really about. The only person who didn't seem to be rattled by today's developments was Vincent, who had quietly watched events unfold and efficiently ushered her into this meeting.

"This is a most surprising development for Grayrock," said one of the suits—a top-tier player. Chandra didn't know him by name, mostly because he was in a department she rarely "interfaced" with. The fact that he would not look her in the eye made it clear that he was out to nail her. "I mean, prime-time television? We don't even advertise on the boob tube. We don't need to, as I'm sure you all know that our customer base is a conservative demographic."

"An exclusive group that might not appreciate such exposure," added Doris Gordon, a smooth-talking personnel director.

Heads nodded. Fingers punched Palm Pilots. The collective groan was clearly turning against Chandra. She had to jump in before she was condemned without trial.

"First of all, let me state that I was pursued by this TV show, and that I did not elicit their attention," Chandra spoke calmly, remembering to make eye contact with every person at the table. "Second, although I have no interest in appearing on the show, I take exception to the notion that we want to keep our customer base small. Haven't we all sat through meetings in which one of the corporate goals is expansion of our services so that Grayrock has a wider appeal? How else can we meet the projected goals by two thousand five, if we don't—"

"Exactly! That's exactly it! Being associated with *Big Tease* wouldn't mar our corporate identity at all!" cried a slight, balding man across the table. Biedermeyer from Public Relations. Chandra had never been crazy about the man and usually thought of him as a beady-eyed little mole, but at least he was on her side today.

"Our involvement with a popular prime-time television show is the perfect chance to demonstrate to the American public that we are not a big, bad financial institution, but instead we are a team of real people. People with real lives and emotions and everyday heartbreaks."

Quiet swept the conference room. Clearly Biedermeyer had taken everyone by surprise, as the subject of the meeting had been damage control, not damage debate.

"You know," said Chandra's boss Willard Ritter, "Biedermeyer's proposal is an interesting one."

Proposal? Chandra cupped her hands around her Palm Pilot. What proposal? The guy was just putting in a plug for television advertisements.

"Perhaps it is time for Grayrock to emerge from the corporate world to the real world," Ritter went on. "A little dose of our own reality programming." He smiled.

The suits chuckled.

Under the table, Chandra dug a fingernail into the cuticle of her thumb. She felt herself losing control of the situation, but didn't want to jump in and steal the volley from her boss.

"Exactly," Biedermeyer sniffed, puffing himself up. "Imagine the return on such a proposal. The free exposure on prime-time television, which would normally require a large portion of our advertising budget—free. The visual of a friendly, accessible corporation embodied by Ms. Hammel—free. The subliminal product placement—free." He held up his hands, as if holding a gift. "What more could we ask for?"

"Point well taken," Doris said, choosing the flavor of the moment. "This is a rare and valuable opportunity for Grayrock." Meeting Chandra's eyes, she flip-flopped slightly. "Or at least, it might be."

"Before we pursue this any further . . ." Chandra held up her hands. "We are not here to debate whether I will go on the show. The answer to that is no. Absolutely not. I am a private person with a professional reputation to protect."

"Point well taken," Doris repeated apologetically.

"Absolutely," baldy Biedermeyer chimed in. "We respect your privacy, Chandra. We really do. And I think I speak for many of the executives here when I say how much we value you as an employee just as we value your contribution to Grayrock. If I didn't know the depth of your loyalty to Grayrock, I wouldn't feel comfortable even broaching this subject. However, since your unflagging dedication to this company is not at issue, I feel well in line asking you to consider tolerating a teensy-weensy invasion of your privacy to serve the greater good of the corporation."

Chandra felt a burning desire to shove her Palm Pilot right down his throat. The very idea that she would sink so low just to score points for the corporation . . .

"Now wait . . . just wait . . ." Alfred Lipton, the biggest cheese in the room, hung his head. "I'm afraid, perhaps, this is too much to ask of an employee." Silence. "But the opportunity is ripe and rare." He lifted his head slightly to gaze at Chandra. "You've always been a team player, Chandra. I want you to know that, should you refuse, no one will question your loyalty to Grayrock."

Loyalty to Grayrock. The words echoed as her heart began to hammer in her chest. Jeez, she'd always been willing to do just about anything for the gain of the corporation. That is, anything legal and ethical.

"This is quite a bit more than we ask of the average employee," said Ritter. "But then, Chandra, you are anything but average. Far from it."

Oh, jeez, couldn't you save remarks like that for when I come up for my annual review?

"Let's talk about sacrifices," a female board member said. "Don't all executives sacrifice a certain level of personal convenience for the good of the corporation?"

The big cheese held up his hands. "Let's not put undue pressure on her. It's up to you, Chandra," he said, his face looming before her like the image of the wizard in the land of Oz.

Under the table Chandra dug her nails into her palms. How was she going to find a way out of this when they kept shoving textbook management theory at her? And their faces: a study in compassion and hope.

It's my funeral, she thought. *Yes, life as I have known it is over as of now.*

"I'll do it," she said, adding, "and I'll do it well."

"Of course you will!" Doris cheered. Easy for her to say. She wasn't going to have a camera crew squatting on her bedroom floor.

Their voices seemed distant as they gave assignments, summarized and concluded the meeting. Then the meeting began to break up and Chandra felt her knee nudged as baldy Biedermeyer slid into the chair beside her.

"This is so exciting!" he said, dripping enthusiasm. "I understand that the first date is oh-so important on this show, so let's make sure yours is a winner! I was thinking that we could put together a list of high-profile candidates who are solid contenders in the financial markets."

Staring at him, Chandra realized he must be a fan of *Big Tease.* Somehow, that thought made her feel even more like a pawn.

She was going to kill him.

Her hands tensed around her Palm Pilot. But instead of using it to whack Mr. PR, she pressed the button to send Maggie an e-mail:

Show is a go for Grayrock.

I hate you, but you have a lifetime to make it up to me . . .

And you're going to need every single minute.

In the meantime, chocolates will help. Godiva dark, please.

Part Two

Two Ways to Meet the Hippest Hotties

19

"Let the dating begin!" Maggie cried, waving a fat hot pretzel in the air. The smoke of roasted chestnuts wafted up from a vendor's card, adding to the feel of December in the air. Maggie adored Christmas in New York: the bells jingled by Santas on street corners; the sparkling white lights that dressed up trees and windows; the fat ribbons of red, silver and gold that adorned everything from entire office buildings to desserts at Aureole. Even New Yorkers changed in December. There was actually goodwill among the shoppers who bustled along with bags dangling at their sides. Once Maggie had actually seen a man give up a cab to another shopper because he was juggling so many FAO Schwartz shopping bags. That was the Christmas spirit for you.

"I was so not ready to be followed by the camera tonight," Chandra said. She reached toward Maggie's pretzel. "Give me a piece of that. So what's the deal?" she asked Max, who was tailing them along with Boone the cameraman. "We're not going on dates—it's just girls' night out."

Max gave a tight grin, clapping Boone's shoulder. "I'll explain later."

Apple lifted her camera to snap a shot of them as people brushed by in the evening rush on Fifth Avenue.

"I hate this," Chandra muttered, forcing a smile for the camera. "Did I mention that I hate this?"

"At least a million times," Maggie said. "But you do tend to overstate things. Just pretend they're not there." Maggie had gotten used to having Boone around over the past few days, and she had loved every minute of the background shooting they had done both at the office and in her apartment. The worst part had been backing off from quick sex while the camera was watching. How long had it been? Three days without a guy! Maggie was sure she'd be sprouting gray hairs any minute, but she did make a promise to her friend. Plus, Jonathon had secretly reminding her that her exploits were now part of America's viewing pleasure, and she wasn't going to gain viewer votes by flying the slut flag the first week out.

Now, as they headed toward Rockefeller Center to join the crowds gathering to watch the lighting of the tree, people occasionally stopped to stare. Some asked about the three women being filmed.

"Did you hear them ask about me?" Maggie huddled with her friends, giggling. "They think I'm Sandra Bullock." She grabbed Chandra's sleeve and shouted to the fans, "Hey, and this is Halle Berry!"

"Maybe they think we're getting footage for a music video," Apple suggested.

"Right." Chandra gave her a deadpan look. "We're Destiny's Mothers."

Apple winced. "We're not that old!"

"Why don't you have a little thingie on the camera that tells people what the show is?" Maggie asked Max. "You know, the way the news crew trucks are all painted up?"

"We don't want to attract attention to Boone," Max said. "Actually, while we're filming, we don't want to attract attention at all. We'd prefer to have our audiences tuning in on Wednesday nights."

"Oh, you're no fun," Maggie said, waving him off. She linked arms with Apple. "Don't you love this? We're celebrities already."

"Sometimes I love it," Apple said. "Other times I just want to hole up in a closet with some back issues of *Elle.*"

"Invasion of privacy," Chandra said. "I can't believe we have willingly given up one of our constitutional rights."

"Oh, it's just for a few weeks, and they don't film the really personal stuff," Maggie said as they cut across the plaza of a tall building where the dandelion-shaped fountains were still in operation. Any day now the fountains would be shut down for winter, but at the moment they sprayed cold mist onto anyone who passed. "I can't believe this thing hasn't been drained yet," Maggie said, pausing downwind of the spray. "It must be a sign; we have to make wishes."

Apple reached into the pockets of her safari-style vest. "Three coins in the fountain? I think it's been done."

"But we've got a new millennium concept." Maggie dug in her coat pocket for quarters.

Chandra didn't even open her tiny Coach bag. "I only have plastic. I'll have to owe you."

"No, no, it's not a loan, because that would mess up the wish." Maggie handed Chandra a quarter. "It's my gift to you."

"Probably a hell of a lot more practical than the Christmas gift she's getting you," Apple told Chandra.

"I buy great gifts!" Maggie argued. "Creative and thoughtful."

"*Mm-hmm.* We won't talk about that pet rocks or the knock-off watches that said: Rolax. Like a laxative."

"You remember that?" Maggie laughed. "What did we call it? The watch that tells you when it's time to go."

Chandra smiled. "But thanks for the quarter. What are you going to wish for?"

Tossing her black scarf over her shoulder, Maggie faced the fountain, determined to channel positive vibes into her coin. "My wish is for the Ultimate Guy. I want to fall in love, heart, head, body and soul." It was something she'd been thinking about over the past few days, most likely an impossible dream;

but it seemed like the only way out of the thorny rut of empty sex she had gotten herself into. She kissed the coin, then tossed it into the fountain, where it landed on the second tier.

Beside her, Apple squinted into the fountain thoughtfully.

"What's your wish?" Maggie asked.

"Nothing so idealistic," Apple said. "I want to win that money to buy my freedom." She hauled back with her primed softball pitching arm and launched the coin into the fountain.

Chandra flipped the coin in the air and caught it with a snap. "One wish for Mr. Right, another for freedom. You guys are a tough act to follow."

"There's got to be something that would make you happy," Apple said. "Your heart's desire . . ."

"There's always that million-dollar prize," Maggie reminded her.

Chandra shrugged. "Money isn't everything."

"But it can take care of a lot of problems," Maggie said. "You know that, Chandra. You used to be just like us, the middle-class kid who had to save her allowance for a Schwinn racer."

"As I remember it, I had to save longer than most. How many times did I have to borrow from you guys or throw myself at the mercy of the . . ." Her voice trailed off as she seemed to notice someone. The camera.

Yeeps. Maggie realized Chandra had revealed more than she wanted to on camera. Time for damage control. "Okay, Chandra, what's your wish?"

Taking a breath, Chandra composed herself. "What do you expect? My wish is the same as usual: a promotion to the top tier at Grayrock."

"Oh, that's so boring," Maggie said. "When are you going to stop bumping your head on that glass ceiling?"

"Excuse me?" Chandra frowned at Maggie. "Since when did you become the editor of wishes?"

Maggie was about to answer when she noticed Max watching approvingly, his arms folded over his down vest. Oh, the camera was eating up their conversation, which was evolving into an argument. No wonder Max was salivating. He probably thought a cat fight would boost ratings.

"But we love each other, don't we?" Maggie said, draping her arms around her friends and ushering them down the street. "I don't want them to see us arguing on camera," she said under her breath. "Make like we're friends."

"We *are* friends," Apple said.

"And if those cameras are going to follow us around, they're going to see us argue." Chandra broke away from Maggie to wave at the camera. "Yes, we argue all the time. Did you pick up on that?"

Behind the camera, Boone remained silent. Glancing up from his cell phone, Max frowned. Or was that his permanent scowl? Maggie wasn't sure if she'd ever seen the guy without that sour puss. "Easy, now. Try to forget we're here. The best footage will come when you're not self-conscious."

They were coming up to the entry to Rockefeller Plaza, where the tall, dark tree loomed ahead of them. The mall here was decorated with delicate spun angels lit by twinkling white lights. Christmas music wafted from heavy duty speakers down by the rink where a famous figure-skating pair was performing, but Maggie's attention was drawn to a platform on the plaza that was cordoned off to the public. Having attended this event nearly every year of her life, she knew that was the hub of activity. A few large television cameras from most of the networks were already set up in front of the podium, waiting for the lighting ceremony to begin. Various spots on and around the platform were lit by handheld cameras as familiar TV anchors interviewed celebrities.

"Oh, wow," Apple said, her hands gripping her camera. "Great photo ops. Is that Alec Baldwin?"

Maggie squinted. "It's definitely one of the Baldwins."

"And look over by the tree," Chandra said, nudging Apple. "Brooke Shields and Sarah Jessica Parker."

"You guys are getting good at this," Apple said as she adjusted the settings on her camera. She handed Maggie her camera bag.

"Hold this. I'll be right back." Darting through the groups of people, she homed in on her marks, snapping shots as she went.

"So Chandra," Maggie said. "I imagine you've been doing extensive research and mapping out strategies and stuff for *Big Tease.* But tell me, sweetie, who's your first big date for the show?"

Chandra slid her hands into the pockets of her long black cashmere coat. "I'd rather not say."

Maggie couldn't believe Chandra's evasiveness. "Oh, come on! It's me, Mags!"

"Right. And you're the competition."

"That and your best friend."

"Can we just not talk about it?" Chandra turned away from Boone's camera. "We're not going to let this show divide us, right?"

"Oh, forget them," Maggie said, flopping a hand toward Boone and Max. "They have no power over us. But really, you're not going to tell me anything?"

Apple ran up to Maggie and grabbed her camera bag. "Tell you what?" she asked breathlessly.

"I don't think we should talk about the show or our dates," Chandra said firmly.

Apple grinned as she changed film. "You've always had that fierce competitive streak, Chandra. It's what makes you so successful in business."

"But still," Maggie said, "she could—"

"She can't help herself," Apple interrupted. "Chronic competitiveness."

Chandra rolled her eyes. "Don't make it sound as if it's a psychological disorder."

"Ooh, you guys!" Maggie bit her lower lip in frustration. It wasn't so much that she minded not knowing as that she wanted to dish with her girls. "Well, in the spirit of 'I don't care if the enemy camp knows my strategy,' guess who's going to be my first on-camera date?"

From the corner of her eye Maggie saw Boone's camera swing

from her to Apple, then to Chandra for reaction shots. And what great shots they were. Open mouths and expectant, wide eyes.

"Tom Cruise?" Chandra asked.

"After what he did to Nicole?"

"Harrison Ford?" Apple guessed.

"Too old, and you guys are way off track." Maggie glanced over at the stage, where a cluster of men in dark overcoats stood together talking. "There he is," she said, pointing. "There's my next date."

Chandra squinted. "John Cusack?"

"John Corbett?"

"No, you idiots, the one by the podium." Maggie couldn't believe they didn't see him. "Tan coat? Tall, lean and mean? The mayor of New York."

Apple and Chandra exchanged a look of horror, grabbed each other and shrieked: *"Eeeyeew!"*

That was the problem with childhood friends: Sometimes they refused to leave childhood habits behind. "I should have known. What are you guys, Republicans?"

Chandra pressed her fingers to her mouth, trying to keep from grinning. "Suffice it to say, we are anti-tyranny, and your guy has all the charm of a factory foreman."

"Which I think her father used to be," Apple added.

Maggie raised herself up, a wall of defense. "Giordano is single, certainly not boring, and he's actually attractive in a megalomaniacal sort of way. The man stinks with power. Don't you just love that? Just because his staff admits he's a tyrant doesn't mean he's a bad guy, right? Somebody's got to get the job done."

"It's just that he is miles away from anyone I'd expect you to choose, Mags," Chandra said. "But a really interesting choice."

The phrase *interesting choice* made Maggie nervous. That was what they said about artists who had just painted themselves out of a career.

"You know," Apple said, "after Bill and Monica, I promised my therapist that I'd stop thinking of politicians in sexual terms. Too many of those guys are my type, and I just found myself thinking all the wrong things when I was supposed to be listening to them talk about strategic defense or tax cuts or welfare reform." She tucked her long hair into the collar of her jacket and adjusted the camera strap around her neck. "I'm going to run for more shots. If I can't find you guys, we'll meet at Joe Allen's after the ceremony."

"Okay," Maggie said, turning back to study the stage area. Elliot Giordano stood by police barricades talking with two blond women. Okay, with a nose like that he wasn't knockout gorgeous. But there definitely was something attractive about the man and his French-cut shirts and his aura of power. He was Elliot the Great, Big El, El Politico, the mayor of New York. "There's definitely power in those pants," Maggie murmured.

"As I said, I'm surprised," Chandra said, slipping her arm around Maggie's shoulders. "And more than a little impressed."

"You're just saying that."

"Nope," Chandra insisted. "He's a good match for you. Broaden your demographics and voter appeal."

Maggie turned to her. "I'm dating, not running for office."

"In a way, it's an election, isn't it?"

Thinking about it, Maggie nodded. Toward the end of eight episodes of *Big Tease,* viewers were asked to either e-mail or phone in a vote for the woman who was the most "worthy" date, whatever that meant. "It's one big popularity contest," Maggie said.

"Yes," Chandra agreed. "And I have to admit, I'm jealous."

Good, thought Maggie. *That means I made the right choice.*

20

For Apple, eating at Joe Allen's was like hanging at a friend's place. The bar was a loud, boisterous affair where you could get a full dinner and a round of drinks and easy conversation. Here celebrities mixed with theatergoers and people were quick to warm up to you, even if you were alone and toting a camera. Across an exposed brick wall divider was the dining room, the see-and-be-seen epicenter of Broadway. Over the years she'd taken advantage of a fair share of photo ops here—Andrea Martin, Bebe Neuwirth, Nathan Lane, Matthew and Sarah Jessica, and Tom and Nicole back when they were still an item. Yes, Apple felt comfortable here, but she was having trouble getting beyond the anxiety that twisted in her chest every time she thought of *Big Tease.* And it definitely didn't help to see Boone and Max sitting opposite Maggie and Chandra, Boone's camera whirring.

"Nothing personal, but are you guys joining us for dinner?" Apple pulled out a chair and placed her camera bag in a safe spot under the table. "Because if you are, we usually split the bill three ways. And we always leave twenty percent tip. And I won't let you shoot if I've got watercress in my teeth."

"Sit down," Max told her, authoritative as a boss. When she

gave him a look, he added, "Please. We have a few new rules I'd like to go over."

"New rules?" Maggie slathered butter onto her raisin bread. "You can't change the rules. Not when everyone knows how it was last season."

"Ah, but I can, and I will." Max folded his hands on the table. "It's in your contract. Didn't you read your contract?"

Never one to labor over fine print, Apple had signed hers. Maggie swallowed hard over a bite of bread. Apparently, she hadn't paid much attention, either.

"Can I get a drink?" Apple asked, gulping down some water. She had a feeling she wasn't going to like this. She managed to catch a passing waiter, who promised to bring her a Cosmopolitan pronto.

Chandra cocked an eyebrow, staring dead-on at Max. "He's right," she said. "He's allowed to tailor the show. Adjustments can be made at the request of network demands or viewer feedback . . . changing market, focus groups." She turned to Maggie. "He's got us."

Max cocked a dark eyebrow at the girls. "Glad to see *somebody* read her contract." He leaned forward, elbows resting on the table, like an amiable pitchman. "So here's the deal. One of the reasons you three were so appealing to our show was that you've been childhood friends. And as you know, our show isn't as much about sex as it is about the dynamics of relationships. Most people don't want to watch another couple making out or going at it. The interesting part is what leads up to sex. The discussions. The fights. The promises. The seduction. The big tease."

Maggie plucked a raisin from her bread and flicked it onto the table. "Don't tell me you're looking to film a three-way."

Apple nearly choked on her water. Where was that drink?

"He can't change the show that much," Chandra said confidently. "We may be indentured, but we're not enslaved."

"Small consolation," Apple muttered. Oh, why had she agreed to this whole thing? She had never liked being in front of the camera. Now she would be exposing herself, sharing her life with millions of strangers. She knew her parents would not approve, not to mention the fact that they'd find out she was living out of her studio again. Oh, man. Well, at least her drink was here. She crushed the lime wedge and took a deep sip.

"Okay, hotshot." Maggie licked her lips. "What's the big plan?"

He rubbed his hands together, as if ready to conjure something between his palms. Max reminded Apple of a wolf. Hungry. Half-smiling. Always assessing. Definitely not her type. Too shifty, and way too young, sort of thirty-ish.

"In this season of *Big Tease*, we want to shift focus—just slightly—from the dating mill to the relationship among the three friends in this race to find the perfect man. How competitive are you, and how will that competition affect your relationships with your friends? How will your friendships help you? What kind of emotional support do you give each other? How much can you really trust your best friends?" He cupped one hand, lifting the circle to his eye like a lens. "We want to focus on the three of you. Whenever you're together, we want to be there. So the new rules are, no gatherings with each other off-camera. When two or three of you are meeting, we'll tape it."

"So our party becomes your party," Maggie said, snapping a cracker in half.

Max nodded. "Exactly." He reached across the table for the bread basket.

Apple looked at her friends, wondering if she was missing something. It didn't seem so bad to have the camera on when they were together. Actually it seemed much scarier to have the camera follow her when she was on a date. Meeting new people was such treacherous territory for her. It would be that much worse to have the world witness her anxiety firsthand. Oh, why did I agree to this?

Beside her, Chandra tossed back the rest of her Cosmo and lifted her chin to the waiter. "We should order," she said, totally unrattled.

Maggie wasn't quite so loose. "Are you planning to change any of the other rules?" she asked Max. "Because I'd sort of like to know up front."

He tossed off the question with the wave of a breadstick.

"That's it for now, but I'll be sure to let you know if anything changes."

Maggie rolled her eyes, though Apple was surprised that a string of expletives didn't burst out. Obviously, Maggie was exercising supreme restraint. She ordered the meat loaf. Chandra wanted the grilled chicken.

"I'll take the couscous salad," Apple said, as the waitress turned to Max.

"Just pretend we're not here," he said, gesturing toward the camera guy.

"Right," Maggie said. "No entrées for our friend here, but he'll pitch in for the bread." She handed the waitress her menu and turned to her friends. "So, guys, spill all. You know about my big date. Who's it gonna be for you?"

"I don't know." Apple felt a twinge of anxiety.

"Don't be coy, Apple," Maggie prodded.

"I'm not. I really don't know." Anxiety swelled as she looked up and found the lens of the TV camera facing her. She took another sip of her Cosmo, sour, gripping. She could do this. She was just talking with her friends. "I actually don't have anyone in mind, and I feel like I'm lagging behind. I just can't think of any high-profile guys I'd like to date."

"Don't think about the pressure. Think about it as a chance to shoot for the stars—literally. Isn't there some celebrity you've always been interested in?"

"Brad Pitt," Apple said. "But at the moment, he's taken."

"What about that photographer?" Chandra ran her manicured nails over her chin. "The guy who did that show on trees. What was his name . . . Teague?"

"Fleming Teague?" Apple felt her face heat up. "He's not a guy; he's a god."

Maggie laughed. "There you go. Ask him out."

"I couldn't. He's like this guru of still photography and I'm a crappy little portrait photographer who's never had a show."

"Excuse me?" Maggie squeaked. "You are talented. And gorgeous. And smart, though men never appreciate that in a woman, do they?"

Chandra was nodding. "And Teague is just a man. He'd probably flip to have a young beauty like you ask him out. Go for it, girl."

Apple winced. "Do you think?"

"Definitely." Chandra nodded, then glanced at the camera. "How bizarre is that? I'm bolstering the competition. God, am I losing my edge?"

"But helping your friend," Maggie pointed out, pretending to erase Boone and the camera. "Just forget about that. Wipe it from your mind. We're not going to let this show splinter our friendship."

"I can't believe it," Apple went on. "I'm going after Fleming Teague. I must be crazy."

"You and me both," Chandra said. "I'm dating way out of my league. Me, going out with a billionaire financier. That is, if the date ever happens. One of the team managers at work is trying to negotiate the whole thing."

"Ooooh! I knew you'd let the dogs out!" Maggie toasted Chandra with her water. "I can't believe you wouldn't let me pry this out of you earlier. So, what's the big guy's name?"

Chandra closed her eyes and announced: "J. Reginald Pringle."

Apple felt her lower jaw drop. "The Brit with the private jets?"

"Hell, that guy owns an airline." Maggie gave Chandra a series of tiny punches in the shoulder. "Pringle is huge! Just one of the most successful black men on the globe, and the man is a total jet-setter. Last time I checked he was dating some Saudi oil heiress. He's been linked with princesses and actresses and now you, Chandra!"

"We'll see." Chandra folded her hands on the table, quietly stressed. "The whole thing is being handled like a corporate merger, and those things never go smoothly."

"Don't worry! It'll be fine." Maggie reached over and rubbed Chandra's shoulder. "Can you believe the three of us? Dating captains of industry and art."

"We'll see about that," Apple said, feeling her trepidation rise again at the thought of approaching Teague. She had seen him around the Village and at galleries, but they'd never been introduced. How was she going to make this happen? Why had she agreed to this? "I don't know how I'm going to do this," she said, thinking aloud. "I'm in way over my head."

"Aren't we all?" Maggie said. "But it's good for us. This is how you learn to swim."

"Or drown," Apple muttered, wondering how she would ever summon the nerve to go after her idol. Yes, she could hear the waves crashing over her now . . .

21

Maggie had always longed for a foray into *Metro*'s clothes closet, and now that the door was open, she wasn't going to be bothered by the fact that Candy had made a lavish ceremony out of handing her the key.

"For the staff here at *Metro,* a visit to the clothes or cosmetics closet is a rare treat," Candy said, pressing the key to her chest. Maggie's eyes were drawn to her boss's pewter gray nails and black gauze tunic. A gauze tunic? Maggie thought, working hard not to wince at her boss's attire. Yeck. What was Candy thinking? Then again, Candy usually wore black, going for that slimming effect in photo ops beside skin-skin-skinny models. Hey, the camera really did pack on the pounds. "I am delighted to offer Maggie this festive foray into fashion for her delightful date on *Big Tease!*"

The woman was a walking headline.

"Well, thanks for that," Maggie said, taking the key from her boss's hand. The skin on Candy's knuckles was fine and papery, and Maggie would have advised her to moisturize if she were anyone else. With the key pressed into her palm, Maggie looked toward the door, hoping that Candy wasn't planning on sticking around. That would definitely ruin a good time. "Thanks a lot!"

Maggie reiterated. "This is really exciting! Guess I'm off to shop for my date, but I'll let you get back to your editor-in-chief duties." All those lunches and phone calls, Maggie thought.

Candy's face fell, only slightly, thanks to the work of New York's finest plastic surgeons. "Oh . . . well, yes, enjoy, then!"

As soon as the boss retreated, Maggie had dashed to Jonathon's office and plucked her friend from a tedious story on "10 Ways to Tantalize." "I've got a deadline," Jonathon mewed.

"Oh, like we haven't done that story a hundred times," Maggie argued. "You can write later. It's time to shop!"

"But-but-but . . ." His protests died as she unlocked the door to an array of color and texture. Like ghosts from issues past, the racks of clothes called out to be considered. Spangles and feathers and beads beckoned.

"Oh, my, Dorothy . . ." Jonathon pressed a finger to his chin. "I don't think we're in editorial hell anymore."

"Hey, watch your language, cowboy. We're on tape."

Jonathon gasped. "Oops!"

Maggie grinned as the tulle lace of a gown whispered between her fingers. Maybe this was worth giving up daily sex.

In minutes, Jonathon was singing. "I feel pretty! Oh so pretty! I feel pretty and so full of joy!" He danced around Maggie, sweeping a chartreuse feather boa around her neck.

The bright yellow-green clashed miserably with Maggie's taupe Georgette dress, but she played along. She grabbed the boa, whipped it behind her, and rubbed it over her butt like a stripper. "Chickee-boom, chickee-boom."

"Oh, that's the look," Jonathan said, touching his chin. "Part call-girl, part parakeet."

"I was thinking of something a little more politically correct, yet feminine," Maggie said as Boone backed up into a rack of coats. As usual, the camera was on though Maggie had begun to ignore it. "You know, like a pinstripe suit with a slit up the side."

"Smart, but so not you." He sifted through a group of hanging clothes. "Leather, silk, chamois, embossed velvet . . ." He embraced a clump of garments. "Pinch me, I'm in a couture closet in heaven!" He pulled a quilted vest from a rack and slipped it on over his black silk shirt.

"Just a minute, there," Maggie said, pulling a loose thread from the vest. "I'm the one going on the date."

"Oh, shut up and let me enjoy a few minutes of fashionista fantasy."

Boone swung the camera from Maggie to Jonathon, attentive to their exchange. Over the past few days Maggie had gotten a sense of what was hot and what was not simply from watching Boone's body language as he filmed. He seemed to like her exchanges with Jonathon, as well as the girl talk when she was with her girlfriends. How would he react when she was on her first date with the mayor? she wondered, realizing that much of the slant of the program came from the enthusiasm of the cameraperson and the input of the person in the editing room. Who did the final edit? Most likely Max the grouch, who now stood in the doorway of the clothes closet, arms crossed, trying to look objective and interested despite the distant quality in his dark eyes. Jeez, he was going to be a tough one to win over.

"Isn't this great?" Maggie asked Max.

He nodded, always reluctant to have his voice or face on camera.

"Everything in here was acquired or donated for fashion spreads in the magazine," Maggie explained as she opened a drawer and lifted a tiny gingham bikini bottom. "This, believe it or not, is underwear worn by Claudia Schiffer. I remember the shoot." She twirled it around her fingers and tossed it to Max, who caught it with an annoyed look. "Imagine what that would fetch on E-Bay."

Max tossed it back without a word. God, it was hard to break the guy! He refused to talk, and that drove Maggie nuts.

"Who cares about Claudia's lingerie when we have an ocean of possibilities?" Jonathon pressed two fingers to his chin. "I'm envisioning something demure yet strong. Vera Wang meets Buffy after she's just staked a few vamps."

"Perfect!" Maggie snapped her fingers and pointed at him. "With a slit up the side, of course."

"Don't worry," Jonathon said as he started sorting through a rack. "We'll find something that shows off your legs . . . and all your best attributes." Once he began to focus on an ensemble, there was no stopping Jonathon. He sent Maggie back to her office with an armful of clothes.

"Hello!" Maggie called out. "I am not a size two, and I won't have my self-esteem deflated by trying to squeeze into something that was obviously designed for a woman who lives on grapefruit and laxatives."

Jonathon caught the garment as it came whizzing out the door. "Okay, okay."

In the end they decided on an elegant two-piece Charles David ensemble in sumptuous black silk. The top was cut low in a deep V and cinched to accent Maggie's full breasts. And for the skirt Maggie got her wish with a side slit cut up, up, up to her hip. "Guess I'll need to wear a skimpy pair of black panties," she said, pivoting in front of the mirror. Glancing behind her, she saw Max watching, arms folded, expressionless. She tipped her head back, eyeing him in the mirror. "Oh, come on, Max. Like you didn't hear that? Or are you so used to girl talk that nothing registers anymore?"

He didn't answer, but his eyes were dark and dangerous. As if he were angry.

"What are you pissed off about?"

Without a word, he stepped out of the room.

"Looks like our producer is having a bad day," Maggie said as Jonathon fussed over a pin on her lapel.

"He's entitled," Jonathon said. "Not all of us are Cinderellas off to meet our prince. So . . . are you nervous?"

"Of course not."

"Good for you. Now me, I'd be in a tizzy. Wondering what we'd talk about. Worried that we had nothing in common. Sure I'd clam up at the worst moment."

"Ohmigod, would you stop giving me ideas?" Maggie pressed a hand to her chest and breathed deeply to ward off the flurry of nerves. Her date was tonight and she hadn't spent any time working up a conversation agenda. Not that she usually did, but she usually did not date the mayor of New York.

"Don't worry." Jonathan soothed. "You're a talker. Always a talker."

It was true. Maggie's soliloquies were legendary. At age five she stood before the mirror and conversed with herself. When she was an adolescent, her mother tried to shorten her stories by telling her to start in the middle. Maggie could talk her way out of a sack with her hands cuffed.

Handcuffs . . . no, there would be none of that. No sex. Oh, why had she made that promise?

"Your palms are sweating," Jonathon told her.

"What if he's a creep?" Maggie raked her dark hair back and checked her face. "I feel a breakout coming on."

"Not before tonight."

"The media calls him a despot. His staff resents him. City workers want to impeach him. And I'm going out with the man?"

"Because you can see beyond all the muckraking," Jonathan said.

"Is that a joke?" Maggie couldn't tell. But suddenly it occurred to her that she was going into her first date with a major handicap: no sex. Her first on-camera date, and how in the world would she get through it without seducing the man? This deal with her friends was so unfair. Without sex, she was like an injured ball player . . . a pitcher with a torn rotator cuff.

If they weren't going to have sex, what would they do?

"Ohmigod . . . what do sexually inactive people do on dates?" she whispered to Jonathan.

He straightened and folded his arms thoughtfully. "Oh, sweetie beans, you've been working here way too long."

22

"I found him," Apple whispered into her cell phone. "I wasn't even looking and I . . . well, I called a friend at the gallery that represents him, but she didn't call back. Anyway, I wasn't getting too far tracking him down, and I was on my way to the Gramercy Arts Center and the Farmer's Market is going on in Union Square. And guess who's buying cheese?"

"Who?" Chandra asked from her office phone. "What are you talking about?"

"Fleming Teague!"

"Oh . . . the god of photography."

"He's shopping in Union Square Park. Sort of browsing. It's definitely him. What do I do?"

"Talk to him."

"But I don't know him."

"This is New York," Chandra said. "New Yorkers always talk to people they don't know. Ask him about the weather or the cheese or something."

Phone pressed to her ear, Apple turned back to the cheese stand and panicked. "He's gone! Oh, no! Where did he . . . ?" She swung around and spotted him near a flower truck. "I'd better go before I lose him."

"Don't stalk him, just be friendly and eclectic."

"How do I do that?"

"I don't know. Just go."

Apple clicked off and took a deep breath as he browsed at a fruit stand. No, not fruit . . . apples. Well, was that corny or what? But it was a connection. Better than nothing. She crossed the asphalt, approaching him slowly. "Excuse me? You're Fleming Teague, right?"

"That's what my driver's license states." He had a slight accent. Actually, it was more an affectation. He pronounced his words so carefully, he sounded like a distant cousin of the Brits.

"I know this is going to sound like a strange coincidence . . ." she began, her voice stiff.

He polished an apple on his sweater—a thick, textured fisherman's knit. "Are not all coincidences strange?" he asked, his gray eyes clear and pale. Apple liked the way they matched the gray in his beard and the tiny bristles of hair that circled his head like a Roman crown.

"Well, the coincidence is that my name is Apple. And you're shopping for apples." She grinned, a stupid grin. Absolutely idiotic. Wincing, she reached for a clip in her hair. Maybe she should have worn it down today . . .

"Really?" Teague squinted at her, then tossed the apple back into the bin. "And yet I see another coincidence. You're carrying a camera. Indeed, you are being followed by a man with a moving camera. And I am a man who composes photographs for a living. In a random universe, what are the chances of that?"

She reached behind her to swat at Suki's camera, worried that the TV crew would scare him off. But Teague didn't seem frightened. His demeanor was stoic, solid. "Life is amazing," she said.

He cocked an eyebrow, studying her. "Indeed. At times it takes my breath away."

Click.

There it was—that moment. Like the quick opening of the aperture. A single flash of energy connecting one person to another. Apple felt it; she knew he felt it too.

She was connecting with Fleming Teague!

Part of her wanted to do a happy dance right in the middle of Union Square; the other part felt cool, composed, willing to tease. She crossed in front of him to peer into the bin of apples. "What are these, MacIntosh?"

"The sign says Fujis," he said, turning to watch her.

"Good. Fujis are good. Delicious, though not to be confused with Delicious apples, which I always find disappointing by the time I've eaten to the core."

"Maybe you can help me," he said. "I like my apples crisp. And juicy."

She palmed a fat Fiji. "You are looking at a very juicy apple," she said, feeling her heart race. The innuendo was a turn-on. "Very juicy. Crisp and tart."

"But not sour?" His eyes were piercing, captivating.

She had to remind herself to breathe. "Never sour," she whispered, sure that neither of them were talking about fruit anymore. He leaned close to smell the apple in her hand, his elbow brushing her breast, leaving a tingling sensation. His beautiful head was nearly in her arms. She was tempted to touch him, but resisted.

He leaned back, looking from the apple to her face. "Lovely. Exquisite."

She smiled, hoping he was referring to her. Or was it the apple? Something about him made her feel off-balance, the magical moment suddenly dissipated. In a wave of awkwardness, she handed him the apple, then wiped her hands on her jeans. "Well, then, that's probably more than you ever wanted to know about apples."

He glanced away, smiling. "I think the lesson is just beginning." He turned the Fiji apple in his hand and took a deep bite, all the time watching her. The action was so incredibly sexual, Apple felt herself heating up as he chewed and swallowed.

"Sir? Sir! You have to pay for apple!" the vendor called.

"Yes, yes, I'll be right with you," Teague told the man. Then he licked his upper lip.

Apple knew that now was the time to act, but she wasn't quite sure how to proceed. Should she ask him out? Ask him to meet her for drinks or coffee? It had been a year or so since she'd dated, and the regular rituals seemed trite in the shadow of such a great man.

"I've much to learn about the world of apples," Teague went on. "One Apple in particular—if that is truly your name."

She nodded. "It's a long story."

"And I shall hear all of it." He reached into the pocket of his jeans and extracted a business card. "Call me."

She took the card and shrugged, feeling like a gangly teenager. "Okay." She reached up and adjusted a clip in her hair. That was easy. "Okay . . . I will." She turned and walked steadily across the square, not wanting to turn back and gape.

Fleming Teague!

Suki caught up and walked alongside aiming the camera at her. "I just met Fleming Teague!" Apple told the camera. She felt uncharacteristically light. God, she hadn't felt this way since . . . since she'd met Coop. The wind whipped her hair in her face, and she let out a long breath. "Thank God he likes apples!"

Chandra had spent the afternoon buried in computer-generated reports about Gem, Inc., one of the many holdings of J. Reginald Pringle. The company appeared to be a little gem, a property that would fit nicely into Grayrock's empire. *Easier said than done,* thought Chandra as she struggled to put the plethora of information into some semblance of order so that it could be presented to top-tier management.

There was a polite knock on the door. "Come in!" she called, wondering if it was the camera crew from *Big Tease,* whom she'd relegated to the outer office. How was she supposed to work with the camera rolling and the wise-ass producer constantly dialing up friends and family on her cell? Actually, Chandra didn't mind Mule as much as Nayasia, a round, solid black woman who dressed in rapper-style ghetto chic. Definitely a suburban mall queen turned funk wannabe. "Listen," Chandra had told her, "I don't mind you filming me, but I can't work with you and your cell phone right in my face. Why don't you 'chill' outside and I'll call you in should any dating matters arise?"

"Yeah, uh-kay," Nayasia had agreed. "Long as we get footage of you in daily life. You know, out on the streets, going home or what-not whatever."

Now Chandra braced herself for Nayasia's oversized tinted glasses and leather duster, but instead Vincent appeared, his dark face expressionless as he took in the papers scattered over the desk, credenza, and low-nap carpeting.

"Is there a meteorological wind phenomenon unique to this office?" he asked solemnly.

"I've been wrestling with paperwork for this Gem, Inc. presentation all day."

"Ah, yes, and it appears that the paperwork is the victor in this match."

Chandra laughed, then noticed that Vincent did not seem amused. "That was a joke, right?"

He nodded. "If you like."

"You can loosen up a little, Vincent. I enjoy my job, and it's okay to have an occasional laugh in the office. It's healthy. Eases the tension."

"If you wish."

"I wish," she said, determined to find his sense of humor one of these days. She gathered up the papers on budget projection and handed them to him. "Maybe you can help me out here. If you can work on the operating costs, I'll summarize the projected earnings and growth potential."

He sifted through the papers. "Let's see . . . we have contractual obligations, existing deals . . . *hmm* . . . and this is all in British pounds."

"Right. You'll have to factor in foreign exchange discrepancies," she said, grabbing a stack of papers from the floor. "We're supposed to meet on this early next week."

"The date has been moved up," he said. "There's an e-mail from Biedermeyer."

"Biedermeyer?" Chandra turned to her desk to click on her e-mails. "What's he got to do with this? The man works in PR."

"It appears he's been matchmaking."

"For me? That man is so interested in my love life, he's beginning to give me the creeps." Staring at the screen, Chandra located Biedermeyer's message and clicked it open as a flurry of motion came from the door.

"Sounds like you need us in here," Nayasia said, cracking her gum. "What's this about some guy hookin' you up. And with who? Who's your date gonna be?"

Chandra resented the inquisition, especially coming from this twit, but she was busy reading Biedermeyer's memo:

I did it! I got J. Reginald Pringle to agree to a meeting ASAP regarding

a. our interest in Gem, Inc.

b. his interest in our own Chandra Hammel

Pringle is flying in on the Concorde for a "merger" of aforementioned business and date this Friday.

"This Friday?" Chandra winced. "There's no way we can have the RFPs on Gem, Inc. done by then. We're going to need . . ."

"Don't thank me!" came the voice of the man Chandra considered among the most annoying on the planet. Biedermeyer rushed in, his head gleaming in the light of the high-hats. "I just want to be invited to the wedding."

"What wedding?" Chandra was so concerned about getting her paperwork and research on Gem, Inc. in order before the meeting, she wasn't connecting with his logic. "Do you have any idea how much preliminary work has to be done before we can meet with J. Reginald Pringle on this matter? Without our research, the entire deal is in jeopardy, and you've thrown us into—"

"Oh, please, Chandra." He held up his hands. "Don't shoot the messenger. I've been working on this under Lipton. Direct orders from the top. I guess he's confident that your team can pull the requests for proposal together in time for our meeting with Pringle." Biedermeyer moved past Vincent to sit on the edge of Chandra's desk. "If you ask me, our CEO seems to have utmost confidence in you, both in the acquisitions field and in the playing field." He winked.

"Oh, God." A feeling of horror swelled as Chandra reared back from Biedermeyer. Was Grayrock really placing so much importance on this silly dating show? The company CEO was involved in the matchmaking?

Mule swung from Biedermeyer to Chandra to soak up her reaction. The camera whirred.

Even Nayasia and her cell phone were silent.

Chandra wanted to explode at Biedermeyer and Nayasia and Mule, with his cold, shiny lens. She wanted to tell them to get the hell out of her life and never come back. She didn't need this show, not in the least. But then, she did need her friends.

Damn them.

"Okay then," she said, clicking onto her calendar and bringing up Friday's schedule. "Looks like Friday's going to be a very full day." She typed in the meeting with Pringle, then turned to Vincent with a pleading look. "Till then, you and I have a ton of work to do."

Vincent nodded, expressionless as he stacked the papers in his arms. "It will be my pleasure," he said cordially.

I wish I could say the same, Chandra thought as she watched Biedermeyer espouse his own virtues to the camera. He recounted his maneuvers—the phone calls and e-mails—as if he were the first man to arrange a meeting. A premature meeting. A meeting that was really not in his jurisdiction. How she longed to point her finger at him and yell: *You really are an annoying little man!*

Instead, she sat back in her chair and contemplated the stacks of paper circling her. It would be another late night.

23

Maggie felt aglow with glamour as she climbed the steps of City Hall in her Manolo Blahnik heels. She turned to the TV camera, tossed her fabulously sleek hair, then did a little shuffle on the top landing, throwing out her arms like a tap-dancer. "He told me to meet him at the office," she said, gesturing toward the tall columns. "So . . . here I am at City Hall, just meeting my guy at his office."

Standing behind Boone, Max shoved his hands into the pockets of his leather bomber jacket and nodded toward the entrance, hurrying her along. Damned if the guy didn't appreciate a little theatricality. If she paid attention to him, she was going to get nervous again, and she couldn't let that happen. Hard to believe he was the executive producer of one of the most-watched shows on television.

Oh, he'll love me in the editing room, Maggie thought as she smoothed down her black skirt and chatted up the cop who opened the big door for her. Heck, if she was dating the mayor, didn't that make her a potential first lady of New York? Now *that* was sexy.

The guard directed her to the second floor, where she was supposed to find Guy Fernandez, the deputy from the mayor's office who had set everything up. The stone stairs were ancient, with dips worn by countless footsteps. Maggie held onto the handrail for dear life; when good old Manolo designed these whimsies he wasn't planning to have the beauties do anything so banal as climb stairs.

Men in shirtsleeves stopped in mid-conversation and stared as Maggie led the camera crew down the hall. She smiled at them all. Hey, everyone was a potential voter—and her race to a million dollars promised to be far more competitive than the last mayoral election.

"You must be Maggie!" cried a willowy man with short-cropped hair bleached a buttery shade of blond. "We've all been looking forward to meeting you," he said, ushering her into a room jammed with cubicles. "And the mayor is so excited about your meeting. We're all excited. You are all we've thought about all week." He smoothed the lapel of a dark suit that shouted Armani, smiling at the camera. Maggie liked the way his cerulean blue shirt matched his sparkling blue eyes. Guy definitely had a sense of style. "Hey, everybody, this is Maggie McGee, the mayor's date for *Big Tease!*"

At once, people hung up and turned away from their PCs to gather round. Here was a group of people who probably snubbed camera crews on a regular basis, but now, with the possibility of getting their faces on a hit show, their resolve had turned to Jell-O.

After a round of handshakes and grins, Maggie followed Guy to a small, fluorescent-stark office for a "briefing," as he called it.

"A briefing?" Maggie asked, wondering where the mayor was now. She was about to tell Guy she wanted to get into the man's pants, not his politics, but it was just the sort of comment that would broadcast "slut!" across the nation, and she needed to think twice about sounding like a hooker on national television.

"Well, then . . ." He settled into the desk across from Maggie, suddenly hesitant. "I'm sorry," he said, holding a hand out to block the camera, "but can you turn that thing off for this portion of our meeting? Some of this is sensitive information."

"It's part of the date, isn't it?" Max asked.

Guy took a breath, then shook his head. "Really? This is nothing you want to air. A real ratings killer. Trust me."

With a shrug, Max pointed Boone out. The camera was shut off and the two men retreated, leaving Maggie alone to face the glittering eyes of Guy Fernandez.

"Okay, then," Guy began. "Before you meet the mayor for your"—his fingers sliced quotation marks in the air—"date, let's go over a list of suggested topics and utter no-nos. If your meeting is going to be on camera, every conversation will be grist for the political mill, and we want to keep this upbeat and friendly." He lowered his voice, confiding, "According to the last Canopic poll, twenty-eight percent of registered voters perceive Mayor Giordano as cold and unsympathetic. It's something we're trying to address."

"Gotcha." Maggie bit her lower lip. "We'll go for warm and fuzzy. Lots of cuddles and candlelit rooms. He *is* in on this plan, isn't he? And actually, where the hell is he, anyway?"

"Yes, and he's in a meeting, but patience, patience." He opened a folder and handed her a crisp sheet of paper. "Okay, then . . . Recycling and re-opening the Fresh Kills Landfill are out. As is any talk of taxes—commuter, sales, property or otherwise. Any discussion of the German artist who tried to drape a parachute over Gracie Mansion is positively verboten. As is talk of the closing of those day-care centers in the Bronx."

Maggie snapped her fingers. "If you're looking for warm and fuzzy, I'd start with those kids."

"Eh-eh-eh . . . can't go there! The mayor feels for the little dears, believe me, but there are budget constraints. Anyway, here's the rest of the list, which you'll need to commit to memory since we can't have this sort of thing floating around. God knows, I shouldn't have even printed it, but—call me a wild and crazy risk-taker—I wanted to help you out."

Maggie checked the list. "Hmm. Not sure I can swing the conversation around to PCBs in the Hudson, not unless he orders fish for dinner."

"I know you'll do your best," Guy said.

"Right . . . which reminds me. Are we actually having dinner? I mean, we're getting out of here, right? I just don't see a lot happening if we spend the evening spinning around the leather chair in his office."

"Of course, of course! We've got you slated for a groundbreaking of a new elementary school downtown, then a reception at NYU."

Maggie pursed her lips, careful not to smudge her lip gloss. The schedule was a far cry from club-crawling, but it would probably look good on camera. "Okay." She handed him the cheat sheet. "You can shred this. I usually fly by the seat of my pants, anyway." She stood up, smoothed her skirt, checked her leg in the pleat. Her shoes were heaven-sent. But would the mayor even notice?

It took an additional forty minutes before Maggie and the camera crew were ushered into the mayor's office, where he sat, tie loose and sleeves folded up, working with a colleague. He glanced up and took in the scene with a dark glance.

"I'm so sorry, Mr. Mayor, but they're waiting for you to start the ceremony downtown." Guy sounded so apologetic, Maggie felt sorry for him.

"It's okay, Guy, someone has to keep me on schedule. And who might this be?"

"I'm Maggie McGee." She stepped forward and offered him her hand. He shook hands, assessing her. The man definitely had charisma. She felt the clouds of importance billowing around him.

"She's your date, sir. *Big Tease?* The TV show."

"I never miss it!" The mayor deftly buttoned his cuffs and slid on his suit jacket. "And I'm pleased to meet you, Maggie. Shall we?" He gestured to the door.

She noticed a crimp in his collar and reached over to smooth it out. The man seemed surprised to be touched . . . then intrigued. "Just trying to straighten things out, Mr. Mayor," she said.

As she withdrew he grabbed her arm, letting his fingers slide down to her palm. "Elliot." He paused a moment, gathering attention. Then, he laughed. "And believe me, City Hall could use a woman's touch."

Bingo, Maggie thought as she led the way out of the office. If the mayor was looking for someone to warm up his cold image, she could turn up the flames.

Low. Medium. High . . . the heat was on.

Four hours later, Maggie's toes felt pinched and her ego felt bruised. In the mad crush of reporters and stuffed shirts the mayor had barely spent three minutes with her, and that was in the limo while Guy had done his briefing, supplying names of the power players the mayor would be seeing that night. Once they sprang from the limo, Maggie had been left to eat the man's dust as Guy ferried him about for handshaking with muckety-mucks. Thanks to roving waiters, Maggie had helped herself to champagne, cheese puffs, sushi and new potatoes stuffed with caviar. Divine hors d'oeuvres, but what's a party without a boy to share it with? Besides, at this point Boone had way too much footage of Maggie eating and drinking. One bad day in the editing room and Max had the ammunition to portray Maggie as a total porker.

Raising her champagne flute to her lips, Maggie stood on the landing at the ancient NYU building, looking down at the huddle of men surrounding her date. "That's the downfall of dating a popular guy," she said, smiling at the camera. "Everybody wants him."

"Only the men," came a voice from across the landing. A round woman in a royal blue evening gown rustled over, one hand on her hip as she gestured to the room below. "See the way they flock into little clusters, then break off and regroup? It's a lot like the players on a football field. Or pigeons in the park."

"Sounds like you've been studying this phenomenon quite a bit."

"All my life. My father was a player—politics, not football—and now I'm married to one." She thrust out her hand. "Roxanne Barrow."

"Ron Barrow's wife?" Maggie smiled, recognizing the name as someone connected to the City Council. "I'm Maggie McGee. And this"—she gestured toward the camera—"this is Boone and that's Max sulking in the corner there. From *Big Tease.*"

"How juicy for you." Roxanne winked at the camera. "So you're dating the mayor, Maggie? Got your eye on the prize, do you?"

"I've always admired his . . . grit."

"Is that what you call it?" Roxanne grinned. "Well, I have to give you credit for taking on a tough one. When it comes to relationships, the man is Teflon-coated."

Maggie raised her glass. "Turn up the burner enough and even Teflon will melt."

Roxanne laughed over a mouthful of champagne. "That's an interesting way of looking at it."

"I write for *Metro.* Relationships are my thing," Maggie said, thinking that her "thing" was actually sex, but again, she had censored herself for the camera.

"And how is your relationship with the mayor going?" Roxanne asked.

"Well . . . so far it's really not, since we haven't been able to talk all evening. But there was definitely electricity in the first few minutes. I'd say he passed my ten-minute test—you know, if you can spend ten minutes with a man without screaming? So there's definitely potential."

"And you're not afraid to pursue that. Good for you," Roxanne told her. "Come on. You should meet the girls." Roxanne placed her empty glass on a marble ledge and took Maggie by the hand. Maggie felt a little giddy as the woman led the way up to the second floor where the hall narrowed into darkness but for a small pool of light. The name on the office read Dr. Isadora Woodley. Inside, women in evening gowns covered the furniture and window sills like doves perched on a belltower.

Maggie grinned. "This is where the real party is."

"Time to clean it up, ladies," Roxanne announced as she gestured toward Maggie. "We have a special guest tonight. Maggie McGee and her perpetually silent companions from *Big Tease.*"

The women whooped and laughed and groaned, some proclaiming that they loved the show, others telling Maggie how lucky she was. Maggie enjoyed their welcome. It occurred to her that she was surrounded by women of wealth—the ladies who lunch—but in many ways the vibe was just like her favorite chicks huddled in the corner booth at the Monkey Bar.

"And you're dating the mayor?" a woman in black beaded gown asked. "You're sure to win the million. Such a deal? You can ditch the man and keep the money."

Boone and Max followed Maggie inside, but one woman stood up to block the way. "Sorry, no men allowed," she said, taking a drag on a cigarette. Maggie couldn't help but notice her surprising display of cleavage; it seemed to spill out of her dress like budding flowers.

"That's just sour grapes, Camille," Roxanne insisted, adding, "Camille's a little bitter because she hasn't won her million yet. Or should I say, hasn't snagged her millionaire?"

"Oh, I've got him, all right," Camille said, stubbing her cigarette out on the sole of her high heels. "It's just that I haven't gotten him to the altar." She lifted her chin to Maggie. "He suffers from failure to commit."

"Been there, done that," said Maggie.

"Haven't we all," Roxanne said. "I need another drink."

"Let the guys stay!" someone else declared. This woman was a study in silver, from her shoulder-length hair to her shimmering gown. "Tell them, Izzie. It's your office, and they can stay, right?"

"Isadora is a professor here," Roxanne explained, "and she's kindly let us use her office so we don't have to assemble in the mouse hole of a ladies' room."

A fortyish brunette slid her feet off the desk and extended her hand. "Isadora Woodley." Maggie shook hands with Dr. Woodley, though none of the other women were so formal. They stayed at their perches on credenzas and windowsills, smoking and lounging, swinging their legs and rubbing their feet. "And I don't mind if the crew comes in, as long as they don't talk politics."

"Our lips are sealed," Max said, stationing himself in the doorway. No doubt for a quick exit, Maggie thought. Although Max always pretended to be low-key, she sensed that he was a total control freak.

"Here you go," Roxanne said as she handed Maggie another glass of champagne. "We know you're not driving."

"This is great," Maggie said. "So you're all friends?"

"I wouldn't push it," Roxanne said. "But we see each other at all the occasions."

Maggie had a million questions, but the conversations darting around her were so intriguing . . . talk of a face-off with a mother-in-law, a meeting with an old boyfriend, a couple who were in the throes of a custody battle over possession of their pet Labrador retriever.

Definitely intriguing.

She was engrossed in the story Roxanne was telling, about a friend who had slipped in the shower because of the saffron oil his wife had used on him, when Guy appeared.

"Ah, there you are, Maggie," he spoked quietly, not interrupting Roxanne. "The mayor is waiting. It's time to leave." He offered a strained smile for the women, but no one seemed to notice him.

Maggie thought about ditching the mayor. This was definitely more fun than eating his dust. But that would make her look like a supremo bitch, and America was watching. Well, they would be in a few weeks.

"Hey, gotta go," she told Roxanne.

"Duty calls?" Roxanne asked. "Till next time."

They gave each other an air kiss on each cheek, then Maggie slipped out. "Okay, Guy," she said as they descended the stairs to the ballroom. "Where are we off to now? Visiting a hospital? Dedicating a statue?"

"Home," Guy said. "That's the end of the mayor's public appearances for today."

"Really? So why don't we stop off at the Martini Bar or Nobu? Someplace quiet for a few drinks?"

"I don't think that is going to happen," Guy said as walked steadily toward the door. "The mayor doesn't frequent bars."

"Must be hell on his social life!" Maggie struggled in her heels, lagging behind.

"It's something we're trying to address," Guy said, then he cut through the crowd outside the door. As she maneuvered the weathered steps, Boone ran ahead of her and scuttled into the limo. Max got in and slammed the door behind him. So much for chivalry.

"Hey!" She tapped on the window. The driver jumped out and opened the door for her. "Sorry, miss."

Maggie ducked her head into the limo, glaring at Guy until he scooted down so that she could sit next to the mayor. She took a deep breath, trying to control her anger. "You know, I don't expect doors to be held open for me because I'm a woman," she said. "But I also don't expect them to be slammed in my face!"

"Sorry." Max grinned, showing that he wasn't sorry at all.

"No, Maggie, it's my fault," the mayor said. "I wish I could have escorted you to the car myself, but for security reasons, they're always hustling me out at inopportune times. I am sorry."

Maggie softened. "It's not your fault." She patted the mayor's arm, glaring at Max across the limo. "It comes with the job, right?"

"I'm glad you understand," the mayor said, taking Maggie's hand in his. Boone zoomed in, and suddenly Maggie realized that the date was about to end.

She turned in her seat to face the mayor, his face a bland smile. Midwestern handsome. "Okay, Mr. Mayor . . ."

"Elliot, please."

"Okay, Elliot, the thing is, the date is just about over and we've barely had a chance to talk. Can't we stop off at a club or something?"

He shook his head. "I don't do the club scene. Security. Public image."

Smelling failure, Maggie tried to think fast. How to save the date? Especially with Max smiling smugly in the seat across from her. She put her hand on the padded shoulder of Elliot's suit and gave a little pout. "I just hate to see the night end," she said, leaning her head against his chest. When she lifted her face, he was there, ready to kiss her.

Maggie poured it on. Okay, she was kissing by the numbers. Moist lips. Gentle press. Touching his earlobe and jaw. Kissing wasn't her thing, anyway—not without attachment—but she had to salvage this date.

She could feel Elliot responding, his shoulders tensing, his breath loud in her ears. She could feel the camera whirring. Max watching.

Oh, this is really sick, Maggie thought as she made out with the mayor. She was enjoying this not for the sensual thrill, but for the voyeurism of it. She nibbled his earlobe and licked his neck. She kissed him deeply, then turned to the camera. "Maybe you should turn that off, before this goes too far," she said with a satisfied smile.

"Right. We're out of here." Max banged on the glass and the driver pulled over.

"See you tomorrow," Maggie called, mostly to Boone, who gave a little salute before Max slammed the door.

"Let's get you home," Elliot said, running a hand over her knee.

Maggie rested her head against his shoulder. "Sounds like a plan."

What an odd feeling, Maggie thought as the mayor followed her up the stone stairs of her apartment building. How weird. He wants to come in and I want to get rid of him. I never want to get rid of a guy . . . at least, not until after the deed.

She keyed her way into the vestibule, then turned to him. "Hey, it was an adventure. We'll do it again, right?"

He shouldered the door and stepped in. "Why don't I walk you up?"

"That's okay. It's the fourth story, no elevator. You know the old brownstones."

"I don't mind the climb," he said, backing her against the mail slots. "You're worth the trip." He was kissing her again, pressing into her, and Maggie was at a loss as to how to stop him. She'd never had to stop the show before. She'd never wanted to.

But now . . . okay, she'd made a promise to her friends. But it was more than that. She just didn't feel like sleeping with the man. Maybe some other time, but not tonight.

She broke away from his lips to utter, "You know, I have an early meeting in the morning."

"So do I." He slipped his hand into the low-cut V of her dress and ran his fingers over her breast. Somehow, it was more like a breast exam than a sexual overture. His fingers tickled her nipple and she squealed. He pulled his hand back.

"Sorry, but I'm very ticklish," she lied.

He smiled. "Why don't we go upstairs so I can find all the ticklish places?"

"No, really. Not tonight." She could see from his face that rejection equaled failure. "The thing is, I have this rule about not doing it on the first date." Another lie.

"But you know my record," he said, running his hands up and down her waist. "I'm the mayor who breaks rules."

"Not this girl's."

"Oh, I'd be happy to go toe-to-toe with you," he said, pressing his hips against hers.

Yes, he was ready for more than toe action. But Maggie's hormones were on hiatus. "Some other time, Elliot. Don't worry, you'll get a chance to see if you merit the nickname Big El."

But he wasn't budging. He pulled her hips against his and took a deep breath. "You know, you're very beautiful, Maggie."

Oh, not that tired line!

"And I have a reputation to uphold," he went on. "I don't want to be known as the mayor who couldn't rise to the occasion." He nuzzled her neck. "I can see the headlines now. MAYOR LETS DATING-SHOW GIRL DOWN!"

Oh, don't be an egotistical ass! she thought as she pushed at his head. "That's a lot better than MAYOR RAPES DATING-SHOW CONTESTANT. Which is where you're heading if you don't get off me."

He lifted his head and looked in her eyes. "You're serious?"

"Dead on, tough guy."

He raised his arms and backed away. "Okay, okay, put your mace away. I'm going."

"Don't be a poor sport," she said.

He frowned.

"No sulking allowed. Call me. Or have Guy call me."

"I'll do that," he said stiffly, then flew out the door.

Maggie didn't know what to think. Was he angry, or just disappointed? Boy, the man had real rejection issues, but then, what had she expected, taking on the tyrant of taxation? "You know," she told herself, "you got a lot of nerve sometimes."

And what was the deal with her lack of carnal response? Had she lost her mind, or was this the game most women played? She pulled off her heels and climbed the stairs barefoot, listing a little toward the rail. *Woo-ee!* Champagne will do that to you.

Upstairs in her apartment, she went to the window and looked down. The limo was gone. She wondered if the women were still gathered in Professor Isadora's office, and thought longingly of grabbing a cab back to join them. Nah. It was late, and Candy had been on her ass lately about crawling into the office after ten. She pulled open the fridge and popped her head inside. Take-out Chinese. Take-out Thai. Cold pizza. Her fridge was the frigging United Nations of take-out.

Maggie grabbed a cold wedge of pizza, sat on the radiator cover by the window and wondered how her date with the mayor would come across on TV. One thing was for sure: She'd had too many glasses of champagne and not enough of those appetizer thingies. Next time, the mayor would have to spring for dinner.

24

"I've been reading about this exhibit," Apple said as Teague led the way into the Museum of Modern Art. She couldn't believe she was on a date with the world-renowned photographer. She couldn't believe she was attending the very exclusive opening of an invitation-only exhibit. She'd been kneeling and peering through the keyhole into the art world for years, and now, in a matter of days, Teague had unlocked the door and thrown it open before her.

That door being the metaphysical one, as he slipped in the MOMA entrance without even glancing back at her. Apple grabbed the door and held it open for Lucy Ng and Suki, then hurried in her chunky boots to catch up with Teague. Was it her imagination, or was he treating her like an assistant?

But then, he seemed to treat everyone with a tinge of condescension, from the cab driver to the museum docents to the other artists who milled around the exhibit. All the charm he'd exuded the other day in Union Square seemed to have escaped him. Watching him hug an earth-mother type and trade jabs with a fab artist in plaid coat and matching eyeglasses, Apple wasn't sure that Teague was a nice person at all. He didn't introduce her to his friends or even acknowledge her as he toured the exhibit. No, something was off about this guy . . . and she was intrigued to discover the source of his torment.

Aptly titled "Blue," the exhibit was an eclectic collection of blue items from the world of art, fashion and film. The walls were swathed in cornflower blue drapes, and a fat banner of blue stripes was suspended from the ceiling in a gentle wave. Threading from room to room, it was the motif that tied the collection together. The small crowd was a mixture of museum academics and New York art chic, and though a full house was expected, so far attendance was light and Apple was able to move about freely.

As Teague talked with some friends, Apple glanced over the exhibit brochure. On the second page she spotted his name, Fleming Teague, and winced. He had a piece in this show? She glanced over at him as he stroked his beard, and imagined his ego swelling under the blue river of cloth. He'd brought her to an exhibit featuring his own work?

Passing a gown once worn by Jacqueline Kennedy Onnasis, Apple joined Teague at the glass case of an Egyptian relic. "I've always loved the brilliant, electric hues of faience," she said, admiring the statue of a pharaoh cast in the color that always reminded her of Caribbean beaches.

"Faience?" Teague stroked his beard. "No, no, my dear that's turquoise."

"No," Apple said gently, "see the notes? It's faience, a clay indigenous to that part of the world. It turned bright blue when it was fired in the ovens."

"Yes, yes, I'm familiar with it," he huffed.

Just chill, Apple wanted to say. She wasn't trying to compete or show off; she was just setting the record straight. Then, in the glass covering the relic, she saw the reflection of Suki and the camera behind her. So that was it . . . she'd embarrassed him on camera. Although she often forgot that Lucy and Suki were there, that ever-present lens could be a real pain in the neck.

Teague merely snorted as he passed the blue gingham dress Judy Garland wore in the *Wizard of Oz.* The man really was a big, fat snob, Apple thought as she paused in front of the dress, feeling nostalgic. Watching the movie had been an annual tradition when it came on, and she still remembered her frustration when the travelers fell asleep in the field of poppies, her fear when those flying monkeys pulled the stuffing out of the scarecrow. Was it possible that Teague had never seen the movie? Or was he just a cold bastard?

Teague gravitated to a Picasso—something from his blue period, of course—and stroked his beard. "He was definitely onto something," he said. "It's unfortunate the man churned things out like a factory worker."

You're so critical, Apple thought as she passed the Picasso and followed Teague into the next room of the exhibit.

"Teague! I knew you'd be here!" The cry came from a woman with a shaved head, dressed in a sarong and dangly earrings shaped like snakes. She ran up to him and threw her arms around him. "Saw your photograph, love. Love it, love it! I didn't know you were into hand-tinting."

"I'm not 'into' anything, mind you," he said crossly. "Every piece calls for its own treatment. 'Cabinet' was a work that wanted hand-tinting."

"Of course, of course!" the woman appeased him. As she spoke about her flight from London, Apple realized she looked familiar.

"Aren't you Lena Ettinger? The sculptor?"

"Why, yes, I am." The woman tilted her head, studying Apple. "And you are . . . ?"

"Apple Sommers. I came with Teague."

He swung around, his eyes narrowed at her. "I've never seen her before in my life," he told Lena.

Apple frowned. The man was joking, but it was a sad little joke.

"Oh, you!" Lena slapped his shoulder. "You always were a bastard. So tell me, what do you think of the exhibit—apart from your own magnificent work?"

"It's totally derivative," he groused. "Nothing provocative. No new statements or explorations."

"But aren't hand-tinted photographs derivative, too?" Apple

pointed out. "We've had Manipulated Photography since the 1970s. Lucas Samaras treats wet emulsions like fingerpaints. Witkin scribbles on his negatives . . ."

"Tell me, dear," Teague asked, "are you interviewing for a docent position here at the museum? Because I'm not enjoying the guided tour."

Apple felt as if she'd been slapped.

"Come now, T," Lena said, trying to smooth things over. "She isn't one of your art school flunkies. Retract your claws." She turned to Apple, the creases in her forehead so apparent beneath that shiny pate. "Don't you want to kill him sometimes? He's such a bear."

Teague rolled his eyes. "Can we carry on? I'd like to see that 'Cabinets' has been installed properly."

Hmm. Maybe there was some legitimacy to his bringing her here, Apple thought. Of course, the artist would want to check that his piece was properly hung and lit.

"Of course, T," Lena said, tucking her program into the fold of her sarong. "We'll catch up later."

Apple followed Teague to where his work hung. True to its title, it was a photograph of cabinets, interesting because there were nearly a dozen weathered doors stacked in compact rows. Whether it was from a doll house or an apothecary shop, Apple wasn't sure, though she liked the gradations of shading that had emerged when Teague tinted the photo blue.

"It's lovely," she murmured. "The textures, the composition . . ."

He crossed his arms over his chest, scowling at it. "They've installed it adequately," he said. "Well, then . . . we should go."

"Can we stay, just for a while?" She anticipated a fight, but she would probably never have a chance to return here. "I'd like to see the rest of the exhibit. And right now, I'd just like to sit and soak up 'Cabinets' for a few minutes." She sat down on an empty bench facing the photograph. To her surprise, Teague sat beside her.

She tilted her head sideways, letting a lock of red hair dangle over one eye. "I've always believed that art provided a glimpse into the mind of the artist."

"A dangerous statement." Gently, he pushed the hair out of her eyes. "What if you glimpse something you don't want to see?"

Apple let out a breath. God, she was always seeing things she didn't want to see. Wasn't that why she loved being behind the camera, able to choose her angle and adjust the focus? Manipulate the photograph and you can manipulate life. "I change focus," she said. "Pull back. Find something else in the background. Change the shot."

He groaned. "My dear girl, you have much to learn."

25

"Before anyone says anything, I want you to know that I have been working like a dog for the past few days and my nerves are raw, so keep your claws retracted. Also, my date is set for today and I don't think we should talk about it. Any of it," Chandra said as she joined her friend at a table in O'Neill's for their breakfast meeting.

"Okay, we can't talk," Maggie said, not bothering to look up from her newspaper. "So why are we here?"

Usually they only did breakfast on weekends, but Chandra had felt the need to see her friends before her endeavor with J. Reginald Pringle. She was meeting him today, and ever since she'd woken up to the alarm she'd felt a knife of pain in her gut. She was scared stiff.

She took a chair opposite Maggie and Apple, who sat together on the banquette. Max and Boone were at chairs off to the side, the ever-present camera rolling.

"We don't have to talk about your date," Apple said, glancing up from her open camera case. "Don't sweat it. We ordered for you. Your usual granola and fruit."

Maggie tossed back her orange juice, turned the page, then

nearly choked. "Here it is, here it is, on Page Six! All about my date with the mayor."

"I thought we weren't going to talk about this stuff." Chandra rested her sunglasses on the table.

"What's it say?" Apple asked, reading over Maggie's shoulder. "Mayor Dates *Metro* Sexpert! Missed It? Tune in Tomorrow!"

"Ohmigod! There's a picture. Look at me in the Charles David suit! And no skin sheen. That powder-base foundation from the cosmetics closet really saved my ass."

Chandra snatched the paper away from them. "Watch your language, Mags." She bit her lip, glancing at the column. Maggie was getting press, and she felt jealous. She read it aloud: "Who was that sassy someone whose entourage was extensive enough to rival the mayor's security team? It seems that Maggie McGee, an editor from *Metropolitan* magazine, is at the top of Mayor Elliot Giordano's agenda these days. Along with her crew from *Big Tease,* the hip TV show that follows women in search of the most romantic date, Maggie wowed the city's highest official. So much, we're expecting to see them again in public. Especially after the sizzling e-mail Maggie sent Mr. Mayor after their date.' "

"My e-mail! I can't believe they know about my e-mail!" Maggie laughed. "Definitely one of my better messages. I always got *A*s in creative writing."

Chandra continued reading. "'We haven't seen the text, but sources close to the mayor said it was so hot, they're surprised his hard drive didn't melt!'"

Maggie burst out laughing. "I'm going to pee my pants!"

"It's not that funny," Chandra said, sliding the paper back to her.

"That last line . . ." Maggie swiped at her tears. "He definitely had a hard drive going."

"More information than I need to know," Chandra said, although she did want to know how the date went. As the waiter passed out dishes of crispy waffles, steaming omelets and granola, Chandra tried to bite back the question. Unsuccessfully.

"So what was he like?" she asked Maggie. "Is he nice, or a true tyrant?"

"Hard to tell . . . I barely saw him." Maggie raked her bangs back and sighed. "I mean, the most interesting part of the date was the chick clique upstairs. Who knew that wealthy women had the same issues we do? All I know is, the mayor doesn't like to hear no for an answer. Not in the boardroom, not in the bedroom."

"He made it to your bedroom?" Apple asked, her eyes wide open with wonder.

"I cut him off in the hall, which I know is totally uncharacteristic of me, but I did make that promise to . . ." She trailed off, noticing the camera. "I'm not going to delve into a sexual relationship without love," she said, right into the lens. Then she turned back to her friends. "So I knew he was pissed. Sent him that sizzling e-mail, and the rest is history."

"Documented on Page Six of the *Post,*" Chandra said. She doubted her date with J. Reginald Pringle would warrant that much publicity. *Stop being so competitive!* she warned herself. Unfortunately her self didn't always listen.

"Lucky you, Mags," Apple said. "I went on a date with my idol and learned why you should never put a person on a pedestal."

Maggie stabbed a fat square of Belgian waffle with her fork. "This is why I try to go into each date with low expectations," Maggie said. "That way, you can only be affirmed or pleasantly surprised."

"It started when he took me to an exhibit that featured *his* work. Then we had to go to *his* favorite restaurant, where the staff fell all over *him,* and somehow I got stuck with the check. And the whole time, he treated everyone like shit. Including me."

"You must have been so disappointed," Chandra said. "You always admired Fleming Teague."

"That was before I knew he was a bossy, opinionated bastard who has no respect for women. For anyone . . ."

Max swung his chair around and joined them at the table. "I

usually don't interrupt, ladies, but I think this would be the perfect time for us to review some of our video."

"Pardon me?" Chandra squinted at him.

"That doesn't happen until the end of the show," Apple insisted.

"Not this time." Max wiggled his eyebrows, à la Groucho Marx. "We decided to change the rules. Stir the pot a bit. Let you ladies check out the competition, so to speak."

"You can't do that!" Maggie said indignantly. "No, no! We don't want to be more competitive than we already are! That's not fair."

"Remember the contract?" Apple held her coffee cup against her cheek. "He doesn't have to be fair. This is so unfair!"

"We hate you," Maggie told Max, then popped a strawberry in her mouth. "I'll bet you were one of those kids who took his ball away just when the game was getting good."

Chandra rubbed her temples. "This is exactly what I don't need today."

"You got that cued up?" Max asked Boone, who was pushing buttons on the equipment.

"Hold on . . . okay, here we go," Boone said, turning the equipment around so that the women could view the monitor. Then he propped his camera up to capture their reactions.

Never a dull moment, Chandra thought as she waited for the video to roll. It was getting to the point where she expected a videocam to pop out of her medicine cabinet while she was brushing her teeth. There was a flash of fuzz on the screen, then Maggie's face beamed, her dark hair shining, her lips glistening with ruby red gloss.

"Now there's a cover girl moment," Chandra said, thinking that she'd better stop at Bloomies and update her makeup before this afternoon's meeting with her date.

"So you want the first date play-by-play?" Maggie teased the camera. "Hmm . . . if I were calling a Yankees' game, I'd say we got to first base. He was pushing for a double, but I held him off with a strong defense. I

mean, what's sex without the emotional underpinning of a meaningful relationship?"

"*Woo-hoo!*" Apple yelped. "You go, girl."

Chandra was clapping. "Gee, Mags, you don't adopt a philosophy, you embrace it."

"Thank you, thank you!" Maggie bowed, but everyone grew quiet again as the video went on.

"It's not that I'm not into him," Maggie said. "It's just that I don't know who he is. I mean, I spent more time with the waiter toting cheese puffs than I did with my date. Understandable, because he's the mayor. He's El Politico. But my thing is, who is Elliot the man? Our date was surrounded by so much hoopla and grandstanding, I felt like I was watching from the bleachers. I want to get closer, and I think that's going to happen on our next date, providing I get past his 'handlers.' "

As the tape ended, Max stood up. "That's Maggie. What do you think? Tough competition, huh?"

"Nice job, *Metro* girl," Chandra said, patting her friend's shoulder. "So you're really going out with him again?"

"Tonight," Maggie said. "I'm leaving work early to get a manicure."

"Tonight is Chandra's first date," Apple said. "Maybe you guys could double."

"Nah, that'd be no good." Maggie waved off the idea. "Chandra and I would dump the guys and go bar-hopping together."

Chandra smiled at Max's look of concern. "Don't think it hasn't been done," she said.

"I hope it won't be happening tonight," Max said with a hard look. "But we're not through here, yet. We still have Apple's post-date briefing."

"Aw, I don't think you need to show that." Apple crossed her legs and curled back into the booth. "I was so tired that morning, and it's not like I covered new ground or anything. The whole thing is . . . derivative."

"How about if your friends are the judge of that?" Max said, cuing Boone.

The video screen blinked, and there was Apple, looking frank and fresh and beautiful. Unlike Maggie, she wasn't wearing any makeup, but the shadows trimmed her cheekbones in just the right way. Her lips seemed swollen and red—from kissing? Chandra could only wonder. Her hair was pulled back from her face with a band, but long spiral strands cascaded down over her shoulders, framing her face like an ornate headpiece.

"I don't know," she said. "I think I put him off a bit, with my knowledge of the art world. He was mad. Definitely not happy with me at first. But then . . ." She shook her head, her eyes gazing off in the distance. "There was this spark between us. A certain chemistry. We acted on that. I mean, why be demure?"

"Ohmigod! You slept with him?" Maggie blurted out.

"You slept with the bossy, opinionated bastard who . . . who . . ." Chandra couldn't bring herself to say it, especially on camera.

"Who treats everybody like shit," Apple finished for her. "It's not the way it sounds. I mean, he's not all bad."

"Apparently not, if you can get his grundies off," Maggie said as the video of Apple rolled on.

Chandra listened as Apple described her night with Teague. She made a sexual encounter sound like a collaborative dance of two artists.

"He asked me to stay," Apple said on the tape, "and the next morning he bought me a toothbrush. Looks like I'll be staying."

"You moved in with him?" Maggie demanded.

Apple shrugged. "Not that anything was really said one way or the other, but his place is so big—a full floor in Soho with a private bedroom. You could get lost in all the artwork there."

Chandra folded her arms and sighed, wondering how she was ever going to compete with her friends in the dating arena. Already she was sure she'd made a big mistake in agreeing to date J. Reginald Pringle. The man was a financier, not an artist or a leading politician. A numbers man. Boring. Dry. Deadly dull.

"I don't believe you," Maggie said, giving Apple a little shake. "You tell us one thing about Teague, and meanwhile you're already shacked up with the guy and picking out china. What, are you nurturing a double-life or something? You must be hell in therapy!"

"Sorry!" Apple winced. "I was going to tell you guys. I just figured I'd wait till I was more comfortable about it. I mean, I don't know what the hell I'm doing. Do you think I have any control over these things?"

"Typical Apple," Chandra said. "She goes on a date and ends up with a four-thousand-square-foot loft in Soho."

26

"I've been a nervous wreck all day, but right now I'm starting to feel relaxed about this," Chandra said as she stared out the floor-to-ceiling window of the British Airways terminal at JFK Airport. "I've realized that this is, first and foremost, a business meeting, and that I need to conduct myself with the same composure and focus I possess in all business dealings."

A few feet away, Mule filmed her musings with his videocam while Nayasia chased the airline personnel with her endless questions. When would the Concorde be in? Was this the right terminal? Was the flight on time? Did they have a manifest of the passenger list? The woman was so tightly wound; one snapped thread and she'd be ricocheting off the walls of the terminal.

Take a lesson from the frazzled one, Chandra thought. *Easy does it.*

Which was easier said than done as the Concorde landed and its passengers began to emerge from the jetway. Not so easy to keep her heartbeat even as J. Reginald appeared, looking more attractive and animated than he seemed in photos. His thick silver hair caught the light, and his warm brown eyes seemed to cut through all the formality that separated Chandra from him.

"Mr. Pringle," she said, stepping forward. "Welcome to New York."

"Please, call me Reg," he insisted, taking her hand and holding it between his palms. "I'm delighted to be here, Chandra." He glanced up at the videocam; then he turned his attention back to Chandra. "In a perfect world, we should all mix business with pleasure, shouldn't we?"

"Definitely," she lied, feeling charmed by the way he held her hands. American men didn't linger beyond a handshake. This was nice. Nerve-racking, but nice.

"I can't talk." Chandra spoke in guarded tones from the phone at Vincent's desk, watching as Vincent served J. Reginald Pringle tea in her office. "I'm officially on my date, though he's having tea in my office with the cameras rolling. Nayasia actually told Vincent to get her some coffee. Can you believe her? Plus I'm about to go into a meeting with Mr. Pringle and the top-tier management of Grayrock." She'd only taken the call because it was Apple.

"Is he cute?" Apple asked.

"Very. But it's Weirdsville. Dating in the office. Totally not me."

"I just wanted to apologize if I seemed to be holding out about Teague at breakfast," Apple said. "I'd never lie to you guys. And it's not as good as it sounds, the part about my moving in with him."

"What's the downside?" Chandra asked.

"He really is a manipulative bastard. And he couldn't bring me to orgasm. Is there something wrong with me?"

"No, honey! No, no, it's not your fault."

"But he tried so hard, Chandra. The guy worked on me for, like, an hour. It's a wonder his tongue isn't in traction."

Chandra shifted uncomfortably. She hadn't been with anyone since Jeff. Sex had been off her menu for so long, she wasn't exactly the best person to give advice regarding failure to orgasm. "Maybe you should have this conversation with Maggie."

"I did, and she was incredibly sympathetic, but she doesn't understand how it feels. She thinks I should drink some wine and masturbate. Talk about something that's way low on my priority list."

"What about fantasizing?" Chandra asked, trying to focus on the problem as Vincent emerged from her office. She bolted up in the chair, feeling guilty. "I'll be off in a minute," she said, gesturing toward his desk.

"No problem at all," he said. "Mr. Pringle wants a newspaper. I'm off to find him a *Wall Street Journal.* And I promised Nayasia a cup of coffee." He headed down the hall, his posture perfect, his shoulders broad and straight.

"I really can't do this now," Chandra said, "but we'll definitely talk. Until then, don't be so hard on yourself. I mean, it was your first time with the guy; he doesn't know what pushes your buttons yet."

"Though God knows he tried. Every button, lever and bell."

"How disappointing for you. And for him, I guess."

"Nah." Apple sighed. "In the end I faked it. I couldn't let him think he'd wasted four hours. Besides, I wanted to go to sleep."

"Sleep is definitely underrated," Chandra said as J. Reginald poked his head out and gave a curious look. "Gotta run. We'll talk later."

Although she still felt uncomfortable, she joined him for tea, during which they talked about Grayrock's past acquisitions. Chandra wasn't sure if he was making conversation or fishing for information, but she maintained a cautious demeanor. She was all too conscious of the rolling cameras and the staff lining up to meet with this man within the hour.

Inside the conference room, Mule was allowed to film, but not record sound in deference to the confidential nature of the meeting. Chandra introduced J. Reginald to Alfred Lipton, the head of the New York office, as well as Willard Ritter, her boss. J. Reginald struck up a conversation about golf with Alfred, which left Chandra off the hook from introducing him to go-with-the-flow Doris Gordon and the ever-pushy Biedermeyer, who was so excited to be included in the meeting he was almost salivating on the shiny mahogany conference table.

As Grayrock players filed in and took their seats, Chandra was disappointed to see that she was seated opposite J. Reginald . . . so far away. But then again, this was a business meeting, wasn't it? *No, no . . . you've got your presentation,* she reminded herself. This was totally schizoid.

After introductions were made, she began her presentation. "Although this is still in the preliminary stages, the executives at Grayrock have been interested in meeting you, Mr. Pringle, regarding Gem, Inc., one of the companies in your corporate group." As she went on, Chandra began to feel a bit more like herself again. Calm. Confident. Grounded.

Once she wrapped up her presentation, J. Reginald Pringle responded, saying he thought Grayrock was a perfect fit for Gem, Inc. There were questions from Alfred and Willard, some banter, a few pale jokes about the camera following them. But once the pressure was off—when Chandra realized her presentation had been a success and the meeting was going well—she found her thoughts drifting to J. Reginald.

What would it be like to kiss him?

His lips were thin, his chin strong and angular. His skin looked smooth, though she imagined that by the end of the day there would be some stubble of a gray beard. She thought of Apple's words about a tongue in traction. What would it be like to have that face down . . .

No . . . no. She couldn't go there. Not now.

But as J. Reginald reached across the table to hand her a memo and his hand brushed hers, she knew there was chemistry between them. From the twinkle in his eyes, the way she wanted to smile at him, the way he cocked his head to the side to study her . . . yes, they definitely had it going on.

What would happen if she stretched across the mahogany table, pulled him out of his chair by his necktie, and started making love to him right here and now? She could imagine the shock on her boss's face. Or maybe not . . . maybe Willard would want to watch as J. Reginald slid his hand up along her black silk stocking, gently caressing her inner thigh, moving up, up . . .

Enough with the fantasizing, she told herself, digging her nails into her palm under the table. What was with her? Her first date in two years and already she was fantasizing about performing in the boardroom. It was as if her libido were trying to make up for lost time.

Take it one step at a time, she thought. *One step at a time.*

If Chandra had any doubts about J. Reginald's feelings for her, they were chased away when they went to dinner alone at the end of the day. Although they were seated opposite each other at a quiet table in the Four Seasons, J. Reginald asked her permission to give up his chair and join her on the banquette.

"Sitting across from you feels far too adversarial," he said as he sat next to her. Was that the heat of his body, or were her hormones lighting up again? "Far too similar to the boardroom, where you are an adversary to be feared, I see."

She laughed. "Not if you've got your numbers in line."

"Oh, if I worked for you I would be lined up and at full attention at all times." His shoulder pressed into hers, softly, intimately. "I hear the caviar is quite good here, as well as the champagne. Or would you like to order something else to start?" he asked.

"Who could argue with caviar and champagne?" Jeff had helped her acquire a taste for caviar by mixing it with a lot of sour cream and hard-boiled egg at first.

She turned and saw that he was smiling. "J. Reginald . . . what should I really call you? That seems so formal."

"It's what my mother named me," he said. "Actually, she named me after some biblical character, then abandoned that when she lost religion. Jeremiah was my given name."

She nodded. "And now your mother calls you . . ."

"Simply Reg."

"Okay, Reg."

"Yes, Chandra Hammel, and where did you get that perfect name? It's like a film star . . . almost made-up."

She wasn't about to tell him that her name was a fabrication. "I was going to be a film star," she said, "but I found business far more glamorous. When I opened the *Wall Street Journal* and started reading about international expansion and tax shelters"—she took a deep breath—"oh . . . don't get me started."

He touched her thigh, rubbing it gently. "How about diversifying holdings? Global markets? Stimulated economies . . ."

Chandra felt herself heating up. She'd been joking, but somehow the joke was turning into incredibly stimulating dinner conversation. "All those things," she whispered. "Those were the things that attracted me to the business of finance." She could feel her cashmere dress sliding up under his fingers.

"It sounds as if we have quite a lot in common," he said, squeezing her knee. "Quite a lot."

27

Across town, Maggie was heaping her plate with savory dishes from a large buffet table and wondering when the mayor would arrive. She was officially attending this Hanukkah celebration as his date, though she'd been escorted here by one of his assistants, a party-hearty guy named Steve Dombrowski. "I didn't know the mayor was Jewish," she said. "Not that it matters. I'm such a lapsed Catholic, the church would probably spontaneously combust if I went for confession."

"He's not," Steve said. "But when you're mayor of New York and you're invited to party with an ethnic group, you attend. That's the deal."

"So, when do you think he's going to arrive?" Maggie asked as she helped herself to a serving of kugel. Not that she'd be polishing it off. The Versace ensemble she'd scored from *Metro*'s wardrobe closet showed off her abs to advantage, but it didn't leave much room for snacking. As it was, Maggie had to remind herself to keep her shoulders up, her stomach tucked. The scarlet red midriff top was cut low with the waist and neckline embroidered with gold and pink. Beneath her navel hung the simple red sheath skirt, clingy and dripping from her hips. "Aren't you just the Little Red Engine that Could!" Jonathon had gushed when she'd modeled the ensemble for him. She'd told him: "This is the gown a girl does crunches for," Maggie said. "I won't be able to sit down all night, but it'll be worth it."

And yes, the ensemble is paying off, Maggie thought as she caught Steve eyeballing her cleavage and oh-so-bare belly button.

"I'm sorry," Steve said with a guilty grin. "What was the question?"

"Hizzoner, the mayor. When do you think he's going to grace us with his presence? I mean, we've been here for two hours and still no sign of his majesty."

"What's the matter? You don't like me?" Steve lowered his head and pretended to cower, though that was nearly impossible with those big brown eyes. He was tall and lean, with a large nose that would be unfortunate on most men, but somehow Steve managed to carry it with comic relief. "Not for nothing, Maggie, but you're going to give me a complex."

"Ooh, don't be that way! It's not that you're not a lot of fun, Steve. You are chock-full of fun. The original fun guy." It was true. In the short time they'd been together, she'd learned that Steve liked the Yankees. Steve liked beer by the pint, though he could pack away a good deal of Manischevitz, too. Steve liked to pull practical jokes on his friends and family members. And that little earphone thing he wore in his ear was so darned sexy. Maggie swung round to face Boone's camera. "It's just that, I'm supposed to be dating the mayor, and I'm having so darned much fun with you I feel like I'm two-timing him."

"Not a bad idea," Steve said, dancing her away from the buffet table.

"Hold on, hold on." Maggie extracted herself from Steve to put her plate and wineglass down on the table. As she turned back, she noticed Max scowling, hands in his jeans as usual. What a miserable camper.

"Come on, Maggie, my girl!" Steve called, "I'm not getting any younger."

Ignoring Max, Maggie swung around and hurried over to Steve, who was already in the throes of a passionate tango.

"You're quite a dancer, Steve. Dancing, eating, drinking. You really do enjoy your job, don't you?" she said as they danced cheek-to-cheek.

"Maggie, my girl, I enjoy everything."

She turned to catch the expression on his face. Yes, there was a subliminal message there. "I'll just bet you do."

All too soon the driver appeared to announce that the limo was waiting. Reg helped Chandra into her coat, then took her by the arm out to the limo. "I can't tell you how much I regret the need to return to London tonight," he said. "Business demands."

"I understand," she told him. "But it's hard to say good-bye." *Did those words come out of my mouth?* she wondered as he helped her into the limo. A two-year dry spell, and now she was getting romantically involved with a man in a matter of hours?

Still, the attraction swelled as he climbed into the car beside her and put his hand on her knee. "We need to leave and it appears your cameraman is detained elsewhere."

There was a tap on the window, where Nayasia's face loomed beyond the tinted glass.

"I can't get Mule outta the john," she said, cracking her gum. Her rhinestone sunglasses twinkled in the light of the streetlamps. "So go on to the airport and we'll meet you there."

"Excellent idea." Reg said, closing the window and instructing the driver to go ahead.

As the car began to roll, Chandra realized that she was off-camera—unwatched and inches away from a man who made sparks fly whenever he touched her. *Thank God for tinted glass,* she thought as she turned to him. By mutual consent, their faces came within inches of each other, his brown eyes so intense.

"You are so damned beautiful," he said. Then the heat between them pulled her forward and they kissed. They kissed and held each other close.

Chandra ran her hands over his smooth brown jaw, his neck and shoulders, studying the curves and angles of his body. She couldn't get enough of him.

"Can you imagine the benefits of a merger?" he whispered as

he slid a hand up under her dress. "The overriding risk factors are low, and the profits have the potential to shoot sky-high."

For a moment Chandra thought he was talking about Grayrock and Gem; then she realized he was speaking metaphorically. Sex talk. Actually, the business school version of sex talk.

"You'd have to examine the collateral carefully," she said, working his belt buckle loose. She reached inside, adding, "You don't want to touch the investment until you know it's solid. Rock-hard and solid."

They talked on as they explored each other, reaching under clothes, tracing the line of bones, caressing smooth skin. By the time they exited the Belt Parkway for JFK, Chandra was consumed with heat, wanting him closer, wanting to make love to him. She didn't want him to take his hand away from the sweet spot between her legs, but they were minutes away from the airport . . .

"That feels incredibly good, but we have to stop all discussion of a merger," she whispered roughly. "We're almost there."

"In so many ways," he said, sliding his hand across her thigh, then squeezing it. "Talk about bad timing. Where the hell is auto traffic when you need it?"

As they pulled up at the terminal, Chandra smoothed back her hair, straightened her dress, and took a deep, calming breath. Reg fastened his pants and straightened his tie. "I promise you, next time we will finish what we started," he said. "Perhaps at the Ritz Carlton or the Plaza?"

"I'm going to hold you to that," she said as he leaned forward to kiss her forehead.

As they walked through the terminal a feeling of disappointment gripped her. Chandra hated to leave anything unfinished. She prided herself on wrapping up everything in her life. Neat and tidy. Maybe it was one of the reasons she'd avoided relationships since Jeff. Relationships were so imperfect.

Inside the airport, Mule and Nayasia caught up with them at the British Airways counter. Mule's hair was scraped back from his pale face, his eyes pinched and puffy.

"Mule, are you okay?" Chandra asked him while Reg checked

in at the British Airways counter. "You're looking a little washed out."

"I think it's the flu," he said, closing his eyes. "Nayasia's pissed, but I've got to get home."

"We're almost finished here," she said, with a longing look toward her date.

"Mule!" Nayasia stomped over. "Did you get that? Why aren't we rolling?"

"Easy, now," Chandra told her, patting Mule's arm. Despite Nayasia's tendency to annoy, the big guy had grown on her. "It's okay. I'll do a repeat performance if you want."

She had to say goodbye to Reg at Immigration. They hugged like old friends, then kissed one more time. With a sigh, he leaned back, his gorgeous eyes twinkling. "Till next time, Love."

Chandra held her breath as he walked down the corridor. A true cliffhanger. She was hanging by her French-manicured fingernails.

"Did you get that?" Nayasia barked. "Did you get it, Mule?"

"Yeah, yeah." He snorted. "Can we go now?"

"In a minute." Nayasia cracked her gum. "Give us a reaction, Chandra. How do you think the date went?"

"Well, he told me he liked to combine business with pleasure, and we certainly managed to do that."

Nayasia lifted her rhinestone glasses. "What do you mean? Did something go on in the limousine on the way here?"

Chandra smiled. "Let's just say we . . . we both seem to want the same thing right now. And he certainly left me wanting more. Much, much more." She glanced back down the corridor, then turned away. "I usually don't open up to a man so quickly, but I really think we clicked."

"Okay, cut!" Nayasia said. "That's it. Let's go."

"Finally." Mule lowered the minicam and rubbed his face. "I don't think I can drive."

"Come on," Chandra told him. "I'll have my cab drop you."

"What the hell is wrong with you?" Nayasia complained. "You made us miss whatever went on in the limo."

"I'm sick!"

"Whatever!" she said, stomping off.

"Man, oh, man . . ." Mule groaned. "She never gets off my case. Blinded by ambition, that's her problem. Did you ever know anyone like that?"

Chandra bit her lower lip. "I used to, Mule," she answered as they walked toward the cab stand. "I used to."

"What is this, an instant replay?" Maggie asked as the mayor nibbled on her neck. They were making out in the vestibule of her apartment, having spent all of twenty minutes together at the Hanukkah celebration, and most of that time she'd shared him with a few hundred other revelers. Not that she didn't have a fabulous time hanging with Fun-Guy Steve. But here she was, being squeezed and suckled by her hotshot date, a man who was still a total stranger. "What's that Yogi Berra-ism? This is like déjà vu, all over again!"

The mayor stopped nibbling to say: "Only this time we've got a camera crew tailing us."

"Oh, yeah, I almost forgot." Maggie lifted her head and licked her lips as Boone moved sideways behind the videocam. "Boone is so quiet; he's sort of my shadow. My conscience. Hi, Boone!" she waved. Max was somewhere outside, most likely sulking on the steps or grabbing a cup of coffee at the corner deli.

"I know one way we can lose the shadow," the mayor said. He ran his hands over her back, massaging her spine, but Maggie wasn't in the mood to melt in his arms. "So, what do you say? Aren't you going to invite me up? I mean, we can leave your entourage behind if things are going to move to a more personal level, correct?"

Actually, she was beginning to find his routine a little insulting. Even during a one-night stand, she felt a strong wave of interest from the guy she was about to boff. But the mayor's focus involved Maggie McGee from the waist down. Maggie as an afterthought. The Maggie cordial—enjoy a shot of her in a brandy snifter before hitting the sack. "You know," Maggie told him, "I don't think tonight it's going to happen tonight."

"What?" He seemed surprised. "Come on. You can at least ask

me up." He rubbed her shoulders affectionately. "Then we can take things from there."

"No dice." Maggie frowned. "I hate to disappoint you, but I don't want to rush into a physical thing when we still barely know each other." She leaned away from him and pretended to pummel his chest. "Come on, big guy. When are you going to give me more than ten minutes? A real date, instead of a sound byte."

He closed his eyes and let out a deep breath. "Occupational hazards."

"I know, Mr. Mayor, and I'm not complaining. But I'm also not going to play Hide-the-Salami with a sausage I've never met."

He snorted. "You do have a way with words, Ms. McGee."

"That's why I rack up the long hours and rake in the low pay. I'm a *Metro Girl.*"

"Okay, then." The mayor extracted his hands and held them up, as if Maggie was about to frisk him. "Much as I hate to concede, and my constituency knows that well, I respect your feelings, even if I don't agree. You probably know I don't take kindly to dissension, but I will work to swing you around to my point of view. I'll have a talk with my aides about clearing some space for you. Time for a real date." He leaned closer and whispered, "Because I wouldn't want you handling any strange salami."

"Thanks for hearing me out." Maggie gave his hand a squeeze, then backed out of his arms. "Have your people call my people."

"Will do." The mayor nodded at her, nodded at the minicam, then headed out to his waiting limo where Steve sat with his oh-so-sexy earphone in place. "'Night, Boone," Maggie said with a little wave.

Boone lowered the minicam. "Catch you in the A.M., Maggie."

Maggie hitched up her red Versace skirt and climbed the stairs, humming a song that she and Steve had danced to. As she fished in her tiny beaded bag for her keys, she wondered how long it had been since she'd had sex. "It's got to be a world record," she said to herself.

She opened the door, slid out of her satin mules and tossed her purse on the bed. "You turned down the mayor, not once, but twice!" She reached for the phone. Apple and Chandra needed to hear about this. She was dialing them up when another thought popped into her head. "Ohmigod." Maggie covered her mouth. "I'm a tease! I'm actually a big, bold tease."

And then, so untrue to form, she giggled.

Part Three

You Can Be the Object of His Desire: Show Him How to Push Your Buttons

28

"Have yourself a merry little Christmas," the singer crooned as she leaned over the baby grand piano and touched the white poinsettias, one of many floral arrangements that Kitty's party planner had placed strategically around the room. Maggie nibbled on another fat cocktail shrimp as she surveyed the room. Kitty, otherwise known as Katherine Wade-Clemson, had really outdone herself this time. The white flowers were just accents to the fake snow she'd had blown into the corners of the penthouse where Christmas scenes of "Old New York" rivaled the displays in Lord & Taylor's windows. There were mechanized dolls skating on the pond in Central Park. A family riding a sled down Fifth Avenue. Nuns filing into Saint Patrick's Cathedral. Maggie crumpled up shrimp tails in a napkin and crossed to her friends. As she walked, the skirt of her sapphire Ungaro gown sent flecks of fake snow swirling on the parquet floors.

"I like the special snow effects, but I do hope these flakes don't stick to my Manolo Blahniks," Maggie told her friends.

"Love the shoes," Apple said. "But the snow . . ." She rolled her eyes. "I'm going to have another talk with Kitty about excess and environmental friendly snow. I think this stuff is Styrofoam."

"It won't get you anywhere," Maggie said, lifting a beaded

shoe to swipe at the heel. "I borrowed these bad boys from the closet at *Metro,* and Candy demands them back or else."

"Every time I see you, you're wearing something new," Chandra told Maggie. "Some of us have to recycle." She was wearing a black halter gown with a bodice made of emerald green satin—a Herrera that Maggie had seen before, though Chandra always managed to pull off the classics.

"Recycle-shmykle," Maggie said. "You look stunning, dear."

"I can't believe Candy is still letting you dip into the wardrobe closet," Chandra said. "She must have been bitten by the Christmas spirit."

"It's called publicity," Maggie said. "Candy is all smiles when Boone's there with his camera. Behind the scenes she still sends me poisonous e-mails about deadlines and my schedule, but e-mails are easy to ignore."

"This place must be a feast for the camera," Chandra said, nodding at Boone. "Where's Max?"

"Slinking around somewhere," Maggie said. "I think I saw him pitching a show to some cigar-smokers on the terrace."

"It's truly decadent," Apple said, marveling at the motorized statue of a boy lifting an ornament to a Christmas tree. "Kitty always goes overboard for parties, but this year it's way too much. How do you think she's going to get rid of this fake snow when the party ends?"

"What does she care?" Chandra said. "She'll be off in the islands or in Europe or Aspen."

"While the servants spend weeks sucking up snow with industrial vacuums," Maggie added.

Apple shook her head, her gray eyes wide and naive. "I just can't imagine what this sort of thing would cost."

"Neither can Kitty," Chandra said. "Laurence gets the bill."

Noticing Boone's camera on her, Maggie raised her champagne flute for a toast. "To Kitty and Laurence—and their fabulous parties!" Chandra had met Laurence in business school, and somehow the three friends had been added to Kitty and Laurence's guest list, a list that included the upper-crust Manhattan society. Over the years Maggie had always expected Kitty to give them the boot one day, but she seemed genuinely interested in their lives whenever they connected. Which happened to be the three or four times a year that Kitty and Laurence threw a party. How else would they chance to meet? Kitty wasn't the sort of person you'd run into at the corner deli or Starbucks. Kitty had "people" to take care of those menial tasks.

The pianist paused as the singer went in for the kill. "And have yourself, a Merry Little Christmas now . . ."

"It's not going to be a Merry Little Christmas for me," Maggie lamented. "I haven't had sex since . . . like forever. Ever since you guys backed me into that promise. And I've got to say, though sometimes it works for me, other times I feel like I'm going to shrivel up and blow away like those papers that streak up Seventh Avenue and swirl around in doorways. I mean, how long has it been? You do the math."

"Let's see," Apple said, tossing a clump of hair back over a bare shoulder. She was wearing a flowing Valentino gown, a soft flesh-colored silk so naughty that from far away, she looked deliciously nude. Her hair was scraped back from her face and fastened with a tortoiseshell clip, accenting her high cheekbones and freckled skin. "Since that was, like, just after Thanksgiving, I'd say you're going on two weeks, but barely."

"Is that all?" Maggie touched her temple. "It seems like so much longer. The buildup of hormones must be affecting my brain."

"Try going without for a few years," Chandra said as she accepted a glass of red wine from a waiter. "Set your timer on, say, two years, then give me a call."

"How did you ever do it?" Maggie asked, trying to imagine the unimaginable. "I mean, I know you were devastated over Jeff. We all were. But to totally abstain . . ." She shook her head. "I would applaud you if I wasn't juggling this champagne glass and this napkin full of shrimp tails. Where do I dump this thing?"

Chandra nodded toward the waiter, whom Maggie gifted with her balled-up cocktail napkin. "But it's not as if I was so noble,"

Chandra went on. "More like nothing was going on. I mean, there was no fire down below. Not a flicker. Not a spark. Until I met Reg."

"Reg," Apple said in a gooey voice. "I can't wait to meet him. You two sound so right for each other. Did you talk to him last night?"

Chandra tried to hold back her grin as she nodded.

"You did? Again?" Apple covered her mouth to suppress a giggle.

"What's so funny about a phone call between London and New York?" Maggie asked, looking from one friend to the other. Clearly, Chandra was embarrassed. Then it hit her. "Phone sex? You've been having phone sex with J. Reginald Pringle?"

"A little louder, Mags," Chandra said, shielding her face with a cocktail napkin. "I don't think the guys over by the terrace heard you."

"Well, that's nothing to be embarrassed about," Maggie said, though it was taking her a minute to process this development. She couldn't get past the feeling that Chandra was now passing her in the race to romance. Especially considering the little promise that was holding her back from doing the deed. Well, sort of. So far she really enjoyed stringing the mayor along, but her libido was crying out from lack of attention. "I'm just surprised, that's all. I didn't peg you as the type to heat up a guy's cell phone."

Apple blinked. "You have us stereotyped? What am I—the orgasm-deficient man-pleaser?"

"Really," Chandra added. "If I didn't know you better, I'd say you're a little jealous."

Maggie bit her lower lip. She hated that her friends could read her so well. "I want happily ever after for you, sweetie," she told Chandra. "I really do. But it would help to have some real intimacy with the guy before you go picking out china patterns. I mean, phone sex can get you over the humps—or, actually, the lack of humping—but there's nothing like the real deal." Even as the words came out, Maggie wondered at herself. Here she was, the Queen of the Quickie, giving out intimate advice. Thank God, her friends were used to her know-it-all attitude.

"I'm on top of the situation," Chandra insisted. "That's why I'm going to London Wednesday. Well, it's for business, too. Some of the other Grayrock managers are flying over, but I can't wait to see Reg again and spend a little quality time with him."

Maggie took a sip of champagne, savoring the pop of the bubbles. "Okay, I'll bite. I am jealous. You're both in relationships, both likely to have regular sex, and here I am out in the cold. Well, maybe, maybe not. I might have met someone I can connect with." She lifted her chin and added in a snooty voice, "Someone with whom I can share a meaningful emotional and physical relationship."

"The mayor?" Apple asked. "Are you finally getting through his shell?"

"Forget the shell." Maggie waved at the air, as if swatting a gnat. "I can't get past his press corps and security team. But there's someone on his staff who's a real pip—Fun Steve. Actually, I invited him tonight. The guy's definitely got potential. I spent an entire evening with him and didn't hate him one bit."

"That's a rave," Apple said. "I wish I could say the same for Teague. He can be so sweet, but sometimes he just . . ." She curled her hands into claws. "It's like he can't leave nice-nice alone. He's always got to dig in and find some sore to pick at till it's bleeding again."

Chandra's eyes opened wide. "Apple, you're scaring me."

"Really," Maggie added. "Where did you get that imagery?"

"I don't know, it just comes to me. Am I crazy, or is it too much to ask for a quiet evening of dinner or a movie or a party without having to stage an argument?"

"What do you guys fight about?" Maggie asked.

"You name it, Teague will argue about it. The other night he was bashing the relevance of Fabricated Photography. And yesterday he slammed the contribution of the German Dada artists to photo montage. And at the movies—the merits of buttered popcorn versus plain."

"You lost me on the Dada guys," Maggie admitted, "but I get the point. Sounds like the god of photography has fallen from his pedestal."

"Oh, he's still a fine artist. Just a poor excuse for a human being." Apple hung her head to the side. "He just wears me down."

"Don't let him do that," Maggie insisted. "Dump him."

Chandra nodded as she sipped her Merlot. "Really. Cut him loose."

"I can't." Apple gazed off in the distance, clearly tormented. "There's something that attracts me to him. And we're living together now. It's already so complicated."

"Hold on, there." Maggie touched Apple's elbow. "Don't use the apartment thing as an excuse. If you need out, you can always stay with me or Chandra. You are not his indentured servant. Do you understand?"

"Yes, yes, but it's not all that bad. There are some good things. It's all such a big fat jumble of good and bad."

"See, this is the problem with shacking up with a guy," Maggie insisted. "I know it's worked for you over the past few years, but it adds a burden of closeness that most early relationships can't bear. Not to mention the fact that you feel indebted to him. Don't you? I mean, you're dependent on the fucker."

Chandra was nodding. "Apple, it's so true. You're always the first to rank on the trust fund babies who live off their inheritance, and this is so similar. Don't you ever feel the need to have your own space? Your own place?"

Apple frowned, her eyes clouded. "It's never been a big problem."

Maggie didn't believe her, but she felt as if they'd pushed enough for now. "Well, when it becomes a problem, you can bunk with us."

"Just remember," Chandra said. "We're here."

Apple nodded as Max joined them. "Ladies, ladies, I've got some news for you this evening." He stroked his stubble. Max always seemed to need a shave. "Starting tomorrow, you'll see your faces in TV promos and billboards around town. And I'm pleased to announce that our first episode of *Big Tease* will air at the end of next week—December sixteenth."

"Really?" Maggie beamed. "That's the date of my tree-trimming party. We can all gather round the set after we trim the tree. Talk about a traditional Christmas."

"You must have been a busy boy in the editing room," Chandra said. "I hope you made us all look fabulous."

"Really," Apple said. "We know you can kill us if you use the wrong shots."

Max rubbed his chin thoughtfully. "I think we've settled on an accurate and fair depiction of our three contestants."

"Well, that's hardly encouraging," Maggie said. "It sounds like a disclaimer."

"Trust me." Max held out his hands like a priest about to administer a blessing. "Didn't I pull off a fair depiction of the three contestants last season?"

Chandra shot a desperate look at her friends, apparently not willing to admit she'd never seen the show.

"It was pretty even-handed," Apple admitted.

But Maggie wasn't fooled, not one bit. Something about Max bothered her. "Can't wait to see the promos," she said, deciding not to press her point here lest Max-the-grouch linger any longer. *Besides, I've got bigger fish to fry,* she thought as she spotted the new object of her affection across the room at the bar. He was already lifting a bottle of imported beer to his lips as he related a story to two guys there. She excused herself and cut through the crowd. "Steve!" She zeroed in on him just as he delivered the punch line. The guys laughed, and one of them slapped Steve on the shoulder.

"Good one. I've never heard that before."

"That's because it really happened to me," Steve insisted, and the guys laughed again.

Maggie squeezed his arm affectionately. "I'm so glad you made it. There's someone here I'm dying for you to meet."

"Oh, really?" He grabbed his beer and let her guide him through the crowd. "Big El didn't show, did he?"

"Nah, our secret's still safe," she said, realizing that Steve had more to lose than she did if the mayor found out they were seeing each other behind his back. She could lose her high-profile date; Steve could lose his job. "Come on . . ." She led him past the foyer then down a corridor. "Right in here." She pushed open the door, then pushed Steve in. Maggie followed quickly, shutting and locking the door behind her.

Steve took two steps toward the double vanity, then turned back to Maggie. "This is a john!"

"I know, I know, but I thought we should have some privacy before I showed you my jingle bells."

"Say what?"

With her back to the sink, Maggie hoisted herself onto the vanity and proceeded to lift the skirt of her gown to her knees. "Jingle bells. I've got little tiny bells on my garters. Wanna see?"

Although he didn't speak, his answer was apparent in the steadfast attention he was now giving her. He hunched over, open-mouthed, as she bunched the skirt up to the hemline and eased it up over her thighs. She passed two little red garters with green ribbons and tiny bells. "These are my jingle bells," she said. "Want to give them a ring? Go ahead?"

He reached forward and batted one with his finger.

Maggie lifted her skirt higher, and his eyes followed. She loved the amazement on his face when he saw that she wasn't wearing panties. That always got them. Rubbing her inner thighs, she sighed. "Okay, there's my Christmas surprise. How about you? Got any jingle balls to show me?"

He stared at her.

"What's wrong, Steve? Don't tell me I've left you speechless."

He handed her his beer and reached for his belt buckle. "I . . . I just didn't expect Christmas to come so early."

She took a swig of his beer, then pushed it away on the counter. "Yep. Here I am, wrapped in bells and bows," she said, barely able to restrain herself from jumping down and ripping off his clothes. She'd gone way too long without sex. But it was worth the wait, wasn't it? Waiting for the right guy, the right moment when . . .

There was a knock on the door, and Steve froze.

Maggie sneered at the door. "Be out in a minute," she called, pulling a condom out from between her breasts. Lowering her voice seductively, she told Steve, "I brought a green condom, nice and festive for the season."

"Gives new meaning to that song, 'Greensleeves,' " he said as he dropped his trousers. While she unwrapped the condom, he sang: "Greensleeves was what his dick wore . . ."

"Oh, damnation, promise me you won't sing during sex," she said, reaching into his shorts to stroke him. "Oh, look at you!" That shut him up.

He was hard, firm . . . very nice. *I missed this!* she thought, stroking him furiously. She was wet with wanting, wet and ready. He pulled down his striped boxers, breathing tensely as she rolled it on. She was ready for him, burning to have him after her period of abstinence. The prospect of doing it in Kit's bathroom in the throes of a Christmas party only increased the thrill.

She pulled her knees apart and beckoned. "Come on, big guy."

He worked himself into her and thrust his hips.

"Ach!" she gasped, so glad to have him. So . . . she was going to have a Sexy Little Christmas after all.

29

Chandra knew the doorman was getting suspicious. He was so unaccustomed to seeing her return home before six on a weekday, he didn't know what to make of her daily lunchtime appearances. "Are you feeling okay, Ms. Hammel?" asked Oscar.

"Just fine," she said as she breezed by. "I've been adjusting my schedule a bit lately. Throwing you off, right?"

"I'll say," he called after her as she pressed the elevator button. "Used to be able to set my clock by you. Never home from the office before seven. Now I'm all off-kilter."

Chandra leaned against the elevator wall and sighed as the doors whooshed closed. This daily rush home was wearing on her, but she didn't feel safe talking to Reg from the office. Not with the type of phone conversations they'd been having. Although she could lock her office door, she didn't want to compromise her state of mind in the office. Not to mention the other considerations. What if her calls were being monitored or taped? What if there were cameras hidden in the building? She knew her fear bordered on paranoia, but with all the hopped-up corporate security in the past few years, anything was possible.

No, she was better off limiting phone sex to the privacy of her own apartment, even if it did mean rushing home each day at lunchtime.

She slammed the door closed, kicked off her shoes and stomped into the bedroom. Her coat landed on the floor in a heap as she collapsed on the bed and took a deep breath. She was getting so used to this, it was scary. She felt the heat rising during morning staff meetings as unbidden thoughts of Reg swirled in her mind. Reg kissing her neck. Reg bearing his chest. Reg moving his fingers up her legs and pushing inside her . . .

Quickly she peeled off her Hermès scarf and suit, down to her skimpy bra and panties. She was sliding between the sheets, loving the feel of soft cotton on her skin, as the phone rang. She clicked it on without saying a word.

"Are you naked?" he asked.

"Almost," she whispered. "I've got my bra and panties on, but I want you to do the rest."

"I'm the man for the job. Under my management, profits have been rising significantly. I anticipate them hitting an all-time peak soon."

She slid her hand under her panties, loving the wetness there. "I'm ready for the merger. All divisions have been briefed and primed. I wish I was there to help you stroke the corporate engine."

"You are stroking it," he whispered. "It's your hand, love. Your hot cunt. You are in this with me, Chandra, and we're going all the way. Are you ready to take me on?"

"Yes, I'm ready." Her fingers rubbed gently, a slow, steady force. She tossed her head back against the pillows as the feelings surged within her. "Let the merger begin."

Stomping past a candle-themed shop window that said: PEACE ON EARTH, GOOD WILL TO MEN, Maggie was feeling nothing but bad will for Max Donner, who trailed her, with Boone straggling behind.

"I resent the way you keep getting me in trouble with Candy every time I want to leave the damned building. Slipping out of there is like trying to lead a kid past a toy store. Why do you have to attract so much attention?"

Max grinned, as if her annoyance fanned his amusement. "Film crews attract attention. Besides, it's not our fault you hate your job."

"I don't hate it. It's just that I require more . . . more freedom than the position allows. But I've never had a problem before. I was able to come and go without the whole world knowing about it. Until you bumbled along," she said as she dropped down the subway stairs.

"Where are we going?" he asked. "Aren't you taking a cab?"

"Item two: cab fare. I'm tapped out this week, thanks to my incredibly busy social life and the fact that your show never springs for cab fare."

"We're not a car service," Max said, fishing in his pocket for something to get through the turnstile. "Boone, let me use your Metrocard?"

"Only if you pay me back," Boone said, swiping his card a second time for Max.

"Don't I always?"

"No. You usually forget."

"Tell Lucy to give it to you from petty cash," Max muttered as he pushed through the turnstile.

"Well, I'm glad to know you're cheap with everyone, not just me," Maggie railed. "If you're not going to spring for cab fare, at least you could split. Share a cab. Really! Who knew the producer of a hit show could be such a cheapskate?"

"I'm not cheap." Max hurried to follow Maggie down the stairs to the downtown platform. "But it's not the intent of the show to change your lifestyle. If you usually take the subway, then so will we."

"Ugh!" Maggie rolled her eyes. "Don't you get it? The cost of three subway fares is probably more than the entire cab fare!"

"Whatever." Max looked down the tracks toward the dark tunnel of the N train. "Where are we going, anyway?"

"I'm meeting Steve for . . ." Maggie hesitated, not wanting to reveal to America that Steve had asked her to meet him downtown for another rendition of Jingle Balls. "For lunch," she finished.

"Ah . . ." Max rubbed his hands together. "This being the Steve you're fooling around with behind the mayor's back?"

"Well . . ." Maggie hesitated, wondering how to spin it into a positive situation.

"The truth," Max warned. "You know we'll crucify you if you lie to the camera."

"Steve and I do have a thing going. But it's not that I'm cheating on the mayor, especially since I've never taken my relationship with the mayor to that level." She paused, adding for good measure, "I've decided that the mayor and I will remain good friends."

"Oh, really? Will you be seeing your 'good friend' anytime in the future? Aren't you scheduled to accompany him to that big A-list party at the Plaza tonight?"

He was gloating. She hated it when he gloated.

"Attending public events with the mayor, but sleeping with Steve on the sly," he said. "Is that how it goes?"

She grabbed the front of his leather jacket and pulled. "Listen, you big beef jerky. I am tiptoeing around to stay on high moral ground, and I'll be damned if I'm going to let you slice me into a slut in the editing room."

"Don't give me any ideas." He plucked open her fingers and straightened his jacket. "I could always go back and change what I've done." He started to walk away.

"Which is . . . ?" Maggie chased him. "How did the editing go? I mean, you've been doing this a long time. What do *you* think audiences want to see? Sincerity? Or distant, complicated women? Wild, free lust, or prudence?"

"Are you nuts!" Max winced. "I can't talk about this."

"But I was just wondering . . ."

The noise of the approaching train ended their conversation. Inside the car, Maggie added, "It's just that, I'm not always the way I appear to be, and . . ."

"Enough!" He waved his arms as if he were flagging in an aircraft. "I am not going to talk about this?"

The other passengers in the car watched, riveted by the man and woman being filmed by the minicam. "Okay." Maggie shrugged. "You can't blame a girl for asking."

She fell silent until they reached the City Hall stop. As Maggie headed out of the subway station with the guys in tow, she realized how lukewarm she felt about meeting Steve. Not that the sex in the bathroom was bad. It had been as satisfying as ever. But now it seemed like something was missing from their relationship.

Fun Steve wasn't the one. He was simply one of many.

She hiked up the stairs and bounded into the sunlight and searched the square to get her bearings. There was City Hall. She crossed the street near a Santa who was playing a Christmas carol on a clarinet.

The music stopped. "Maggie?" he called.

"Santa?" She spun around and searched his face. Wide brown eyes, thoughtful lines on the forehead. A nice face, vaguely familiar. "Do you know me, Santa?" she asked. "I mean, aside from the fact that you brought me that twelve-speed the year that I begged and pleaded for it."

The Santa pulled his beard aside. "It's me! Les."

"No way!" Maggie had dated Les for a time before she'd fallen in with Deuce. Les, the low-key jazz musician. The things he could do with his lips. Yes, that boy could blow. "What are you doing here? Are you still performing."

"Yeah, performing in the Village and teaching at the New School. Thought I'd do the charitable thing for the holidays." He thanked someone for a donation, smiling broadly. "Hey, I saw you on a billboard at Time's Square. You're gonna be on TV!"

"Yup." She grinned, feeling happy to see him again. "And look at you . . . so cute in your Santa suit." Suddenly, she had zero desire to hook up with Steve.

"Hey, I get off here in about ten minutes. Why don't you stick around and come back to my place with me? Got some new tunes to play for you."

"Sounds great," Maggie said, feeling the lure of ex-sex. She remembered how easily Les could go from making love to his clarinet to making love to her. Of the many times they'd tumbled over the mattress on his floor, making love under the batik-printed clothes draped overhead . . .

Max cleared his throat, as if to remind Maggie that her conscience was present. "Let me just make a phone call," she told Les as she pulled out her cell to call Steve. She spun around to Max. "I thought the show wasn't supposed to interfere."

"Just wanted to remind you that we're here, documenting your infidelities for posterity."

"I have no one to cheat on! I'm not married or engaged or . . ." Someone answered. "Oh, hi. Steve Dombrowski, please," she said, making a face at Max. The man was infuriating, a total pain in the butt. "You know," she told him as she waited for Steve to come on the line, "I think you take your job too seriously. Way too seriously."

30

Why do I let myself get caught in these situations? Apple wondered as she strolled through the gallery for the third time, her throat dry, her palms sweating. Her black duster billowed over her jeans as she swung around, conscious of Lucy and Suki hanging in the background. The afternoon had grown dull; Suki had stopped filming half an hour ago. Somehow Apple felt responsible for their boredom. It was time to go.

"Teague?" she called. He prattled on, holding his hand up for her to wait.

Why are we still here? she wondered. There were only twelve pieces in the entire show, and yet Teague had lingered here for an hour, musing over them, talking with the gallery owner, acting as if there were something more here than one man's handicraft of Elmer's Glue and ribbons. For that's what the pieces were—three-dimensional displays of shaped ribbons. Very colorful.

"Arte Povera" the exhibit called itself. Apple recognized the phrase coined by an Italian art critic back in the sixties. It meant "poor art" and was meant to represent three-dimensional art created from everyday materials, though over the years it was only used to refer to Italian art. The creator of this "Arte Povera" was from Soho.

Strange, Apple thought. No one was *from* Soho. And why did he dig back for the Italian term? Not that Apple meant to be critical, but sometimes it was hard to look at other art when no one recognized your own. Her portfolio had been to half a dozen galleries, but so far no one had expressed an interest in taking her on. It was one of the reasons she preferred museums to galleries; at least she could understand why the paintings of the Impressionists and the Masters were considered precious.

Apple walked to another piece, clenching her fists. She hated the way Teague deserted her when they were in public. He didn't even introduce her to the gallery owner, and he'd deliberately excluded her from the conversation. What a bastard.

Apple was about to interrupt Teague to tell him she was leaving when a handful of people came in. The quasi-art crowd. Apple knew them well enough to know that she was not accepted in their circle with their designer eyeglasses, rumpled clothes, cynical attitudes and bank accounts replenished by trust funds.

Suki swung her camera up. As if on cue, the newcomers began to perform.

"Oh, look at this," one of the guys said, walking over to the first piece. He turned to Apple. "Do you know the artist?"

"No."

"Good, then I can trash it." He laughed. "I'm sure I've achieved more texture and balance with the spaghetti on my plate."

Apple sighed. She had to get out of here.

"Hey, I know your face," one woman said. "Are you an actress?"

"No."

"But I know you. Wait, you're Apple. On that TV show. 'Find out what's at Apple's core!' I saw the billboard downtown."

"Oh, great." The ads for the show were out. Apple could just imagine the variety of ways the copywriters had played with her name.

"You're an actress?" someone asked again.

"I'm a photographer."

"Really? Who represents you?"

"I . . ." She didn't want to admit the truth. "Right now I'm talking to a few galleries."

He nodded. "Wow, I'd love to see your work. Right now my gallery is doing a show on ethnic photography. They've got a few by Atget and Doisneau. A couple by Manuel Alvarez Bravo."

Apple nodded silently. His gallery. That meant he had a dealer. He was legitimate; she was not.

"Misha's dealer is Nancy Greer. Lizbeth is with the Whittley, and Hoshi's dealer offered her a one-person show," he added, nodding at the slender Asian woman in his group. "She's probably going to do it in the spring, at Harold Freeman. You have to come!"

"I'd like that," she lied, feeling like an outsider. These artists had the vibe of trust fund kids; wealthy offspring who pretended to rough it downtown while they dabbled in art.

But they have dealers! her mind shrieked. *They're represented by galleries!* She was definitely doing something wrong.

"We'll send you an invitation?" he asked. "Do you have a card or something." She fished out a business card and he thanked her. "Hey, what's this? Professional portraits?"

"I pay my bills by doing portraits and weddings."

"*Really?*" The woman, Hoshi, squinted at her. "So you're a commercial photographer."

"No," she said, wondering why she bothered to argue. "I'm an art photographer. The other stuff just pays my bills."

"Ehh . . . you can say that, but it's just lip service," Hoshi argued. "An artist creates art. A photographer takes pictures. There's a difference."

"Are you saying photography is not art?" Apple asked her.

Hoshi's eyes rolled to the side as she considered. "No. I'm merely saying that commercial photography is . . . well, commercial. Commerce. And if you don't pursue your artistic calling, then . . . well, how are you an artist?"

Apple turned away from her and focused on one of the pieces—twisted clumps of gold and green ribbon rising to the top. A matted jungle dance. The shapes swirled before her along with the words. *How are you an artist?*

"How are you an artist?" her father insisted. "You take a few fuzzy pictures of your grandmother, now you're telling me you want to drop out of Bennington to . . . what? Take more fuzzy pictures? It's a lousy student exhibit!"

The exhibit had been called "Dignity," which Apple felt captured her grandmother's light within the body that could no longer serve her. Clementine Sommers had suffered from Pick's disease, a neurological disorder similar to Alzheimer's, that had robbed her of the ability to communicate or follow through on tasks as simple as preparing a bowl of oatmeal. During Apple's visits, Granny had been so grateful for a warm meal, happy to have someone to take her for a walk, content to sit for her portraits, but she'd had no clue that Apple was her granddaughter. "That nice one with the red . . . you know," Granny used to say as she patted her head. That nice one with the red hair.

Some days Granny was barely responsive. But in the finished photos, Apple discovered subtle characteristics that were not apparent in person. The lifted corner of her lips. The papery texture of her skin. The pinpoints of light in her eyes. Apple had stared at the finished pictures, awed by what they revealed. It was as if the small ticks in the photos offered glimmers of Granny's spirit.

Her advisor had agreed, as had two or three critics who'd seen the show.

But her father had never seen it. He had been blind to the beauty of those photographs. Blind to his daughter's talents and his mother's ever-present though diminished spark.

He was still blind.

"What do you do?" another woman in the group asked, switching back and forth on her very high platform boots. The question jarred Apple from her thoughts. "Like, weddings and bar mitzvahs and things? Have you done any famous people?"

Apple shook her head. "I had my own exhibit when I was nineteen."

"Really? Where?"

"At . . . at . . ." At my school. A college exhibit. Yes, I peaked when I was nineteen. It's been downhill ever since.

"Commerce," Hoshi repeated. "It's an age-old conflict. Commerce versus Art."

"She's right," came a heavy voice. Teague approached the group, the heels of his boots clacking on the tile floor. "You are currently engaged in commerce, my dear Apple. For all your grandiose thoughts of your own artistry, you have yet to prove your talents to the world."

Yeah, but I have to pay my bills! she wanted to shout to all of them.

She dared to face Teague, wondering at the steely resolve in those gray eyes. How could he? He didn't even have the metal to defend her against these art school twerps? These . . . these people who had found their niches in galleries, who were probably selling their work through art dealers while she toiled in her studio trying to cajole cranky babies and their crankier mothers to sit for a portrait. It was so unfair. They were probably even subsidized by Daddy's money while she had to make her own way . . .

Her throat tightened on the realization. The art flunkies she so resented were subsidized, but so was she . . . living with the Teagues and Coops of the world who were willing to pay the way to have her revolving around them.

Oh, shit. I'm arm candy. A parasite. She could barely breathe as she turned and headed for the door, the outside. Escape . . . but to where?

Maggie walked into the Frick Collection, flashed her membership card and followed the path she knew so well. The building had been constructed back in 1913 by millionaire Henry Clay Frick, who had told the architect he wanted "a small house with plenty of light and space and land." The result was a magnificent stone mansion that now housed Mr. Frick's extensive collection of paintings, sculptures and furnishings.

They always met under the Renoir painting of the mother and children, ever since Apple had started dragging them to this old mansion in times of trouble.

And there was Apple standing under the painting rendered in soft blues and greens and lavenders. Looking like a work of art herself, Apple wore low-slung jeans, a black duster, and a gold tunic top beaded and embroidered in silver, navy, pearl and gold. Like something from a royal tapestry, the shirt followed the long line of her body up to her graceful neck, her sad, pale face.

"I love when we do this. It feels like a covert operation," Maggie said as she approached her friend. "Meet me at the Frick. The crow flies at dawn. The red sun also rises. Or is that a Hemingway novel?"

Apple didn't even seem to hear her, but distractedly glanced over Maggie's shoulder. "Where's your crew?"

"Max and Boone split when they found out I was meeting you. They figured that your crew could cover us, but they're going to be on my tail later. I've got a party with the mayor tonight."

"Must be nice to have a few minutes alone." Apple turned to stare up at the painting. "I'm beginning to feel like a caged animal."

"Is that what's bothering you?" Maggie asked, reaching up to untangle a lock of Apple's hair from the beading on her shoulder.

"That and . . . like, everything else."

"Did you have a fight with Teague?"

"Not even," Apple said. She recounted the afternoon—Teague's argument with the waitress at lunch, then the scene at the gallery. "It's not so much that he didn't defend me," Apple said as they walked out to the garden court, "but he joined in the criticism."

Maggie was nodding, hating every word she heard about Teague. "Definitely! The guy's a big weenie!"

Apple sat down on a stone bench and rested her chin on her fists. Her hair swung down, a curtain of wavy orange. "He's making me crazy. I mean, if he doesn't approve of what I do, if he doesn't see my potential in the art world, why is he with me?"

"Oh, Apple." Maggie bit her lip, not sure where to begin. "There are a million reasons a man might want to be with you.

You're gorgeous and smart and you see things that everyone else misses, but I'm not sure Teague is onto any of those qualities. He's an older man, right? It may just be the arm-candy factor. He could be the type who enjoys walking down the street with a young hottie at his side. Or maybe he thinks he's going to mentor you and shape you into an artist, so that he can take all the credit for your artistic success. Whatever it is, this isn't working for you. Look at yourself. He's making you so unhappy."

Apple groaned. "I don't feel unhappy. Just displaced. Like I'm in the wrong body, or the wrong life. Nothing really makes me happy or sad anymore." She lifted her head. "You know, when I came in the door here, I didn't feel anything. Not the ghost of Henry Clay Frick or relief at being here or the thrill of sitting in the big dining room. Nothing."

"Oh, no. No, no!" Maggie insisted. "You can't give up on the Frick! You love this place. We all do! This is our little mansion on Fifth, right? The dining room where the Fricks used to entertain two dozen guests twice a week. How many times have we walked through here pretending this was going to be the place we would inherit? You turned me onto that game, Apple. You can't give it up."

Apple dropped her head again. "I wish Chandra were here."

"I know." Maggie rubbed her friend's back, thinking of Chandra in London, pursuing her financier. "But Chandra would back me up on this. You've got to get away from Teague. This relationship is definitely not working for you." Maggie dug around in her purse—a square Dior bag. "Look, take my key. I'll get the extra key from the super."

"I can't go to your place."

"Why not?" Maggie pressed the key into Apple's palm and squeezed her fingers around it.

"All my stuff it at Teague's."

"How lame is that? We'll go get it tomorrow. For now, you need some space."

"But what about your space? What if the mayor brings you home and . . ."

"I don't think his majesty is getting any action tonight."

Maggie knew she was more likely to bring home Fun Steve or Les, The Piper, but she didn't want to get into it at the moment. "Hell, I'd break up with him if the man would give me more than two minutes. But my friend Roxanne is supposed to be at this bash, along with the whole chick clique. You'd like them. And . . ." She checked her watch and winced. "Ooh, I'd better go." She felt awful leaving Apple behind. "You want to come back to the apartment with me now?"

Apple shook her head. "I'm fine here. Really."

Big, fat liar, Apple thought as she rode the bus down Fifth Avenue. Nothing was fine about her life. Nothing.

She had just gotten a call on her cell from her assistant, who had told her that she'd missed a photo session scheduled for that afternoon—an author portrait. "The man was pissed," Juanita said, "but I talked him into rescheduling." Apple banged a fist against her knee. She had to pull herself together; she couldn't afford to miss work.

The bus rolled past glittering lights. An entire building was wrapped in gold, with a fat red ribbon wrapped at its center. A man squeezed onto the bus carrying fat bags of toys from FAO Schwartz. "It's starting to snow," the man announced, and the passengers oohed and aahed. But Apple hugged herself and turned toward the window, wondering why the things that used to soothe her now pissed her off.

Lucy tapped her shoulder from the seat behind her. "Is this your stop?"

Apple had told Lucy and Suki that she was going to get off here and take the crosstown bus to Maggie's. But now she didn't feel the momentum to make it there.

"No. No, I'm going back to Soho."

Snow was falling, a furious barrage of white, as Apple trudged down the street, the camera crew following her.

Teague was in the loft, smoking a pipe. He pulled off his reading glasses and threw out his arms. "My dear Apple . . ." He hugged her against his fuzzy sweater, which smelled of tobacco and spice. "Your hair is wet."

"It's snowing."

"Sit," he said. And she did. He toweled her hair off as the camera rolled. Apple felt as if there was something very important to say, but she couldn't seem to get to it. She was an actor in a scene without a script. Lost.

"I've got the kettle on," Teague told her. "You're to have a hot cup of tea, then off to bed."

Lucy cleared her throat. "We'll be going, then."

Apple nodded at the women as they left the loft.

"There you go." Teague handed her a mug of tea.

So lost. Apple pressed her palms against the mug, eager for its warmth. Her life was totally fucked up. She knew that. But how could she begin to fix it?

So lost.

31

London. Chandra kept her face to the window as the car passed a double-decker bus, then rows of tidy attached buildings. And there was Harrod's, the famous department store. She had always dreamed of traveling here, and now that it was a reality she savored every sight, sound and smell. Even the air seemed different here. Thicker, richer, laced with the damp fog she'd read about. The car was on its way to Reg's headquarters, where other executives from Grayrock were gathering for a meeting about the acquisition of Gem, Inc.

Chandra had flown in a day before the meeting to see some of the sights, and Reg had insisted on taking her around in his limousine to the Tower of London, St. Paul's, Picadilly Circus. "I love playing tourist!" he insisted. Reg befriended two gray-haired ladies at Windsor Castle, whom they gave a ride back to their hotel.

"If we had more time, we could take the Chunnel to Paris," he said.

Paris. The word itself had the power to melt Chandra's heart, not that Reg wasn't already doing a good job.

After touring, their evening had begun with a quiet dinner at the Ritz, dancing, and then to Reg's Kensington Gardens town home for sherry, where her date had ceremoniously removed her shoes and massaged her feet. After that Reg discreetly dismissed the TV crew. Thank God! Chandra felt like she'd been waiting way too long for the night of lovemaking that ensued.

"Tell me about it!" Maggie had probed during their brief phone call. "Tell me everything."

But Chandra wasn't one to kiss and tell. "It was wonderful. That's all I can tell you."

"I'll get the details, even if I have to ply you with Cosmos," Maggie had insisted.

Chandra had laughed. "It's a date."

Now as the car pulled up to Pringle Headquarters, Chandra marveled at the turn her life had taken. Was she really leading Grayrock into an acquisition that could change the face of the company? And dating one of the most influential financiers in the European market?

This is my life, she thought, smiling at the driver who opened the door. She stepped out and looked up at the gleaming glass building. *Life is good.*

Inside, Chandra was ushered to a suite of offices that would be used by Grayrock for the meeting. CEO Alfred Lipton was having coffee with Chandra's boss, who waved Chandra in to join them. "Come!" Willard called. "Have a cup! Or a spot of tea, I should say. We're all feeling festive today."

"Glad to hear it," Chandra said. "So your flight went well?"

"Better than that," Willard said. He looked around to be sure no one was listening from the hall. "Most of the reports came in yesterday. Vincent was going to e-mail you, but I figured we'd bring them along and surprise you. Anyhoo, Doris's group checked out Gem's contractual obligations and expiration of existing deals, and it's looking good. Quite good." He handed her a folder. "I think we might have a deal here."

"Excellent news!" Chandra glanced into the folder, then stood up and tucked it under her arm. "Let me go take a look at this before the meeting. But thanks for making my day."

She went to the office next door where her associate Vincent

Singh sat at a desk typing on a laptop as if he were back in his own office. "Good morning, Vincent."

He darted a look up from his laptop. "Good morning. You received the reports from Doris's group?"

"Got 'em right here," Chandra said, tapping her coffee cup against the folder. "I was just—"

"Good morning, love." Reg came up behind her and planted a moist kiss on her neck.

Chandra smiled. It tickled. It felt great. But she had to maintain a degree of professionalism. "You shouldn't do that. Not here."

"I know," he said, "I might make you spill your coffee."

Chandra laughed. She couldn't help it. The same behavior she usually found so offensive was charming in Reg. Vincent didn't laugh; in fact, he didn't even seem to notice. But it made Chandra wonder if her perspective was totally skewed because she was falling in . . . no, no, she had a meeting to run!

As the meeting began to wind down, Chandra deferred to Alfred Lipton. "Something to add?" she asked.

"Just that it's been a very positive meeting for Grayrock and Gem, Inc. We need to take this information back to the States and present it to our board. No one can guarantee how our members will vote, but I think it's safe to wager that we may be partners in a few months' time." Alfred pushed his glasses up on his nose and extended his hand across the table toward Reg.

"Yes, that would be lovely, wouldn't it?" Reg said, his brown eyes shining. He clapped Alfred on the back, then went around the table, shaking hands. When he reached Chandra, he delicately lifted her hand to his lips and kissed it.

I'm blushing, she thought, noticing the smiles of her coworkers.

"I've invited Alfred to see my indoor putting green," Reg told her. "We shall return forthwith."

"No problem," Chandra said. "I want to check in with the office." As the board room grew quiet, Nayasia sidled over to Chandra.

She wasn't her usual brash, smug self. Her oversized glasses were stuck on her head, her sleeves rolled up. "I'm not supposed to talk like this," Nayasia said, "but I cannot get over what I've seen going on here. You have landed yourself some kind of catch here, girl. You know what you got?"

Chandra pursed her lips. "He's a great guy."

"And he's crazy about you!" Nayasia ran her finger over the smooth conference table. "I don't know how you stayed focused on your meeting with him in the same room."

"It wasn't easy."

"What were you thinking about? Last night at his place?"

Chandra shook her head as the fantasy returned. "Actually, I was thinking about the two of us making love right here . . . on this table."

Nayasia froze, then jabbed at the table. "That's what you were thinking? Girl, you surprise me. And I took you for a straight-arrow type."

I have my moments, Chandra thought.

Nayasia turned to Mule. "You got that? You got the fantasy?"

"Got it," Mule said from behind the minicam. "Sorry, Chandra."

"Wait a second . . ." Chandra felt her throat go tight as she scowled at Nayasia. "You did that just for the camera? Just to get me to talk about . . . you tricked me?"

"I work for *Big Tease,*" Nayasia said, pushing away from the table. "And we needed a little fantasy to spice up your segment, honey."

Feeling betrayed, Chandra glanced up and noticed Vincent standing in the doorway with a folder. "Sorry to interrupt," he said. "I mean, if you want to continue discussing your fantasy, I will return at another time."

As if I were interviewing with CNN, Chandra thought, marveling at Vincent's steadfast demeanor. But somehow, the fact that he was unfazed by Chandra's revelation made her feel a little better. "No, Vincent, it's okay. I've talked enough. What's up?"

"I checked in with Brianna and there are a few things we should go over. The numbers are in from Tokyo, and there seems to be a conflict with a project manager in the San Francisco office."

"Great! You saved me some work, as usual." She extracted balance sheets from the folder. "What would I do without you, Vincent?"

"Most probably you would have had to call Brianna yourself."

She shook her head, smiling. "We've been working together how long? Nearly a year, and I still haven't gotten used to your dry sense of humor."

He cocked an eyebrow. "Who is being humorous?"

"The martinis are wonderful here, Chandra," Reg said as she slid into a booth covered with faux zebra skin. "Shall I order for us?"

"Sounds great," Chandra said, easing against the banquette and relaxing to the soothing jazz music. CeeCee's was one of London's hottest clubs, and of course Reg was one of the privileged who could skirt around the line and walk right in the door.

I'm dating a millionaire, she thought. *In fact, I may be falling in love with a millionaire.* Pretty swell for the little girl who grew up in Gramma's house in Queens. She wished her friends were here to share the fun. When would they ever get to meet Reg? She was headed back to New York in the morning, but Reg had to stay here, at least until next week. Gem, Inc. wasn't the only company owned by Pringle, Ltd., and he had mentioned a few other pressing matters he'd had to put off to entertain Chandra.

Glancing up, she noticed Mule and Nayasia seated discreetly at the table across from her. This camera thing was getting tiresome: the ever-present eye of the lens, probing, insatiable. But she refused to let it ruin her night with Reg. She ran her hands over the smooth gold linen and admired the fresh flowers on the table and looked toward Reg, who was talking jovially with the bartender. She didn't want to leave. The thought of going home made her throat go tight. How wonderful it would be to stay here, in the glow of Reg's love, in this charming city. She couldn't remember the last time she'd felt so ecstatically happy. Had she ever been this happy?

She bit her lower lip as the image of Jeff came to mind. Yes, she had been happy with Jeff. He had made her laugh; he had shared her passion for work and antiques and jazz music. They had been a team, totally in synch, easily moving from work to the gym to their favorite restaurant without a snag in the day. She'd never realized how perfect their life together was until it ended.

And now there's someone else, she told herself as Reg made his way to the table bearing two sexy martini glasses. *But Jeff would understand. He would have wanted me to fall in love again. I always knew that, but I wasn't willing to move on from his memory.*

"Here we are," Reg said, placing the glasses gracefully before her. "This one is yours. And I daresay you've earned it, Chandra, bringing Grayrock and Gem together. Have you any idea of the magnitude of this deal? I don't think you do, just as you seem hardly aware of your incredible beauty."

She touched the slender stem of the martini glass. "You say the sweetest things. But I was just doing my job. Mergers and Acquisitions."

"Mmm. And where do I fit into the grand scheme of M and A?" he said, sliding his hand over her thigh.

She took a sip, and the martini hit her throat with its cold sting. "Let's see. We've already merged," she teased him. "More than once, and quite satisfactorily, I'd say."

He was nodding, his brown eyes glimmering. "I'd have to concur with those findings, and suggest that we explore other mergers in the near future."

She leaned into the warmth of his body, loving the feel of him beside her. "I'll check my calendar, but I think I can take a meeting in about . . ." She let the words trail off as the flicker of something in her martini glass caught her eye. Twirling the glass, she saw the olive bob amid a twinkle of silver. "What . . . ?" She leaned in for a better look. "There's something in my martini," she said. "A ring."

He cocked an eyebrow. "An engagement ring."

Her heart began to race. This couldn't be true. It couldn't mean . . ."There's an engagement ring wrapped around my olive?"

"Yes, yes, I do hope you don't mind the surprise. Personally, I hate to have things sprung on me, but I purchased the ring for you and when the bartender was making up the drinks, I simply couldn't resist."

She tipped the glass for a closer look at the marquis-shaped diamond. "What exactly does this mean?"

"Oh, dear Chandra. I love that you're so literal."

"No." She reached in and retrieved the olive. "It's just that I want to hear you say it." She sucked the liquor from the olive, then popped it out of the ring and bit into it seductively. "Here," she said, pushing the other half past his lips.

"Mmm. Then it's official. If we've shared an olive, we'll have to marry."

She held the fat diamond ring away from her, watching as it winked in the dim light. "What was that? I can't hear you."

With a laugh, he took her hand in his and slid the ring onto her finger. Then, leaning so close his lips were nearly touching hers, he whispered, "Chandra, will you marry me?"

She took a deep breath. She loved being with Reg. And Grayrock would certainly approve of making the merger a marriage. Not to mention that this swelling romance would certainly give her the edge for *Big Tease.* (Not that she was counting, but she did love to win.)

"Yes," she said, throwing her arms around his shoulders. Yes, yes, yes!

32

After a busy morning in the studio, Apple decided to take advantage of a break in the afternoon schedule and go looking for photographs to add to her portfolio. Which was probably the wrong approach since, in her experience, art just sort of happened, but she was frantic to prove herself. That woman in the gallery had uncovered a grain of truth: if she didn't pursue her art every day, how could she claim to be an artist?

"Are we almost done out here?" Lucy Ng stepped out of a doorway and wrapped her scarf over her mouth. "I'm freezing."

"I have another hour to kill," Apple said. Kill being the operative word. So far she'd spent most of her time fending off new fans who'd seen her on billboards or TV promos. She resented having the camera crew follow her. They killed any inspiration that wasn't already frozen by the bitter wind whipping down Seventh Avenue.

But I'm not going to give up, she thought as she squatted down to change the lense. A cell phone bleeped, and Apple, Suki and Lucy immediately reached for their pockets. "It's me," Apple said, flipping her phone open and pressing the cold piece to her ear. Like she needed one more distraction. "Yes?"

"Hey, Booboo," Maggie gushed. "Did you hear?"

"She left a message on my voice mail. Isn't it wonderful?"

"Wonderful?" Maggie's voice squeaked over the phone. "She's known J. Reginald Pringle for about ten minutes. Unless you count reading about his exploits in business school."

"But she's so happy," Apple insisted. "After all she's been through, losing Jeff, and all the stuff before that with . . ." She was about to mention Chandra's mother, but realized that Suki was shooting her. "She's been through a lot, and now she's found someone who makes her happy. Sounds to me like she's in love."

"I don't trust him," Maggie said. "Gorgeous millionaires do not fall out of the sky like that."

"He wasn't dropped by parachute; they met because of a business deal." Apple paced in front of a novelty shop called Crystals 'n' Condoms. Apparently a venue of New Age safe sex. She paused in front of a photo of a bare-chested man holding a crystal to the sky. Maybe that's why she wasn't achieving orgasm. Was everyone else onto New Age sex and here she was stuck in the conventions of the former generation?

"Besides, I'm mad at you," Maggie said. "You never showed last night. Don't tell me you went back to that Screwy Louie."

Silence.

"Don't let me near him, okay? If I ever meet that bastard, I'm gonna let him have it, right in the short and curlies. Wait! Are you bringing him to my tree-trimming party next week. Don't tell me . . ."

"Okay, I won't tell you."

"Apple, are you okay?"

"Fine. I'm just freezing my tah-tahs off, getting some shots in the Village. But I need to run. Gotta get back to the studio by three."

"Okay, but remember, you have my key. If you want to come, come."

"Come, come. If only it were that easy," she said. Apple glanced back in the shop window at the display of rainbow-colored condoms. Red. Orange. Purple. Somehow the image of a purple penis had little appeal for her.

"What?" Maggie asked, then gasped. "Oh, right. And how is the orgasm thing coming along? Did you read those articles?"

"I'm sorry, but you've exceeded your allotment of personal questions," Apple said. "Please call back another time."

"All right, back to work. God knows, I've got plenty of it. I'm so far behind deadline I have to duck into the ladies' room whenever Candy sweeps by."

"Later." Apple put her cell phone away and scoped out the scene around her. A swarm of cars and yellow cabs. People walking, bundled against the cold. And the beautiful patchwork-quilt architecture of New York.

"Can we finish here?" Lucy asked, cowering in her fake fur. "My toes are falling off."

"How about that building over there?" Suki suggested. "See the way the sunlight edges the windows? The way it forms a grid?"

Apple snapped off a few shots, but she wasn't thrilled with them. "The rhythm is nice, but it's very Hamann."

"Ha—who?" Lucy asked.

"Horst Hamann," Suki said. "He does buildings. Skylines. The lines of skyscrapers, the grids of windows."

"The problem is," Apple went on, breathing hot air onto her fingers as she searched Sheridan Square, "every building in New York is derivative of Horst Hamann. He's shot them all."

Lucy was now shifting from one foot to the other. "Okay, you two talk shop. I'm ducking into Café Figaro for a latte."

As Lucy hurried into the café, Apple noticed the newsstand at the center of the Square. It was a hovel of junk: decals and newspapers, magazines and candies. Apple took a picture, then went to the curb to cross the street and get closer.

"Do you know the work of Eugene Atget?" she asked Suki.

"French," Suki said, pursing her lips. "The man who photographed old Paris?"

"Right. He captured the flavor of the city in realistic street scenes. Shots of vendors and streetlamps. This newsstand reminds me of his work."

Suki nodded. Apple knew she'd attended a few courses at the New School.

"But of course, that's derivative, too." Apple shook her head, frustrated. She needed to innovate. She'd been on to something with those portraits of Granny, but somehow she'd gone off-track.

Wind roared through the square, whipping up papers and debris and blowing them uptown. A newspaper swirled in front of a restaurant on Christopher, menacing a small group of people who were emerging. Two couples, arm-in-arm. Apple lifted her camera, then lowered it again as she noticed the familiar gait of one of the men.

Teague?

Her stomach twisted as she watched. Yes, it was him, definitely with another woman. Feelings swelled inside her, feelings of hurt and betrayal. She wanted to run over and pummel him, but no . . . not in front of Suki, not on camera.

She forced herself to turn away, but too late. Suki had noticed her reaction.

"Isn't that your boyfriend?" Suki asked.

Apple turned back to see him and a new wave of anger rose. She had to confront him. She flew across the square, holding her camera to keep it from banging against her stomach. "Teague!" she called, but he didn't turn around. She had to move close and touch his shoulder. "Teague!"

His head whipped around, his eyes alight with fury. The woman beside him eyed Apple curiously, almost amused.

"What are you doing here?" Teague demanded of Apple, as if she were the one out of line. He shook her hand off with disgust. "Go back to the apartment."

"Wait a minute," Apple said. "What's going on here? What the hell are—"

"I said go home!" he roared, stopping her with a scowl. Bossy and disapproving, just like a father. Just like her father.

Apple felt the energy drain from her as the two couples turned their backs and walked east. Without explanation. Without another word. She was supposed to go home like a good little girl while her lover went off with his grown-up friends.

How she hated him.

Sitting in the office of *Metro*'s editor in chief, Maggie felt like she'd run into a wall. Lately she could do no right by Candy, save for the fact that she'd landed this plum gig on a TV show, which provided a big, fat booty of free advertising for *Metropolitan*. Still, Candy had always been short-sighted, and at the moment all she seemed to see was the fact that Maggie was late on a few deadlines.

"We simply cannot operate this way," Candy said. "Late stories mean overtime fees for everyone, from the copy editor right down the line to the printer."

"I know, I know. I'm sorry," Maggie said. "But those two pieces are coming together. I just need two more expert interviews and I'm done."

"No, Maggie, not this time."

"What do you mean?" Maggie dug her fingernails into her palms. Was she getting the axe?

"I mean that I've reassigned those stories to Tara," Candy said, folding her manicured hands demurely for the camera.

"Tara?" Maggie couldn't believe it. "She's never written or edited anything!"

"She's green, but she's eager, and I believe she's already gotten in touch with her experts. In fact, I have her finished copy for 'Grisly Guys We Hate to Love' right here." She opened a folder and slid a printout across her shiny desk, but Maggie didn't bite. She couldn't stand to look at it. That was her story, her creation, her pitch. Okay, maybe it wasn't the most original idea in magazine publishing, but it was based on previously published stories that had scored well in reader polls. She knew that. She had known that back when Tara was back home sleeping in Underoos and getting her boogies wiped by Mommy.

"All righty, then." Maggie stood up, wondering where to go from here, wishing there wasn't a minicam documenting this most humiliating moment of her career at *Metro.* Candy was such a bitch! She'd invited Boone in, knowing he'd be privy to Maggie's humiliation. Somewhere, under that primped and tucked mask of a face, Candy was gloating, enjoying this.

"Let this be a lesson to you," Candy said firmly. "If you don't get back into the swing of things and produce for *Metro,* you can't be a part of the magazine. Everyone here does his or her part."

"Right," Maggie said, feeling numb.

Candy smiled at the camera. "No hard feelings."

Maggie dragged Jonathon into her office, where Max was using the phone. As he hung up and squeezed into the corner with Boone, Maggie closed the door and grabbed her Buddha statue. "I wish, I wish, I wish she would have this incredible epiphany, during which she finally sees my vast talents."

"What did Candy do now?" Jonathon asked, squinting at her over his glasses. "Don't tell me she made good on her threats and fired you?"

"Ooh, she makes me so mad! She took away my stories and gave them to Tara!" Quickly, Maggie recapped the details of her talk with Candy. "I can't believe it," she said, picking up a folder. "These are my notes on 'Boys We'd Love to Boff.' The damned story is almost finished. Finito."

"Mmm." Jonathon brushed a speck of lint from his soft gray flannel trousers. "Somehow I think your stories aren't the core of the issue here."

"Oh?" Maggie put the Buddha down and picked up a leather catcher's mitt, which she used for softball in Central Park each summer. "Sounds to me like you've heard something."

He shrugged. "Candy's not shy. Everyone on this floor knows how she feels about you right now."

Maggie slammed a fist into the glove. "What gives, spy guy?"

"It's the fact that you've been missing deadlines. Late every morning. Disappearing during the day."

"But I've got a show to do!" Maggie insisted. "I've got to come up with the winning date!"

"Without compromising your job," Jonathon suggested. "I believe that's the intent of the show. But the truth is, you're hardly in the office. It's apparent that you no longer love this job. You're always tied up with the show and society bookings and finding the right handbag to bag the boy."

"Ugh! Jonathon, you're right! You're right, you're right, but I can't help it. My heart is definitely not with *Metro* anymore, but I can't quit. I need this job. See, that's all the more reason I need to do well on the show. I need to win that million dollars. I have to win the million. I need the cash—and the emotional boost."

"Is it the money or the mere fact of winning that has you in such a tizzy?" Jonathon asked.

"Both!" Maggie insisted, pounding her glove. She pulled on the rawhide string, then pressed her face into the mitt, loving the smell and feel of the worn leather. She inhaled deeply. "Oh, to hide forever in rawhide . . ."

"Come on out, cupcake," Jonathon called. "You can't hide from Candy's wrath."

"I'm meditating. I need to rethink my dating strategy." She dropped the mitt and faced Jon. "I think it's time to dump the mayor."

"No! He's such a great catch!"

"But there's no chemistry. No real connection. We just attend the same functions together, usually on different sides of the ballroom—sometimes in different rooms. Afterward he takes me home and tries to score, but so far he's barely made it to first base."

"Really?" Jonathon seemed intrigued. "He still hasn't gotten out of the vestibule? How unlike you."

"I know." Maggie took the glove off and tossed it onto the counter. "What can I say? The guy turns me into a tease. Unlike Fun Steve, who pushes the right buttons in bed and at the bar. He's a pip, but I don't think Steve can go the distance. I mean, once you scratch beneath the surface, there's nothing."

"Now, bring me up to speed, here. Does the mayor know you're sleeping with Steve?"

"No, which was part of the allure in the beginning. Secret sex."

"Which is more or less exciting than Santa sex?" Jonathon prodded.

"That I wouldn't know," Maggie said, "since Les and I just listened to some music and kissed a little." When Jonathon gave her a doubtful look, she held up her hand. "Scout's honor." It had been a surprise to Maggie, too, but somehow her sexual sensibilities had changed, beginning with that ridiculous promise to Apple. When she finally went to bed with Steve, the sex had seemed hollow, like a frothy entertainment. After the physical pleasure of orgasm had worn off, she found herself entangled with a rangy comedian who refused to leave the party—literally and figuratively.

"So Steve is the man you're targeting now? Or is it the mayor?" Jonathon touched his chin. "You need to re-explain your strategy. I'm so confused."

Maggie picked up the phone and started punching in the number for City Hall. "I have to break up with the mayor."

"So you can be free to see Steve?"

"No, I have to break it off with him, too."

"I may be math phobic, but it seems to me that two minus two is still zero. Zero being the number of men in your life at the current time."

"I know, I know, but I'm never going to meet the right guy if I'm hooked up with these other charlies." She asked for the mayor's office, but was put through to Guy Fernandez, who told her that a phone conversation was out of the question. "Would you like to speak with Steve?" he asked. "He was just talking about you."

"No, no, no," Maggie said quickly. "I'll catch up with both of them later." She hung up and sighed. "I guess it wouldn't be PC to break up with someone over voice mail?"

Jonathon shook his head.

"All righty, then. There's tonight. I'll see them both, knock them both off, then I'll be free to move ahead."

"Break it off with both of them . . ." Jonathon said thoughtfully. "And this is your strategy for getting a date?"

33

Apple had to give herself credit. After the scene with Teague she had returned to the studio and managed to hold herself together to do a portrait of a whiny baby and her whinier mother. And after that she'd even called a few clients back to set up sittings or book weekend weddings and bar mitzvahs.

She had held herself together . . . until now. Now as she climbed the musty stairs and fumbled with the key to Teague's loft, she felt sick. She didn't want to be here, but she felt compelled to come back, as if she somehow needed to follow Teague's order. Maybe she was just curious, but she had to come back, even if it was just for a few minutes to gather her things. In the pocket of her coat was the key to Maggie's apartment. She would spend the night at Maggie's.

Inside, classical music was playing. The smells of tomato sauce mixed with the tang of acrylic paint. Over by the brick wall, Teague was painting in long strokes on a large canvas. Nude.

"It's about time you got in," he called, not bothering to turn around.

Good. She didn't like to look at him full-frontal naked. The sight of his flabby, hairy buttocks was quite enough.

Oh, why was she here?

"You did a very bad thing today," he said, turning slightly to give her a stern look. "Very bad."

She clenched her teeth. How ludicrous to be punished by this man. The last time she'd heard those words had to be when she was ten and she'd tossed a dirt clod that hit Craig Mullens in the head. She hadn't meant to hit him; she was trying to throw higher than Sharon and Maggie. It just happened that Apple's dirt clod landed where Craig was playing. The resulting stitches had earned Apple the wrath of her father for a week. "That was a terrible thing you did!" he rumbled. "Where were you raised, to be such a deprived animal?"

Up in her room, she had looked up the word *deprived* in the dictionary.

"Yes, I'm deprived," she told Teague. Which seemed to throw him off.

"Well, you will not disturb me again while I'm conducting business," he said.

"Who was she?" Apple asked, then wanted to take it back. What a dumb question. What was he going to say? She's my *other* girlfriend.

"She's an artist's rep, and I was mortified. You were quite the embarrassment."

Apple nodded. That's me: the embarrassment.

Just as her mother always said, "You don't even have a real job," Cherry bitched. "What are we supposed to tell people?"

"Little Apple hasn't grown up yet, dear," Dad said. "She's always had impractical notions for living. I tried to tell her that years ago, but does she listen?"

"Now, run along to the bathroom," Teague said. "Take your shower so we can make love. I'm horny like you won't believe."

Apple slid her hand into her coat pocket and felt the key to Maggie's. She should go. She knew it. And yet . . . damn it, she couldn't. She had to stay here. She had to do as he said.

"Go on, now," he said, spreading a fan of vermillion over the canvas.

Apple slid off her coat and let it fall to the floor. Then, plodding toward the bathroom, she thought of the white pills in her cosmetic bag. Two Xanax . . . that would help. That would get her through the night.

"So you understand why we can't see each other anymore?" Maggie asked Steve, who leaned against a wall, arms crossed, sexy little earpiece hanging from his hair. "I mean, I always have a great time with you, but with the camera crew following me, and your job with the mayor, and . . ."

"Take it easy," Steve insisted, patting Maggie's shoulder. "It's not like we were engaged or anything." He ran a hand over the spaghetti strap of her scarlet red Ralph Lauren gown and peered down at her cleavage.

She loved the way his fingers teased her shoulder. Hell, she wouldn't mind one more round in one of the posh rooms upstairs, but that was not the sort of thing you were supposed to do when breaking up with a guy—a definite mixed message.

"We were great together," Steve told her, "but you're right. I shouldn't have been dicking around behind the mayor's back. Hopefully, he'll take it like a man when he finds out. You know, if those producer guys end up showing us together."

"Oh, we will," Max called from behind Boone. "You can count on that."

"Yeah, thanks for that," Steve called, adding under his breath: "Douche bag."

Maggie was glad that Steve took the news so well, but she wasn't so successful with the mayor, who still hadn't shown up to the gala affair. Not that Maggie minded making new friends as she dined on veal medallions and exotic vegetables. She managed to squeeze into a table with Roxanne and Isadora and Camille and Eloise and Shelby, and she enjoyed dancing with their dates, an array of men whose only shared trait was that they wore tuxedos. There was Roxanne's husband, Lou, who served on the City Council. Isadora's husband was an archaeologist just returned from a dig in South America. Camille's longtime boyfriend was the heir to a jewelry store dynasty. Eloise's husband, Kermit, was a programming director at CBN ("Loved you in the promos!" he told Maggie), and Shelby was married to the CEO of a large pharmaceutical company. The men were interesting; the women fascinating. When the guys went off to smoke cigars, the girls began to dish, and Maggie listened attentively.

"How could she not know he's cheating on her?" Camille said of Mrs. Howard Middleton, whose husband Howie had brought a young, blonde "coworker" to the party.

"She knows," Roxanne insisted. "Of course she knows. She's probably torturing him by refusing to divorce him. You know, you can do that. Just keep saying no until he ups the ante."

"Like Marta."

"No, Marta's case was different. She thought she'd make him squirm by crossing her legs. Unfortunately, her husband found plenty of women willing to go along for the ride. I hear he socked a lot of cash away in the Cayman Islands so that she couldn't get her hands on it."

"Are we talking about Marta Keller?" Maggie named a famous TV journalist.

Roxanne nodded smugly. "Poor thing. I think she's doing some morning show in San Diego now. But I feel for her, and her kids."

"She's better off without him," Eloise said. "You're lucky you're not married, Maggie. Men are so much work. You do everything for them, and still they don't get it. They never get the big picture."

"But do tell," Roxanne said, squeezing Maggie's arm. "How goes it with the mayor? Should we be expecting any formal announcements soon?"

"Don't hold your calendar open for that event," Maggie said. "It's just not happening for us. I'm planning to end it . . . if I ever see him again."

Isadora lowered her voice. "Is he gay?"

Maggie blinked. "Not that I know of. Actually, I find him to be a bit of a hump-hound, though we've never done the deed. He's persistent enough, but I don't think we have the right chemistry. That coupled with the fact that I never had more than ten minutes to talk to the guy—you get the picture."

Eloise gasped, lifting a hand to cover her mouth. "The mayor is a horn dog!"

"Given the right circumstances, they all are," Roxanne said cynically.

"I would have never thought it of him," Eloise insisted.

"They got it all on camera," Maggie said, nodding toward Boone and Max.

"My husband likes to do it on camera," Shelby admitted. "The first time he set up the videocam in our room, I slapped him silly. I thought he was a perv!"

"Did he give it up?" Camille asked.

Shelby shrugged. "I got used to it, though the camera does add ten pounds." With a sidelong glance at Boone and Max, she adjusted the bodice of her gown. "That's a nice dress," she told Maggie.

"It's a Ralph Lauren. I love the cut of yours."

"Vera Wang," Shelby said. As they went around the group, chiming "Valentino" or "Ungaro," Max gave a grunt and walked off.

"What a rude young man," Isadora remarked.

"Tell me about it," Maggie said. "And I have to put up with him twenty-four-seven."

"He probably needs vitamins," Eloise said. "I read that vitamin deficiencies can make you grouchy."

"You don't need vitamins if your diet is right," Isadora said. "Has anyone tried that new anti-oxidant diet? With the chocolate and green tea?"

They were up to the grapefruit diet when Max returned. "Boone!" He whistled. "You can pack up and call it a night. The mayor isn't coming."

"How do you know?" Maggie asked.

"Just talked to one of his aides. Not the guy you were boffing. Fernandez. He says the mayor had to cancel. So we're out of here."

"But I want to stay," Maggie said.

Max shrugged. "So, stay. Don't think you'll get any action hanging with these crows, but it's your choice."

"Excuse me . . ." Maggie put her hands on her hips as she stepped up to face Max. In her Manolo Blahnik heels, she was eye-to-eye with him. She felt her friends circling around her along with other partiers. Battle lines were forming. "What exactly is your problem? Besides the fact that you have no respect for women."

"Coming from a chick who has no respect for men, that holds no weight, honey."

"What the . . . honey? You really don't understand women, do you?"

"You act like men are a different species, a race of mental midgets . . ."

Maggie smiled. "And that would be wrong because . . . ?"

"Honey, if you can't figure it out, I'm not the person to explain it to you," he said, his dark eyes wide with fury.

His attitude infuriated her. She felt her hands balling into fists. How she'd love to deck him . . . but this was not the place. She was above all that. . . . Really, she was!

Max went on, "Maybe there just aren't enough brain cells in that pretty head of yours to process it all."

"Oh that's just too much!" Maggie's fists railed at her sides. She stamped a foot and turned away before she hit the man. Then, noticing the enticing glass of champagne bubbling in Roxanne's hand, she snatched it away and turned to Max. "Maybe this will cool you down!" she said, pouring champagne down his shirt in an illustrious display.

The crowd gasped and murmured. Lights were flashing—cameras? Maggie wasn't sure. She was savoring the moment of Max's degradation. He held his hands out as tiny drops of the liquid ran down his gray flannel dress pants to the parquet floor.

"Well," he said, yanking a linen napkin off a nearby table. "That was a waste of some terrific champagne."

"Oh, no. It was worth it." Maggie held the glass to her cheek demurely. "It was worth every drop."

34

On Saturday morning at Royal Canadian, Chandra broke tradition and ditched her granola for the satellite-size pancakes.

Maggie was shocked. "I don't think I've seen you carbo-load since junior year of high school when we spent the night eating that twelve-scoop sundae in the parking lot at Baskin and Robbins."

"How do you remember these things?" Chandra said, digging into a pecan pancake with maple syrup and butter.

"I have a very good memory for food. Food and sex. If there was ever a game show centered around food and sex, I'd be the all-time champ."

Apple arrived with a newspaper tucked under one arm. "Hey, bride!" She leaned across the table to hug Chandra, then slid the paper over to Maggie. "You made Page Six. Again."

"I . . . what?" Maggie rifled through the pages to find the story. "Ohmigod! It's me and . . ." She puckered as if she'd sucked a lemon. "Max?" She shot a look at Boone's camera. "Is that why he's not here this morning?"

The camera nodded up and down.

"Big chicken-livered scaredy cat," Maggie said, skimming the article. Of all the guys to show her with. They couldn't pick Fun

Steve or Les, the musician with the smokey eyes and baby dreads? No, they showed her with sour, dour Max. Proof of how hard it was to shape a public image.

"Twice on Page Six?" Chandra stabbed a pecan with her fork. "Aren't you the publicity maven."

"We all are, Chandra. You just don't know it because you've been out of the country," Apple said. "I keep getting stopped because people recognize me from billboards or TV commercials. We're all over Times Square."

"I did see a *Big Tease* sign on the way back from the airport," Chandra admitted. "Our heads were huge."

"Ugh!" Maggie winced at the newspaper. "You big buffoons! I wasn't fighting with my date! He was *not* my date."

"What does it say?" Chandra asked.

"Apparently Maggie and Max got into a little tiff at the Plaza last night," Apple explained. "Maggie used her prime pitching arm to toss a glass of champagne down Max's shorts."

"Down his *shirt,*" Maggie corrected. "And I can't tell you how disappointing it is to be pictured with the most despicable man in the world."

"It could be worse," Apple said. "You could be living with him."

Maggie stabbed at a wobbly piece of egg. "I thought you were moving in with me, Ap. I keep telling you, but I can't make those decisions for you." When Chandra looked up in concern, Maggie added, "Control issues. Plus he's a big-time bastard. She saw him having lunch with another woman yesterday."

"I hate him," Apple said.

"So why do you stay?" Chandra asked. "This worries me."

"I'm working on it." Apple sighed. "Boo-hoo. Don't let me drag down our reunion breakfast. Not when you've got such great news," she said, grabbing Chandra's left hand to check out her engagement ring.

The single marquis diamond glimmered. "It's a whopper, all right," Maggie said.

"We're so happy for you," Apple told Chandra. "I'm so excited about shopping today. Do you think he'll want to help you pick out patterns, or do you have full authority?"

"I don't know," Chandra said. "We never really discussed those details."

"What?" Maggie prodded. "You guys were too busy crunching numbers to iron out the prenup?"

Chandra smiled. "We enjoy going over the numbers together. We both love to talk shop." She lowered her voice, eyes down on the table in embarrassment. "Reg is the first man I ever met who actually . . . he actually gets off on it."

"Oh, great! A guy who thinks the backbone of his financial empire is in his pants!" Maggie shook her head. "Men have such high opinions of their penises."

"Do you have to put it that way?" Chandra frowned, clearly annoyed.

"She's just jealous," Apple said, patting Maggie's arm. "Chandra, you're the only one of the three of us who's having good sex. And it's hard for a 'sexpert' to pass on her crown."

"I'm not passing on anything. I wish the best for all of us. And now, with this press," Maggie said, pinging the newspaper, "I'm more motivated than ever to find my own Mr. Right. Which reminds me, you're both coming to my tree-trimming party this week, right?" Maggie's Christmas party was an annual tradition: a way to get friends to help decorate the tree; a way to get guys to her apartment. "I'm working on this connection Jonathon knows. This guy says he might be able to get Billy Joel to come."

"Really?" Chandra blinked. "Wow, you really are becoming a celebrity."

"Oy! If I could only get on Page Six with *him,*" Maggie said, folding up the paper. "So, where do we start today? Tiffany's? Bergdorf's? Macy's?"

"Definitely Tiffany's," Apple said. "You've got to register there."

"Good, because there's a handbag I want to check out across the street at Bergdorf's. They've got the new spring Fendis in. I'm dying to touch them."

"I thought you were giving up cheap sex and expensive bags?" Chandra asked Maggie.

"Oh, please," Maggie said, lifting her coffee cup. "I've lived like a saint for the past few weeks, but a girl can only conquer one demon at a time."

"It all seems so pretentious," Chandra said to her own reflection in a shiny Mikasa plate from the lovely display upstairs at Tiffany's. The clerk had been incredibly helpful, but Chandra couldn't think with the woman lingering nearby. Thank God for Apple, who seemed savvy with these things. She had told the clerk they'd search her out when Chandra was ready to register. Meanwhile, the handsome plate decorated with dark blue and gold starbursts gleamed mockingly at Chandra. "To expect people to buy me something so expensive . . . It seems rude. I should find something more reasonably priced."

"But this is the one you love," Apple insisted, lifting the gold-edged saucer one more time.

"She's right," Maggie said. "Stick with your favorite. Besides, do you really think money is an obstacle for any of *his* friends? It's just the opposite; you could embarrass him by picking something too thrifty."

Chandra clenched her teeth, still considering. "I don't know. This makes it feel real, somehow. More real than anything else so far, except the ring."

"And we know that whopper is real," Maggie said, studying the refractions of light in a Waterford bowl.

"Look at all these patterns." Chandra picked up a cup. "It's overwhelming."

"Didn't you go through this with me in high school?" Apple asked Chandra. "When I was so crazy about Glen Thurman and I was sure we'd get married right after graduation? I must have picked out china eighty-five times. I love china. The different colors and textures, the thickness or frailty of bone china. Some of it's so thin you can see your hand through it."

Maggie raised her hand. "I believe I was the one who put up with that crap. Chandra was off taking the SAT review course or getting extra credit by working at the North Shore Animal Shelter."

Chandra didn't look up, but she remembered those days well.

Although her friends had teased her about being a workaholic bordering on nerd, they didn't really understand that she was doing it all to bail herself out of the lower middle-class tax bracket, that her only ticket out of a one-bedroom apartment in Queens was going to come through scholarship money.

"I went through it all over again when Melonie got married," Apple said soberly. "It's never too soon to register. But I can't believe you're not familiar with this stuff. I started picking patterns in eighth grade. When Melon got married I changed my choices three times, though it didn't really matter since I wasn't the one having a wedding."

"And now?" Chandra asked. "If you just got engaged, what would you pick today?"

Apple went to the Limoges table and lifted a cup to the light, as if it were a sacred offering. "This is the one . . . Ivy Renewal, it's called. Though if I got married now, I probably wouldn't have a wedding. I mean, I really don't have a lot of patience for ceremony." She frowned. "Wow, that's disappointing. Not even engaged and already I feel cheated out of my wedding."

"You know," Chandra said, "it just hit me that registering for china is the least of my worries. I'm not concerned about the trappings of a wedding; what I need to work on is the happily-ever-after part, which isn't so easy with Reg across the Atlantic."

"Atta girl," Maggie said. "Keep your eye on the real prize, though you always were so grounded. So if we're done here, can we go across the street and check out the new handbags at Bergdorf's?"

"Just a second," Chandra said, taking her Palm Pilot out of her purse. "I just want to get a few of these names down."

"Hey, that reminds me," Maggie said. "How are you going to work out the long-distance thing? Is he moving to New York, or are you going to London?"

Going to London? The words pinged at Chandra's heart. Could she really leave New York? Separating from New York and her friends and her job had never been part of her future plans, but so much had changed when she met Reg. Or maybe he would relocate to New York? Somehow she found it hard to imagine him abandoning the lovely, sleek Pringle Headquarters built in that highly desirable suburb of London. "I don't know," Chandra said. Was he expecting her to move to his city?

"You don't know?" Maggie turned away from the crystal display. "You guys didn't talk about living arrangements?"

"It never came up," Chandra admitted. "You don't think he's assuming I'll drop everything and move to London, do you?"

"I'd be willing to bet on it," Maggie said.

"Though Reg is rich enough that you guys could be together and jet across the ocean every few days," Apple said. "The trip's a zip on the Concorde."

Chandra shook her head. "I don't think the bosses will be too happy about me floating into Grayrock every few days."

"As if you're going to keep your job!" Maggie grabbed Chandra by the shoulders and gave her a shake. "Wake up, girl! You don't need your stinking job. You're about to marry a millionaire."

"But I like my job," Chandra said, feeling deflated. "And could you not broadcast my success so loudly? I think someone over in Fine Linens didn't hear you."

"You've got some major issues to take up with your guy," Maggie said. "And if you decide to move to London, I get dibbs on your apartment."

"No fair!" Apple objected. "You already have an apartment."

"Not as nice as Chandra's."

"It's a co-op," Chandra pointed out. "I'm not allowed to sublet, and . . . and . . ."

"And the purchase price is going to be way beyond our means," Maggie finished.

"No, I was just going to say that I don't want to sell it. I don't want to leave New York."

"We'll see," Maggie said. "Not that we won't miss you, sweetie, but a few more dates with Reg and you'll be packing for London faster than you can say Eliza Doolittle."

Chandra couldn't believe it; she wasn't ready to leave New York. But if she was going to be a couple with Reg, they would work this out together. A couple. Somehow, after being single for so long, the idea of being on a team again was very reassuring.

35

News of Chandra's imminent wedding had made it back to the States before she did. By the time she returned to the office on Monday, the Grayrock staff was well-versed in the plans of the quiet M&A manager who worked for Willard Ritter.

"I can't believe how fast word got around," Chandra told Vincent that morning as she settled in at her desk with a cup of coffee. "I went to check my e-mail from home last night, and I had more than fifty. And most of them had nothing to do with business—just congratulations from people in the company, from the mail room on up."

"Yes, yes, we also received a flood of phone calls, and I promised to pass along many well wishes to you," Vincent said, his hands pressed flat against her desk. "Of course, my own voice joins in to congratulate you. I hope you will be very happy." His somber brown eyes were downcast, focused on the rug.

Chandra realized this was difficult for him. Was it because it undermined his supreme professionalism to mix personal matters with business? Or was Chandra's friend in accounting right; Mandy Stillwagon had always maintained that Vincent had a crush on Chandra. Whether it was true, Chandra knew from the year or so they'd been together that he was a nice guy, an excellent worker, a good and loyal confidant. Once or twice she had fantasized about what it would be like to touch his beautiful light brown skin, but she would never date a coworker.

"Thank you, Vincent," she said. "I appreciate your support." She turned to her computer, but he wasn't leaving. "There's something else?"

He nodded. "The woman claiming to be your mother . . ."

Chandra felt a tightness in her stomach, but she let him go on.

"She has called many times, having seen the television commercials that feature you." His round, brown eyes were full of concern as he went on. "She has told me that now, seeing your face, she is quite sure you are her daughter. The woman is not a threat, as I perceive her, though she is rather persistent and calls nearly every day now. I was wondering what I should tell her at this juncture?"

Suddenly, the coffee before her seemed way too acidic. Chandra pushed the mug away and took a breath. Damage control. She needed to patch things together and stop this woman. This woman who was her mother.

I should have known, Chandra thought. *I should have realized that my mother would spot me on TV. Didn't I mention that possibility to Maggie and Apple?* And now, Rhonda was making her calls, trying to claim her own prize . . . about to ruin everything.

She's going to ruin my life . . . again.

Feeling sick, Chandra pushed away from her desk and went over to close the door. As it latched shut, she leaned against the hard wood and took in a deep breath.

"I'm sorry, Vincent," she said, nervously grabbing up a gold pen from her desk. "So sorry to involve you in this mess."

"I don't understand."

"The woman who's been calling probably *is* my mother. The truth is, I was born in Philadelphia to a woman I haven't seen since I was an infant. She sort of handed me off to my grandmother, who ended up raising me here in New York. I don't know why she's turned up now, after all these years. I mean, when I was little she never had anything to do with me." Chandra recalled a sunny day, sitting on Gramma's front stoop. She couldn't have been more than four or five, too young to be in school. That was the day she created the fantasy of her mother. Her mother was coming, she told Gramma. That was why she wore her pretty denim jumper with a red T-shirt and her Sunday shoes. She wanted to look nice when Mama came to see her.

"Oh, child," Gramma had said with a sigh, "your mama isn't coming today, or any day. She lives far away in Philadelphia. There's no way she's stopping by."

Chandra did not answer Gramma, but she refused to believe her and went back to the porch to play "Waiting for Mama." When the neighborhood kids asked her to play, she told them she couldn't. She had to sit and wait like a good girl.

That sunny day was the first of many in which she had acted out the waiting game. Sometimes she dressed up, other times she took extra care with her hair or saved two or three cookies in a sandwich bag, just in case Mama was hungry for a snack. And although Mama never arrived, somehow the simple act of playing out the fantasy made her feel better. She had a mama out there, and maybe someday, someday Mama would come to see her.

"This information brings the situation to a new light," Vincent said. "How would you like me to handle it?"

Chandra tapped the gold Cross pen against her palm, not sure what to say. "The thing is, I have no relationship with my mother, and I don't really want one. I mean, there's nothing there." She shook her head. "Why is she coming after me now? Do you think she wants money?"

"She did not mention such a thing during my conversations with her, but perhaps this is her ulterior motive," Vincent pressed his hands together in a supplicant gesture. "If you like, I will speak to her on this matter and try to determine her reasons for contacting you."

"Or maybe it's the TV show," Chandra said thoughtfully. "Maybe it's fame she wants." She pressed her eyes shut. "Of course! She probably wants to appear on camera, make a big splash. Ruin my chances on the show, destroy my reputation here at work and with Reg." She winced. "Reg is not going to do well with this. God, he'll never marry me once he finds out I've got some weirdo mother from the projects of Philly."

"And how would that be a reflection on your character or integrity?" Vincent asked. "Really, Chandra, I worry that Mr. J. Reginald Pringle is not much of a man if he won't accept your background."

"He doesn't like surprises," Chandra said, "and I can't say that I blame him."

"Then perhaps you should reveal this information to him and take the sting out of the possibility of surprise."

Chandra sucked in her breath. "I couldn't do that." She didn't know Reg well enough to sit down and bare her soul. Of course, she wouldn't lie to him if he asked her, but it would just be too embarrassing to spill everything about her mother's desertion, her childhood in Queens as the granddaughter of a house maid. "I just . . . I'm not ready to get into this with him."

"Not to worry," Vincent said. "I will speak to the woman and try to determine her motives. Perhaps she can be deterred from contacting you in the future?"

"That would be great, Vincent," Chandra said, feeling a rush of relief at his offer of help. "Thank you. This is really above and beyond."

"No problem," he said. "I will do my very best."

As he left her office, Chandra wondered if it was ethical, asking Vincent to involve himself in one of her family matters. Then again, all talk of ethics had flown out the window when Grayrock had pressured her to go on *Big Tease. And look where that got you,* Chandra thought.

Happily engaged. Maybe ethics weren't all they were cracked up to be.

36

"Where is Apple?" Maggie wondered aloud as she gazed around her apartment chock-full of guests. She adjusted the off-the-shoulder bodice of her red velvet Givenchy gown, then dodged a big, burly hockey player who was toting four Sam Adams Winter Brews to his buds. She tucked a strand of silver tinsel back up on the bookcase, and then ran into the kitchen to pull another quiche out of the oven.

"Great party," the back-stabbing Tara announced from her perch beside the kitchen sink, which was filled with ice and champagne bottles. "So much better than last year."

"What are you, the party critic?" Maggie didn't even bother to look at the girl as she shoved her hands into oven mitts and made her way out to the buffet table. With any luck, Tara would make a bad move and land in the sink. That would ice her ass! Okay, for once Tara was right. This year's tree-trimming party rocked. The apartment looked great, the food was fabulous, and the guest list was like a Who's Who list in *Time Out New York*. A few of the New York Rangers were cruising the crowd. Roxanne and Isadora had come without their husbands. Les's combo was playing in the hall, where a few dancers from *42nd Street* had done a routine on the stairs. The staff of *Metro* was here, along with a few players from the mayor's staff. The mayor himself was expected later in the evening, but Maggie had learned not to count on him. Chandra was here, with two Grayrock people, but the third musketeer was missing.

"Where the hell is Apple?" Maggie asked Chandra, who was biting into a pumpkin-cranberry muffin.

"I don't know, but these are delicious," Chandra said. "Where did you get them?"

"Don't ask." Maggie leaned closer. "I actually baked. Can you believe it? But I was expecting a big crowd and I couldn't afford to blow it all at Zabar's or Balducci's. I made the muffins, the cookies, the quiches and the salads. The cheese and alcohol were all I had to spring for, and that was plenty. Let me tell you, it's expensive to be a social butterfly. My Visa bill is screaming."

"Maybe you should ask Candy for a raise," Chandra said, nodding over at a cluster of *Metro* editors. Candy's hair was teased higher than ever—definitely in danger of big-hair land—and she was talking right into Boone's camera in that manner that infuriated Max.

"Gack!" Maggie waved at the air, as if she could wipe the scene away. "I don't think promotion is in the cards right now, especially after she spent the week whopping my sorry butt. With all the shit to juggle for the show, I haven't exactly been the exemplary employee. But you know how it is, right? You're probably not getting anything done either."

"You're talking to me?" Chandra said. "I live to work."

"Chandra is the exemplary employee," Vincent said.

"We all wait around for her to make mistakes," added Brianna, Chandra's assistant. "So far, it hasn't happened. We're still waiting."

"All righty, then, I guess it's just me who isn't a multitasker. Then again, I've done a good job juggling my dates, I think."

"Did you manage to break up with the mayor yet?" Chandra asked.

"No . . . not officially, but I sent him an e-mail saying we had to talk. If that doesn't spell it out, then the man needs to hire a cryptologist."

"Maggie?" called Max's voice, irritated as usual.

Maggie frowned. "What bug is up his ass today?" she muttered as Max circled a few of the dancers to join them.

"Where is Apple?" he asked. "We didn't send a camera to her place because she said she would be here. Where is she?"

"The hell if I know," Maggie said. "She promised to come. It's still early."

"But we are minutes away from the airing of the first episode," Max pointed to the television in the entertainment center decked with red ribbon. "And we need reaction—reaction from all three of you. This is the cat-fight part, the core of the show's concept. Where is she?"

"I don't know," Maggie insisted. "I'm not her mommy."

Vincent handed Chandra a cell phone. "I'll call her," she told Max. "But I'm sure she's on the way."

Everyone waited as Chandra let the phone ring. Maggie got impatient, hating that Max was blaming them for the fact that Apple wasn't here yet. He was the show's producer; *he* was supposed to be running the show. "You know, Max, maybe if you provided car service for the show's contestants, you wouldn't be losing track of them," Maggie told him.

Max just grunted.

"See?" Chandra held out the cell. "No answer. She must be on her way."

"I don't like this." Max raked his dark hair back. "Part of the show's format is to show your reaction to the show. All three of you." He glanced over at Boone. "Maybe I should grab a camera and go to her place myself."

"You? Shoot the scene?" Maggie grinned. "That's scary. Careful with those closeups. Pores and nose hairs are so unbecoming."

"I started in this business as a cameraman," Max said.

"She's probably on her way," Chandra insisted. "If you go over to her place, you'll miss her."

Max grunted again, checking his watch. "We're on the air in ten . . . there's no time anyway." He turned on the heel of his Nike sneaker and stalked off. "My ass is fried."

Looks okay to me, Maggie thought, watching his blue jeans swagger away. Jonathon came over, with Guy Fernandez not far behind wearing an earphone plugged into a headset.

"Don't you love those little ear doo-hickies?" Jonathon whispered, nudging Maggie. "I feel like I'm with Clint Eastwood."

"They are sexy," Maggie agreed. "*Love* the doo-hickies." She didn't really consider Guy the macho type, but it was great that Guy and Jonathon had hit it off. Since Maggie had introduced them at the beginning of the party, they'd talked nonstop beside the punch bowl.

"He's on his way up," Guy said. "They're clearing the stairway for him now."

"Who?" Maggie asked.

"The mayor!" Guy nearly spat.

"Oh, really?" Maggie wanted to laugh. "The guy finally makes it past the lobby, and it's too late. I may go down in history as the only part of New York the mayor didn't conquer." She raised her hands like a boxing champ.

"Please!" Guy hissed.

"Really, Maggie," Jonathon giggled, "this is no time to get political."

"Who's political? I just can't believe I was the first one to tell the man no and stick to my guns."

"Good evening, Mr. Mayor!" Guy gushed as Elliot Giordano breezed in the door.

Maggie had to admit, he looked dapper in his navy suit and deep blue shirt. "The guy has such potential," she muttered to Chandra. "Too bad he's so inaccessible."

"So why did you stick with him for so long?" Chandra asked.

"Because he got me into the best parties. I schmoozed with high society, made some great friends. You met Roxanne and Isadora, right? Oh, they're the two chicks over there tickling that hockey player." Maggie straightened the Christmas card display on the credenza before moving forward to greet the mayor. "How the hell are you, El? It's been so long, and I've been wanting to talk . . ."

"One minute to air!" Max interrupted the party, waving his

arms. The combo stopped playing, the crowd scattered, and Max pointed to three folding chairs he'd set up in front of Maggie's television set. "One minute to airtime. Let's go, ladies. Take your seats, here."

Maggie put a finger to her lips and told the mayor, "Hold that thought," then she linked her arm through Chandra's and breezed over to the chairs. "Looks like we're going to be the life of the party, like it or not," she muttered to her friend.

"Not," Chandra said, "but I can always count on you to steal the attention."

"You got it, chick," Maggie said, tucking her red velvet gown and taking her seat as the theme song for *Big Tease* came on. *"You can tease me, you can please me, but we all know how the story goes. You Big Tease! Romance, please! When you're ready for love . . ."*

Suddenly, everyone was singing along, from hockey players to socialites to *Metro* editors. Even the mayor crooned.

"I had no idea this show was so . . . pervasive," Chandra said, crossing her legs with dignity, as if to separate herself from the gushing crowd around her. "It's truly frightening."

"I hear ya, sister," Maggie said under her breath. "I watched last season, but I never, *ever* sang the theme song."

"One of the many reasons we're good friends," Chandra said, crossing her arms and leaning back.

As Maggie settled in to watch the show, she felt a prickly wave of anxiety. She knew her fast-talking, no-nonsense attitude could easily put people off. Shoot, her mother always told her she could be downright offensive. Had Max edited her scenes to soften that, or had he sharpened the blade? She shot him a glare, but he was busy stewing over the fact that Apple was a no-show.

The mayor crept up and took Apple's seat as the commercials ended and the screen showed Apple, Maggie and Chandra listening to Max's explanation of the show. Cut to Rockefeller Center, where Maggie was pointing to the mayor, bragging that he would be her first date.

The mayor grinned in satisfaction, but Maggie found herself wincing. She came off as bold and bratty, trying way too hard.

That wasn't how it felt inside, not at all, but then the show wasn't really about how it felt to be Maggie, was it?

She had to grit her teeth to watch herself dancing in the wardrobe closet with Jonathon, babbling at work, shopping for handbags at lunchtime, reeling off advice to her friends. Oh, how could anyone tolerate the loudmouth Maggie? Still, she wasn't as bad as Max's editing made her look. Was she?

There they were on their first date—lots of handshaking and champagne. The action turned to the chick clique in Isadora's office, which broke the mood in the room as the crowd laughed at the barbs that went flying. Then there was a fashion show, and then a fund-raising event. As Maggie watched herself talking with Fashionistas and society chicks, she realized how much fun she'd had with the people in the mayor's world. Those people were so much more fun than he was. Maybe that was the hardest part about breaking up with the mayor; she was going to miss his social calendar.

The action moved up to Kitty's Christmas party, where the camera caught her stealing in and out of the bathroom with Fun Steve. Despite Steve's explanation on the way out—"My zipper jammed and she was helping me . . ."—the truth was apparent. Everyone knew they'd made "a love connection," as Max put it in his voice-over narration.

"Oh, thanks for that," Maggie muttered as they went to commercial. "Like no one got that."

"Well, well, Ms. McGee," the mayor piped up.

Maggie braced herself, certain that he would lash out at her. How could he not? She'd had secret sex with one of his aides, and she'd never even delivered the goods to the mayor himself.

"I'm glad to see you called upon your city officials for support of your cause," he quipped. People laughed. What a sport.

Maggie turned in her chair to study him.

"I was certainly happy to accommodate you," the mayor went on with a tight smile, "but when I agreed to give you support from City Hall, I had no idea how deep that commitment might go."

"Well, yes, Steve definitely rose to the challenge," Maggie said.

"He's a good man." She had to think of a diversion, help the mayor save face. "But can I just say, Mr. Mayor, I really enjoyed our outings? As your date I was privy to so many different levels of society, and I found it all fascinating. I definitely have to thank you for that."

"You're very welcome." Taking her hand, he leaned close to kiss her on the forehead, then rose. "I have another function to attend, but I didn't want to miss this, Maggie. It's been a pleasure."

The pleasure was all mine, she wanted to say. She'd had the fun. She'd had the secret sex. The mayor . . . well, he just had the power, but apparently it was enough to keep him going. "Hey, happy holidays," Maggie said, shaking his hand. "Thanks for coming," she called after him.

"Sit down, sit down, we're back!" Max ordered.

Maggie rolled her eyes. What a tyrant . . . and a bastard, too. He'd made her look so bad, especially when she'd gone off with Steve. Okay, part of the lure of Fun Steve was the guilty pleasure, the lure of having naughty sex with him while pretending to date the mayor. Very hard to make that sort of thing come across as noble, but people just didn't understand the needs of a sexually actualized girl. Not that Max had even tried to understand, the bastard. She wanted to run out of her seat and pummel him, but the show was starting again and she was curious to see whether he'd edited Chandra and Apple in an equally negative light.

The first shots of Apple were in her studio, with sunlight streaming in through the windows and classical music playing. There was Apple, capturing a portrait with her assistant, Juanita, adjusting the lights. Even Lucy Ng, the show's producer, gave a few suggestions, making the whole piece feel like a tightly woven quilt of emancipated women. And then, there was Apple in the farmer's market, the earth child who seemed at ease among the flowers and breads and colorful bins of apples and lemons and greens. By the time she met Teague, Max's editing had well established Apple as an earth goddess, an exquisitely beautiful artist.

"Can you believe this editing?" she muttered to Chandra. "I've been slammed."

"I don't know," Chandra said. "He managed to capture Apple's sweetness, her innocence."

"Ugh-guh-guh," Maggie chortled as Chandra's segment began in the Grayrock offices. There she was, a picture of composure and confidence. *That is Chandra,* Maggie thought as she watched her friend greet Reg at the airport. *Chandra, a woman in control who knows what she wants and goes for it with gusto . . .*

Ohmigod! I'm writing magazine copy for my best friends. What's happening to me?

And where the hell is Apple?

37

Apple was in her studio trying to do everything in her power to avoid a total breakdown. Having stripped down to her bra and panties, she lay on the floor in a circle of candles examining the fine wrinkles and pores of her skin. The human body was a beautiful thing. Sometimes shimmering with beauty on the outside while evil hunkered in shadows within.

Could the camera capture the shadows and lights within? She spread her legs and stretched her chin to the floor, contemplating her foot and wondering.

She'd been to the Frick, had stayed until five when the guards had politely asked her to leave. Damn that place for closing so early. They should let her in 24/7. They were never open at night, when she needed a place to sit quietly amid undisputed beauty. For that was the lure of the Frick Collection, she'd decided. It was beyond the criticism and controversy of twentieth-century art; it was a body of work by artists who had followed their calling and pursued their art, whether it was to escape into a European landscape or capture the subtle alienation of a prostitute turned society wife. Those artists were unsullied by negativism. Their works were preserved in a haven, a glorious mansion that was home for anyone who could pay the price of admission.

To be surrounded by beauty, that was what Apple needed. She'd found so much ugliness inside her, so much pain and evil in close proximity. Teague was evil. Ugly and evil. And somehow, she was attracted to that darkness. She had joined with him and so was penetrated by his evil.

The phone rang again, and she checked the caller ID. It was Juanita. She arose and began to pace. Should she answer it? Juanita was trying to help, but Apple didn't know if she could deal with her. She had asked Juanita to juggle a few commitments, cancel some appointments. It wasn't clear when she would be able to work again. Nothing was clear.

The machine kicked on. "Look I cleared the rest of the week, but Mr. Singleton is really pissed about Saturday. He says he'll sue you if you ruin his daughter's wedding. I told him I would cover it, but he wants you. I don't know what you want to do. Call me." Then the machine clicked off.

A wedding. Apple paced around the circle of candles, watching the flames stretch in the windsweep she created. How could she shoot a wedding if she couldn't get an angle on the shadows inside? The light of bride and groom, the contrast of dark and light.

And what if their inner lights did not meld? What if there was only darkness? She swept near a candle, loving the glimmer it cast up her bare leg. If the world were rid of darkness, would there be light? If contrast disappeared, everything would be painted a sheen of white. A snow wall. Utter blindness.

Stretching out on the floor, she wondered if that was the breakthrough she'd been waiting for. Overexposures. White upon white. Shades of white. Levels of purity. Focusing on her leg, she snapped off the gentle bend of her knee in a frame. She moved up to the thigh. The smooth curve of her hip. Then down to the toes, amazing digits, like old ladies bundled up and traveling in a snowstorm. She went to the mirror and studied her breasts, stretching her arms high overhead. The lines of her bra gave form to the composition. Bewildering, all those models who spent so much money trying to remove lines and creases, when in truth the lines enhanced the human body. The human form needed lines to parallel and bisect the long bones of legs and arms.

Legs and arms. So slender and pink, wrapped around Teague's back.

It was the last vision she'd had of him in his apartment. Teague wrapped in lithe, linear limbs. The lines of some woman's body.

Another woman's body.

And the oddest thing was, neither of them seemed disturbed by her presence. It was as if she'd been invisible, a ghost woman floating through the loft to pick up her camera and her favorite pair of jeans.

Legs and arms, she thought as she snapped a shot of herself in the mirror. People just didn't appreciate the lines of nature.

Part Four

Have Yourself a Sexy Little Christmas

38

The next morning Maggie sat at her desk trying to shrug off the gloom of backlash as she leafed through the December issue of *Metro*. "Woo-hoo! I'm so glad this piece made it through without Candy sanitizing it," she said.

Jonathon leaned over her shoulder and read: "Feeling Frisky? Fill His Stockings with Sex Toys."

"Don't you love it? I can't believe we've never done anything like this before. After all, we're supposed to be the magazine for sexual pioneers."

"Dick tacks?" Jonathon winced. "You recommend giving him dick tacks and edible underwear in his stocking?"

Over in the corner, Boone and Max were laughing. Maggie glared at them and then turned back to Jon. "What's wrong with that?"

Jonathon adjusted his glasses, searching for the tactful answer. "Some guys don't like to mix culinary with cunnilingus, but hey, that's not everyone."

Maggie slapped the magazine against the counter and groaned. "Ugh! I just go too far sometimes, don't I? Don't I?"

"Your unbridled enthusiasm is to be commended, but yes, you are the author of overboard. Hence the phone call from your mother, and Candy's insensitive proposal at the editorial meeting."

"Grr! I thought we weren't going to talk about that," Maggie said. She was still seething over Candy's proposal to run a readers' survey in the magazine. "We could call it: 'Rate Maggie's Dating Etiquette,'" Candy had suggested that morning. "And the scale could go from: "1—It took a bit of multitasking but she managed to juggle 3 guys, to 5—Sorry, *Metro,* but she's in Slut City.'"

Maggie wasn't ashamed of her behavior with the mayor or Fun Steve or Les, but the mockery of the staff still hurt. Then, to heap the insults higher, her mother had called to critique her hair cut. "I can tell you've been working out, dear, but really, you've got to do something with your hair. It's so flat and lifeless. Now, I was talking to Mercedes and she tells me that her daughter . . ."

"Grrr," Maggie growled again. "I feel so trapped." She grabbed the Buddha and rubbed its tummy. "I wish I could have the day off. I wish I could slink out of here and never come back."

"What's stopping you?" Jonathon asked. "You disappear all the time."

"Candy. She's laid down the law. One more infraction and I get the boot."

"How Republican of her," Jonathon said. "Let's slip some salt into her coffee mug."

"Nah." Maggie put the statue down and raked back her hair. "I'm so depressed. Not even up for a prank. If you didn't notice, I was not thrilled with the way I was portrayed on national television last night." She shot Max a seething look. He just smiled.

"What do you have to be depressed about?" Jonathon asked. "You're the hottie of Manhattan. Everyone knows your face now. You're gainfully employed, dating an adorable hockey player for the Rangers—one with teeth, I might add."

"Kevin is a cutie," Maggie agreed, "but he's not the one. The sex is mundane, and so is the conversation. Last night while he was on top of me, I found myself doing mental inventory on the items in my refrigerator, realizing I needed milk."

As she spoke, Max stood up and slipped out of the room. Maggie hated when he did that, acting as if her thoughts and feelings weren't important.

"This is a bad sign," Jonathon agreed. "Is he that bad in bed?"

"He's fine," Maggie said with a sigh. "It's me." She pointed to an advertisement for *A Christmas Carol* in the open magazine. "I'm the Scrooge of love. Meanwhile, Chandra is making wedding plans and Apple is so engrossed in Teague again, she won't come out anymore. I can't believe she missed my party last night. Which reminds me. I'm going to try her again. If she's not picking up, at least Juanita will answer at the studio." She grabbed the phone, pressed in Apple's number, and waited as it rang. "Ugh! Now the machine is kicking on. Where the hell is Juanita?"

Max returned, his face looking grimmer than usual. "We have a problem," he said.

"What's the matter?" Maggie teased. "Spilled your coffee in the editing room so that it ruined next week's show?" It would serve him right for skewing the perspective on her dates, making her look like a brash big mouth.

"Looks like we've lost one contestant," he said. "Apple has dropped out of sight. She never showed last night and this morning she wouldn't let Lucy and Suki into her studio."

"Maybe she's not there," Maggie said. "That would explain—"

"She's there, all right. Lucy spoke to her, but briefly. Said Apple didn't make much sense, though she was emphatic about staying in the studio. When Lucy contacted Apple's assistant, Juanita said Apple had totally lost it. Told her not to bother coming to work again."

"What?" Maggie whirled around in her chair to face him. Apple was setting herself up to play hermit on the hill?

Max folded his arms. "I guess that's one less competitor for you."

"I can't believe this," Maggie said.

"I knew you'd be thrilled," Max told her.

"You . . . you bastard!" Anger jolted Maggie to her feet so that she flew out of her chair and lunged at Max. He held up his hands defensively, but she grabbed his necktie and gave it a yank. "Where do you come off thinking I give a rat's ass about your show? I was friends with Apple long before your stupid show even existed, and that's what matters. My friends. Not some trumped up competition."

"Let go of the tie," Max growled.

She lifted it with her hand, then slapped it against his chest. "People talk about morality and ethics in dating? You need to examine your own morals, Max. To put your show above someone's health and well-being . . ." She grabbed her coat and Fendi Envelope and opened the door. "You are morally depraved." Then, sensing that it was the only way to make a proper exit, she slammed the door behind her.

"Ouch!" Jonathan complained from inside the room. "I was right behind you."

"Sorry!" she called, then hurried toward the elevators.

Maggie leaned on the buzzer for ten minutes before Apple's groggy voice came over the intercom. "Would you buzz me in, already?"

"Who is it?" Apple asked.

"It's Maggie, like you don't already know. Let me in, you big sleepyhead."

The door buzzed and Maggie pounded up the stairs wondering if Apple really didn't recognize her voice. How had she disconnected so quickly? The door to the studio was open a crack, and Maggie pushed her way in to find Apple sitting on the wood floor in an old nubby bathrobe. Light reflected from the large pair of silver scissors in her hands.

"Apple, are you okay? What are you doing?" Maggie asked, noticing that there was some semblance of order to the slices of photos around Apple. Three distinct piles.

"Working on my art. That pile is for legs. This one for arms. Heads and any circular joints go into this pile." Apple looked up, and Maggie noticed the dark circles under her eyes. "It's art. Not commercialism. It's my art."

"I see," Maggie said, studying the piles of clippings as she circled them. Was it art? Was Apple taking a hiatus to follow her muses? Or was she having a breakdown? Venturing over to the desk by the wall, Maggie noticed thirty-seven messages on the answering machine, beside an empty bottle of Xanax.

Art or a breakdown? Maggie thought, picking up the phone. *I would guess a breakdown.* "Honey, did you take all these pills at once?" she asked Apple, holding up the empty vial.

Apple shook her head. "No, but I just took the last two and I would love some more." She touched Maggie's pant leg. "Could you get me more?"

"No, honey. I'm going to get you out of this funk."

"I don't think so. Why did you wake me up?"

"It's almost noon," Maggie said. "We've been worried about you since, since you missed my party last night."

"Oh." Apple turned away, resting her forehead in one hand. "I couldn't do it. I just couldn't face the cameras again."

"It's okay." Maggie kneeled beside her and put her arms around her. "It's okay, Ap. We're going to turn the cameras off, for as long as you want. Right now, you just need to get better."

"I don't see that happening anytime in the near future," Apple said. "I guess you'd better take your coat off."

Maggie called Chandra, who left work to join them in the studio. "When was the last time you ate?" Chandra asked Apple, who shrugged, not looking up from her cutting work.

"I've got leftovers out the whazzoo," Maggie said, grabbing her coat. "I'll go for food and rations and be right back."

"There she is!" the voice called. "Come on."

Standing on Eighth Avenue with her hand up to hail a cab, Maggie saw them scramble over from a nearby doorstep. Max and Boone had been staked out near the vestibule of Apple's building, like vultures waiting to close in for the kill.

"Oh, go away!" she said. "Don't you know when you're not wanted?"

"We have a contract, Maggie." Max stepped between her and the street. "You signed it, baby. So did Apple and Chandra. We are going to film you today and tomorrow and the next day, until we complete our season. And episodes of tears or crises or temper tantrums will not deter us."

"What part of 'Go Away' do you not understand?" Maggie asked, horrified at his persistence. It was as if the smell of Apple's pain made him that much more determined to move in for the kill. "We are so done with you, bud." She turned to Boone and held up her hand. "Put the camera down, Boone. It's over."

"It's not!" Max insisted. "And we are gonna stay on you like white on rice."

"Ohmigod, you sound like a cheap mobster," Maggie said, still staring at Boone. "I said it's over. Camera down. Contract broken. You can sue the three of us, but you're not getting one more candid interview. Go find yourself three more suckers."

Slowly, Boone lowered the camera and nodded at Maggie.

"Thank you," she told Boone. "Thanks for having an ounce of decency." Then she turned and waved at a yellow taxi.

"You can't do this!" Max shouted as she pulled open the cab door. "You can't back out of the contract."

She turned to him and smiled. "I already did."

That afternoon when Maggie returned to the studio, Apple was sleeping on the sofa, her head in Chandra's lap. Maggie unloaded her bags in the kitchen, then poured two glasses of Merlot for Chandra and her.

Handing Chandra the wine, Maggie noticed that the watery gray sunlight of winter afternoon was fading. "*Ugh!* I have to call the office again. Last I heard Candy was pissed, but what can you do?" She took a sip of wine, studying the ringlets of orange hair that spilled over Chandra's skirt. "Did she seem clear to you before she fell asleep?"

"She was lucid enough to let me know that she walked in on Teague in bed with another woman. The man brutalized her emotionally."

"I don't know why she put up with him."

"Apple always does; that's the pattern," Chandra said. "She's got to figure out why she's attracted to these chauvinistic older men who want to control her."

"Father figures," Maggie said. "I bet it goes back to her issues with Nelson."

Chandra nodded. "Here we are, armchair therapists. But the thing is, Apple has got to figure this all out. She's got to do her own digging."

Maggie had brought two sleeping bags, along with leftover muffins and quiche and salads and cheeses. "This should get us through to next Christmas," Chandra said as she looked through the packed refrigerator.

That first night, Apple awoke to eat some quiche, then fell asleep again on a sleeping bag in a puddle of moonlight.

Maggie moved the silver sheers to the top of the refrigerator, then changed into her sweats. "This is like a sleepover," she told Chandra. "In fact, I'll even let you have the couch since you have to go to work in the morning."

"No, I don't think I'm going." Chandra knotted the belt of her robe, then plopped onto the sofa. "I'll definitely take the couch, but I'm going to try to get out of work tomorrow. I think Apple needs us. Sort of like an intervention. She needs us now."

Maggie snuggled into the sleeping bag, thinking of how overwhelming her problems had seemed that morning. How weird that she could escape them all by rushing to Apple's rescue.

Well, at least temporarily. She knew her job was in jeopardy. She'd left Kevin's calls unanswered, and she hoped that Max didn't sue the three of them for backing out of the show. She hadn't told Chandra about that yet; she figured it was low on the priority list right now. She yawned. Her problems would boomerang, but for now it felt good to be here focusing on Apple . . . just Apple.

39

If the past few days had seemed surreal to Apple, Friday morning began just as oddly as she blinked awake to the odd vision of Maggie in her sweats, stooped over, her head buried in a kitchen cabinet. She flopped her head around to find Chandra sleeping quietly on the couch.

She wanted to tell them to go. She appreciated their concern, but they couldn't help her. She would only drag them down with her into the mire of despair, and that was something she didn't want to do. On the table, the answering machine blinked, relentless.

Sitting up, she felt the same swell of pain that had ruined her the past few days. A blunt sharpness in her chest. She scratched her head, muttering, "I need more Xanax."

"You need some cookware." Maggie pulled a fly swatter out from the cabinet and tossed it into the trash can. "I'm looking for a pan to make lasagna. I need a deep, rectangular pan." Maggie pulled open the cabinet under the sink and a bottle of dishwashing liquid tumbled out. "Where do you keep your cooking stuff?"

"I don't. This is where I work and I never make anything beyond a pot of coffee here."

Maggie rolled up her sleeves, assessing the kitchen area. "That is what we are going to work on. It's been here all along, right before our eyes."

Apple rubbed her eyes. "Excuse me?"

"Look at this space!" Maggie flung her arms wide. "You've got plenty of room to make this into a dual living-slash-working space."

Chandra sat up on the sofa and scratched her head. "You know, that's not a bad idea. You'd need something to cover the windows, and a place to sleep." She stretched her shoulders from side to side. "This couch is lumpy."

"I don't know," Apple said. "It's just not a cozy space. It's not comforting."

"We can make it cozy," Maggie insisted. "Oh, and you're going to need some linens and towels and things. I had to dry myself off with a handtowel. Your mother would be horrified." She handed Apple the bottle of dishwashing liquid. "You can use this in the shower. I'll let you borrow my shampoo. Come on, come on, let's go."

Apple stood up, adjusting her bathrobe. "Where are we going?"

"To therapy," Maggie said. When Apple started to groan, she added, "Group therapy. It's called shopping."

Apple looked over at Chandra, who shrugged. "Looks like it's time I bought you a long overdue housewarming gift." When Apple shook her head in confusion, Chandra stood up and marched her toward the bathroom. "Just get it going, girl."

By the time the three friends were showered and dressed, Maggie had talked her hockey player into loaning them his car for the day. They ate Maggie's pumpkin muffins and fruit salad for breakfast, then piled into Kevin's car for a major shopping excursion.

"I can't afford antiques," Apple said, thinking that they were headed out to the suburbs of Connecticut. "I am so strapped right now, I can't afford anything."

"I've had a good year," Chandra said. "I'm happy to put out the plastic, really. But we're not going antiquing. I know it's so yuppy, but we're going to Ikea."

Apple was fascinated by the room settings of furniture. Perfect rooms for a perfect world. How she'd love to snuggle on one of the living room sofas and pretend it was her own personal space. But Maggie and Chandra were driven, on a mission to transform the studio into a home. They found a graceful single bed and a screen to divide off a portion of the room. Maggie insisted on a wardrobe for Apple's clothes, and a beautiful chest of drawers. Chandra supervised the loading of the furniture into Kevin's Navigator, then they were off to the next stop, Bed, Bath and Beyond. While Apple marveled at the spectrum of colors in the bath department, Maggie went wild gathering fat towels and cotton sheets.

Back in the loft, Maggie assembled the bed while Apple found a way to hang some of her enlarged prints from the screen, making it blend in with the studio. "See?" Maggie said proudly. "You have your own personal space without compromising the professional atmosphere of the studio."

Flopping back against the plush pillow, Apple smiled. It was a cozy setting, a world apart from the high windows and metallic equipment. "My own bed. I don't think I've had my own bed since I dormed at Bennington."

"Well, then, it's about time," Chandra said.

Time . . . Apple closed her eyes. Time was slipping away, and she still hadn't produced anything of lasting value. Days went by without progress. She needed to work on her art.

Fortunately, Maggie and Chandra seemed to sense when it was time to talk and when it was not. While Chandra worked on a laptop and Maggie made dinner, Apple sat down and tried to make some order of the pile of appendages she'd been separating. She was beginning to see the pieces more clearly now, beginning to see the form . . . the statements she could make with these pieces.

"Vincent," Chandra said aloud, "you do love to worry, but you can make some decisions on your own." She typed rapidly, then clicked the mouse. "He's a great worker. Look at him, in on the weekend. But he gets so disturbed when numbers don't add up just so the first time." She clicked offline, then pulled some documents out of her briefcase.

Apple admired Chandra's passion for her work She hadn't felt that thrill for so long, the knowledge that she'd accomplished something no one else could do. Not since Granny's portraits.

The phone rang, jarring her concentration. She lifted her chin but did not move to answer it. Maggie and Chandra watched her as the machine clicked on and Cherry Sommers's voice rang out.

"Honey, I don't know what you're doing but it's maddening that you haven't called back. Really, Apple. What are you planning for next week? Your sister's coming in, and we're expecting you. Everyone saw you on the show and you're a minor celebrity around here. Daddy didn't get to watch it, but I taped it for him. Call us."

As the machine beeped, Apple stood up and cautiously approached it. "I can't go there," she told her friends. "And I can't begin to deal with these messages. Some are probably clients, but a lot of them are my mom and . . ." She rubbed her arms. "How do I begin to deal with them?"

Chandra was suddenly beside her, peering down at the answering machine. "Here's how you start." She pressed the rewind button and the machine whirred back, erasing the messages.

"But I . . ." Apple touched her hand to stop her, then thought better of it. "Just erase them?"

"Tell people your machine broke," Chandra said. "It happens all the time. Next week you can have Juanita call your upcoming clients, just to confirm appointments. Anyone else will just have to call you again."

Apple felt lighter as the machine reset itself, the number of messages back to "0." "I like that."

Apple's mother called again that night, then again on Sunday morning.

"Maybe you should talk to her," Maggie said. "At least get her off your case."

Apple looked at Chandra for advice, but her friend waved her off. "Don't look at me. I've got mother issues you don't even want to know about."

"It's not my mother," Apple admitted, feeling the words tumble out on their own. This was not something she wanted to discuss, but somehow it was happening and she was hard-pressed to stop it. "She's just part of the package. A dangerous package."

Maggie's dark eyes were full of rue. "Your father."

Apple felt herself swallow, her throat suddenly tight. "Of course it's him. My father and my endless quest to please him, to gain his approval and validation. But because that never happens, I keep dating guys just like him. Even though I hate him." Tears stung her eyes as the truth burned inside her. "I really hate him. Christ, it's all so Oedipal, I'm skeeving myself out." She laughed, swiping at the tears on her cheek.

Maggie hugged her, but Apple had to articulate her feelings for fear of losing the clarity of vision.

"I have to stop living with my father," Apple said. "That's what I've been doing. Going from one paternal enabler to another. It's time to stop, time to stand up on my own two feet."

Chandra nodded, listening carefully. Apple could always count on her friends to listen. "Christ . . ." She let out a breath. "You guys don't need to hear this shit."

"We've all got baggage," Maggie said. "But not everyone has the courage to dig through it."

"I have to deal with this," Apple said. "Otherwise it's going to swallow me up."

"I know," Chandra said. "God, do I know."

40

On the fourth day at Apple's place, Maggie was beginning to enjoy her new role as chef. She was up to her elbows in oatmeal batter, eager for the cookies to be baked so that they could pig out.

"Can I ask a question?" Apple said. It was Monday morning and Apple was sitting on the floor of her studio, her grandmother's photos spread out around her. Chandra was in the shower, having debated whether she should go to the office. "When are you guys going back to your lives?"

Maggie flung a wad of oatmeal cookie batter onto the pan and laughed. "What, are you getting sick of us?"

Chandra stepped out of the bathroom in a cloud of steam.

"I know you have lives to go back to." Apple pulled herself up straight and faced Chandra, her neck a long, slender line. "Vincent's all worried at the office, and Reg is flying in. I know you have an important meeting." She turned to Maggie. "And isn't Candy on your case for missing too much work? You'd better stop the baking and get your ass uptown to *Metro.*"

"We're not leaving until you're okay," Chandra said.

"I'm fine. Okay, maybe not fine, but I'm not suicidal or anything. Go. Live. Enjoy."

"We're not leaving until you promise to get your butt out of this apartment now and then," Maggie said, sliding the pan of cookies into the oven. "Shit, now that we've made it all comfy cozy, you may never leave!"

"I went out," Apple said. "Didn't we have that shopping excursion? Christ, I went all the way to New Jersey. And what about tonight? Isn't there some Christmas gala at Tavern on the Green? Max wants us all there for *Big Tease,* right?"

Maggie gulped. She hadn't told them that she'd nixed the show, but then she never really expected Apple to let the cameras follow her again.

"That's right," Chandra said as she pulled on her boots. "Reg is flying in for it. Well, he's mostly coming for the meeting, too. Which I really need to get to." She glanced down at her black silk baggy pants and matching blazer. "I never thought I'd see the day when I wore pants to the office. Slumming, but I don't have time to go home and change."

"Pants are totally acceptable in the business world," Maggie said emphatically. "It's just that your personal dress code is so strict. I mean, even if you work for a conservative company in this day and age, you can show toe cleavage."

Chandra shook her head. "I beg to differ, but I don't have time to argue. So . . . are we on for tonight?"

"The party is on," Maggie said, "but I don't think the cameras will be there. I sort of told Max to back off."

"Sort of?" Chandra pressed. "Or did it come out in typical over-the-top Maggie fashion?"

"He was being a pain in the tush, and I wasn't going to let him chase Apple around. I mean, it was out of the question."

"So that's why they haven't been hounding us the last few days." Apple shifted two portraits. "You know, we were halfway done—four weeks into it. It's definitely worth finishing."

"Call Max," Chandra told Maggie. "You can patch things over with him."

Ohmigod, I'm going to have to grovel, Maggie thought. "Why don't you call him?" she asked Chandra. "You're so much better at negotiation."

"It's always a mistake to bring in a new party halfway through a deal," Chandra said, slipping on her coat. "Just call him and straighten things out, and I'll see you guys tonight."

Maggie licked a lump of cookie dough from the bowl and sighed. Straighten things out with Max. She would rather stick needles in her eyes.

Why is it that everything is crumbling around me? Maggie thought as she rushed uptown to the office just before noon. There was no way she was going to go begging to Max Donner, but she'd have to deal with that later. For now, there was the matter of a job to salvage. She dodged moving cars to run across 57th Street against the light and entered the building with trepidation. What if the security guard refused to let her up? What if her PC was dismantled, her voice mail disconnected, her Roladex gone? She was afraid Candy might have made good on her threat to fire, and everyone knew those horror stories of employees returning from lunch to find their office disassembled without a trace of their career left behind.

But the guard just nodded, and other staff members said their usual hellos as she hurried in to find her office still intact. "Damn, did I really pull that off?" She collapsed in her chair, unbuttoning her coat as she rang up Jonathon. "Hey, I just slunk in. What's the word?"

"Candy's pissed at you, but she hasn't come in yet today. Some shoot downtown, with rumors that Brad Pitt might stop in."

Maggie unbuttoned her coat and threw it off. "Hey, meet me in the wardrobe closet. I've still got the key, and I'm in need of another delectable dress."

"Aren't you pushing it? Isn't there something, like, maybe *work* on your desk?"

"Bring your bad self, and you can leave your Puritan work ethic in your office." Maggie hung up and headed off to the wardrobe closet, hoping for a smashing ensemble for tonight's party. She was rummaging through a rack of gorgeous suede skirts when Jonathon appeared.

"What are we tonight—formal, semi-formal or downtown chic?"

"Do you love these shoes?" Maggie waved a pair of leather strap sandals with a gem buckle past Jonathon's face, and he snatched at them.

"Love them. What are they, Dolce and Gabbana?"

She nodded. "And they're gorgeous. I have to wear them tonight." She slid out of her shoes and slipped them on. The heel was so high she had to hold onto Jonathon's arm for balance.

"Totally impractical. Your feet will freeze and you'll wobble around all night, but yes, you should wear them," he agreed. "Who could resist?"

"And with this Donna Karan suede skirt and matching blazer?" She pulled on the chocolate suede blazer and modeled it for him.

"Divine," he agreed. "But I thought you were off the show?"

"Shh! No one needs to know that. Apple and Chandra haven't even accepted it yet. They're still in denial," she confided.

"Are you in there, Maggie?" Maggie and Jonathon turned to face Debbie, who entered hesitantly carrying her notorious clipboard.

"Just scoping out wardrobe for tonight," Maggie said, talking quickly. It was rare for her boss to come looking for her, and Maggie's instincts told her this was not a good sign. "There's a big photo op at Tavern on the Green."

"Great!" Debbie forced a smile. "Love the shoes. Listen, there's no good way to tell you this . . ." From the way her face was clenched taut, Maggie knew.

"Oh, no!" Maggie shrieked. "Candy put you on the task of firing me?"

Debbie winced. "I'm sorry. I couldn't talk her out of it."

"Ugh! She's so awful, but it's not your fault. I sort of saw it coming." Maggie stepped forward and gave Debbie a quick hug. "Thanks for everything. You're a great boss." She lifted a foot and moaned. "My poor shoes."

"Take them!" Debbie insisted. "Take a few things. You may be fired, but since you have the key to the closet I say you're entitled to one last dress-up spree. Consider it a consolation prize."

"Ooh! Will you ax me, too?" Jonathon begged.

"Sorry, Jonathon. One firing a day is my limit."

Maggie slipped off one Dolce & Gabbana and kissed the heel. "Thank you, Debbie. God bless you!" She might be unemployed and dumped from the hottest network TV show around, but at least, tonight, she was going to look fabulous!

Maggie's spree in the wardrobe closet produced more attire than she could carry, so she grabbed a cab for her last ride home from the office. As the driver pulled up in front of her brownstone, Maggie tensed at the sight of a man on the steps. It had been a while since she'd seen a homeless person on the steps, and it wasn't an occurrence she . . .

Wait . . . it was Max Donner. He sat on the steps like *The Thinker,* rubbing the dark stubble on his chin.

She paid the driver, unloaded three shopping bags of shoes onto the sidewalk, and glared at Max. "Where's your sidekick?"

He held up his hands. "No camera today. I come in peace."

She handed him one of the wardrobe bags, then slammed the door of the cab. "Help me lug this upstairs and maybe I'll accept your peace offering." As they climbed the stairs, Maggie's heart danced with the realization that Max needed her. He'd already aired the first episode with Apple, Chandra and her; he could hardly pull the plug on things now. Yep, the show would go on—no groveling required.

"I was thinking," Max began as she unlocked her door, "that it would really serve you well to stick with *Big Tease.* Last week's ratings shares were great, and though I was just following the show's policy, I do understand why you wanted the cameras off."

"No, I don't think you do," Maggie said as she hung a wardrobe bag in the hall closet. "My friend's welfare was at stake."

"Got it, got it! It won't happen again, I promise. And we're going to turn the whole thing around to your advantage, make you look like gold. We'll run the footage of you giving Boone and me our walking papers. We're going to do this whole friendship theme—about how the friendship among the three of you was more important than your interest in the show. Friendship surpasses all. Friends say no to a million dollars. Of course, the prize is still on—*if* you agree to stay with the show."

Maggie's answer was always going to be yes, but she had enjoyed watching him work for it. She let out a dramatic sigh. "Yeah, okay, I guess."

He walked to the door. "Don't bowl me over with your enthusiasm."

"I said okay," Maggie groused, "don't push it, Max. I'll talk to Chandra and Apple, but I think they'll go along with it. That's what friends do."

He paused in the doorway. "Don't bother, I already talked to them." He wriggled his eyebrows. "They saw you as the holdout."

Ooh, he'd gone behind her back; she wasn't sure how she felt about that. She folded her arms. "My friends know me well. I'm not as simple as you think, Max."

"Don't waste your time with me," he said with a smile, "tell that to Kevin."

As he disappeared into the hall, she was about to say "Kevin, who?" when it hit her. She was supposed to go to the party with Kevin the hockey player and it was probably too late to get out of it. Damnation! That had to top the list of reasons to get out of a relationship. Hmm . . . not a bad list. Maybe she could sell it to one of *Metro*'s competitors.

Top Reasons to Get Out of a Relationship

1. You caught him playing grab-ass with your best friend.
2. He can't get off Mommy's lap.
3. You like Mac; he's a PC man.
4. You forgot his name. Whose name? What? Where?

* * *

41

The music swelled around her as Maggie negotiated her way through the partygoers at Tavern on the Green, looking for her date. Boone and Max followed her, and Maggie sensed that Max was trying to be on his best behavior, perhaps afraid that she would pull the plug on the show again. The restaurant was its usual fairy kingdom, with sparkling lights, glimmering crystals and shiny mosaic tiles that cast reflections everywhere. The atmosphere was festive, but despite the boost from her Donna Karan attire, Maggie didn't feel like partying yet, not until she'd finished with the dirty work. The sooner she found him, the sooner she'd be able to dump him and move on.

And moving on was what Apple already seemed to be doing, quite successfully. She'd hooked up with a crew of young men from an Australian yacht racing team—young being the operative word, for Apple usually didn't even notice men under the age of forty. At the moment, Apple was dancing with one of them, her blush silk Valentino gown billowing behind her. "Save some for me," Maggie called, toasting her with her champagne flute. Suki climbed onto a chair, trying to follow Apple and her guy on the dance floor.

Over by the grand piano, Chandra and her fiancé held court,

surrounded mostly by men in suits that screamed Wall Street. The minute Maggie arrived at the party, Chandra had made a point of introducing her to J. Reginald Pringle, who had shaken her hand warmly and joked about how happy he was that Maggie was willing to share her friend with him. Maggie and Apple agreed he was witty, attractive, charming.

"I'm so jealous, I could spit," Maggie had said.

"Relax," Apple had told her, "he's not your type."

Ah, Maggie thought, *but who is? That's the problem.*

"Maggie! So glad you joined us!" Roxanne said, and she and Maggie exchanged air-kisses. It was Roxanne who had finagled three free tickets for this society bash, actually a fund-raiser for a children's charity. She followed Maggie's gaze to the group of people on the dance floor. "See anything you like? Or are you here with someone?"

"I was supposed to meet my date, Kevin what's-his-name. You know, the guy on the Rangers?"

"Yes, we met him at your party," Roxanne said. "Loved the hockey players! What fun."

"Fun, yes, but not for me."

"What's that? You've taken a turn for the serious?" She touched Maggie's arm. "Maybe these boring affairs are getting to you. Aren't you sick of all this?"

"Love it! Love it! No, it's not the social life, it's the men I'm having trouble with. Am I too demanding, or is there a profound shortage of guys with brawn plus brains?"

"I hear you," Roxanne said, nodding so that her diamond earrings bobbed. Watching her, Maggie spotted Kevin over her shoulder, whispering into some model's ear.

"There's the bad boy of the ice," Maggie said. "I hate to break his heart, but it looks like he's rebounding already."

Roxanne glanced surreptitiously at Kevin. "Let him down easy, especially if he's going to fall for a model next. Devastating."

"If you'll excuse me," Maggie said, stepping away. She managed to make quick work of dispensing with Kevin, who wasn't acting like her date anyway so why was she bothering to break it off with him? Now that she was trying to play by the rules, the rules seemed to be changing by the minute.

As Kevin sauntered off to join the modelizers, Max folded his arms and grinned. Not a large gesture, but enough to annoy the hell out of Maggie. After the way he'd edited her in the first installment, she hated being near him. Hated that he thought she was loose and without moral scruples. Of course, he'd never said as much, but she knew it from the way he'd shaped her "on-air" personality. Every time she looked at Max, she was reminded that she was a loser, a failure of a date who couldn't sustain interest in the hottest men of Manhattan. A social misanthrope, unable to ever, *ever* fall in love and maintain a balanced relationship.

She glared at Max. "What was that about?"

He held up one arm defensively, shielding his champagne against his shirt.

"Oh, you . . ." She snatched away his glass of champagne and he ducked reflexively. Maggie stopped herself from flinging this time. Instead, she downed the entire glass of bubbly stuff, handed him the empty, then walked away wondering how she was going to survive four more weeks with him on her tail.

Standing beside Reg, Chandra felt as if she were marrying into royalty. Men sought him out for his advice and influence, eager to bask in the glow of his charisma and power. And the men who sought him were no strangers to power, men who brokered global deals, players from Wall Street and huge conglomerates. Old money and new.

A few yards away, Mule was on the job filming her, while Nayasia had wandered off somewhere with her cell phone. Today Chandra didn't mind the cameras. In fact, she would be glad to have this incredible night on film to watch over and over again.

". . . and what type of diversification did you say Grayrock was interested in?" a bearded man asked her.

"That's difficult to say, although we're looking to expand on international—" Chandra was interrupted when a slight woman stepped in front of her.

"I'm so sorry to interrupt, but I just had to speak with you." The African-American woman was slender, petite . . . much like Chandra herself.

Looking into her brown eyes, Chandra recognized her. Oh, no! Not now! She couldn't believe this woman had come here . . . her mother.

"My baby," the woman said, her voice cracking with emotion. "You don't recognize me, but I would know you a mile away. My daughter, Sharon. My little Sharon has grown up!" She reached out to grasp Chandra's arm, and two men from Reg's security team stepped forward and grabbed the woman, ready to escort her outside.

Oh, no, not a scene! Chandra sucked in her breath, holding a hand up to stop the men. "No, no, it's okay." She caught a look of alarm from Reg, but she just nodded to him, letting him know she was all right. She nodded toward the hall and told the woman, "Why don't we discuss this outside?"

The woman had no choice but to follow Chandra to the ladies' room, though she didn't seem to be put-off at all by the lack of an audience. Sitting on one of the upholstered chairs in the lounge, Chandra took control. "You shouldn't have come here, Rhonda. We really have nothing to discuss. You didn't take the hint when I didn't return your phone calls?"

Her mother let out a breath. "I know, but I was dying to meet you. So curious to see how you turned out. You'll know, when you have a child of your own, you'll know that you never stop thinking of them, never stop loving them."

"Love is not an issue here," Chandra said. "We're strangers. It's been so long since I've seen you, I don't even remember what you look like. We've had no association. We have no relationship. Gramma was my mother—my only mother—and you didn't even make an appearance when she was sick, or when she died. I'm sorry, but that's the way you wanted it back when I needed you."

"You're right, and I'm the one who should be sorry." Rhonda reached out and touched her hand. "I am sorry."

Chandra lifted her chin and found herself looking into a reflection of herself, with deeper creases around the mouth, darker lines under the eyes. She wanted to give this woman what she had come for, but she felt as if she had nothing to give. There was no love between them. Only years and years of waiting.

Closing her eyes, Chandra thought back to the days when she'd waited on the porch steps for Mama to come. Oh, why didn't you surprise me back then? Why didn't you come to me when I needed you, when I scraped my knee or aced a test? When I struck out at bat and lost the game for the entire softball team? When my first boyfriend broke my heart?

"Maybe I've no right to have these feelings," Rhonda said, "but I can't help the swell of pride I feel when I hear about all that you've accomplished. I saw your office and your apartment on television. A doorman, you have! My daughter lives in an apartment building with a doorman! Honey, you've come a long way from the projects of Philly. I just can't help feeling proud."

Chandra swallowed hard over the knot in her throat. She didn't want to get emotional over this. She refused to give her mother the satisfaction of knowing that she had ever cared, that she had cried about her mother, that she had lain awake nights wondering why she'd been "given away" to relatives.

"I need to get back to the party." Chandra stood up, but the woman's hand didn't fall away from hers. "This is really not the appropriate time for this."

"I'm sorry, Sharon."

"My name is Chandra now." She couldn't help the icy tone of her voice. She felt no warmth for this woman.

"Yes, okay." Rhonda dropped her hand. "I had to see you, but I won't bother you anymore. That's a promise."

Chandra left the ladies' room, wishing she could erase the last thirty minutes of her life. It wasn't fair. It wasn't right that she should have spent her entire childhood suffering for this woman, then that she should have to suffer again when her mother showed up.

It just isn't fair, she thought as she straightened her jacket and headed back to the party, her Christian Louboutin pumps clicking against the tiles of the hall.

Back in the party room, the men of Reg's circle whispered behind Chandra's back, eyeing her curiously. What a change from their attitude of a few minutes ago, she thought as Maggie and Apple joined her.

"You okay?" Apple asked. "That woman has some timing."

She nodded, searching the group. "Where's Reg?"

"Ms. Hammel," a woman interrupted. "I'm Nell Lindquist, for *New York Living*. Can I ask you, what do you make of your fiancé's hasty exit?" Chandra felt her throat tighten as the reporter's words began to register. "Is it over between the two of you?"

"Excuse us," Maggie said, grabbing Chandra's elbow, "but we're not giving interviews."

Chandra glanced around the room, trying to blink back the tears that stung her eyes as Maggie led her away. Where was he? Had Reg left without telling her?

42

Apple had always considered the ladies' room a safe refuge from the world, which was one of the reasons she didn't want to let Boone and Max come in to film them. "No way!" she said, pushing them away from the door. "Girls only. If you can find Suki we might let her in, but you guys don't have a prayer." She pushed the door shut and turned to Chandra, who was sitting at a vanity table. "Better talk fast, before we're on *America's Funniest Bloopers* again."

"What did she say to you?" Maggie asked. "I can't believe she showed up after all these years."

"She just said she wanted to see me. That she's always been curious, and somehow seeing me on television gave her the push to go through with it," Chandra told her friends. "There's one good thing about meeting her. At least I know she's not a stalker type. She promised to leave me alone from now on. As if that'll do any good. The damage is done." She dabbed at her cheek, trying to remove streaks of mascara. "Where did Reg say he was going?"

"Something about having to take a call back at the hotel," Apple said. Somehow that sounded better than the reality, with Chandra looking surprised and stressed, Reg surprised and uncomfortable. It seemed apparent that Reg left to avoid the aftermath of Chandra's personal drama, but Apple didn't have to tell that to Chandra, at least, not right this minute.

"I'm going to go talk to him," Chandra said. "I'll take a cab to his hotel and lay everything out for him. He hates surprises, but if I tell him the truth I know he can handle it."

"Of course he can," Apple said. "You're worth a minor inconvenience."

"Do you want some company?" Maggie offered. "I seem to be dateless at the moment."

"No, this is something I need to do alone," Chandra said, staring at herself in the mirror. She smoothed her hair and straightened her shoulders—trying to pull herself together, Apple realized. "Help me think of something witty to say to him."

"Take it from me, the truth is all he needs to hear," Maggie insisted. When Apple and Chandra turned to her, she got defensive. "Okay, I know I'm not an expert on long-term relationships, but I have good instincts."

"Great instincts," Apple said, turning to Chandra. "Tell Reg the truth. If he really loves you, that's what he needs to hear."

They walked Chandra out to the entrance and saw her off in a cab. Then they linked arms and returned to the party.

"Are you going to introduce me to your Australian friends?" Maggie asked. "How old are they? Drinking age yet?"

"They're all in their twenties, though I suspect they might be on the short side of twenty-five. But they're dying to meet you. You were their favorite on *Big Tease!*"

"Which proves only that they like fast women," Maggie said, following Apple over to the group. "Let me at 'em!"

"I see you've snagged us a celebrity," Jeremy said, stepping forward to shake Maggie's hand. "I'm Jeremy Tisbane, and contrary to what you might think I have no connection to any of these hooligans who are most certainly over-imbibing. Although I have met Ms. Apple Sommers, much to my delight." Apple felt giddy as he smiled at her. With short dark hair, round green eyes and high cheekbones, he looked younger than his years and so full of life. The kind of guy you just wanted to nudge so that he'd nudge you back and chase you down the street.

Apple introduced Maggie, and then sat back with Jeremy and watched as her friend joked with the guys, entertaining them with her usual routine of self-deprecating jokes. It felt good to be out, good to be rid of Teague and all the domineering, pompous men like him, good to have a place of her own to go home to when the night ended.

She thought of her mother's last phone message. "We're planning on having you for New Year's, too. Your cousins are coming from Boston, and they want to see you. God knows why, the way that show portrays you. Like a lost little vagabond. How is that fat artist you're living with?"

Mom was a few episodes behind. Apple decided to call her in the morning and put her out of her misery. She was not going home for Christmas or New Year's; she was not a vagrant; and, Christ, would it kill her mother to be a little kind to her own daughter?

Jeremy turned to her, flashing that adorable smile of his. "Your friend is a riot," he said. "I'm so glad she came along to entertain the troops. Now I can have you all to myself."

"Watch out," Apple told him, "I can be dangerous to operate while you're under the influence of alcohol."

She loved the way he tickled her neck when he leaned close and whispered, "Good thing I'm not driving."

Maggie had been sitting under the spangly chandeliers and giant Christmas bulbs of Tavern on the Green for much of the evening, joking with the Australians whose stories of walloping storms and close races were quite amusing. But despite the lively exchange, she found herself unattached as the crowd thinned and the band began to pack up.

Alone and unattached. *Ugh!* She'd never had this problem when she was a woman of loose morals. Damn her newfound dating ethic!

The Aussies were making noises about moving the party to the bar at the Parker Meridian, but Maggie wanted out. There were no prospects for long-term relationships in sight, and she wanted to go home and lick her wounds and—for once—get a good night's sleep.

"You coming with us?" Apple asked, her arm linked through Jeremy's.

"No, I'll catch up with you tomorrow," Maggie said, turning toward the coat check. "I've got an early morning tomorrow . . ." Yep, I have to get out of bed and update my résumé, Maggie wanted to say, but she hadn't told her friends about getting canned from *Metro* yet, not wanting to spoil the evening. Hell, there was nothing they could do about it, anyway.

That seemed to be Boone and Max's cue, as Boone lowered his camera and said goodnight, while Max disappeared without a civil good-bye. The bastard.

Bundled up in her coat, Maggie walked out of the restaurant and cursed at the long line for a cab. Better to walk over to Central Park West and try her luck there. The wind whipped her hair back and quickly froze her bare toes, which were no longer happy in their Dolce & Gabbana sandals. "The price we pay for fucking beauty," she muttered as she finally reached the avenue. A pack of cars were headed her way, and seeing the white light of an available cab, she thrust up her fist.

The cab cut across two lanes and screeched to a stop in front of her, just as she noticed a man up the avenue bolting toward it.

"It's mine, buddy," she said, stumbling in her heels as she reached for the door.

He dove in front of her, banging his hand over the door handle. "I've been waiting five minutes, and I'll be damned if you're going to . . ."

The familiar voice made Maggie pull back reflexively. Max. Dammit!

"Oh, Maggie. I guess we can share," he said, as if it were this magnanimous gesture. It was her cab! He pulled open the door and stepped aside as she climbed in and hobbled across the back seat. It wasn't so easy to slide in suede.

As Max dropped in, she gave the driver her address and folded her arms. Geez, did this mean they had to talk? The last thing she needed was one of Max's diatribes.

"You know," he said, "I offered to share with you. You don't have to be so petulant."

"I'm not petulant," she said, refusing to look at him as she rubbed her arms. "I'm tired."

"Tired? Or is that just an excuse because you didn't score tonight?"

She shook her head. "You know, Max? I don't have to like you. It wasn't a requirement for being on your show—thank God! You can't make me like you, and anything you say now is only going to make me dislike you more."

"Then I don't have much to lose, do I? Because quite frankly I don't see where you come off acting like a total bitch with me. What, do I bring out the worst in you? Why do your claws emerge whenever I'm around?"

"Grrr." she growled. "Maybe it's your animal magnetism." Ha!

"I just don't get you, Maggie. You know, when I first read the three essays on your application, yours was the one that really grabbed me. It was *you* who got the three of you on the show."

Well, that's rich, since I wrote all fucking three of them! she stewed. But she wouldn't say it. She refused to look at him, and she wasn't going to encourage him to vent. Not about her!

"I know you can be a decent person," he went on. "I've seen the video of you when I'm not around, and I know that you are a true and loyal friend. But what is it about me that brings out the bitch in you, can you tell me that? What is it?"

She turned to him and grabbed the lapels of his leather jacket. "It's chemistry, okay? Some kind of weird, fucked-up chemistry between us!"

There was shock in his eyes . . . shock and something else she couldn't quite decipher. His nose was an inch from hers, his breath warm on her face. She could see the little stubble of his beard as she pressed forward and . . .

POW!

They were kissing. *Ohmigod. Oh, God. Oh, oh, no, no . . . not this.*

Her heart was pounding, thrumming in her chest, overwhelming every cell in her body. It pounded, pounded, not from the realization that she was about to disqualify herself from winning a million dollars. Not from caffeine or MSG or forty minutes on the Stairmaster. No, it was from Max. His touch. The chemistry. His kiss.

Oh, shit!

43

"So . . . this is your room?" Apple said as Jeremy gave her the grand tour of the hotel room's sitting area, the closets, the bathroom, and the king-size bed. She toyed with the ice-bucket tongs, intrigued by the dynamic between them. For the first time, she felt as if she had the upper hand in a relationship. It was nice to be in control.

"Right," he said, leaning against the bar. "Hard to believe that a half-baked racing team would be put up in such swell lodgings in North America's off-season, isn't it? But some wealthy heiress wants us here to pander for her Christmas party. Seems we're to be the party favors, and we've no choice but to make an appearance as this unnamed heiress provides a good deal of financial support for our crew." He gestured toward the tongs in her hand. "Are you planning to use those, or do you have a secret obsession for sharp objects?"

She laughed, placing the tongs on the bar. "Am I making you nervous?"

"It's not you; it's me." He slid his hand across the bar until his fingers touched hers and started a gentle climb up her arm. "The thing is, I'm saving myself for the right girl, and I don't usually make it a practice of inviting young women up to my room. Don't want to mislead you." He was up to her neck, beginning to touch her hair, the cascade of ringlets. "I do want you to know I have a strict moral code."

"I guess I shouldn't have come up here," she said, "because I can't be trusted. Men have accused me of being wild and salacious." She ran her fingers over the line of his jaw, loving the feelings that suffused her body. Warmth. Want. Power.

The air around them was charged with energy as she leaned forward and pressed her lips to his. Jeremy was delicious, but the vibe was different from the usual dynamic when she was with men. Instead of feeling dwarfed by him, he made her feel wild and dangerous, as if she was the potent force here.

Apple liked the power. She liked it so much, she decided to press her body against his and deepen the kiss. A very dangerous move. The power surged between them.

"You're going to take advantage of me," he said. "Aren't you?"

She ran her hands over his shoulders and back, loving the feel of her partner. "Only if you want me to."

"Making me beg?" he whispered, kissing her neck. "Okay, I want it. I want you, Apple."

She closed her eyes and sucked in a deep breath, loving the power. The power was hers; she had always possessed it. How had she missed that before?

Amazing, the power of a kiss, Maggie thought as Max gave his address to the driver, who sped on without turning onto Maggie's street. Somehow one kiss had turned into twenty. One kiss had brought down the walls between them, leaving them vulnerable and honest with each other.

"God I hate you," she whispered, nipping at his ear. "How I've hated you all these weeks."

"Only because I can see what everyone else misses," he said. "I know you, Maggie. I know your flaws and your excesses and your big mouth and your little bursts of enthusiasm. I see the good and the bad and I want you the way you are."

"No way! I hate you."

"You hated that you couldn't have me."

She ran a hand over his thigh and ventured between his legs, loving the tightness there. "Okay, okay, Mr. I-know-everything. I am dying to get in your bloomers. Why are we going to your place?"

"Because I don't want to be caught by Boone now or in the morning," he said, slipping a hand under her coat to elicit tender sensations from her breast. "I sent him to your apartment, thinking you'd hook up with one of the Australian guys."

"You bastard!" She pressed her teeth into his neck. "You are so evil!"

"And you love it."

"I do," she admitted, hitching up her skirt and swinging around to straddle him in the cab. "I do."

"Hey, keep your pants on," he said, kissing his way down to the hollow between her breasts. "I'm not one of those exhibitionists."

"Okay, okay," she said, grinding against him, "just a little lap dance till we get there."

He leaned his head back, smiling. "You are too much."

"You love it," she said, leaning her face down to his. "Shut up and kiss me again."

They kissed in the elevator on the way up to his floor, then he lifted her off her feet and carried her down the hall, nearly falling into his apartment.

"Don't drop me!" she murmured as he kicked the door closed and pulled open her coat to dip inside.

They tore at each other's clothes, kissing and nibbling and laughing as they stumbled into the hall. "Where's the fucking bed?" she asked, passing the living room and kitchen. "Where's your bedroom?"

"Don't tell me you need a bed. Maggie McGee does it in bed?" he asked as he ran his hands up and down the curves of her bare waist. "How mundane. Don't tell the other editors at *Metro.*"

"Fuck *Metro.* And I was thinking of you, Max. Don't want to injure your sorry ass when I pummel you into the ground."

"There's that mouth again." He pulled her against him and she thrilled to the hard-on that pressed into her. "Such nasty words coming out of this succulent, kissable mouth."

He pressed his mouth against hers, stealing her breath away with his gentle, moist attack. Oooh! He was good. Way too good. She couldn't stand it. She had to rub against him, had to have him inside her. Holding onto his shoulders, she hoisted herself up, and nudged her wetness against him. That did it.

"Ugh . . ." he moaned, cupping her buttocks to hold her there.

She reached between them and nudged his cock to the right spot. They both moaned as he slid in.

"Oh! This is so good!" she said, rocking on him. "I've never fucked someone I hated so much."

"Oh, Maggie . . ." His eyes rolled back. "You have such a way with words. And your pussy feels so good."

"Now who's doing the nasty words?" she said as she rocked on him, her muscles and nerves and hormones singing in glee. Doing the nasty with Max. Un-fucking-believable.

44

It was all so civilized, so incredibly decent that Chandra felt as if she were dating a protocol officer instead of a real man. When she arrived at Reg's hotel, she had been allowed up to his suite only after careful screening from his "security personnel," two indifferent men with shaved heads and cynical eyes.

"But I'm his fiancée," she said as they insisted on frisking her. "I was just with him at the dinner party. Don't you remember me?"

"We can't be too careful," one of the men claimed as he patted down her hips.

Inside, Reg seemed tired and distracted. "Chandra, dear, you shouldn't have come," he said. "There's no privacy here." He kissed her hand, adding between gritted teeth, "I'm sorry to say you cannot stay, and even a moment alone is out of the question." He turned to the sitting area, where a man was seated beside the table, earphone dangling over his shoulder. "Trevor will be with me through the night."

"What's wrong?" Chandra asked. "Has there been a breach of security? Some threat?"

"No, no, just the usual measures," he said. "Trevor felt that the party was growing too unstable, too high a risk, so I had to depart. I do hope you enjoyed yourself."

Chandra bit her lower lip, still not convinced of the need for the sudden security measures. "So your departure had nothing to do with the unexpected arrival of the woman claiming to be my mother?"

Reg's face tensed, though his eyes never moved from her face. "Yes, what was that about? I didn't have a chance to catch it all."

Chandra took a deep breath. "The woman was a stranger to me, too, but I do believe she is my birth mother. I was raised by my grandmother, and my mother has not had any contact with me since I was an infant. Until tonight."

He nodded, his eyes sharp with concern. "I see."

"I was not a child of privilege. My mother gave me up to my grandmother in Queens, who found work cleaning people's houses. Everything I have came through hard work, not inheritance. I've never talked about it much because I've always been ashamed of my background, and quite sure I could overcome my past through hard work. But tonight I learned that you can't run from who you are. You can't obliterate the past."

"Indeed." Reg smiled. "You are a woman of character, Chandra." He slid an arm over her shoulder and guided her to the door. "I'm glad to know the real you. I wish you could stay, but it seems that I've got to put up with Trevor baby-sitting me while I'm here in New York."

"I understand," she said, though she didn't. She sensed Reg's distance and had hoped that her admission would close the gap, but instead she now felt farther away from him . . . far away and drifting by the moment.

"Good night," he said, forcing a smile.

You bastard, she thought. *You can't take the bad with the good. One little ripple in the pond and you're racing for the safety of shore.* Her feelings were strong, but she wasn't in the mood to stage a futile argument.

"Good night," she said. "And good-bye."

Apple couldn't believe where this was heading. He had touched her in a most intimate way, his lips on her, his tongue massaging her sweet spot until she'd exploded from within, gasping in ecstasy and surprise.

He had made her come!

When was the last time she climaxed with a man? She could barely remember. Christ, was it back in college? Not that it mattered as she'd stretched out naked across the bed, her hair falling over the side, her nails digging into the smooth cotton sheets as his mouth made magic. At the moment of climax she had called out in ecstasy; then she burst out laughing.

He'd risen, kneeling before her, confused as he wiped his hand over his chin. "I must say, I've elicited a variety of responses in my day, but none so hysterical."

"I'm just so happy," she said, still shaking. "So happy to come."

"Oh, right, then." He smiled, the look in his eyes still tentative. "If you're happy, I'm happy, too."

And now she was riding Jeremy, her legs straddling him on the bed, easing up and down in an excruciatingly delicious rhythm. It was going to happen again, she could feel the swell inside her, the ever-heightened sensations. He was moaning now, and she knew he was close to a climax, too. Maybe they could come together.

She rode him, rocking the bed, breathless and expectant. "I'm going to come," she whispered, not breaking the rhythm. "I'm going to . . ." He growled and she screamed with abandon as they ventured to a place Apple hadn't visited for way too long.

It was good to be back.

45

"Any messages for me?" Chandra said the next morning as she breezed past Vincent's desk. She'd had a rough night, sure that Reg would call her to offer some explanation or apology or clarification, but the phone had remained silent.

She had lain awake, thinking of her tenuous future and her mother's poor timing, but her tortured thoughts had let her only to anguish until she'd finally popped two Tylenol PM at one in the morning and eventually dozed off.

Vincent glanced at his PC screen and frowned. "It's not yet eight-thirty, but no, there have not been any calls for you this morning."

She let out her breath, unbuttoning her black cashmere coat. "Oh, okay." Walking into her office, she felt unsettled. This thing with Reg was undermining her usual composure. She said good morning to Mule, who put down his bagel and began filming. Usually she kicked him out, but this morning she didn't even have the aplomb to manage that.

"What seems to be the problem?" Vincent asked, following her into her office. "If I may so rudely ask."

Chandra pressed her lips together, and then decided to spill. Okay, it was probably unprofessional, but aside from her girlfriends Vincent was one of her most trusted and loyal confidantes. "I'm not sure whether Reg and I are still engaged." She hung her coat in the closet, then closed the door, her eyes going to the marquis diamond sparkling on her left hand. She shook her head. "I just don't know how he feels . . . or how I feel."

"I see." He glanced through a stack of folders in his arms and handed one of them to her. "You may want to base your decision regarding the marriage on this report. I've compiled a summary of the reasons Grayrock should not proceed with the acquisition of Gem, Inc. There were inconsistencies and omissions in the data supplied by Mr. Pringle's company."

"Inconsistencies?" Chandra opened the folder, wondering why she didn't get an inkling of this when she went over the early numbers.

"Gem, Inc. has liabilities that were held off the balance sheet," Vincent said. "Turns out they have been cited in export violations by the government of South Africa on numerous occasions. There's also the issue of failure to pay export taxes, as well as suspected smuggling and black-market activity."

"Slave wages . . ." Chandra's pulse quickened as she read on. "They've been paying slave wages in the mines, despite protective labor laws? Oh, Lord, this is a can of worms. Not even worms . . . snakes! I would hate myself if we . . ." Her voice trailed off as the magnitude of this possible mistake hit her. It was an offense to her personal ethics, not to mention the mission of Grayrock.

"If the deal goes through, Grayrock stands to lose millions," Vincent went on. "And the damage would not end there, as we would risk losing many of our shareholders who would disapprove of . . ."

"I know, I know, you're right," Chandra said, still stung by the realization that Reg had tried to cheat her. "You're sure this information is accurate?"

Vincent nodded, his dark eyes sober. "Absolutely. I've had it verified by two outside sources."

"Okay, then." Chandra flipped the report closed and sat down at her computer. "I've got to e-mail the top-tier executives right away." She clicked on her address book and started highlighting names.

"I'm sorry," Vincent said.

"Don't be," Chandra said as her fingers flew over the keyboard. As she typed she thought of the many distractions that had taken her away from her work lately. There was Reg and the show and Apple's breakdown. If her head had been in the right place, she would have picked up on these discrepancies before the situation was so far advanced. Instead, she'd fallen for Reg, fallen into a daze. She finished the memo, read it to Vincent, then clicked on SEND.

"There, that will alert everyone. Next, I'm going to go from office to office with your file. People need to see the details in black and white; they need to have these numbers in their face before lunchtime. Maybe if we work fast, we can get the lawyers to draw up a severance agreement to present to Reg at this afternoon's meeting."

She grabbed Vincent's folder and pushed out of her chair. "You're due for a big promotion," she told him sincerely. "This was excellent work."

"I was only doing my job," he said humbly.

Always so low key. He didn't want the praise, but Chandra was grateful to Vincent for saving her career and her soul. So grateful that she reached out and hugged him. "Thank you," she said, pressing her face against the shoulder of his crisp, dark blue shirt.

His arms rested lightly on her back, but suddenly an alarm sounded in her head. Breach of protocol! EEOC complaint! Lawsuit! This was not behavior condoned in Grayrock's employee relations manual.

But a second alarm sounded, surprising her even more. Vincent felt . . . lovely. Lovely to be in his arms. Like a sighing wind over a river.

She pulled away, trying to read his face but seeing his usual neutral expression. "Well, then, I'd better head upstairs and get this file to everyone." She wondered if there was more she should say, but couldn't bear to prolong this awkward moment. Wondering what had possessed her to touch him, she turned away and headed out of her office.

That was when she noticed Mule filming from the couch by the window. Oh, damn it. Caught on tape.

Well, right now *Big Tease* was the least of her worries. She had to save Grayrock from her humongous mistake, and maybe, in the process, she'd be able to salvage her own career. Just maybe.

46

Max couldn't believe it had happened. Maggie was here, in his arms, in his bed, in his life.

He would never forget the way she'd woken him this morning, the incredible warmth of her mouth on him, working him up to a frenzy before she straddled him. Light streamed in from the edges of the shades, pale winter light, just enough to warm the angles of Maggie's body as she rode him like a wild cowgirl. "Woo-hoo!" she'd squealed, reaching back to smack his thigh. "At last I have a chance to wallop you!"

That had been their first encounter of the morning, their third since she'd come home with him last night. Man. His cojones were so fried at the network. He'd broken all the rules, but if it meant being with Maggie, he didn't care. She was amazing, outrageous, brash and loud. But he'd known that all along, watching her these weeks. He'd known he loved her long before she kissed him.

Right now Maggie's head lay on his chest as his breathing began to even out. He stroked her dark hair, twisting it over her neck and shoulder. She wore this little white lace camisole thingie that was an incredible aphrodisiac as it revealed her taut, dark nipples when they were erect. Which seemed to happen whenever he rubbed his fingertips over them. "I can't believe this," he said. "I can't believe we're together."

"Tell me about it," she said. "The most unlikely couple to succeed. I was always so sure you hated me. How come you acted that way? Always pissed. Always walking away during my interviews, acting like my personal feelings were so unimportant."

"I had to get out," Max admitted. "I had to leave the room, get myself far away. I couldn't stand to hear you talking about having sex with another guy. God, that tore me up. It was so bizarre, as if I had any right to care. But it killed me, thinking of you with someone else, knowing they were so wrong for you."

"Max . . ." Maggie purred. "That is so damned sweet."

"I don't think you were thinking 'sweet' at the time," he said. "I still haven't gotten the stains out of those pants you doused. My gray flannels."

"Oh, poor baby." She leaned up and kissed his chin, then nuzzled into the hollow of his neck.

God, she was incredible. A real handful, but the payoff was worth every moment of torment and anguish Maggie had put him through. He wanted to possess her, to thrill her, to argue with her, and to have wild sex with her. He wanted to keep her in his life, although he hadn't quite figured that one out yet.

The phone rang and Max groaned.

"Don't answer it," Maggie said.

He glanced over at the caller ID box. It was Boone. "I have to take this one. No, stay," he said, keeping her head pressed to his chest as he scooted across the bed to reach the phone. He pressed the cordless phone to his ear and answered, "Hey, Boone."

"Max, I'm at Maggie's and there's no sign of her," Boone said as Maggie reached under the sheet to stroke his cock.

"*Mmm* . . ." Max closed his eyes, trying to concentrate. He couldn't let on to Boone that he was with a woman . . . especially since that woman was Maggie. But the way she was touching him . . .

"She never came home last night," Boone said as Max sucked in his breath and glared at Maggie. She pulled her hand away with a grin, slipped out of bed and headed down the hall to bang around in the kitchen.

"Coffee?" she called as Max covered the mouthpiece of the phone with one hand.

"In the fridge," he answered as Boone went on.

"There are no signs of life this morning. I don't even think she's in there. Must have gone off with one of those guys, just like you thought."

"Right." Max could see her down the hall, leaning against the kitchen counter, stretching up into the cabinets to search for coffee filters. She wore only that lace thingie on top and skimpy white G-string underwear on the bottom, revealing more than a handful of round, succulent butt. To see that sensual beauty slinking over his mundane kitchen counter . . . Max had to turn away before he lost his train of thought again.

"What do you want me to do?" Boone asked.

"I don't know . . ." Max rubbed the stubble on his chin. "What time is it? Is it cold out? How long have you been waiting?"

"Ten-thirty. A little nippy but no wind today. I've been here for about an hour."

"Look . . . I'm running a little late today, but I'll see if I can track her down."

"Should I hang here?"

"I don't know. You want to head back to the studio?"

Silence. Boone hated being off his assignment. "Naw, I'll wait here awhile, see if she shows."

"Whatever. Okay, I'll check in with you by noon and we'll plan from there." As he hung up, Maggie darted across the room and jumped up on the bed.

She thrust her hands in the air and did a little dance atop the quilt. "You've got to track down Maggie! You've got to track down Maggie!" Her face was alight with mischief as she dropped down on her knees beside him.

"You were listening to my phone call."

"Oh, your job is so hard!" she taunted him. "How long are you going to make Boone suffer out in the cold?"

"Hey, I feel bad about lying to him. He's a great employee."

"Of course he is. Love the Boonster."

"And we've got a show to film." The show. Shit. He knew

something was hanging over him, bearing down on him. "Which leads me to the plan." He took her hand and squeezed it, memorizing the trusting look in her wide, dark eyes. He had a feeling she wasn't going to like his strategy, but there was no way around it. "I'm thinking that you can't afford to give up *Big Tease* at this point. I mean, you just lost your job, and although I know I'm irresistible and everything, I'm thinking that you should go back home right now and we can pretend this never happened. I'm willing to keep the secret."

"You are, are ya?" She swung her knee over his hips so that she was straddling him again. God, he couldn't have this conversation with her wet folds pressing against him. "Well, you big beef jerky, you may be willing to stage a ruse, but not I. I'd rather blow the show and stay under the covers with you." She leaned down to lick one of his nipples, adding, "Or I could blow you *and* blow the show. How's that for a full day?"

"Ugh . . . Maggie, stop." He touched her shoulders and she lifted her head. "I need to get to work."

"Don't mind me. I'll just wait here till you get home, being unemployed and everything. Maybe I'll be able to figure out where you keep your coffee mugs by the time you get back."

He sat up, shifting her off his hips so that she was kneeling in the bed quilt. She looked so sexy and vulnerable in that white thingy with the quilt bunched between her smooth legs that he had to turn away and pull on his boxers. He hated himself for what he had to do. If only there were another way . . .

He turned back, steeling himself. "You'd better go."

"No way. I'm parking it here, buddy."

"I can't let you throw it all away."

"For what, a million dollars? It's just a show."

"It's important," Max argued. "Important for your future. I'm not going to stand in your way. Right now you need the show."

"Screw the show," she said, her voice revealing her rising emotion. "I don't need it."

He turned away to pull on his jeans, then went to the closet for a sweater. God, she was making this so difficult. Sheer torture. He didn't want to be a bastard, but she was painting him into a corner. When he turned back, she was still poised on the bed, but her composure was cracking. She nibbled on the cuticle of her thumb.

"You're still here?" he asked.

"Yes, and I hate you again."

"That was inevitable."

"Are you always this schizoid?"

Only when I fall in love, he thought, though he couldn't say it. He picked up her lavender suede skirt from the floor and handed it to her.

She snatched it away from him indignantly. "You know, I should have stuck with my first instincts about you. I knew you were a prick."

He didn't answer. He couldn't. He could barely keep himself from stepping forward and yanking away the skirt and pulling her back into bed. Instead, he just shoved his hands into the pockets of his jeans and disappeared into the other room to let her get dressed.

Halfway down the hall, he heard her shout: "I hate you! I really hate you."

Join the club, he thought. *At the moment, I hate myself.*

47

Maggie cried all the way home on the subway, and she didn't even care when an old woman cast her a look of pity.

Yes, it's awful and I am pathetic! She wanted to say. *I'm in love and he kicked me out . . . kicked me out while the bed was still warm. Oh, jeez, it's too awful.*

As she walked up her street, she saw Boone waiting on the steps of her brownstone. Of course, of course, insult to injury.

"Hey, Maggie." He winced when he caught sight of her face. He looked down at his camera, tentative. "What do you want to do?"

She pulled her coat closer around her and looked down at her gorgeous heels. Her toes were freezing again. "Okay, Boone, why don't you come upstairs and we'll do a quick interview. Then I need a shower. Desperately. Can I do that alone, please?"

"Aw, Maggie, you know I try to stay out of your face."

"I know, Boone." She walked past him and started up the stairs. "Come on."

Inside her apartment she paused in front of the mirror, noticing the dark smudges of mascara under her eyes. "That's what you get when you cry on the damned subway." She tried to rub the black smears away, then realized it was useless. She needed a good steam cleaning to purge herself of the pain.

But first . . . the interview. Sitting on the sofa, she crossed her legs and leaned back to admire her Dolce & Gabbana shoes. The damned beautiful shoes had been her downfall. If she'd had sensible shoes on she could have run to the cab long before Max showed up. Tears stung her eyes, surprising her, as she thought she'd gotten all that out on the damned subway ride. "Okay, Boone, I guess you want to know where I've been all night. That being the night I went to a party at Tavern on the Green with a well-known hockey player and left the party alone. Well, I left alone but then on the street I ran into . . ."

What could she say? She was willing to tell all and disqualify herself from the show, but wouldn't that put Max out of a job, too? If she really cared about him, she couldn't do that to him. She had to go down on her own stinking sinking ship.

"Truth is, I met up with someone I've known awhile and we shared a cab. And during the ride we discovered that . . . that there's this amazing chemistry between us." She shook her head. "It's the sort of thing that I've been writing about in *Metro* for years. *Lust Plus!* and *Finding the Hottie Who Can Heat Up Your Bed AND Warm Your Heart!* The attraction between us was intense. It was . . ."

Suddenly she couldn't squeeze words past the knot in her throat.

She thought of the look in Max's eyes—the shock when she kissed him, the torment when she touched him, the love as she held him.

The love.

No matter what he said, despite his denials, they had connected. Together they were the best combination of physical attraction and intellectual stimulation one could imagine.

Maggie's voice was hoarse as she choked out the words, "I think I fell in love." Then she was sobbing, shaking with emotion. Leaning over the pillow, she buried her face in her hands and cried.

A moment later, Boone was at her side, handing her a tissue like an awkward older brother. "You okay, Maggie?"

She lifted her head and sobbed, then noticed that he'd turned off the camera. "Oh, Boone!" was all she could say as he patted her shoulder awkwardly.

Apple bit her lip as the name flashed on her caller ID: Greer, Nancy.

Nancy Greer? The art dealer, calling her? How could that be?

She picked up the phone. "Apple Sommers."

"Apple, hi! Nancy Greer, here, from the Greer Gallery. I don't think we've met, but I saw your work on *Big Tease* and I find it utterly intriguing. I'd love to arrange a show for you, if you don't have representation. When are you available to meet so that I can go over your work?"

And just like that, Apple had a date with an art dealer.

"And not just any art dealer," Apple told Jeremy that afternoon as they walked through the Village to meet his friends for coffee at Café Reggio. "Nancy Greer has an amazing reputation for getting collectors interested in the work hanging in her gallery. She's a dealer who also knows how to sell."

"That's fantastic!" Jeremy said as she paused to take some shots of the Christmas trees leaning sadly against the brick wall outside a flower shop. Waiting beside her, Jeremy seemed to muse over the camera crew shooting them from a respectable distance away. "Can they hear what we're saying? Is everything we say going to air on television?"

"Not necessarily," Apple said, glancing back at Suki and Lucy. "It's edited down, so you might not make it past the cutting room floor."

"Interesting." He swung back toward Apple. "But that's not to diminish your fabulous news, your rise to artist's stature. You know it only confirms my idea that you must come back to Australia with me. This is your chance to explore something totally different. You can't imagine the images you'll find there; the creatures and the landscape are quite a departure from the sights of Manhattan."

"I'm sure it's wonderful," she said, imagining Jeremy on a dusty plain, "but I can't afford a trip like that right now."

"What's to afford? I've got enough air miles to send myself to the Moon time and again, and you're welcome to have them. And once there my parents would be happy to put you up at their ranch. They raise sheep. Not nearly as warm and fuzzy as it seems, but it does stave off the creditors."

"I don't know . . ." Apple said, barely noticing the traffic that whizzed down Seventh Avenue as they waited for a light to change. She didn't want to be under any man's thumb, not anymore. "We just met, and you're going to put me up? How do you know I'm not a lunatic?"

"If you turn crazy, we can put you out with the sheep," he said, smiling. "Think about it."

"I will," she said, glancing over to Sheridan Square, scene of Teague's crime. No, she wasn't going to let him ruin the Village for her. Maggie had given her that tip: "If you connect every landmark to a bad relationship, you'll never be able to leave home!"

Jeremy stopped at a street vendor to check out some sunglasses; then they moved onto Waverly Place where a trio was playing Christmas music. Apple lifted her camera, taking shots of the tinsel star hanging from an apartment window, an American flag made out of Christmas lights, a man in a watch cap walking a dog wearing booties, a girl in oversized hip-hop clothes bouncing a rubber ball alone on the playground. Manhattan was fertile ground for a photographer, but maybe it would be good to explore some place completely different.

She changed focus to catch faces in the crowd around the musicians. The relaxed stance of an elderly man. The full smile of a mother pushing a stroller. A pompous scowl . . .

A scowl she knew too well. Pulling back, she saw that it was Teague arm-in-arm with a well-known actress—a woman who was about a head taller than Teague. Apple wanted to laugh, but she restrained herself long enough to get a few shots.

She was lowering the camera as Teague noticed her, his irritation obvious. *Hmm . . .* was that actress still married?

Fury burned in his eyes, but she simply smiled as she swept

past him. "Maybe you'll see yourself on Page Six again," Apple told Teague, turning away from his look of disgust.

As she headed to the café with Jeremy, she laughed. Was that the man she found intimidating? That fat moosh ball? Well, she'd managed to break his spell. She no longer needed approval from Teague or from her father or from any man.

Independence day in December. Why not?

As Maggie handed the shopping bags into the coat check at O'Neill's she felt pleased that she'd made good use of her first full day of unemployment. With no money coming in, she'd managed to spend more than two hundred dollars on gifts and ornaments and candles at the Christmas store in Bloomies. Not to mention that irresistible cosmetic counter downstairs. Damn, unemployment could be dangerous.

But that was where she'd run into Roxanne and Eloise, who insisted they join her for lunch. Glad for the diversion, Maggie had accepted and now she was listening as the hostess suggested various tables in the busy restaurant. "I can't put you at that banquette because the people at the next table would not appreciate your cameraman."

"What are they, mob?" Roxanne asked, squinting into the dim dining room.

"Let's just say they left their spouses at home. How about the round table over there?"

Roxanne nodded. "I guess it will have to do."

"And I'm buying Boone lunch," Maggie said. "It's the least I can do."

"No," Boone said awkwardly, still behind his camera. "You can't."

"I insist!" Maggie said. "You've been traipsing around after me in the cold for weeks. I owe you, big guy."

"Thanks, but no. Really. I can't."

"He really can't," Eloise said as they sat around their table. "My husband works at CBN, too. Not on *Big Tease,* but even so network policy is the law. Maggie, if you buy him something, it could be construed as a bribe to make you look better on the show."

"Well that's just lousy," Maggie said, grabbing an onion roll from the bread basket and popping a piece in her mouth. Hell, with the prospect of kissing on the outskirts, onion rolls were in. "Okay, Boone, I won't mess with your career. You can pay your own tab. But I do recommend the onion rolls."

After the waiter took their order, Roxanne started in with questions about the Australian yacht racing team at last night's party. "They looked so cute, but I didn't get a chance to meet them."

"Hotties, all of them," Maggie said, giving the women a rundown of the crew. "Apple hit it off with Jeremy Tisbane, though I haven't heard the final score on that yet. Of course, there was the mysterious departure of one British financial mogul who shall remain nameless. Again, more on that as it develops. The music was delightful, but the show was definitely stolen by the semisweet chocolate Christmas trees decked with edible ornaments."

"Love the way you sew the evening together," Roxanne said.

"Really, you should apply for that TV columnist spot at the network," Eloise added, tucking into her apple-and-Brie omelet. "You make yet another boring fund-raiser sound like a hootenanny."

Maggie stabbed at her Cobb salad. "I had a great time."

"And she met someone," Boone said. "Tell them."

"Boone! I thought you were supposed to be the anonymous eye?"

"Ooh, do tell!" Roxanne insisted. "Do I know him?"

"I'm not talking about it until . . . until it gels into something worth talking about," Maggie said firmly. "But tell me more about the job at the network. How do you know about it?"

"From Kermit, of course. You remember my husband, the hotshot at CBN? He says that Tell-tale Tina got canned last week, though it's all still very hush-hush. They're looking for a replacement—Dare I say?—gossip columnist? But you put such a positive spin on things, Maggie, you'd be perfect for it. Reporting New York events."

"Really?" Maggie felt her heart race a bit, but she knew better than to enthuse over something that might be out of her reach. Okay, she couldn't help it. A TV columnist? She would give her best Fendi bag for a job like that. "How thrilled would I be to give up writing about orgasms and cheating boyfriends for a gig on TV? It's too exciting. I can barely eat. Okay, maybe just one more bite." She forced herself to sit and chew her salad. This was not the place to break into a happy dance. Besides, the job wasn't hers—yet. And there was still the matter of Max, though landing this gig at CBN might get her out of that pickle jar. If she was employed by the network he wouldn't have to worry about breaking their rules and having it all on his conscience.

"You can't take a job with CBN," Boone piped up. "That would disqualify you from *Big Tease.*"

"Excuse me?" Maggie glared at him. "Anonymous perspective? I love you, Boone, but this is one time you really need to put a cork in it!"

48

I can't believe it's over, Chandra thought. Running on autopilot, she had made it through the meeting with J. Reg Pringle, countering his claims and cutting off his veiled threats with suggestions of countersuits. The outcome was promising, with the top-tier Grayrock executives seemingly relieved, and Reg withdrawing from the proposed deal.

As Chandra sank into her desk chair, she realized her hands were now shaking. It was over, but she was just now beginning to succumb to the incredible stress brought on by this entire fiasco. Across the room, Mule filmed quietly as he snacked on cheese and crackers left over from the meeting. She pressed her hands onto her knees so that he couldn't see them.

It was over, and she had survived. Just barely, but with Vincent's help Grayrock had been saved from making a huge mistake. She recognized Vincent's voice coming down the hall.

". . . although I am not sure if she can see you under—"

"Of course she'll see me," Reg boomed, "she's engaged to marry me." He appeared in the doorway, his head thrown back as if he were a gladiator about to conquer the office. "Chandra." The dark eyes that had once energized her now seemed cold and calculating. "I never expected such underhanded behavior of you."

"Shall I call Security?" Vincent offered.

"Don't be ridiculous!" Reg said, dropping into the chair opposite her desk.

"No, I can handle it," Chandra told Vincent, realizing that this would make two life-altering confrontations in less than twenty-four hours. But at least her hands had stopped shaking. "Tell me, Reg, what do you consider underhanded? The fact that I checked out the reports that were falsified by your staff? Or maybe it was the notion that I refused to lead my corporation into an investment that would have had a devastating impact? Or was I supposed to close my eyes and forge ahead because you and I had a handshake deal?"

"You could have let me know if some of the details didn't check out," Reg said. "Really, I can't be aware of every little mistake my people make."

"These were not little, and they weren't mistakes," Chandra insisted. "Your people intentionally misled us into believing that Gem, Inc. was a thriving operation that complied with local laws and regulations. Without going into the details you prefer to overlook, it's neither of those things."

"Oh, stop being condescending, I know damned well what's going on at Gem," Reg said, folding his arms. "I thought you were intelligent enough to realize it long ago, but I supposed I overestimated you. Of course, it's over between us. I could never marry a woman who backed out of a business deal. Imagine what it says of your character?"

His words were infuriating, but Chandra wasn't going to let him get to her. "My character?" She lifted her chin. "Right. Trustworthy. Loyal. Hard-working."

"You backed out of a deal!"

"You misrepresented an entire corporation," she countered. "Come on, Reg, did you really expect me to close my eyes on this one? Do you realize some of your employees could be jailed for these practices?" With some satisfaction, she noticed a muscle in his jaw twitch; good, she was getting to him. He probably didn't fancy life behind bars, slopping up the floors and dining on prison gruel.

"Well, it's hardly a pity as the wedding would have been called off, anyway." He rose, straightening his impeccably smooth navy suit jacket and swinging around to grin one last time. "I would never marry into trash."

"Neither would I." Anger seethed inside her as she grasped the fat diamond on her left hand. She slid the ring off and tossed it at Reg, who didn't have the grace to catch it. It bounced from the lapel of his jacket onto the floor, where he scrambled to pick it up. It gave her some satisfaction, watching him fumble on the floor.

"Go on, fob your ring off on some other fool. It probably came from the back of the slaves at Gem, Inc. anyway."

He straightened and dangled the ring in front of her. "That was good enough for you at one time, though, wasn't it?"

"Get out!" She searched her desk for something heavy to fling at him, but she didn't want to risk breaking the alabaster clock she'd discovered during an antiquing expedition. Instead, she swung round and chased him to the door. "Get out, and don't ever come near these offices again." Although her voice sounded strong and steady, she was shaking inside as she turned away and leaned against the doorjamb. How could he fall so low? How was it that a man who had seemed like the perfect mate turned out to be a hurtful, heinous beast?

She collapsed in her chair and let the tears stream down her cheek. This was so unprofessional. She had never cried at work, but with Reg she had made the mistake of combining work with her personal life and . . .

And there was Mule across the room, capturing her humiliation on film for posterity. Lord, her life was a mess! She buried her face in her hands and let out a sob.

"Let me close the door." She recognized Vincent's voice and his light shuffle on the carpet.

She grabbed a tissue and pressed it against her face. "This is so embarrassing."

"I am sorry," Vincent said. "I apologize for the fact that things went so badly. I should not have allowed the man access to these premises."

"No, no, it's not your fault." Swallowing hard, Chandra waved the tissue at him. "If it weren't for you, we'd be deep into the Gem deal." She could feel her emotions swelling again, her voice rising for no good reason. "No, you've done fabulous work, Vincent. You always have. Things worked best in this department when we were a team, the two of us."

"Yes, yes . . ." Vincent's dark eyes seemed distressed, but he quickly glanced away from her. "Yes, I must admit, I would like to be on your team. I would like to be on your team all the time. What I am trying to say . . . *uh!*" He covered his face with his hands.

Chandra dabbed at the tears, trying to focus on him. She'd never seen Vincent so uncomfortable.

He shook his head and sighed. "Once again I must apologize. That was totally out of line. And also corny. I am far too melodramatic."

"What are you talking about?" Chandra paused as a tiny door opened and a glimmer of light trickled through. Vincent. Of course. He was attracted to her. *Duh!* Sweet, composed, repressed Vincent. She had always known he guarded his feelings and complexities; there was so much that he hid from the world.

A calm stole over her as she rose and went around the desk to him. His eyes were squeezed shut, as if he couldn't bear to witness her reaction. How exquisite his cheekbones, how lovely the mocha shadows of his face. He flinched as she took his hand tentatively in hers. "Vincent . . . we are a team, aren't we?"

He opened his eyes, his jaw working as he tried to form the words. "I have always wished it would be so. It was a dream of mine, a foolish dream that snowballed as we became more and more accustomed to working together. So many moments when I should have kept my mind in my work, but instead I let my thoughts venture off until they became a jumble of romantic notions. I didn't intend for it to happen, Chandra, but somehow I allowed myself to fall in love with you."

"No, I've been the fool." Her throat tightened as tears threatened again. "You've been here all along, by my side, but I've never seen you clearly. I was the fool." Chandra was trying hard to maintain a professional demeanor but her need for him was so overwhelming that she had to step forward and hold him, pressing her face against his, feeling the protective cover of his arms.

She needed him in her life. She wanted him in her life. She wanted to be with him, to explore the man she knew so little about.

He kissed her cheek, rocking her in his arms. "It's been torture seeing you with him," he whispered. "You are a far better person than he is. You have a conscience and a soul."

A conscience . . . that reminded her of Grayrock's policy on dating coworkers. "We may have to convince the people in HR to rewrite that chapter on internal fraternization." She sunk her fingers in his rich dark hair, loving the silky feel of it.

"We'll work on that." He kissed her brow, her cheek . . . the side of her neck. "We'll address that policy just as soon as we go over the monthly status reports."

"Mmm . . ." She leaned her head back as he kissed the tender spot behind her ear. The conversation served as an aphrodisiac, and she wondered if she and Vincent would ever be able to leave the office at the end of the day. "Now that the Gem deal is off we need to explore international expansion again. Maybe we should investigate some new territories . . ."

"Yes, I've noticed some areas that deserve attention," he whispered. "A few territories are quite ripe for exploration . . ."

49

Although hot toddies in the Oak Bar at the Plaza were a Christmas Eve tradition for the three friends, Maggie wasn't sure she could go through with it this year without breaking down under the mistletoe and crying in her Cosmo. In the past few days she'd turned her life inside out and upside-down, taking a new job, disqualifying herself from *Big Tease,* and shedding her "temporary celebrity" status for, what she hoped would become, a long-term celeb thing on the air as CBN's new tattler on *Connecting with Maggie.* The wheels of fortune and fame had turned for Maggie McGee; it was the wheel of love that had broken off its axle.

But she pasted herself together and decked her body in Christmasy red velvet, trying to rise to the occasion. She'd thought it would help to have one of the adorable Kate Spade bags that she'd been provided by the show (FREE, as long as she wore it on the air once—such a deal!), but despite the halls decked in red, gold and green, she felt totally blue.

"It's about time!" Apple called, waving her through the crowd to where the two women sat at a round table, the object of Suki's camerawork, while Lucy Ng leaned against the wall of the bar, toying with her flowing red scarf as she talked to two men. "Sit your butt down and give us the update, Mags! Do you still have deadlines? Less writing, right? How are the hours?"

"I hope your boss is nicer than Candy," Chandra said as Maggie sat down.

"Bitch!" Chandra and Apple said together.

"My new boss is a man named Harv," Maggie said, trying to make the most of things. She could do this, right? She wasn't going to let a man ruin her good time with her friends. "He's a sweetheart. Bald and married and so interested in everyone and everything in a genuine way. What a difference. He's a pleasure to work for." She ordered a Cosmo, then looked from Apple to Chandra. "But don't get me started on the boring stuff. Tell me what's been going on with you guys? Who are you spending Christmas with?"

"I'll be with Vincent," Chandra said. "We're just going out to dinner if anyone wants to join us."

"Right," Maggie said. "Tag along with the love birds."

"You're welcome to come," Chandra insisted.

"Nope. Wouldn't want to interrupt your plans for that house in the suburbs and the two point five kids. Little Vince on the soccer team. Baby Chandra taking tap." When Chandra pursed her lips, Maggie squealed. "No way! Tell me you're not already talking marriage."

"Maybe a little." Chandra shrugged. "We've known each other for more than a year, so it's as if a lot of the preliminaries of courtship were covered long ago."

"And you're happy?" Maggie asked as her drink arrived.

"Very. I think he's good for me."

Apple added, "Vincent convinced Chandra to give her birth mother another chance. I think it's nuts. Who needs family?"

"But I'm open to it," Chandra said. "Not that we have to be friends, but there are some questions that could be answered. It might be helpful for me and for Rhonda."

Maggie hoisted her Cosmo. "Here's to happiness all around." She nearly choked on the words, wondering how she'd turned into such a mush ball. Somehow the fact that she'd been touched, but briefly, by love had made her more susceptible to sentimental toasts.

"Here, here!" Apple said as they clinked glasses. "Happily ever after!"

"Aren't you chipper?" Maggie tossed back half of the drink, trying to kill the pain. "I take it you're still hooked up with Mr. Aussie?"

Orange curls bobbed as Apple nodded. "I'm going to Australia with Jeremy on New Year's Day. Planning to tour and shoot the landscape, maybe come up with something new for my show at the Greer Gallery."

"What a coup for you, Ap." Maggie touched her friend's elbow. "You really deserved a break. See, something very good came out of the show. With Suki shooting in your studio all the time, she got your work on national television."

"Thank you, Suki!" Chandra said, waving.

"Who knew?" Apple said. "And listen to this, Madame Sexpert." She flashed a huge smile, lowering her voice to add: "I'm having orgasms again. All the time. Jeremy does it for me."

"That's great," Maggie said, wondering if her skin were turning an illustrious shade of telltale green. "Oh, sweetie, that's fab! What a great way to start the new year, coming, coming and going off to Australia."

"So . . . tell us everything," Apple pressed Maggie. "Like . . ." She lowered her voice again, "Has Max called you?"

Maggie felt a knot form in her throat. "Okay, we're not going there, but I will tell you that I have the most wonderful job on the planet, with the freedom to cover any New York event I want, whether it's a Madonna concert or a dinner party or the birth of a baby baboon at the Bronx Zoo. The hours are flexible, the pay is great, the profile huge." There . . . her voice was evening out a bit. Thoughts of the job could definitely perk her up; they just weren't enough to sustain her when she started to think of him. "Oh, and I get to keep wardrobe and the handbags I use on the air, and I make it a point to carry a bag to every event I attend. It's sort of my trademark. Fendis and Pradas and Coach bags in delicious shades of cherry and chocolate and olive."

"Add a shot of vodka and I think you've got a Mexican coffee," Apple joked.

"Love the Kate Spade," Chandra said, lifting the bag off the table.

Apple patted Maggie's hand. "What a great job. It's perfect for you, right?"

Maggie nodded, forcing a smile. "It's wonderful! I'm just so . . ." Her voice cracked with emotion as tears threatened. "I'm just so damned happy!" she blurted out over a sob.

"Oh, shit!" Apple's face scrunched up. "What did we say? I'm so sorry, Mags. Is it about the show?" Chandra fished in her bag and handed Maggie a stack of tissues as Apple babbled on, "Oh, Maggie, do you miss being on *Big Tease?* Are you upset that your show on the same network disqualified you from—"

"She doesn't miss the show," Chandra interrupted. "This is about a man. Maggie's fallen in love."

"Oh, Christ!" Apple lifted her drink. "We'd better order another round. I didn't realize you'd fallen for Max."

"I didn't want to dump on you," Maggie told Apple. "You've been so happy, going around with Jeremy these past few days and I didn't want to complain, but it's true. I actually took the network job purposely. I figured that if I was already disqualified from the show, Max would see that I was free and clear." There was that knot in her throat again. "I thought he'd come running. He didn't. I'm crushed!" she sobbed, pressing the tissues to her eyes. This was going to be murder on her mascara.

"Oh, Maggie," Chandra said, patting her back. "I wish I knew what to tell you. The real thing is painful when it doesn't work out. And I admit, I feel a little guilty for pushing you toward a serious relationship. We pushed, you fell, and now look at you."

"I wish there was something we could do," Apple said helplessly.

"Wishing was what started this," Maggie wept. "That was my big mistake—throwing a coin in the fountain and wishing for love, but forgetting to wish that the guy would love me back."

Suddenly, Chandra dropped her hand away from Maggie's back.

Maggie swallowed hard, trying to catch her breath, "If I could just . . . just . . ."

"Turn around," Apple interrupted her.

"What?" Maggie sucked in a whimpery breath and turned toward the street entrance to the Oak Room.

There he stood, tall, dark and brooding. Max.

"Ohmigod!" It was Max and he was looking at her, his eyes intense, connecting with hers. He was walking toward her. He was taking her by the hand and pulling her into his arms and pressing her lips to hers in the most amazing kiss that . . . *"Mmm."*

In the distance, Maggie heard Chandra say: "Santa Claus is coming to town."

EPILOGUE

Maggie

"And now, live from our Rockefeller Center studios, here's the final episode of *Big Tease!*" the announcer shouted against the rush of applause.

Maggie reached over to the next chair and squeezed Chandra's hand. Thank God, Max had been persuaded to let her appear on the final episode despite the fact that she was no longer a competitor. Jeez, that boy was stubborn as dandruff, but she'd done a little convincing sidework under the sheets to win him over. It helped that she had the network bigwigs behind her, as they wanted to promote their new society columnist whom many had been calling "Midnight Maggie" based on her penchant for late-night parties.

As the stage lights flashed, Maggie felt a surge of excitement. It didn't hurt that Max was crossing the stage in that sexy swagger of his, microphone in hand. After all these weeks with him, she still wanted to get into his boxers. Was that love, or what?

"And tonight," Max was saying, "we are fortunate to have one of the original competitors with us—one of my personal favorites as you may have heard her say, but also a woman who committed a game-show taboo and got herself disqualified."

The audience groaned.

"Oh, as if you didn't already know that," Maggie piped up. "Though I'd like to add that I was happy to place myself out of the running, since it meant accepting a plum job *Connecting* on CBN."

"They call her Midnight Maggie," Max said seductively. "Why . . . I wouldn't know."

Maggie faced the camera and smiled. "What, do I need to make flash cards for you?"

Apple

It was so weird being on the show through a studio feed. She could hear the laughter and roar of the pumped-up New York audience through her earplug, but here in Sydney there was only a quiet studio with Jeremy sitting off-camera beside the sound guy.

Jeremy . . . they'd clocked in some major mileage together. He was the sort of person who needed a project or a quest or a journey every day. Adventure ruled his soul, and Apple enjoyed being along for the ride.

Okay, maybe Jeremy wasn't a forever guy, but he was so sweet and young, and her relationship with him had unlocked the door to outrageous, mind-blowing orgasms, the kind she'd only read about in Maggie's *Metro* articles . . . until Jeremy. He was now pacing at the edge of the curtain of studio light, impatient as always to get on with things, and that was fine with her. They were hoping to catch a train across the outback today, off to Alice Springs, and although Apple didn't know where the trail would lead from there, it wasn't something she needed to worry about anymore. Jeremy smiled, pointed at his watch, then waggled his fingers beside his head and made a face at her.

Apple laughed. Hey, who was to say he wasn't a forever guy? It was too soon to say. For now, he made her laugh, and that was enough to . . .

"Apple!" Max was saying in her earplug. "We're thrilled that you could join us from Down Under. For those of you who have been orbiting in the space station for the past month, Apple followed the intrepid Jeremy Tisbane back to the Australian bush where they've . . . no, Maggie, it's okay to say bush in that context, really!"

Chandra

Oh, please, let it be over, Chandra thought as the studio audience booed yet one more time in response to a videoclip of Reg seductively chewing the engagement olive. It wasn't so much the humiliation of seeing herself smitten by the man; she'd come to see her interlude with Reg as a valuable learning experience, both in business and in love. What Chandra really hated was sitting on this stage like a beauty pageant contestant vying for a crown. Really . . . it was tedious and a little embarrassing.

"And now for the moment we've all been waiting for . . ." Max said theatrically. "The decision of our audience members who have been phoning and e-mailing in their votes for the past two weeks. Let's see the tally board," which was a fake-looking screen with Apple and Chandra's names beside a place for the scores to register. At Max's command, digital numbers flashed and . . .

"Lord . . ." Chandra muttered, through clenched teeth. She was the big-time winner.

"Chandra Hammel is our winner, the woman most worthy of a date on *Big Tease!*" Max shouted as he took Chandra by the hand to center stage and held the mike to her.

"I have to say, I'm surprised," she said. "Especially considering how they hated J. Reginald Pringle."

"Ah, but people we polled told us they were swept away by your romance with Vincent. They swooned over the man some called the 'Bombay Babe' or the 'Indian Love God,' and chicks were taken with the Cinderella appeal of the story, or should I say, 'Cinderfella' with Vincent being the everyday mouse who carried the torch so quietly."

Putting up a hand to shield her eyes, Chandra searched for Vincent backstage. "There he is." She motioned him out, and he crossed the stage reluctantly. She had always been surprised by Vincent's Zen attitude about being videotaped. "I believe my actions are responsible and correct," he had told Chandra, "so having them recorded on tape does not change the integrity of my behavior." Lord, you had to love the guy!

Personally, Chandra was looking forward to having videocams out of her life: to walk down the street alone with Vincent and talk privately, to eat without worrying about spinach sticking in her teeth, to shop in Balducci's without causing a scene . . . it was going to be heaven.

Maggie appeared with a giant check for a million dollars, which Max handed to Chandra. "Congratulations, Chandra!"

"Thank you," Chandra said, turning to the audience to add, "and thank you. It's been an adventure." She handed Vincent the giant check and linked her arm through his as the director cued everyone to wave good-bye.

Chandra smiled at the camera, glancing down to check the time on her Rolex. If they got out of the studio quickly, she could get to the bank before it closed and deposit the check in the escrow account she had set up just after Thanksgiving. An escrow account bearing the names: Chandra Hammel, Maggie McGee, Apple Sommers. Chandra had drafted the deal memo at the onset of the show when the girls had decided to split the prize money three ways, no matter what. Despite the lure of the money, each woman had known that she couldn't let a cash prize tear her apart from her girlfriends.

"This is the weirdest three-way I ever got involved in," Maggie had e-mailed Chandra when she'd read the deal memo.

Chandra had e-mailed back: "Just shut up and sign!"